No Remorse

Heath Gunn

ISBN: 978-1-9162957-4-2 (E-Book Kindle)

ISBN: 978-1-9162957-5-9 (Paperback)

A CIP catalogue record for this book is
available from the British Library

Front cover image by Stuart Bache, Books Covered.

First printing edition 2021.
Page Turner Publications
20-22 Wenlock Road
London
N1 7GU
www.heathgunn.com

DEDICATION

For my kids, Mitchell and Kayleigh, who have been simultaneously making me feel young and old at the same time for twenty-four years.

ACKNOWLEDGMENTS

There are so many people, who knowingly, or not, contribute towards the writing of my stories. The people below were a great help in bringing my ideas to reality.

A huge thank you to my editor Jane Hammett, who did a fantastic job in helping me to polish this book into the final version you are holding now.

Thank you to Graham Bartlett gbpoliceadvisor for taking the time to advise me on the technical aspects of policing, surveillance and interviewing, without making it technical at all.

Thank you to Jane and Matthew Pound for patiently talking me through how aspects of the prison service and their investigations work, answering lots of random questions along the way.

A big thank you to my Gunn Club Crew, you know who you are and I hope you know how much you helped me tweak the final story.

Thank you also to Tracey Mackenzie for doing a great job of proofreading and picking up my typo's.

1

Tuesday

Monica Silverman heard muffled voices from outside her cell door, accompanied by the rattle of keys.

'I wish they'd leave me the fuck alone,' she said under her breath.

The hatch slid open and Bob Anderson stuck his cheery face into the gap.

'Monica, it's Bob Anderson. We're going to open the door – please stand at the back of your room.'

She thought Bob was all right, as screws go. He didn't give her any hassle and was always polite enough – but she just wanted to be left alone.

'What's she doing, Bob?' Monica recognised the new voice. It was Gill O'Leary – a chubby, middle-aged woman with curly brown hair and thick-rimmed glasses, who grated on Monica's last nerve.

Monica chose not to react to Bob's instruction, then she heard him say, 'Nothing. She's just sat on her bed, staring at the floor. I fucking hate it when she doesn't move.'

She allowed herself a smile. She knew that her inaction would wind them up. *If I sat still for long enough, maybe they'd fuck off.*

'Ask her again,' said a squeaky woman. A new voice.

'Monica, we need to come in and speak to you. Can you please stand against the back wall of your room?'

For fuck's sake. Well, if they're not going to leave me alone, I'm going to have some fun.

She stood up from her bed and walked to the back of the room without looking in their direction. Then she sat on the floor, cross-legged, rested her hands on her thighs and closed her eyes, as if she was ready to meditate. Bob let out a heavy sigh.

'What is it, Bob?' asked the squeaky one.

'She's fucking meditating at the back of her room,' said Bob.

Monica took his exasperation as a small victory.

'Oh well, it could be a lot worse,' said Gill. She was right. Monica could make life a lot worse. She opened her eyes just enough to see through her eyelashes.

'Come on then, in we go,' Bob prompted his colleagues. The door handle turned slowly.

Bob and the two female officers stepped into Monica's cell in a V formation, the women standing at Bob's shoulders, primed and looking ready to pull him out of the cell.

They took another step forward. As they did, Monica slapped the floor, hard. All three screws jumped back half a step. Bob gasped. Monica saw him. She saw them all. They absolutely shit themselves. She lifted her head to look at them and couldn't resist a smile.

'That wasn't funny, Monica.' Bob shook his head.

It fucking was. I just about managed not to laugh out loud.

'We've been sent to bring you to the office, so I need you to get up, slowly, and turn around, so we can put some restraints on you,' Bob told her.

'If she wants to speak to me, why doesn't she come down here?'

'You know that's not how it works. Now come on, let's not make this difficult.'

'Why would *we* make it difficult, Bob? After all, we're all friends here, aren't we?' She watched Bob, unmoving. She looked from one screw to the other, figuring out who she could have the most fun with on the way to the governor's office. The squeaky one was new. Her ID said she was called Beth, and she looked young and a bit ditzy.

Monica Silverman was a convicted serial killer who, in the judge's words, had 'carried out multiple heinous acts, including abducting, torturing and dismembering a number of women' before being caught. She'd been inside for three months. In that time she had assaulted six prison officers – one, they said, was unlikely to ever work again, such was the extent of her injuries. She'd also assaulted quite a few inmates.

She'd learned a long time ago how to appear removed and cold. This made her almost impossible to read. To date, no one in prison had come close to giving her anything resembling trouble. She was bigger than most women – not out of shape, just big. Monica had been a champion hammer thrower before she got locked up, and this gave her a massive advantage over her peers in terms of strength and power.

'Come on then, Monica, let's get on with it,' Bob said. He glanced over his shoulder at the two officers on either side of him, who stood, poised.

Right, time to have some fun, Monica thought.

Beth and Gill nearly jumped out of their skins when Monica thrust her arms out in front of her, pressed the sides of her feet into the floor and sprang to a standing position, as flexible as an Olympic gymnast. Bob instinctively took a step back; Beth and Gill moved with him. He didn't take his eyes off Monica. She just stood there: statuesque, grinning at the three of them. They all looked freaked out.

'Turn around and face the wall,' said Bob, clearing his throat and trying his best to sound authoritative.

'Oh, I love it when you're masterful.' She laughed. 'Don't you two just love it?'

'That's enough, Monica. Now turn around and face the wall.' Bob raised his voice.

'Oh all right, calm yourself. I was only having a bit of fun.' She decided to play along for a minute and see what happened next. She turned and faced the wall of her cell and, without being prompted, put her hands behind her back. Monica heard the screws shuffle forward together, staying in formation, in case they needed to restrain her. Bob closed the ratchet handcuffs around her wrists and turned her around to leave the cell. As Bob guided Monica, Beth and Gill moved around to his flank. They started to walk her towards the cell door. About a metre from the door, Monica realised their mistake. She grinned.

They'd fucked up – and put her between them and the doorway.

She kicked the door frame hard, throwing herself back into the guards, bowling them over like skittles.

Beth was on her knees in front of Monica. Monica kicked her with full force, catching her under the jaw, forcing her head back. It smashed against the cold, hard, floor.

One down, two to go, she thought.

Before they could stop her, she rounded on Gill, who was scrambling to her feet. Monica swept Gill's legs out from under her then stamped on her forearm as she lay on the floor. The crack of breaking bone, and her accompanying scream, gave Monica a real buzz. Bob was bigger and slower than his team-mates. When Gill screamed, Monica grinned at Bob, then threw herself towards him, driving her forehead into his face, splitting his nose and smashing his top lip against his teeth. She rocked back onto her knees as he instinctively raised his hands to his bleeding face.

He looked defenceless. She was enjoying herself.

She dived forward again and sank her teeth into his forearm, biting down and ripping out a chunk of flesh. Bob let out a blood-curdling howl.

Monica stood and looked at the three of them, on the floor, all helpless. She didn't want to kill them, even though she could easily have done so. To her, it was just a bit of fun.

Monica stood for what felt like an age, staring at Bob.

A full response team came racing through the door, summoned by Gill who'd pulled her alarm. Monica looked at them, unflinching, her face smeared with Bob's blood, spitting out bits of his flesh.

***

Bob watched, holding his arm, as the team took Monica to the floor. She didn't fight back; she just grinned. They dragged her to her feet and marched her out of the cell. Bob didn't move.

Next, a team of medics came rushing in, accompanied by more prison officers. Beth lay motionless on the floor. Ignoring his own injuries, Bob scrambled to her side and took her wrist, checking for a pulse.

'We need to get Beth out of here and to hospital, along with you and Gill,' said Charles, one of the prison medics. 'Can you walk? Gill, what about you?'

They nodded. Gill was cradling her arm, her face contorted in pain. Bob had blood streaming from his face and arm, and was starting to feel drowsy. He swayed back and forth, then his legs crumpled beneath him. He crashed to the floor beside Beth, aware of the frenzied activity around him but unable to focus, unable to speak. His head swam. The room became a blur of lights and noise, which all seemed to be getting further and further away. He tried to speak, tried to call for help, but nothing came. No sound, no words. His eyes closed slowly – he was too weak to hold them open. Then the sounds around him ebbed away to nothing and all went black.

2

The response team bundled Monica into an isolation cell. For sport, she managed to bounce one of them off the door frame as they steered her inside. As soon as she was inside the cell, she felt the familiar release and speedy exit of the prison officers. They were all afraid of her and she knew it.

The heavy steel door banged closed and an out-of-breath voice barked a meaningless instruction at her through the observation hatch. She didn't catch what they said before they slammed it shut.

She was alone again.

She allowed herself a brief smile of victory, stepped backwards until her back touched the cold door, then slid down it to sit on the floor. Monica found the solid doors reassuring: she knew that, while they stayed locked, she had the solitude she craved and no one placing demands on her.

Monica was three months into five life sentences, set to run consecutively. She knew she would never get out of prison. She'd decided she was smarter than most inmates and that her crimes, and her physicality, made her a formidable prisoner. She was pretty sure she was feared by fellow inmates and guards alike. This amused her. For the first couple of weeks she'd used the communal exercise yard, dining room and showers as her own private playground, picking off victims at will, with no one quick enough or strong enough to stop her - always making sure she was out of the sight of Guards. She'd carried on just as she had done before her arrest: picking on the petite and the timid, girls that reminded her of her mother, with their perfect hair, swaying hips and annoyingly perfect bodies. She didn't feel the need to kill them; she just had some fun with them.

In week three things had changed. As she was dragged out of another session of isolation by visibly anxious guards she was told something she hadn't expected to hear.

'You're going up to see the governor,' one of the three prison officers said as they handcuffed her hands behind her back.

'May I ask why?'

'Because I was told you are. Now get a move on, Silverman.'

She found his tone rude and noted his name ... for later.

She was pushed roughly along the corridor towards a steep set of metal steps, through two heavy locked doors and into a carpeted corridor. The lead officer leaned around her and knocked on an office door, then they walked her through into a basic reception area.

'Monica Silverman to see the governor,' the guard said to a stern-looking woman in her fifties with tortoiseshell glasses and a high forehead. Monica stood silently, compliant.

'Go through, she's expecting you,' Tortoiseshell replied, nodding towards another door. The three officers marched Monica into the governor's office then took a step back to line up behind her. The office smelled of expensive perfume and leather chairs – not overwhelming, quite nice.

'Monica Silverman, please take a seat.' A woman in a smart navy skirt suit sat at the desk. Monica did as she was told and sat down in a comfortable grey chair, in front of a curved grey desk. The woman, who had straight, shoulder-length blonde hair, smiled at her. Monica didn't get smiled at very often. She noticed that the governor had nice teeth.

'I'm Governor Dominicali, and you, Miss Silverman, are causing too many problems for my team. This is something that will not be tolerated, whether you have a five-year sentence or five life sentences. You pose a unique problem for an establishment such as this. My officers, as well trained as they are, are not used to the level of aggression that you are displaying. In addition, your fellow inmates have a different idea of what makes a formidable prisoner – well, at least they did until you arrived.' She paused. Monica felt the governor's eyes inspecting her, as if she was searching for a reaction. Monica returned the searching look with an emotionless stare.

'Am I going to have a problem with you, Miss Silverman?'

'Probably, Governor.'

'Hmm.'

Dominicali didn't rise to the bait. Instead she shifted her attention to the three officers and said something that surprised Monica.

'Leave us,' she said flatly to the officers.

'Ma'am, are you sure?' the lead officer stuttered.

'Yes, quite sure, thank you, Mr Stevens.'

'OK, we'll be outside, ma'am.'

'Thank you. Do close the door on your way out.'

The three guards turned and left, as instructed. As soon as they had closed the door, Dominicali got up and walked around towards Monica, then perched on the desk. Monica felt a spike of arousal as the split in the governor's skirt opened, revealing a glimpse of a well-toned thigh. The governor clearly looked after herself. Monica moved her gaze up to meet Dominicali's, who smiled at her again, making it clear she'd seen her looking.

Monica wasn't bothered.

'You and I need to have little chat,' the governor said.

Monica sat up straighter and looked her in the eye. 'Oh?'

'You have a unique set of skills that, if given the right level of focus and direction, could be very useful.'

'I don't follow, Governor.'

'You will. Stay with me.' The governor returned to her own side of the desk and sat down. 'We have some prisoners here who, for whatever reason, were given completely inappropriate sentences by the presiding judge. The result is that these low-lives squander tax-payers' money and we just have to smile sweetly and take it.'

'So, where do I come in?'

'You, my dear Monica, are in the perfect place, with the perfect opportunity and the perfect set of skills, to help me rebalance the scales.'

'Sorry, I still don't follow.' Monica was deliberately being obtuse. The governor sighed and steepled her fingers in front of her face. Monica decided it wasn't a kind face, or one to be trusted, so she decided to stick to her vague, non-compliant approach.

'OK, let me spell it out for you. We have women in here who are serving very little time for crimes that should've resulted in life sentences. And, if the law had any balls, death sentences. What I'm proposing is, that in exchange for some bespoke privileges and a more comfortable time in here, you help me by clearing out the trash. How does that sound?'

'Like an abuse of power?'

Dominicali rolled her eyes. 'And you, of all people, are in a position to turn down such an offer? I think not. Let's face it, you have a talent for what you do. You evaded capture for long enough to allow you to kill repeatedly and you're stuck in here for life, whether you like it or not.'

'So when you say you want to rebalance the scales, or clear out the trash, what you're actually saying is that you would like me to kill my fellow inmates on your behalf?'

'Kill, torture, frighten – it depends what's called for, I guess.' The governor said with a shrug.

'And who decides what's called for? You?'

'Of course. Who do you think?'

'I'm not good at following instructions – or hadn't you noticed?'

'Ha ha, yes, that had come to my attention on more than one occasion. I don't have to be prescriptive. I can give you the target and you can pull the trigger, so to speak, in any way you see fit.'

'OK. Let's say, hypothetically, that I'm interested in your offer. What's in it for me?'

'What would you like?'

Monica paused, just long enough to judge that Dominicali was becoming uncomfortable with the length of the silence. Then, just before the governor filled the quiet, Monica spoke.

'A more comfortable cell, for a start. The hole you've thrown me in is crappy.'

'OK.'

'And access to the gym. The screws stopped me going after I accidentally hit someone with a dumbbell.'

Dominicali laughed. 'It was hardly accidental. You hit her around the side of the face with a twenty-kilo weight.'

'I meant to hit her in the nose, ergo, an accident.'

'Anything else?' asked the governor, clearly not impressed by Monica's counter.

'Only one thing.'

'Yes?'

'You let me deal with them in whichever way I see fit. No interference.'

'Fair enough – on one condition. You don't make too much of a mess. Nothing that can't be cleaned up ... and nothing that can get back to me.'

'Oh, don't worry, Governor, you'll be safe, up here in your ivory tower.'

'Don't push it.'

'So who's first?'

'I'll let you know by the end of the week. I've got some files to review and sentencing guidelines to check.'

'How will you let me know? I can't come up here every two minutes.'

'Oh, don't worry. You'll know.' With that, the governor held up an open hand to Monica, ending the conversation. She leaned over her desk and pressed an intercom button on her phone, asking her PA to send the officers in.

They came in and flanked Monica. She glanced from one to the other, wondering whether to elbow one of them in the face, then thought better of it. She was keen to see if the governor's offer was for real, and didn't want to mess it up for the sake of an ungratifying brawl.

The governor was true to her word. Monica was moved to a much nicer room, complete with a TV, and given access to the gym, although she had to use it on her own, in the presence of two prison guards, both of whom stayed well away from her while she was heaving weights around

A week after their initial meeting, a note was passed to Monica in a sealed envelope. When she opened it, written in stylish handwriting were the words 'Alba White, 13b, exercise yard, 3.30 p.m.'

It had been easy. Two guards she'd never seen before came to collect Monica from her cell and took her to the yard, where Alba was walking on her own. The guards turned towards the wall, as if deep in conversation. Monica made her way over to Alba, who looked wary as the much bigger woman approached.

'Have you got a ciggie I can bum?' Monica asked.

Alba gave her a relieved look and reached into her pocket. As she looked down at the packet to retrieve a cigarette, Monica punched her hard in the side of the head. She felt the familiar buzz of excitement as her prey crumpled to the ground. As soon as Alba hit the floor, Monica crouched beside her and pressed her forearm against the smaller woman's throat, slowly squeezing the life out of her.

When she was sure the job was done, she lifted her arm and glanced over towards the guards, who were still facing the wall. She looked down at Alba, shrugged and walked back to the guards. One of them looked over at Alba's lifeless body, then at Monica. He didn't say anything. Neither of them did.

They walked her back to her room in silence, escorted her inside and locked the door. There was some gossip around the prison about Alba, saying she'd been offed. But nothing about Monica.

This pattern had been repeated a couple more times in the weeks that followed. Each time, the same two guards collected Monica and took her to what she assumed was a prearranged place, where her unsuspecting prey met their fate. Then she was walked back to her cell in silence.

3

'Boss, there's a call for you from the prison,' DS Drew Taylor said to DI Lomas Baxter.

'The prison? What do they want?'

'I don't know. They said they wanted to speak to you directly, wouldn't elaborate.'

Lomas nodded and picked up the phone. 'DI Baxter, how can I help?'

'Is that Detective Inspector Baxter?'

He rolled his eyes. 'Yes, how can I help you?'

'This is Mike Button, I'm the Head of Custody at HMP Brookham. Would you be able to come up to the prison? There's been an ... incident ... and I was told to call you.'

'Oh? Why would that be?'

'It involves Monica Silverman and she says she'll only speak to you.' The caller let the name hang on the line.

Lomas broke the silence. 'OK, tell me what happened.'

'Three of our officers went into Miss Silverman's room to collect her for exercise. Two are on their way to hospital with injuries caused by Miss Silverman...'

'And the third?'

'The third is dead.'

There was a short silence.

'OK, I'm on my way. Has the coroner been called?'

'I'm calling them next. Will you bring a team to inspect the scene?'

'Yes – our guys will look at everything. I'm assuming the cell is locked down?'

'The room is locked, yes, Detective Inspector.'

Lomas noted the clipped tone in Button's answer, but ignored it.

'Good. Can you collect Miss Silverman's clothes and bag them up for our forensics team? She'll also need swabbing, so can you make sure she doesn't get access to a shower?'

'Yes, of course. She's in isolation at the moment, so there's no danger of her showering.'

'OK, great. We'll see you soon.' Baxter hung up and spun his chair round to face Drew. 'Right, Drew, grab your coat. We're going to prison. It seems Miss Silverman has killed a prison guard.'

'What?'

'Yep, two hospitalised and one dead. She's told them she'll only speak to me. I guess, on the plus side, at least we don't have to hunt her down this time.'

On the way to the prison they were both quiet, immersed in thoughts about Monica Silverman and the gruelling investigation their team had gone through to catch Monica and put her behind bars. An investigation that saw them both taunted and threatened by the monster that was Monica.

It had taken a year and a half to get the case to trial, and three months to hear it. Monica had only been inside for three months.

Lomas had worked many cases in his years on the force, but the pressure that had mounted during the hunt for Monica Silverman, as the death toll rose and she became more brazen, had been intense. The press and public were always fascinated by serial killers, and Monica Silverman had been no different. She had gained celebrity status by the time she went to trial. He hated the way the UK press sensationalised killers, feeling that their treatment took little to no account of the feelings of the victims' families and friends.

Soon, they were parking at the prison.

'Right, let's go and see what Monica's been up to this time,' Lomas said.

'More of the same, isn't it? Just a different place.'

They walked into the prison, showing their ID and signing in. Lomas was impeccably dressed as always, in a smart navy suit and white open-collared shirt. Drew wore a thigh-length grey coat over black trousers and boots, her long red hair pulled back into a neat ponytail. They waited for about five minutes then were met by a smiley man in his mid-fifties, with a round belly and blushed cheeks. Mike Button shook their hands.

'Lovely to meet you both. It's been a hell of a day. Can I check you've left your phones, keys and other belongings in the lockers provided?'

'We have. We just have the recording equipment to take through, and one of your officers has just checked it,' Lomas answered, familiar with the protocol.

'Fantastic. This way, please.' Button swiped his ID against a card reader and an automatic door swung open, taking them into a double-door airlock. They stood together, waiting for one door to close before the next opened. The three of them went into a sterile-looking corridor that smelled of cleaning fluid, with grey doors set into the walls at intervals.

'It's the next door on the right – room three.' Button pointed at a grey door. 'I'll be on the other side of the glass. There's a table at the side of the room for your recording equipment.'

'And Miss Silverman?' Asked Drew.

'Already in the room waiting for you. We had her brought up when you arrived.'

'Thank you, that's very efficient,' said Lomas, pleasantly surprised.

'Thank you, DI Baxter. We try.' He swiped his card and held the door open for them. As soon as they walked through the door, Lomas saw Monica grinning at them, her wrists connected to the top of the desk by handcuffs.

'Detective Inspector Baxter and Detective Constable Taylor,' Monica said, beaming at them.

'Detective Sergeant Taylor,' Lomas corrected. 'Hello, Monica.'

'Congratulations, Drew – a well-deserved promotion, no doubt. You must be very pleased. Well, I must say it's lovely to see you both – and you look so well.'

Lomas pulled out a chair and sat.

Drew set up the equipment, they went through the formalities of starting the interview, then Lomas dived in. 'It didn't take for you long to revert to your standard behaviour, Monica.'

'I'm sure I don't know what you mean, Detective.' Monica's dark eyes narrowed and she tipped her head to one side.

'You've only been in here three months and already someone is dead. Bob Anderson, a guard at the prison, died earlier today in your cell.'

Monica's expression changed as Lomas said Bob's name. What looked like a genuine look of surprise came across her face. 'Oh, that is sad. I liked Bob. He was one of the ones you could have a joke with, and there aren't many of them in here, let me tell you.'

'You mean, you didn't know Bob Anderson was dead?' Drew asked.

'Nope, I had no idea. They don't tell me much. They marched me off to a different part of the prison quite quickly, then I guess they called you.'

'But you did attack three prison officers, Monica, so it can't be a complete surprise that they didn't leave your cell fit and well?' Lomas sounded sarcastic.

'I guess so although, to be fair, I would have expected the squeaky one, Beth, or Gill to have come off worse. I bit a little piece out of Bob's arm, but not big enough for him to bleed out, unless he had a blood thinning condition, I suppose.' She looked thoughtful.

'Initial indications are that Mr Anderson suffered a heart attack, brought on, no doubt, by the encounter with you in your cell.'

'They call them rooms,' Monica said.

'Sorry?' Lomas said.

'Rooms – they call them rooms, not cells. Apparently it helps the women feel less threatened and vulnerable if the place they're imprisoned in is termed a room. Personally, I couldn't care less, but there are some fragile little things in here.'

Lomas continued. 'So, to be clear, you don't deny attacking the three officers? And you now understand that your attack on the guards led to the death of Bob Anderson?'

'Well, when you put it like that it's hard to dispute. I suppose you've got me, Detective. Although I'm not entirely sure what you think you're going to do about it. I'm never getting out of here – my sentence will still be running long after all of us are dead. So frankly, what does it matter?' She turned her palms upwards and shrugged as she spoke.

'It matters because an innocent man who came to work today, to do his job, is dead.'

'When you put it like that, it does sound more dramatic. He has a way of making the mundane sound like a drama, don't you think, DS Taylor?'

'No, Monica, I don't.' Drew's voice was stony.

'Oh well, suit yourself. Is that all, DI Baxter? It's just that I've got a busy day ahead. You know, reading, looking at the wall, counting the hairs on my arms, that kind of thing.'

'That's all for now, Monica, but we may need to come back and talk to you again. Don't leave the country, will you.'

Monica smiled, looking amused.

They ended the recording. Lomas eased his chair out from the table.

'Before you both go and before my *bodyguards* come in to collect me, you need to know something. There's much more going on here than you realise.'

'Meaning?'

'Meaning there are forces at work within these walls that are far darker than I, DI Baxter. Guard!' With that, Monica closed her eyes, signalling the end of the conversation. Lomas heard the door being opened.

Lomas and Drew looked at each other as smiley Mike appeared in the open doorway.

'All done? Right, this way, please. Monica, the team will be in to collect you shortly.'

'Who are you calling shortly?' Monica said without opening her eyes.

Lomas smiled as the expression on Mike's face remained unchanged.

'Tell me, Mike, is the governor around? I'd like to give her an update on our chat with Monica.'

'No, she's off today. But I'll let her know you'd like to speak to her, if you wish.'

'No, that's fine. I've got her email, I think. I'll drop her a note, but I'll leave her my card. Could you pass it on?'

'As you wish.'

They made their way back to reception and collected their belongings from the lockers. It wasn't until they were back in the car that Drew broke the silence. 'What do you think she meant by that last comment?'

'I don't know, if I'm honest. Either she has something she wants us to know, or she's trying to divert our attention away from the fact she just killed a prison officer. But this is Monica Silverman. She's not stupid. Evil? Yes. Stupid? No.'

'I know she's not to be trusted, but it sounded like she had something she wanted to share, then she thought better of it.'

Lomas had to admit that he felt the same. They'd spent hours interviewing Monica after her arrest. Although the crimes she'd committed were heinous and reprehensible, she had never tried to shift blame or duck the responsibility for her actions. This had earned her a modicum of respect from Lomas, although he would never tell anyone this.

Just before they got back to the station, Lomas had decided what he wanted to do. 'Do a little bit of digging into the prison, Drew. See if there's been anything out of the ordinary happening – especially with anyone connected to Monica.'

'Anything in particular you want me to look for?'

'Well, given that it's Monica, I'd look for anyone who's died.'

4

Wednesday

Niamh Dominicali paced as she waited for Mike Button to arrive in her office. She'd arrived half an hour earlier, at 7.30 a.m., and had been told by her PA, Claire Kidson, that the police had been at the prison interviewing Monica following Bob Anderson's death. Niamh thought that Claire had taken a little too much pleasure in letting her know. She knew that Mike should have called and told her. As Head of Custody, it was his job to deal with this kind of thing, but Dominicali hated being blindsided by anything. Button had called her and told her about the attacks, so why the hell hadn't he let her know he'd asked the police to come in? She knew that he was just following procedure which he did to the letter, always, but she was still enraged to find out what had happened from Claire – with her smug smile, looking disapprovingly at Dominicali over her tortoiseshell glasses as she spoke.

Her phone buzzed and she tapped the intercom button. 'Yes, Claire?'

'Mike Button here to see you, Governor.'

'Thank you. Please ask him to come in. Could I get a coffee, please?'

'Of course, coming right up.' She could hear the smug tone in Claire's voice and could only imagine how she'd spoken to Mike when he arrived.

The door opened slowly and a sheepish-looking Mike Button edged into the office.

'Mike, come on in.'

'Good morning, Governor.'

'Take a seat. We need to have a chat.'

'Is it in relation to the incident from yesterday?'

'Yes, it is. You see, while I appreciate the fact that you called me and let me know that Miss Silverman had attacked three of our officers, with terrible consequences, what I did not appreciate is that Claire was the one who told me this morning that the police had been here yesterday to interview Monica.'

'Well, of course they were, Governor. As per policy. In the event of an assault resulting in serious injury or death, the police must be notified immediately.'

'I know what the fucking policy says, Mike! The point is, you didn't let me know when they were coming to interview Monica. Had I known, I would have made myself available. When something this significant happens, I want to know about it. Do I make myself clear? This is my fucking prison, so make sure I know what the hell is going on. Got it?'

Mike didn't make a sound as she ranted at him. He just sat looking at her, his face becoming redder than normal.

'I'm sorry, Governor, but I did call you. Your phone went to voicemail. I left you a message informing you that I'd contacted the police and the time they would be here.'

Niamh grabbed her mobile from her bag and punched her thumb against the bottom edge of the screen. Nothing happened. She hit the screen again. Still nothing. Her battery was dead. A wave of embarrassment swept over her. It didn't last long and was quickly replaced by anger.

'You could have emailed me and marked it urgent. I would have read it immediately.'

Mike, still red-faced, looked as though he was going to protest some more. Niamh glared at him, almost daring him to argue. After a few seconds, he spoke. 'I'm sorry. My mistake – it won't happen again.'

Dominicali was almost disappointed. She'd half wanted to keep venting at him, but she would take the victory.

'OK, well, let's not dwell on it. These things happen, I guess. So what did they have to say?'

Button shifted in his seat, looking as if he'd sat on a drawing pin.

'What is it? Don't tell me there's something else I don't know.'

'No, it's not that. It's just that they asked if they could see you after they'd finished interviewing Miss Silverman.'

'They always want to eyeball the governor – want to ask a few leading questions about systemic abuse or prison officer procedure. There's always something. They don't dig around for meaningless shit as often as the press, but they still like to have options when it comes to blame. That's why you should have let me know.' She knew she had to stop driving the point home before she made Button cry, but she was pleased with how the conversation had gone full circle, from her having a flat battery to Mike being wrong for not calling her. Niamh decided to have one more dig before she put him out of his misery. 'Anything else I need to know about? Any more surprise visitors?'

'No, that's all, Governor.'

'OK, thank you. You can go now.'

Without another word, Button got up, put DI Baxter's card on the edge of her desk and scurried out of the office, his head bowed.

Niamh flopped into a comfy armchair in the corner of her office and steepled her fingers under her chin, thinking about how the police interview with Monica might have gone. She would have to talk to Silverman, but she would take her time to plan how the chat would go. She needed to make sure that Monica knew who was boss, and that she wouldn't let the cat out of the bag on their arrangement in exchange for a lesser punishment for killing Bob.

Only then did her thoughts turn to Bob. Niamh had liked him. He'd been really helpful when she'd arrived at the prison. To begin with, she knew it was because she had long hair and tits and wore a skirt to work. It was nothing new to Dominicali; she'd had to deal with it during her rise through the prison system. But Bob had quickly got past that and had become a trusted confidant who had helped her find her way in the prison and had given her all the gen on prisoners and guards. Within weeks, she'd known who the corrupt ones were, like Bell and Rodriguez. It had been easy for her to get them on-side in her arrangement with Monica. They were the only ones she asked to take instructions to Monica, and they were always the ones who collected her and brought her to see Niamh.

She walked over to her desk and pressed her intercom. 'Claire, could you order some lovely flowers for Irene Anderson, please? And could you get me a card so that I can send her a personal note?'

'Certainly. Would you like your coffee now?'

'Yes, please.'

She'd forgotten about her coffee while she'd been chastising Mike. Claire had clearly known that it wasn't the right time to come in. She secretly liked Claire, even if she could be officious at times.

Niamh drained her coffee and asked Claire to get Bell and Rodriguez to come and take her to see Monica.

'You mean, in her room, Governor?'

'Yes, that's precisely what I mean. I don't think it sends the right signal, getting a prisoner who has committed such an awful act of violence brought up to my office, do you?'

'No, I suppose it doesn't. I'll get hold of them right away.'

It didn't take her two henchmen long to get there. She'd only had time to deal with a few emails, including one that was a notification of the incident involving

Monica. Claire buzzed through to let her know her escorts were outside. She grabbed her suit jacket from the back of her chair, checked her appearance in a mirror that hung on the wall in a small, private room just off her office.

Bell and Rodriguez were standing on either side of the door. Bell was tall, thick-set, with stubble and perfect black hair. Rodriguez was more or less the exact opposite: short, bald and always looked as though his shirt was about to come untucked. They were both as crooked as they came. When Niamh had approached them about earning some extra cash on the side, they'd been more than happy to do whatever she asked. In the past few weeks, they'd become an essential part of her network. Their collective greed meant they were often around, due to the amount of voluntary overtime they picked up, always willing to cover another colleague's sickness or leave days.

'Where to, Governor?' asked Bell.

'Wherever the delightful Miss Silverman is, please, gents.'

They nodded at each other. Bell led the way, with Rodriguez hanging back to let Niamh fall into step between them.

The three of them made their way to the isolation block, which housed prisoners who presented a risk to themselves – or others. Monica was in the end cell.

Rodriguez checked through the observation panel. He told Niamh that Monica was lying on her bed and hadn't moved. He opened the door and stood to one side to let Dominicali go in.

Silverman didn't move from her bed, or acknowledge the governor's presence. She lay still, as if she was sleeping, but Niamh could see that she wasn't.

'I think we need to talk, Miss Silverman.'

Monica didn't reply.

'I hear you've had a busy day.'

Still nothing.

'Look, cut the crap and sit up. You're not impressing anyone with the thousand-yard stare, so knock it off.'

Monica swung her legs over the side of the bed and sat up, glaring at the governor. Niamh stiffened as the prisoner moved, but didn't flinch. The stare didn't bother her; she had enough experience not to be intimidated by the likes of Monica, although she'd rarely faced anyone with such raw power, or the ability to be physically threatening.

'Could you step outside and close the door, please, gents? I'll let you know if I need you, but I don't think Miss Silverman is up for making things worse.' She said, waving the back of her hand. She waited a moment for the door to close, then turned her attention back to Monica.

'Do you want to tell me what went on in your room yesterday? Killing one of my guards and hospitalising two more is not exactly in the spirit of our arrangement, is it?'

'Bob wasn't deliberate – not that you'll believe that. I was only having some fun with them and didn't mean for anyone to die.'

'No, I believe you. But you bit a chunk out of his arm and have really messed up the other two. And for what? To amuse yourself for two minutes?'

'I suppose so, but it's not like we're in a zero-tolerance environment when it comes to violence, is it, Governor?' Niamh could feel the self-righteousness oozing from Monica.

How dare she try and justify what she did by comparing it with what we've been doing? Dominicali raged internally.

'I think, if that's the angle you're planning on working, you're on very thin ice.'

'I wasn't,' Monica replied.

'Good. Now, what did the police have to say?'

'Oh, they assumed I was guilty. In my position, it doesn't really matter whether I meant to kill Bob or not, does it? I'm a convicted killer. Who would believe me if I said anything to try and defend myself? But, as I said, Bob wasn't deliberate. I actually quite liked him.'

'Yeah, me too. He was a nice guy.' Niamh paused for a second, her thoughts drifting to Bob and his widow. 'OK, well, you're going to be in here for a while and I don't think there will be any little side ventures any time soon. We've had a few too many *accidents* in the last few weeks – it will raise suspicion if there's anything else.'

'OK, understood.'

As Niamh turned to leave, she heard the rub of fabric and felt an arm slip around her throat, pulling her in tight. She grabbed Monica's arm and tried to pull it away, just far enough to catch her breath, but it was no use. Monica was too strong. She felt herself being pulled backwards. Unable to shout, she kicked the door. Bell ripped the door open, Rodriguez behind him, both wide-eyed, clearly not expecting this. Niamh was struggling for breath and thrashing around, without effect.

Bell stepped forward.

'Come on, Monica, this is not the best idea, is it? Let the governor go,' he urged. Niamh could tell that he was trying to stay calm and gain control of the situation.

'Fuck off, Bell-end.'

'This isn't going help anything, is it? Come on, let the governor go.'

'I told you to fuck off. Now get back or I'll kill her.'

Niamh could feel the taut muscle of Monica's forearm against her throat. She couldn't move. She tried to stamp on Monica's foot, and felt a hard fist bury itself in the back of her ribs. It hurt a lot, but she couldn't scream. The thought of what had happened to Bob, Beth and Gill immediately popped into her head and fuelled an uncommon panic in her. She tried again to fight Monica off, driving her elbow backwards towards her attacker's ribs, but to no avail. Bell opened his mouth to speak again, but he was too late. Monica spun Niamh around to face her. As her body turned towards Monica, she saw a fist coming towards her face ... then everything went black.

***

Monica threw the governor's limp body onto the cell floor, as if she was casting aside an item of clothing, then turned her attention to Bell and Rodriguez.

She saw Bell's fists clench as he stepped forward. Monica immediately dropped to a crouch and swept his legs out from under him, stamping on his face as he hit the floor. Then she grabbed Rodriguez by the back of his sweaty little head and bounced his face off the cell wall repeatedly, until he too became limp. She turned back to Bell, who was trying to get up, and kicked him in the ribs, flipping him over. As he spun, his arm flicked up. She caught his wrist and snapped it without giving it a thought. He screamed as she took his arm in both hands and bounced the back of his elbow off her knee. She heard it crack. Bell let out another cry.

She couldn't risk the noise being heard outside the cell so, dropping to her knees, she took Bell's head and whipped it around and back with ease. His neck snapped.

Taking the keys and handcuffs from Bell's belt, she set them on the bed. Then she quickly changed into Bell's uniform, tucking him into her bed and leaving only the top of his dark head showing above the covers.

Once she'd dealt with Bell, she turned her attention to Rodriguez. Monica checked for a pulse. When she found that he had a faint one, she considered her options. She could leave him alive, bound and gagged, or she could kill him and make sure he couldn't raise the alarm. She decided on the latter. Very calmly, she covered his mouth with a towel and applied pressure, then held his nose closed. It only took a few minutes, for the involuntary, self-preservation twitching to come and go, then Rodriguez was gone. She manoeuvred his corpse into a corner, out of view of the door, and briefly wondered whether it had been necessary to kill them both – then agreed with herself that it had.

While Monica sat and waited patiently for the governor to come round, she tidied up her appearance, dragging her hair into a neater style.

As Niamh Dominicali started coming to, Monica pulled her hands behind her back and slipped the handcuffs on her, making sure she could feel it happening.

'It's OK, take a minute, Niamh, there's no need to rush.' She felt like her old self once more. In control.

The governor looked at her, fear written all over her face. 'What have you done?'

'I'm sorry, what do you mean?'

She watched as Niamh frantically looked from Rodriguez's corpse to the lump in the bed that was Bell, then back to Monica.

'You can't possibly think you're going to get away with this.'

With a broad smile and in a calm, hushed voice, Monica said, 'Ah, but that's where you come in, you see. Your phase of our little game is over. Now it's my turn. But my rules are much simpler than yours. You either do exactly as I say, or you die. Simple, really, don't you think? The way this part works is that you're going to help me get out of this hell-hole. And when I say "out", I don't mean out of this cell. I mean *out* out.'

The governor sat in silence for a moment.

'Don't think for too long, or I might change my mind and leave you here with dumb and dumber.'

'Let's say I agree. How on earth are you planning to get from here to the main door and out?'

'It's a straightforward plan – as all the best ones are. All you have to do is play along, smile in the right places and be confident. Which I know you can do. The alternative is, you get cold feet and lose your nerve, then the one thing you can be confident of is that you'll die in front of your staff. I have very little to lose. You, however...'

5

Lomas spun around on his office chair and called Drew.

'You rang, boss?' she said, appearing in the doorway.

'I've been thinking about Monica's final throwaway – or not – comment. She's a slippery one for sure, but the more I think about it, the more it doesn't sit right with me. She's got nothing to gain by flagging something that might be going on, but also nothing to lose. She certainly doesn't owe us any favours. So it must have been triggered by something.'

'I agree. I've looked into recent events at the prison. There have been a few accidents that have resulted in prisoners dying or being seriously injured.'

'You have my attention. Go on.'

'There was a young woman that stands out. Two months ago, a prisoner called Alba White died in the exercise yard. No one seems to know what happened to her – or no one wants to say. The death was recorded as misadventure and the file was closed. There were a couple more, but she's the only one that died in the exercise yard which gives us a thin link to Monica Silverman and her interests.'

'You mean because it was an exercise yard accident? Hmm, very convenient, don't you think?'

'It does look a bit too coincidental – Monica arrives and women start dying, and in the exercise yard too.'

'OK, good work, thanks. Let me have what you've got so far and keep looking. Let me know if you find anything else.'

'Will do.'

Drew closed Lomas's office door on her way out. He turned his chair back around to face his desk, bringing up Monica's file on his PC.

Once they'd got Monica into custody, questioning her had taken days. Lomas remembered it well. She was, without doubt, the coldest, most calculating killer he'd ever interviewed. She had a rationale for most of what she'd done, which she delivered convincingly. She had denied nothing. For some of her victims, she'd given Lomas and Drew an elaborate debrief of what she'd done and – to a lesser extent – why.

The first couple of victims had seemed almost like practice kills. Her account of them was patchy. The women had been from local families that Monica found annoying and didn't like very much. But once she'd got more comfortable and started to hone her skills, she'd focused more on people she took real exception to.

Anna-May Appleby, a twenty-seven-year-old nurse, had been Monica's third victim. Lomas remembered that Drew had found quite tough to deal with, as she had a sad family background. Following Anna-May's death, her mother had died by suicide.

Monica confessed to Lomas and Drew that she'd targeted Anna-May because she'd nursed her mum while she was dying in hospital. Monica's mother had become quite fond of the young nurse during her final weeks – she always went above and beyond for her patients. According to Monica, her mum had referred to the nurse as 'that lovely Anna-May', whereas Monica referred to Anna-May as 'sugary sweet and just as sickly'. Monica had been constantly told how lovely Anna-May had been by her mother. This in Monica's view had been regardless of the fact that it was she who had taken time to come and visit her mother, who she referred to in interview as "the old witch".

She had clearly gained a great deal of personal satisfaction from making Anna-May suffer in the time before her death, and her confession was delivered with venom.

Another victim was Elinor Mary Clarke. Her only crime had been working behind a bar, and giving particularly good customer service, in a local pub where Monica's parents liked to go for a quiet meal. In addition, Monica's dad used to go to the pub for a pint and some solitude. Elinor Mary's attentive nature was enough to make Monica's parents talk about Elinor in glowing terms when they got home. And that was enough for Monica to add Elinor to the list of those who 'had to go'. As with Anna-May, Monica had become convinced that her parents preferred Elinor over her and would obsess over the positive way her parents spoke of both.

Finally, the one that got away. Christina Marley – a name that Monica had almost spat, with a virulent fury, when questioned about her. Her anger had been driven by the fact that Christina had been rescued by Lomas and Drew. Christina's transgression, in Monica's eyes, went back to her days as a student when she had worked part-time in a book shop alongside her teaching degree. It was one of the few places where Monica had gone with her mother, and Christina and Mrs Silverman had built a friendship of sorts on discussing books and authors they liked. This had riled Monica and she had 'stored this one up' to kill later.

Her mum had described Christina as 'cultured, pretty and intelligent', and had apparently once said to Monica that they might have a better relationship if she were more like Christina.

Lomas picked up his mobile and called his wife.

Heidi answered after a couple of rings. 'Hey, you. This is a pleasant surprise. Everything OK?'

'Hey yourself. Yes, everything's good. I was just thinking about you and had a couple of minutes spare, so I thought I'd give you a call and see how your day is.'

'You're very sweet, Mr Baxter. My day's good so far. Work's the same as usual – nothing much happening. How about you?'

'Yeah, it's OK, I guess. I'll tell you about it later.' said Lomas, flicking a fly from his keyboard.

'That doesn't sound so great. What time do you think you'll be done?'

'I should be done about nine. Shall I pick something up on the way home?'

'I'm probably going to eat with the kids. I had an early lunch, but pick some chocolate up if you're stopping. We could try and finish that Netflix series we've been trying to get through.'

'Ha ha, chocolate it is. See you later, love you.'

'Love you too.'

Lomas dropped the phone back on his desk and rubbed a hand through his salt-and-pepper hair. He had been thinking about Heidi and their kids, Ant and Eve. But the reason he'd felt the need to check on Heidi was because he'd been reminded of the steps he'd had to take to protect them all when he'd been hunting Monica. If he was honest with himself, he just needed to hear Heidi's voice.

6

After Monica removed her handcuffs, Niamh Dominicali took a moment to straighten up her appearance before stepping out of the room where the bodies of Bell and Rodriguez lay. Monica followed closely, dressed in Bell's uniform.

Niamh could feel her insides trembling as she concentrated on trying to look as natural and relaxed as possible. She knew Monica would be true to her word and wouldn't hesitate to kill her in front of her team. She also knew that Monica would probably kill anyone who witnessed it too. The weight of responsibility was crippling. She had to keep everyone as safe as she could and just hope that somewhere along the way Monica would mess up.

No one batted an eyelid as the pair walked through the cell block towards the stairwell. As they reached the stairs and turned to descend, Niamh could feel the distance between them narrow, Monica's intimidating presence looming over her.

'Keep walking, Governor, you're doing great,' Monica said quietly behind Niamh's head.

They made their way without incident to the staff changing room. Niamh satisfied herself that none of her officers were in there. Given it was mid-way through a shift, they shouldn't have been. She watched Monica force her way into a series of lockers, looking for clothes that fit her. Niamh stood near the door, where she'd been told to stay, rooted to the spot and terrified of what Monica would do if she tried to raise the alarm or make a run for it. She didn't imagine that death-by-Monica was a pleasant way to go.

She's taking ages. Someone's bound to come in soon, then she'll be fucked. What if I make it into the corridor? I can raise the alarm? she thought.

She waited until she thought Monica was engrossed, casting the contents of yet another locker onto the floor, then Niamh grabbed the door handle and yanked it open. She'd only made it halfway through the door when it slammed against her, pressing her between the door and the frame, knocking the wind out of her and banging her head.

When the pressure of the door was released from her chest, Monica's fist drove into her ribs. She buckled under the blow, her arm instinctively tucking into her side. It was too late; her attempted escape had been thwarted.

Monica grabbed Dominicali by the hair, pulled her back into the changing room and knocked her to the floor with a swift backhand blow.

'That wasn't very smart, was it?' Monica hissed. 'Now, sit there and don't fucking move. We haven't got time for you to fuck about.'

Niamh didn't say anything. She could see the rage in Monica's eyes and knew she was lucky to be alive. Monica turned away from her, clearly confident that Niamh would stay where she'd put her. She was right.

After another couple of minutes rifling through other people's belongings, a triumphant Monica reappeared.

'This should do,' Monica said, holding up a pair of jeans, checked shirt and baseball cap. Niamh didn't reply. The prisoner changed quickly then came over, leaning in close to the governor.

'I'm prepared to overlook that little rush of blood to the head. Because, with the exception of your cracked ribs, it's so far, so good. Don't lose your nerve, Governor, and everything will be fine. Just do it the way I said, be confident and happy, and it will all be over soon. That way, you and your staff won't get hurt.'

'I've got you this far, haven't I? Let's just get it over with.' Niamh winced.

'Happy, remember?'

'Oh, fuck off, Monica!' she replied, temporarily forgetting her fear.

'Well, that's not very nice, is it? You carry on like that and we'll make this journey like groundhog day, with you waking up on the floor next to a couple of dead officers. How does that sound?' Monica's tone was laced with menace.

'OK, OK, let's get on with it.'

Monica nodded. With a smug smile she pushed Dominicali towards the door. Niamh smoothed her hands down the front of her skirt to straighten out any creases, ran her hands through her hair, and they headed back out into the corridor. The pair followed a well-trodden route from the staff changing room to the main exit. They walked in silence, Niamh constantly aware of the threat behind her and feeling shooting pains from her side up into her chest. As they neared the reception area, she forced on a smile and sparked up a conversation with Monica, who, seconds earlier, had moved alongside her.

'It was really good to see you. Thank you for coming all the way down. Hopefully you'll have a decent run back,' Niamh said.

'Thanks for your time, Governor. It really means a lot to know that Claire is in a place that's so focused on her wellbeing. I'll be sure to pass on your best to the family when I get home.'

Monica handed in a visitor's badge that Niamh had seen her pick up from the changing-room floor and headed for the exit. The governor's stomach was churning and she fought the urge to shout for help. She didn't want to be responsible for the deaths of the people around them.

'I'll walk out with you. I'm just popping out quickly, Tony. I won't be long,' she said to a vacant-looking chap who sat behind the reception screen.

'No problem, Governor. I'll buzz you both out.'

And that was it. They walked through the airlock and outside, just as Monica had said they would. No one had so much as raised an eyebrow at Monica in her stolen clothes.

Now for the final bit of Monica's plan, Niamh knew she had to raise the alarm without risking people's lives. Monica had been very clear about the time-lag she wanted the governor to leave.

'Wait for an hour before you start screaming from the rooftops that I'm gone – or I'll make a return trip to your home and your family.' She had left Niamh in no doubt she meant it. However, this was the one part of Monica's scheme that Niamh had no intention of complying with. It was bad enough knowing she'd helped the most dangerous prisoner she'd ever encountered to escape. She wouldn't add to that by staying quiet for an hour, regardless of the repercussions.

'OK, Governor, which one's yours?'

'The grey Audi TT,' she said, pointing to her car.

'Why does that not surprise me? Oh well, a hairdresser's car will have to do. Hand over the keys and your driver's licence.'

'I don't have it on me. It's in the office.' Niamh replied, biting on her bottom lip.

'Huh... What do you have with your address on?' Monica said, looking slightly irritated.

'I'm not sure if I have anything in my car.'

'You'd better have a look, then, hadn't you? If not, don't worry. I can find you easily enough.' The smile Monica gave Niamh chilled her to the core.

She saw Monica look up at the prison walls, clearly checking where the CCTV cameras were, but keeping the peak of the baseball cap low enough to cover her face. They walked over to the car. Once there, Niamh unlocked it and fished in the boot. She found an old utility bill, which she passed to Monica.

'Oh, that's a nice part of town. Thank you. And remember – not a word for an hour, or I'll be paying you and your family a little visit. And before you think the police can protect you from me, they can't, and they know it.'

Monica took the keys from Niamh and got into the car. She watched helplessly as Monica drove steadily toward the gate, which slid back obediently to let her out into the world. As the gate slid closed, Niamh listened to her car drive away ... and then it was gone.

What the fuck have you done, Niamh? she asked herself.

Niamh turned and ran as fast as she could to the main entrance. The familiar buzz of the door release couldn't come quickly enough, and she bit down on her bottom lip, hard. She took a card out of her pocket that DI Baxter had left with Mike Button.

'Come on, come on, stop fucking about and open the fucking door,' she mumbled under her breath.

The door buzzed and she threw herself into the airlock.

'Tony, give me a phone, quick!'

7

'DI Baxter, how can I help?'

'Hi, Lomas, I've got a Governor Dominicali on the line,' said the desk sergeant.

'OK, thanks, put her through. Hello, Governor–'

'It's Monica. She's escaped!'

'What?' Lomas could hardly believe his ears.

'She's out! She killed two more of my officers and forced me to help her get out. She's out, DI Baxter, she's out. What have I done?'

Lomas heard the panic in Niamh Dominicali's voice. 'OK, let's take it one step at a time. You say she's out. How did she get away?' he asked as sympathetically as he could, while waving at Drew to come in.

Drew opened Lomas's office door and he covered the phone, while listening to the governor tell him that Monica had taken her car.

'Can you get the control room to get an ANPR alert put out on this car, please?' He scribbled down the make, model and registration number the governor had given him. 'Then come back in here please.'

‘Will do, boss.’

Lomas turned his attention back to the call. ‘How long ago did this happen?’

‘Just in the last five or ten minutes. She told me not to say anything for at least an hour or she would come back and kill me,’ she said between heavy breaths, from sprinting back to reception.

‘She can’t have got far. We’ll get officers out. Let me call you back. What number can I reach you at?’ He took down the number, ripped the note from his desk pad and leapt out of his chair. Standing by his desk, he called through to the control room. ‘Jim? I need your help. We’ve got an escaped prisoner – in a car, left the prison five to ten minutes ago. Drew just came down to get an ANPR alert out.’

‘I’ve seen the alert, Lomas, and all of our patrols will have it. Do you want us to get the guys to start scanning the CCTV feeds to see if we can locate it leaving the prison and then track it from there?’

‘That would be great.’

‘I’ll get clearance to get the chopper up as well. That will give us eyes in the sky.’

‘Thanks, Jim. Can you get a message out to the patrols not to approach the prisoner if they locate the car? She’s dangerous, and I don’t know if she’s armed.’

'She?'

'It's Monica Silverman, Jim.'

'Fucking hell, Lomas, that's not good. I'll get cracking.'

'Cheers, Jim.' Lomas left his office and bounded up the stairs to DCI Marie Carlton's office. He knocked and, unusually, opened the door without waiting for a reply. Marie spun her chair to face him.

'Lomas, you OK?'

'No, not really. I've just had a call from Governor Dominicali. Monica's escaped.'

'What? How?' asked Marie.

'According to the governor, she helped her to get out. I don't have any details yet, but she's been out about ten minutes.'

'She helped her get out – what the hell? Do we have any idea where she might have gone?'

'Who knows? I'm still trying to get my head round the fact that she's out. Jim's getting the chopper up, pulling the CCTV feeds, and an ANPR has been put out. He's also speaking to uniform to get people out to the train and bus stations. I'm going to go to the prison and see the governor, try to establish exactly what happened and see if Monica said anything that will give us an idea of where she might be headed. I'd also like to get Christina Marley picked up and armed response ready to go.'

'Do you think Monica might go after her?'

'I think she's the only one that got away – and that pissed Monica off.'

'OK. You get up to the prison, I'll get armed response sorted and arrange to have Christina collected. Keep me posted. The shit's going to hit the fan with this one, Lomas. It'll go all the way to the top.' Marie shook her head.

'Yeah, I know. We could do with a quick result on this.' He rounded up Drew on his way out and headed for the prison. As they drove, he called Heidi. When they'd been hunting Monica the last time, she'd taunted him and his family, delivering gruesome packages containing body parts and sick notes to his home. The only way he'd been able to keep his family safe and concentrate on tracking Monica had been for Heidi and their two children to move to her parents' house. He didn't want to panic her, but he also didn't want to risk them being home if Monica decided to head there.

He used voice command to make the call while he drove. As soon as he said, 'Call home' Drew glanced across at him. Lomas was sure she knew why he was calling Heidi.

'Hey, you OK?' Heidi said in her usual bright tone.

'I'm good, thanks. Are you and the kids all at home?'

'Me and Eve are. Ant's out with his mates. Why?'

'Can you get hold of him and all three of you go around to someone's house until I get home from work? I don't want you to panic, but Monica Silverman has escaped from prison and I don't want any of you in the house on your own.'

There was a pause that felt like it lasted forever, then Heidi spoke. 'Yeah, of course. I'll go and pick up Ant and we'll head over to Lucy's. She's in with the kids tonight, and she'll be fine with us going over, I'm sure. Are you OK?'

'Yeah, I'm fine. Drew and I are heading to the prison to speak to the governor. Text me when you get to Lucy's would you?'

'Yeah, sure. Be careful, love you.'

'Love you too.' He ended the call and turned his attention to Drew. She too had been targeted by Monica during her reign of terror, and he needed to check she was OK with getting involved again.

'How are you feeling about this?' he asked.

'I'm not massively chuffed that she's out, if that's what you mean. But we've got a job to do and there's nothing I'd rather do than bring Monica back in.'

'OK. In that case, I guess we're both going to talk to the governor. For your information, she sounded in quite a state on the phone. She said that Monica had killed two more of her officers before forcing the governor to help her escape.'

'Wow, she doesn't do things by halves, does she?' Drew marvelled.

'Nope, she doesn't.'

'Do you think she'll come after us again?'

'I don't know. I'm hoping we can bring her in before that becomes an issue. She's only been gone a little while and we've got every copper in the area looking for her. She can't get far.'

Apart from making a call to check the scenes of crime team were heading to the prison too, they didn't say anything else the rest of the way. When they arrived, Governor Dominicali was waiting for them at reception. Her face was flushed and she looked understandably stressed. She walked them through to a private room and asked one of her team to get them some drinks.

Lomas took a good look at Niamh Dominicali. He couldn't imagine how she must be feeling, but he needed to understand what had happened if he was to have any chance of finding Monica quickly before anyone else got hurt.

They made polite small talk until their drinks arrived. Lomas took a sip of his tea. It was too hot to drink, so he put it to one side and took a small voice recorder from his jacket pocket.

'Are you happy for us to record our conversation, Governor? It will really help when we get back to the station if we can let the rest of the team hear what you've been through.'

'Yes of course, that's fine.' She began to sound flustered again. Lomas knew he would have to tread carefully if he was going to get a useful interview from her. He got them each to introduce themselves for the recording, then began.

'Are you feeling OK to talk about the events of earlier today, Governor?'

'Niamh, please call me Niamh and yes, that's fine. I want to help in any way I can. I feel just awful about what I've done.'

'Let's not worry too much about that at the moment. It sounds like you've been through quite an ordeal, and all the training in the world doesn't prepare you for someone like Monica Silverman. Trust me, we know.' He smiled reassuringly and paused to let Niamh gather herself. 'In your own time, can you tell me what happened, in as much detail as you can remember? The smallest detail can make all the difference.'

'Yes, of course. I asked two of my officers to accompany me to Monica's room. I was escorted by officers Bell and Rodriguez. I went to see what she had to say about the attack on Bob Anderson.'

'OK, so what happened when you got to the cell?'

'She seemed in a reasonably cooperative mood. We spoke about what she'd done to the three officers. She said she didn't know that Bob was dead until she'd spoken to you, and seemed genuinely sorry that he'd died. She made a point of telling me that she hadn't intended to kill any of them. It's like she does it for fun. Anyway, we exchanged a few sympathetic words about Bob and I turned to leave. Then she grabbed me from behind, around the throat. She squeezed so hard, I thought she was going to kill me.'

'That must have been frightening. How did Bell and Rodriguez react?'

'Bell tried to de-escalate her, but she wasn't listening to him. I tried to defend myself, but she punched me in the ribs and knocked the wind out of me.' Her chin creased and her bottom lip began to quiver. Drew passed her some water. She nodded her thanks and took a sip.

'What happened next?' Lomas asked.

'Bell stepped closer and Monica spun me around and punched me in the face. It must have knocked me out, because when I came round, Bell and Rodriguez were both down.'

'When you say "down", what do you mean?'

'Bell was in Monica's bed. She was wearing his uniform. Rodriguez was dead in the corner. He looked as if he'd taken quite a beating.'

'So did you know Bell was dead?'

'No, I assumed he was dead as she'd got his clothes on and had put him into her bed with just the back of his head showing.' Her voice cracked as she finished the sentence. She took a minute to gather herself.

'OK, you're doing really well. Would you like to take a break?' Lomas asked, hovering a hand over the recorder.

'No, I'm fine, thank you.' All the time Niamh was talking she was wringing her hands and tears welled in her eyes.

'OK, take your time. When you're ready, tell me what happened next?'

Niamh took a tissue from her pocket and dabbed under her eyes, sitting straighter in her chair. 'She handcuffed me as I came round – I'm not sure why, as she took them off before we left the room. Maybe it was a power thing. Anyway, next she talked me through how I was going to help her get out. She told me that we were going to make our way through to the staff changing room, where she was going to find some other clothes to change into. Then we were going to walk to reception together. When we got close, she wanted me to chat to her as if she were visiting a family member who was in the prison. Then she told me that she wanted me to keep up the conversation and to keep it as bright and natural as possible, so the reception staff didn't twig. She told me that when we reached reception, I was to walk with her out to the car park and give her my car keys. She told me that if I didn't do any of it, or if I tried to raise the alarm, she'd kill me – and whatever members of my team were witnesses or closest to us at the time.'

'So, when Monica told you how you were going to help her get out, what did you think was going to happen?'

'I didn't think it would work. It sounded too simple and I was convinced that someone would recognise her and raise the alarm, figuring out that I was acting under duress.'

'But no one did?'

She took another sip of water. 'No, it was just like she said. We walked to the staff changing room where she broke into some lockers until she found some clothes. I tried to run while she was looking through a locker, but she was too quick – she slammed the door shut on me and dragged me back inside. She told me she was prepared to overlook that one attempt, but if I tried anything else she'd kill me and my family. We left the changing room with her walking beside me, then we chatted on the walk up to reception. She gave Tony a visitor pass that she'd found in the staff area, and we walked straight out of the door into the car park. When we got to my car she demanded some ID with my address on and, well, then she was gone.'

'It sounds terrifying, Niamh, but could I ask why you didn't raise the alarm when you were in the main entrance, with lots of staff around?' Drew asked.

'I've asked myself the same question, DS Taylor. If I'm honest, I was too scared. Like I said, she told me that if I tried to get help, or raise the alarm, she'd kill me and everyone around us. I knew she meant it – and from what I've seen, I knew she was capable.'

Drew nodded. Lomas waited to see if she was going to ask a follow-up question. When she didn't, he asked Niamh to carry on.

She explained that as soon as she'd heard her car get beyond the perimeter of the prison, she'd run inside and called the police, remembering she had the card Lomas had left with Mike Button. She sounded sincere enough. From watching her body language while she was giving them an account of what had happened, Lomas believed her. Even though Niamh was an experienced governor, she'd clearly been shaken by the ordeal with Monica and had acted under extreme duress.

'OK, Niamh, is there anything else you can think of that we need to know?'

'Only that while she was telling me what she would do to me and my family if I raised the alarm too early, she also said that she was looking forward to finishing what she'd started.'

'She said that?'

'Yes, those exact words. She took my keys off me, and the letter with my address, and said, "Thank you for the temporary loan of the car, Governor, I'll leave it in one piece. But it might be the only thing that is. I'm looking forward to finishing what I started." Then she jumped into my car and drove out of the gates.'

Niamh's hands shook as she lifted the glass to her mouth.

Lomas and Drew exchanged glances.

'Thank you, Governor, that's been really helpful.' Lomas stood to leave, picking up and turning off the recording device.

'You will catch her, won't you, Detective? I couldn't live with myself if my actions resulted in more people getting hurt.'

'We've caught her before, we'll do it again – and this time we have an advantage. We know who she is.' He smiled at Niamh as he moved towards the door, then added, 'I think you could probably do with getting some rest. You've been through quite an ordeal. Be kind to yourself, Niamh. No one knows how they're going to react when they're placed in a position like that – until it happens. You did what you thought was right, for you and your people. That takes courage.'

8

Monica floored the TT and felt the acceleration push her back into the seat.

'Nice car, Governor. Maybe not such a hairdresser's car after all.' She swung out to overtake a slow-moving van. She cranked up the stereo and lost herself for a few minutes in the feeling of freedom, one which she hadn't been sure she would ever have again, until Niamh came to her with her corrupt little scheme. Monica caught a glimpse of herself in the rear-view mirror. The borrowed baseball cap prevented anyone from getting a clear view of her face.

She turned off the main road and headed down a wide country road, moving fast enough to put a good distance between herself and the prison, but not fast enough to attract any unwanted attention. The road wound playfully and she enjoyed the way the Audi handled. She was aware that she would have to ditch the governor's car quite soon as she was convinced that Dominicali wouldn't have waited an hour before raising the alarm, despite her threats. She'd clearly been shitting herself. Monica doubted she would have been able to hold off screaming for help the minute Monica was out of sight.

Seeing a sign showing Andover to her right, she began to get her bearings. Keeping to the twisty back roads, she gunned the TT again and pointed it towards a quiet little place called Ropley, with the intention of heading for Petersfield. She knew the police would be focusing on all major routes around the prison and working outwards, but she also knew that they didn't have the manpower to patrol all the country lanes – and that was where she intended to stay until she'd ditched the car.

Monica thought through her options. If she was to stay undetected for any length of time, she had to be smart. Baxter would already be involved, she was sure of it, and he was no mug.

As the road started to widen and a steady stream of cars and bikers appeared, out enjoying the roads, she took a turn down a narrow, hedge-bound track. She bumped along the track for a hundred metres or so, recognising the TT wasn't built for this kind of terrain. Once she was sure she was out of view of the road, she stopped the car, killed the engine and left it with the keys in the ignition. She ripped both number plates from the car and threw them – some considerable distance and in opposite directions – into the surrounding fields. She thought that the lack of plates might slow down identification of the Audi. Maybe only for a few minutes – but they all counted.

With the baseball cap pulled down and her hands stuffed into her pockets, she set off on foot for the nearest train station.

It didn't take long to work out where she was. Thankfully she wasn't far from the market town of Alton. She remembered it as being the home of steam trains, from days out with her father as a youngster. She made her way to the train station, keeping her head bowed and her face hidden. It was a risky strategy but she had to get to her stashed funds, and that would mean travelling from Alton to Portsmouth. It would take too long to walk and she figured that jumping on and off trains was less risky than hitch-hiking.

Monica stood in front of a train timetable and worked out a convoluted, indirect route that would be difficult for anyone to track. Then she found a quiet corner and leaned against the wall, waiting for her first train.

She spent the next hour and forty-five minutes on four different trains. They took her up to Aldershot, across to Guildford, down to Petersfield and finally on to Portsmouth.

Her plan worked well. She got on the train, listened to the guard announce where they were, then headed to the toilet in the furthest carriage from the guard, only coming out when she heard the station she wanted next announced over the train's speakers.

Only once did she nearly come unstuck. When she stepped out of the toilet as the train approached Petersfield station, the guard was checking tickets. A woman, balancing a baby on her hip while holding on to a shopping-laden pushchair, held out her ticket to him. Monica turned quickly back into the loo, closing the door until she heard the familiar 'Tickets, please' further on, past the toilets. She just managed to get out in time.

Dusk was starting to draw in as Monica reached Portsmouth. She walked out of the station, avoiding a bored-looking police officer who was standing to the left of the main door. The huge metal station canopy hung above her and a line of taxis stood patiently waiting for their next fare. There was a chill in the air and she could smell fast food from across the street. She didn't need to stay here long – just long enough to get to her money and get away.

Walking at a fair pace, which kept out the cold, she took a right and headed through the middle of

Landport. She stuck to residential streets and green areas, staying away from possible CCTV cameras mounted on shop fronts. She could see kids playing in gardens, making the most of the fading light and she ignored anyone who looked her way, focused on reaching her destination without drawing any attention to herself. As she turned down an alleyway, which felt like it went in the direction she needed to go, a couple of youths stepped out from an adjacent alley.

They wore black hoodies, their hoods drawn down over baseball caps, not dissimilar to the one Monica wore. The taller of the two, who had a scattering of stubble, stood in Monica's path. She stepped to the side, but the small one, who wore a big, toothy grin, blocked her way.

'You got a phone?' the taller one asked.

Monica ignored them and put an arm forward to part them. They didn't move.

'Oi! You fuckin' deaf? I said, you got a phone?'

'No, I'm not deaf, and no, I don't have a phone. Now please move,' said Monica.

'She says she ain't got a phone, bruv. What d'you reckon?' the teen said, turning to his smaller accomplice.

'I think she's full of shit. Everyone's got a phone, innit?'

'Yeah, you definitely got a phone. And while you're at it, give us your purse too.'

'Oh, I get it – this is the part where I get all scared and hand over my belongings in the hope that you won't hurt me. Is that the plan?' Monica asked, amused.

The youths shared a confused glance.

'Yeah, that's right, now fuckin' hand it over,' said the short one, raising his voice.

'And if I say no?'

'You don't wanna say no. We'll fuck you up.' He made a gun-like gesture with his hand.

'Is that a fact? Well, if you gents are so sure that I have a phone and money, why don't you come and get them?' Monica threw a lightning-quick jab into the throat of the taller one, who gasped for air and clutched his neck. She turned to his sidekick. Before he could move, she'd grabbed his hood, pulling it down and twisting it around her hand. With complete control of the youth's head, Monica looked into his defiant eyes. Then she brought up her knee, while driving his head downward to meet it. His face bounced off her powerful leg and she felt his nose crumple on impact. She dropped him and let him fall to the ground. Monica turned to see the taller one starting to recover his composure, but still taking in hefty emergency gulps of air. In one swift movement, she knocked him to the ground. When he landed on his back, winded, she stamped on his chest, hearing his ribs crack under her foot. He let out a whimper and coiled into a defensive ball. Monica ripped his hood and cap from his head, grabbed a fistful of his hair and pulled his face close to hers.

'Now you listen to me, you little fuck. Next time you decide to rob some poor bastard in a back alley, remember, there's always someone who will surprise you. So unless you're absolutely sure that you're invincible, which clearly you're not, don't fucking do it. Now, give me *your* phone and both of *your* wallets.' She let go of his hair and he scrambled to his unconscious friend. He rifled through his mate's pockets and got out an iPhone and a scruffy-looking Marvel wallet, then he shoved his hands into his own jeans and produced another iPhone, which looked quite new, and a wad of cash.

'I don't carry a wallet, just foldin'.'

'Well, that'll have to do, won't it? Hand it over.' She looked in the wallet and found an ID card. 'So your friend down there is called Damian. What's your name?'

'Erm, it's ... Paul.'

'Paul what?'

'Paul Daniels.'

'You're shitting me?' she said with an amused smile.

'No, seriously, it's Paul Daniels.' He looked like he'd explained it a million times and was thoroughly pissed off with having to do it again.

'Now that's magic! OK, Daniels, before I fuck off and leave you alone, if you and Debbie McGee here say anything to anyone about this and it gets back to me, I'm coming to his house first, then yours. And what you've just had will be nothing compared to what I'll do to you. Clear?'

'Yeah, yeah, we're clear. We won't say a word. Honest.'

'You wouldn't know honest if it bit you in the balls. Now, sit next to your mate, Debbie, and stay there until she wakes up.'

'OK.'

'One more thing. What's the PIN number for this phone?'

'One, three, seven, nine.'

'Thanks. Now remember, not a word.' Monica held up a cautionary finger. She looked at the wad of cash in her hand. There must have been about £300, which she figured was either their benefit money or they'd nicked it. Then she looked at the battered Daniels, crouched on the ground next to Damian, wincing with pain. She peeled a twenty off the wad and threw it at Daniels.

'Get yourselves some painkillers and something to clean the cuts with.'

She didn't wait for a reply. The shocked look on Paul's face was enough to make her smile. She turned and carried on walking, leaving the pair beaten and bloody on the ground.

The rest of her journey was without incident. She took pleasure from being out in the fresh air, no one barking orders at her or telling her how long she had left outside, as had been the case for last few months.

As she made her way down a long road lined with terraced houses she looked in through the occasional window, wondering about the families who lived there. What kind of lives did they have?

The enticing scent of fish and chips drifted out of an open window, and she realised it was hours since she'd eaten. First my money, then food, she thought. Should she be healthy or bad with her food choice? She reconciled herself to the knowledge that it was going to be a greasy takeaway, for sure.

As she neared her destination, she became hypervigilant of her surroundings, taking in each movement, passing car and noise from nearby windows. It would have been better to do this at night, but she couldn't afford to wait until after dark. She needed to keep moving and the best way to do that was with cash in her pocket.

The abandoned vicarage loomed large in front of her. Monica hadn't been here for almost two years. The last time had been with Elinor Mary Clarke.

She checked up and down the long street as she approached the house. No one was around. She walked around the side, making her way along beside a high fence. Four panels along, she pushed a hand between a post and the edge of the first slat. It came away easily, she smiled. Reaching inside and about two-thirds of the way up the panel, she felt around and located what she was feeling for. A slide bolt, which she pushed away from her with her thumb. With her other hand she grabbed the first fence panel and pulled. A camouflaged gate swung open and she stepped into an overgrown garden. She closed the gate behind her and replaced the loose fence panel. Monica turned and looked up at the big old house. Faded bunting, that looked as if it was left from a party many years ago, hung from door handles and fluttered in the wind. She snorted her disapproval and walked away from the house, wading through the dense undergrowth, feeling the tall grass brush against her hands as she walked.

At the end of the garden, twenty metres from the house, was a rickety old shed, its door hanging off. Monica moved the door to one side and brushed thick cobwebs away as she stepped inside.

It had clearly not been used for a long time. It smelled damp and didn't look like the local kids had bothered with it either, which was a relief.

Confidently, Monica reached into a half open drawer and retrieved a claw hammer. She flicked a bug from the handle and let the hammer hang by her side. Using the torch on Paul's phone, she lit up the back corner of the shed. She counted three floor panels in, then mentally traced a line along the plank until she reached an end-to-end join. She knelt down and put the claw of the hammer into the small gap between the two ends of wood and prised one end up towards her. When it had moved enough for her to get her fingers under it, she pulled the length of timber clear and placed it carefully behind her. She did the same with two shorter planks on either side clearing a hole in the floor. Then she reached in until she felt some plastic sheeting. She pulled the plastic to one side to reveal a black gym bag. Lifting the bag out, she held it in front of her, smiling in satisfaction at her own cunning. Monica replaced the floorboards, stamping them back into place. She put the hammer back in the drawer and stepped out of the shed.

In the garden, she took a look around, to be sure there were no unexpected visitors, which would have been bad – for them. Satisfied she was still alone, she opened the bag. It was filled with bundles of bank notes of various denominations – more than enough to fund her escape. It also contained a sheath knife with a 3.5-inch blade and a walnut handle.

She'd owned the knife for years, having bought it with some of her Christmas money when she was thirteen. Back then it was used to kill small animals – mice, rats, the odd cat. She unsheathed it. Memories of the acts she'd committed with it came back to her as she weighed it in her hand. She could almost see the glazing over of the animals' small black eyes as life drained from their vulnerable bodies.

For as long as she could remember, Monica had known she was different. She'd always been fascinated by death, by how fragile life is, and the power she could have over it.

She'd graduated to humans when she was about seventeen. Her first kill had been a young girl she'd gone to school with, Macy Turner. She'd always annoyed her. The kill had been clumsy and without any finesse. Macy was a popular girl who, along with her entourage, used to tease Monica and any other girl who looked different, who didn't fit in, until they cried, or did something that got them ridiculed even more. Monica had managed to talk Macy into walking with her into town, which meant them going over Southampton's Itchen Bridge. When she was sure there was no one around, Monica had wrestled Macy to the edge of the bridge and pushed her over, then watched her plunge to her death in the icy water, twenty-seven metres below. The coroner had determined it had been suicide, despite the protestations of Macy's parents, and that had been that. Her first victim.

She zipped the bag shut and threw it over her shoulder, heading for Southsea, some fresh clothes, food and transport.

9

'I know you have my team's best interests at heart Marie, but not having me on this would be a mistake. I know her better than anyone. I know how she thinks, and how dangerous and unpredictable she is,' Lomas said.

'Look, Lomas, I know that you are without a doubt the best person to be tracking Monica. After all, it was you who brought her in in the first place. But she places you, your family, and Drew, and probably her family, at direct risk of an attack. She said she was going to finish what she started and we've got to take that seriously. When you arrested her, she was taunting you and Drew. God knows who she'd have gone after next.'

'So if you know all that, why would you take me off the case? There's no one else I trust to keep my family safe. I need to be in the middle of it, knowing what she's doing, so I can take the right steps to keep everyone safe and bring her in.'

'Let's say I did let you lead this. Who do you think is in the frame for being on Monica's list?'

'Like you say, Drew and I are probably high on the list, as is Christina Marley. I would imagine she'll want to get to Christina quite quickly. At least now we've brought her in, we don't have to worry too much about her.'

'OK. But Lomas, you're on a short leash with this one. You keep me in the loop every step of the way. Whatever you know, I want to know, understand? If this goes sideways, Randolph and the press will have a field day with it.' Superintendent Randolph was an over-weight, creepy-looking man who liked nothing more than giving Marie and Lomas grief for the slightest of set-backs. Their combined results made it difficult for him to score too many points, but he always took pleasure in it when he could.

'Got it. Thanks, Marie.'

'Don't thank me yet – we haven't caught her. I've still got to get the NCA out to sort out Christina – and do a press release to get Monica's face out there.'

Lomas left DCI Carlton's office and headed for the briefing room. She was Senior Investigating Officer, and she had every right to take him off the case and insist he stay away from it. He needed to get a result, and quick. Everyone that could be drafted in to help, had been. Activity in the police station since they'd got the news of Monica's escape had been frenetic.

There was a busy hum in the room. As Lomas entered, the noise of multiple conversations petered out.

Drew and the Investigation Manager, Tina, had already set up the front of the room: pictures of Monica, her victims, a brief summary of Monica and what she'd done were already posted on the board for colleagues to familiarise themselves with.

'OK, listen up,' Lomas began, clapping his hands. 'As you know by now, Monica Silverman has escaped from prison.' He let the sentence hang in the air for a moment. 'For those who were part of the original investigation, you'll remember just how dangerous Miss Silverman is. She is *not* to be underestimated. She is highly intelligent, highly motivated and very dangerous. She possesses a high degree of athleticism and strength, which only adds to the level of threat she poses. DS Taylor has notes for all of you. Study them and familiarise yourself with them. She has a four-hour head start. She left prison by car, so in theory she could be anywhere between 120 and 200 miles away, if she's been driving consistently. However, I believe, given her previous behaviour, she won't leave the south coast. As far as she's concerned, she has unfinished business here, and that means coming back to this area. She's also smart enough to know that she can't stay in the car she escaped in, which was the governor's Audi TT. I think she'll have dumped the car and made other transport arrangements.

'So we need to find the Audi. A search of CCTV from public transport has so far given us nothing. Nor have the alerts we sent to taxi and bus operators, or the officers we've had in bus and train stations. Pete, Nick, I'd like you to focus on tracking the car. You'll also need to pull all reports of cars stolen over the last four hours, in case she's swapped to something else.'

'Boss,' Nick Swain replied with a nod. Nick was tall and muscular, a rugby-player type with a nose that had clearly been broken.

'You've all got photos on your phones to help with questioning. I'll make the file on Monica available as a download, should you need it while you're out and about. Gurdeep, can you take a couple of officers and check the places we know Monica's used before?'

'Yes, boss.'

'OK. Questions?'

'I have a question,' said a middle-aged uniformed officer from near the back of the room.

'Yes, Jim?'

'Did Monica hurt anybody getting out of prison?'

'Yes, she killed the two prison officers you can see, at the top left of the board, during her escape.' He pointed to the photos of Bell and Rodriguez, next to photos of Bob Anderson, Beth and Gill from the cell attack.

'She killed them both? With what?' Jim asked.

'Her hands. The photos next to Bell and Rodriguez are of Bob Anderson, an officer who died following an attack by Monica in her cell earlier this week, Gill O'Leary and Beth Jeffries, who were both hospitalised after the same attack. Like I said, Monica is extremely dangerous. Which brings me on to my final point. If you're lucky enough to track Miss Silverman down or come across her, you will not approach her on your own, or even in a pair. You call for back-up and keep her under surveillance. No heroics. We've had firearms teams relocated, should we need them. Monica will add you to her tally of dead bodies without giving it a second thought. Any more questions?'

There were none. The hum of conversation returned and Drew walked over towards Lomas.

'You OK?' he asked the younger officer.

'I think so. I can't believe she's out. We're not going to catch her before she hurts someone, are we?'

'Honestly, I doubt it, but hopefully we'll catch her before she kills anyone. I'm hoping she goes to ground to avoid being found. That way, no one gets in her way.'

10

'That will be eight pounds fifty please dear,' the woman said from behind the counter of the chip shop. Monica handed over a twenty-pound note from a bundle she'd taken out of the bag and stuffed in her jeans pocket.

She'd managed to find a couple of pairs of jeans that looked as though they should fit, along with a couple of T-shirts and hoodies from a charity shop across the road. Monica figured that they were unlikely to have advanced security systems or CCTV.

On the face of it, she was right.

She didn't see any cameras as she flicked through the racks of donated clothes. Monica felt relatively safe as she worked her way along the row of small independent shops that lined Palmerston Road, and she'd changed out of her escape clothes into her new ones in a pub toilet.

Eating her chips as she walked, she glanced at the houses she passed. Inside the houses, families were going about their business, oblivious to the killer stalking their streets. She turned left beside a small school. Monica knew that the seafront was at the end of the road. A grey VW Golf reversed into the road from the driveway of a terraced house that sat at an angle to the road. It stopped just short of Monica as she walked by, unfazed by how close it had been. She made her way to the end of the road and stopped outside a hotel, screwing her chip paper into a tight ball. Monica looked the building up and down and decided it would be ideal for her purposes. She made sure her hair was stuffed inside her baseball cap, threw the chip paper over the wall, then walked in.

She was greeted by a guy in his early thirties, sitting behind a crisp-looking white reception desk with a vase of fresh flowers for decoration. Sign-written on the wall above his head were the words 'Time is precious; waste it wisely'. Monica smiled, thinking how apt that was for some of the people she intended to visit.

'Good afternoon. Welcome to Southsea Rocks – how can I help you?'

'Hello, I wondered if you had a room free.'

'Not free, but I won't charge you much.' He laughed. Monica didn't react. He dropped his smile and carried on. 'Er, of course. How long will you be staying for?'

'Let's start with a week and see how we get on.'

'Great. Can I take a name?'

'Thompson – Lena Thompson.' Monica replied without missing a beat.

'OK, Lena, let's get you booked in. I think I have a room on the top floor which is nice and private. How does that sound?'

'Perfect. How much is it?'

'Fifty-five pounds a night.'

'Excellent. I assume you take cash?'

'Of course,' he said, a friendly smile returning to his lips. 'Here's your room key. Enjoy your stay.'

She took the key, returned the smile, then walked towards the stairs.

Her room was immaculately clean and uncluttered. Monica unpacked her meagre belongings from the gym bag and flopped onto the bed. It felt so good to be in a normal room, on a normal bed. She allowed herself to sink into the thick, squishy duvet, and within minutes she was asleep.

11

Lomas's phone vibrated in his pocket.

'Hi Drew – any news?'

'Yes, we've found the governor's Audi.'

'Excellent – where?'

'It was dumped on a track between some fields near Alton. It had no number plates on it, but apart from that it looks fine. A local farmer found it and reported it.'

'OK. We need to locate the plates. Have them check the surrounding fields.'

'Already on it, boss. I'm getting the Audi recovered back to the lab after scenes of crime have finished with it in situ. They're just setting up lighting now.'

'Good. Anything else?'

'I just spoke to Nick. So far they've had no luck from reports of stolen cars and CCTV feeds, but there's a lot to check.'

'OK, let's keep it up. Good work, Drew.'

'Thanks.'

Baxter ended the call and let out a sigh before calling DCI Carlton to update her. It was progress, but not as much as he'd like. He was standing next to his car, on a petrol station forecourt, and couldn't remember what he'd stopped for by the time he ended his call with Marie. Jumping back into his car he headed out of town and towards Heidi's friend Lucy's house. He pulled up outside Lucy's about half an hour later and sat for a minute in the car, knowing that as soon as he walked in he'd get a barrage of questions from Heidi, the kids and Lucy.

Lomas knocked on the door. As he did, it occurred to him that police officers really did have a distinctive knock. Lucy opened the door, gave him a warm smile and stepped to one side to let him in.

'You look like you've had a rough day. Heidi's through there.' Lucy said, tipping her head towards the kitchen.

'Thanks, Lucy. I've had better days, if I'm honest.' He wandered through to the kitchen, where an Ed Sheeran song was playing quietly on the radio. Heidi was sitting at the dining table with a cup of tea. Lomas walked over, kissed her, then took a seat next to her.

'Hey, how you doing?' she said.

'I'm all right – a bit frustrated, but OK.'

'Tea, Lomas? Or something stronger?' Lucy asked, already picking up the kettle.

'Tea's fine, thanks, Lucy. I'm not staying long.'

'So what happened?' Heidi asked.

'It's a long story and I can't share too much of the detail, but the short version is that Monica made the governor walk her out of the prison, then hand over her car for Monica to get away in.'

'Oh my God! Poor woman – is she OK?'

'She was pretty shaken up, but she's a prison governor. I'm sure she's quite resilient.'

'Have you any idea where she's gone?'

'Not yet, but I don't think she'll have gone far. She's smart, but I'm not sure she'll stray far from where she knows. She grew up on the south coast.'

'Do you think Heidi and the kids are at risk?' asked Lucy, putting a coaster down and popping a mug of tea in front of him.

'If I'm honest, I don't know what she'll do. But she's really dangerous and I'm not taking any chances. Speaking of the kids, where are they?'

'They're upstairs with my two. The girls are watching a movie and the lads are playing Xbox.'

'Sounds about right,' he said, taking a sip of his tea. Their twins, Eve and Ant, were sixteen. Eve was quiet, studious and very bright. She was petite, blonde and pretty, and had recently started seeing a boy from school. Lomas had been given scant details about it. Josh was apparently popular with the girls and, according to Ant, his sister was school-corridor gossip. She didn't care. Ant was the exact opposite: tall, loud, loved football and had no time for girls. Instead he spent all the time he wasn't on a football pitch either gaming or out with his mates. The pair got on well and, in common with many twins, had a special bond that was difficult to define, or infiltrate.

'What are we going to do?' Heidi asked him.

'I'm not sure yet, but while she's out I'm not happy about you all being at home while I'm not there.'

'You can stay here,' Lucy offered.

'Thanks, Lucy,' he said, looking at Heidi for a reaction. 'That's really helpful, but you don't want our two making a mess of your house.'

'They can't be any worse than mine – and besides, it'll give them a bit of normality, if you're wrapped up in finding your escapee. Anyway, it's up to you.'

'We should probably talk to the kids,' Lomas said. Lucy went to the foot of the stairs and called up to Ant and Eve. Lomas turned to Heidi. 'I know it's worrying, but I need to know you're all safe so that I can get this done.' He could see the worry in her eyes.

'It's fine. Lucy wouldn't say we could stay here if she didn't mean it. Why don't me and the kids stay here tonight and tomorrow we'll work out what to do next. I'm guessing you'll be having a late one?'

'Yeah. We've had no sight of her yet. As soon as her face hits the TV screens, all the crank calls and mystery sightings will start.'

'Do what you need to do. We'll be fine. I love you.' She cupped his face in her hands and kissed him. For just a couple of seconds, nothing else in the world mattered.

The kids came bounding down the stairs. Eve gave Lomas a hug as she reached him. Ant said, 'Hi Dad.' As he jumped down the bottom four stairs, he walked past him and asked Lucy if she had any crisps.

'In the cupboard, where they always are.' She smiled.

'Thanks, Lucy. I think he's got hollow legs,' said Lomas, moving through into the lounge, listening to his son rummaging through the kitchen cupboards.

They all sat down, Lucy and her kids too. Lomas took a breath.

'Is everything OK, Dad?' Eve asked. She was bright and insightful, and Lomas had always made a point of not lying to his kids if they asked him a direct question.

'I need to talk to you all about something. Do you remember Monica Silverman?'

'Yeah – how could we forget? She's the killer – we had to go to Nan's because of her,' Ant answered.

'That's right. Well, earlier today she escaped from prison.' He looked from one to the other, gauging their reaction and weighing up how much to divulge. 'She's been out for a few hours now and we don't know where she is. So for tonight, you two and your mum are going to stay here with Lucy. I'm going back to work to try and find her.'

'How did she get out, Dad?' Eve asked.

'I don't want to get into the specifics at the minute – it's an ongoing investigation. But this doesn't happen very often. I've got a lot of resources to help me track her down, and we'll be working around the clock until we do.'

'Is that why we came here earlier on?' Eve followed up.

'Yes. I called your mum as soon as I could and asked that you all get away from our house. I've got to make sure you're all safe, so that I can concentrate on catching Monica. Now, she's going to be on the news and probably on your social media feeds too. I don't want you commenting or sharing the stories that come out. She might be watching to see how much attention she's getting and I don't want your names popping up on any feeds.'

'OK, Dad,' they said together.

'Right, can you give me a minute with your mum, guys?' He stood up and hugged them both then they left the room, Lucy and her two following, closing the door behind them. He turned to Heidi. 'Are you going to be OK?'

'I'll be fine – don't worry about us. Just go and do what you need to do.' They kissed again and he stood to leave.

'Love you.'

'Love you too. See you tomorrow.'

12

Thursday

It was just coming up for 6.00 a m and Niamh Dominicali had endured the most restless night of her life. By the time she got home she'd been grilled by her boss, who'd apparently had a very direct call from the Minister of Justice – and she'd had her mother wailing with worry down the phone for over an hour. To top it all off, as she sat in bed, unable to sleep, and turned on the TV that hung on the wall in her plush bedroom, the first thing that popped onto the screen was the face of Monica Silverman. Niamh threw the remote across the room, regretting it as soon as she heard it hit the wall.

'Convicted multiple murderer Monica Silverman had been only a few months into a five life sentences, when she escaped from prison yesterday. A spokesperson from the prison service said that Governor Niamh Dominicali was unavailable for comment.' The programme cut to a clip of DCI Marie Carlton.

'I would urge anyone who believes they have seen Monica Silverman, or has information regarding her whereabouts, to come forward and speak to us. Any information, no matter how small or insignificant you think it may be, could help us track down this dangerous individual. If you think you have spotted Monica, it is vitally important that you do not approach her. Call the police immediately on 101. Alternatively, you can contact Crimestoppers on 0800 555 111. Thank you.'

The news broadcast cut back to the studio and the newsreader summarised the escape again, describing it as their top story, then handed over to the weather.

Niamh threw the covers off and got out of bed, immediately feeling the effects of the half-bottle of spiced rum she'd downed the night before. Her head was pounding and she felt dizzy. She opened her bedroom window and took in a couple of deep breaths of the cool morning air.

'Come on, sort yourself out, Niamh,' she said. She picked up the TV remote, replaced the batteries that had popped out when it hit the wall, and turned the TV off. She headed for a shower, where she stood under the powerful jet of hot water, clearing her head. It was 7.30 a.m. by the time she was dressed and ready to go.

She booked an Uber and within five minutes a Toyota Prius pulled up outside her house.

She was dreading the day ahead. It was going to be hell. She knew she'd fucked up, regardless of how supportive her director, or the Minister for Justice said they would be publicly, she knew she was in for a rocky ride. They were pissed off, and rightly so. No one let a Cat. A prisoner escape, especially not the governor, and especially not by helping them to get out.

Niamh Dominicali was a rising star in the prison service. She'd been fast-tracked through the graduate scheme and had stood head and shoulders above her colleagues, during her leadership course and afterwards. In a male-dominated environment, Niamh was fiercely ambitious and had developed a reputation for being firm but fair, and for getting the job done. At twenty-seven, after acing her promotional exams, she became the youngest prison governor in England. After four years in the job, people were already talking about her replacing her boss.

She sat in the back of the Uber looking out of the window at people going about their business, wondering where Monica was. She called the prison and asked to be put through to Mike Button. He answered quickly, sounding flustered.

'How is everything, Mike?'

'Morning, Governor. To be honest, I've never seen anything like it. It's a circus. There are press everywhere and the phones haven't stopped all morning. They all either want to speak to you or they want a comment from the prison.'

'And what have you said?'

'I said you're not available for comment and that we had nothing additional to say.'

'Good, thank you, Mike. It's OK – I'll speak to them when I get there, or they'll never leave us alone. Could you ask someone to meet me at the gate as soon as I've spoken to the press, please?'

'Of course. I'll meet you there myself. How long will you be?'

'I'll be there in five minutes.' She hung up and sat back in her seat.

As the car turned the corner towards the prison, she saw a swarm of TV crews, press and photographers. Mike was right; they were everywhere. She sighed and braced herself to get out of the car.

'Could you pull up right next to the gates, please?' she asked the driver, who was eyeing her nervously.

'Yes, of course, miss. Is this where the escape was yesterday?'

'Yes, it is.' Her answer was clipped. She was sure he already knew the answer to his question and that he just couldn't think of anything else to say. 'Just here will be fine, thank you.'

One of the photographers spotted her as the car slowed down, and she heard her name shouted multiple times. Cameras started flashing and TV crews were jostling for position as the cab came to a stop.

'Thank you,' she said. She opened the car door, and a hundred questions were thrown at her at once. Niamh turned to face the cameras, being sure to keep a solemn look on her face. This was not a time to smile.

'Governor, could you tell us how Monica Silverman escaped?'

'Governor, could you tell us if anyone died in the escape?'

'Governor, how did she get out?'

The questions came thick and fast, each one louder than the last. She held up her hands and half a dozen boom mics were thrust towards her.

'I would like to thank you for your help in trying to find Monica Silverman. As you know, she absconded from this prison yesterday. I can't share any details with you at the moment, but we are helping the police in every way we can with their search. They responded immediately when we raised the alarm yesterday and have been hugely supportive. Monica Silverman is a very dangerous woman. As DCI Carlton said in her appeal for information, please do not approach her. If you see Monica, or think you have information regarding her whereabouts, please call the police immediately. Thank you.'

With that she turned towards the prison, ignoring the questions being fired at her. Mike was standing at the gate, ready to escort her inside. With the gate and the press behind her Niamh walked, her head high, towards the prison entrance – and her next challenge. To face her staff.

13

Monica woke early. Daylight streaming through the curtains, which she'd been too tired to close the night before. Still in the clothes she'd fallen asleep in, she stood and looked out of the window, stretching after the first decent sleep she'd had in months. She wandered through to the bathroom and looked at herself in the mirror.

'Well, this will never do, Monica,' she said with conviction. 'They're going to spot you a mile away looking like you. What say we change that look?'

She went back into the bedroom and from her gym bag took a pair of scissors and a packet of hair dye, which she'd bought from a small chemist on the walk down to Southsea. She'd been cutting her own hair for years and it didn't take much effort to crop it from just above her shoulders into a short cut, clipped into her neck and tidy at the sides. Next she massaged in the first of the hair products to turn her hair from its natural dark brown to blonde. While she was waiting for the colour to take, she switched on the TV and was amused to see her own face on the news. She felt a warm glow of victory when she saw Governor Dominicali standing outside the prison, telling reporters that she couldn't share the details of the escape.

'I bet you can't, you corrupt bitch.'

Monica made a coffee from the complimentary supplies and flicked through the TV channels to find better coverage of her escape. It didn't take long to find a rerun of DCI Carlton's appeal for information.

Once she'd listened to DCI Carlton, Monica raised her cup to the TV. 'Good luck with your search, Detective.' She said, assured that she'd made the right decision regarding her appearance.

After she'd left the dye on for long enough, she showered, rinsed it off and put on clean clothes, stuffing a baseball cap in her pocket. She walked downstairs and out past reception, where the guy who'd greeted her the previous night gave her a cheery greeting.

'Good morning, Miss Thompson, have a lovely day.'

'You too,' she replied over her shoulder, pushing the door open and heading out onto the street. Monica walked up Florence Road and towards a garage she'd seen the night before. They had a few cheap runabouts on their forecourt and she needed a car if she was going to get around undetected.

'Good morning, I'm Brad, how are you today?' a man greeted her cheerfully, wearing tobacco chinos and a blue V-neck jumper.

'Hello. I'm good, thanks. I'm after a cheap runabout and you seem to have a few.'

'We've definitely got a good selection of affordable cars. Tell me, what kind of thing did you have in mind?'

'Something with a good size boot and not too expensive on fuel.'

'Hmm, let me see. How much were you thinking of spending? Just so I can point you in the right direction.'

'Preferably no more than £1,500 and it would be cash, if that works for you. My last car just died on me, so I'd like to buy a car to take away now.' Monica saw Brad's eyes light up. He almost looked as though he was going to rub his hands together.

Instead he clapped his hands. 'I have just the car for you. Came in part exchange last week. It's got nearly a year's MOT and was serviced at the weekend by our very own in-house mechanics.' He walked enthusiastically away from Monica. She followed at a more leisurely pace. Brad gestured proudly towards a silver Renault Megane. 'Isn't it lovely?'

'It's a bit smaller than I had in mind, if I'm honest, Brad. When I said a large boot, I need room for–'

'Say no more, let me guess. Horse riding? You're into horse riding and you need room in the boot for all your tack.' He beamed at Monica, with a smile that she found instantly obnoxious and made her want to hurt him. She resisted.

'You're spot-on. How did you know?' she said, forcing a smile.

'You don't sell cars for as many years as I have and not get a sense for people. Forget the Megane – I have something much better suited to you.' He walked her around to the other end of the row of cars and pointed to a grey Ford Mondeo estate. 'She's a little high on the miles, but that two-litre engine is bullet-proof. One owner from new, she has a full service history, a good MOT, and she's ready to go.'

'Could I have a look inside?'

'Of course.' He scurried off to get the keys, returning with the same broad smile across his smug face. Monica had thought of three different ways to kill him while he was gone.

'Here you go.' He blipped the key fob and opened the driver's door for her.

'Thanks.' She got into the driver's seat, took the keys from Brad and started the engine. It was clean, rattle-free and would suit her purposes just fine.

'It says £1,895 on the screen, Brad. But I really don't want to spend any more than £1,500.'

'OK, I'll tell you what, if it means you're not stranded… Never let it be said that Brad Williams left a lady stranded. You said cash, didn't you?'

'I did. I have it on me now.'

'Great, then let's go and do the paperwork.' He held out his hand and she shook it reluctantly.

She followed him into a small office with pictures of sports cars on the walls and warranty brochures in a stand on the corner of the desk. It smelled of takeaway food. She could see a scrunched-up McDonald's bag sticking out of the bin.

'OK, so there's just the money and paperwork to sort out. As you're not having the warranty extended, you need to know it comes with three months as standard from us. Any problems, you give me a shout.'

'Thanks, Brad, that's good to know,' she said, getting the cash out of her pocket.

'Now, I just need your name and address for the order form and warranty book.'

'Jodie Grier.' She answered without giving it much thought. She gave a Portsmouth address, a couple of doors down from the vicarage where she'd stashed her money, with equal ease.

'Well, Jodie, you've got yourself a lovely car there.' Brad counted the money and shook her hand again.

'Thanks, Brad. I really appreciate you sorting it out so quickly for me. I need to get off to the horses now.'

'Of course – no rest for the wicked, eh? Have a great day.'

She stuffed the paperwork into the glovebox of the car and drove off the forecourt, heading for the sea-front. Once there, she dutifully paid for a parking ticket for a space facing the sea. She took a chicken sandwich off the passenger seat, that she'd bought on the way, and watched the waves crash against the shore as she ate. Taking Paul Daniels' phone from her pocket, with a new SIM card installed, she set up a free email address and a Facebook profile for Lena Thompson. Once she was on Facebook, she began to search for what she really wanted.

14

It had been a long night. Lomas had snatched a couple of hours sleep in his office. He'd made Drew, Nick, Pete and Gurdeep go home halfway through the night to get some sleep. All were pursuing their own lines of enquiry and reluctant to let up until they'd found something worthwhile. With the exception of Gurdeep, they'd all been on the original investigation. Lomas understood how personally they were taking the need to recapture Monica. But he also knew that, without rest, they'd burn out quickly.

He was sending Heidi a text, his back to the door, when a soft voice he recognised interrupted him.

'Lomas Baxter, how the hell are you?'

He spun around in his chair and sprang to his feet in a much more energetic fashion than his lack of sleep should have allowed. Stephen Leade was a detective inspector who'd been on the force as long as Lomas. They'd worked cases together when they were coming through the ranks. Leade had a razor-sharp brain and had been tipped for fast-tracking, but in his own words 'couldn't bothered with the paperwork that came with sitting behind a desk higher up the chain'.

'Stephen, great to see you, come in.'

Leade took a seat opposite Lomas. 'I hear you've got a hunt on your hands.'

'You could say that. I'm sure you've heard all about it.'

'I've had the headlines. Prison governor aids escape, serial killer on the loose, Lomas Baxter counting increasing number of grey hairs.' He grinned at Lomas.

'That's about the size of it – definitely more greys. What brings you here this early?'

'I've been doing a piece of work on prison deaths. Your Governor Dominicali has had a few recently. When I heard about the escape it piqued my interest, so I thought I'd pop over and see if you could tell me if you've got anything relating to the recent deaths.'

'Yeah, sure. Like you say, there have been a few deaths at the prison recently. In fact, I got one of my DS's to pull the details on deaths that have happened over the last few months, since Monica arrived. Would that be helpful?'

'I might already have it, but I'll happily take a look at what you've got. You think Silverman is linked to more of the deaths than official reports say?'

'I don't know. She said something odd, when Drew and I went up to the prison to interview her, about an officer who died in her cell after she'd attacked him.'

'Oh?'

'Yeah. I don't know if there's anything to it, but you know when something sticks in your head?' said Lomas.

'I know what happens when things stick in your head, mate. People generally end up inside.' Leade grinned at Lomas.

'Well, it's one of those. We were finishing the interview, we'd turned off the tape, and she said, "You need to know something. There is much more going on here than you realise".'

'Any idea what she meant, or why she'd say that?'

'Not a clue. I've racked my brains and can't think what she'd have to gain from it. Like I say, it's stuck in my head, but there may be nothing to it. She is a psychopath, after all.'

'Fair enough. If I could have a look at what you've got, that'd be great. Now, have you got any decent coffee in this place?'

'Ha – I don't know about decent, but let's go and grab a cuppa.'

They wandered out to the kitchen. Lomas made them both a drink and they sat for a while, chatting about family, life and the job. They'd both seen their fair share of action. It had been a while since they'd had a catch-up. Lomas checked his watch; Stephen drained his cup and stood up.

'Right, mate, I need to get on. It's been good to see you. I'll let you know if I can add anything after I've read the file. We need to catch up properly soon over a beer, not a coffee.'

'Yes mate, definitely. I'll get Drew to send that stuff over today. I'll see you soon.'

They shook hands. Leade headed for the stairs, and Lomas turned and walked towards the open-plan office where his team were working on tracking Monica.

'Morning all,' he said brightly as he walked into the room.

'Morning, boss,' replied those who weren't on phone calls. He made a beeline for the team who were trawling CCTV footage. As he got close, DC Carver, a young officer with thick dark hair, spun around on his chair.

'That was good timing, boss. I think I might have something.'

Lomas grabbed a chair and pulled it up next to Carver. 'OK, show me what you've got, Grant.'

'It's not the best image, as it's from an in-train camera, but if you compare the footage we have of Monica leaving the prison with the person here…' He hovered his screen pointer over an image of someone in a baseball cap. 'I think it looks like it could be her. They ducked into the toilet, came out briefly, and then when the guard appears in the back of the shot, they go back into the toilet and don't come out again until the station.'

'Great work, Grant. Can you zoom in on the figure?'

'I've already enhanced it to improve the image, but yes, I can get in closer.' He dragged his mouse along the pad, zooming in on the figure in the centre of the image.

'Stop there,' Lomas said, leaning in to get a better look. The person in the picture had their head bowed, clearly trying to avoid any cameras, but the clothing and stance looked enough like Monica for Lomas to be excited.

'Clean this up as much as you can, please. Then get some copies printed. Bring them with you to the morning briefing to talk everyone through.'

'Me, sir?'

'Yes, you. You found her. Well done. Now tell me, where was this?'

'The train is just pulling up to Petersfield station, which is where they get off. I've checked the timings and it's a couple of hours after Monica escaped, boss.'

'Why the hell is she in Petersfield?' Lomas pondered out loud.

'I don't know, boss.'

'Don't worry about it, Grant. You've done a great job. Between now and the briefing, can you track back and find out where she got on? And where she went next?'

'I should be able to find her by going through all the cameras.'

'Can you split them and get someone to give you a hand?'

'Yes, we can split the camera feeds and have a look between us. We might be able to follow her using the station cameras.'

'Great. See you in the briefing at 08.30.'

'Yes, boss.' Grant beamed.

Next Lomas went to the team that had been screening phone calls from the TV appeal. They'd been bombarded with false sightings from people who seemed to be genuinely trying to be helpful.

'How's it going, Jenny?' Lomas said to a middle-aged woman with big eyes, sharp features, and brown hair in a tight bun on top of her head.

'Pretty much what you'd expect so far.'

'That bad, eh?'

'Well, so far she's been moving furniture into a house in Norfolk, buying cheap vodka in a corner shop in Inverness, and ten-pin bowling in Liverpool.' She smiled ruefully.

'OK, I'll leave you to it. Give me a shout if you get anything that seems remotely likely, would you?'

'You'll be the first to know.' She turned back to her screen and answering her next call.

Lomas decided to go and see Marie Carlton and update her on the train CCTV image before getting a quick shower and change of clothes, ready for the morning briefing.

Marie had been an early bird for as long as Lomas had known her. They had joined the force together. She'd always been more focused on promotion than Lomas, and he had no doubt that she would make Chief Constable. He knocked on the door and immediately heard her invite him in.

'Good morning,' he said as he walked through the door.

'Morning, how are we doing?'

'Not too bad. The phone lines haven't stopped since your appeal yesterday, which was very good, by the way. You ever considered a career in TV?' he asked with a smile.

'Like you have time to watch TV if I did.' She returned his smile. 'Have we got anything?'

'That's why I came to see you. Grant has pulled some train CCTV and it shows what looks like Monica, hiding in a toilet between stops then getting off at Petersfield.'

'What the hell would she be doing there?'

'That's what I thought. Anyway, I've got Grant and the team trawling the rest of the footage to see where she got on the train and where she went after she got off.'

'That's great intel but the trail's running cold.'

'I know. We got nothing off the car apart from her prints, which we obviously already have. She'd tossed the plates in opposite directions into fields, I guess to slow us down.'

'Did it?'

'No, not really. We'd already confirmed it was the right car. Then we dusted it and checked for anything on site we could use, before we brought it back.'

'OK, so where do you think she's gone from Petersfield?'

'I'm still convinced she's heading back down this way. When we find out what she did when she got off, we'll try and track her from there.'

'OK, good stuff. Keep me in the loop, will you? Oh and Lomas, get changed. You were wearing that yesterday.' She smiled and opened her laptop. He didn't reply, just smiled, shook his head and headed off for a shower.

There was a real buzz about the briefing room when he walked in just after 08.25. Grant sat at the front of the room, looking nervous.

'Morning, boss,' Drew said as he walked to meet her at the front of the room.

'Morning, did you get some sleep?'

'Yes, I managed to get a few hours, thanks. How about you?'

'I grabbed a couple of hours. Have you spoken to Grant yet?'

'Yes, just now. He's got copies of the images he pulled. It looks like he found her, don't you think?'

'I do, yes. I'm just going to check he's OK. I told him he could brief the team.'

'That explains why he's a bit quieter than normal.'

Lomas took a few steps towards Grant, who stood up straight away.

'You good to go, Grant?'

'Yeah, I think so, boss.'

'Good man, you'll be fine. Just take deep breaths and try not to talk too quickly. Remember, you're the surveillance expert in the room – they'll all want to hear what you've got to say.'

'Really?'

'Yes, really. Don't worry, you'll be great. I'll bring them to order then get you to update them on the images. Have you got some with you?'

'I have, and I've got it loaded on the screen, ready.'

"Course you have. See, you've nailed it before you start.' He patted Grant on the shoulder and went to the front of the room.

'Is he OK?' Drew asked.

'He's bit nervous, but he'll be fine.' He clapped his hands at bang on 08.30 and the room fell silent.

'Right, people, good morning. We've had a busy night. The phones haven't stopped since the TV appeal for information went live. We've had nothing useful yet, unless you count a report of Monica ten-pin bowling in Liverpool, but Jenny and the team are screening every call and you never know when we're going to strike gold.' He nodded at Jenny, who was standing near the back of the room. 'Similarly, our checking of stolen car reports hasn't given us anything to go on. Nick, Pete and the team are going to carry on with that this morning. But it looks like Monica has dumped the governor's car, which we've recovered from a track between fields near Alton, and left on foot. So far, the car hasn't yielded anything significant, but the forensics team are going over it with a fine-tooth comb and we'll be updated if they find anything. Which brings me on to CCTV surveillance. Grant, come and update everyone on what you've found.' He took a step to the side to let DC Carver take centre-stage.

'Good morning,' Grant Carver said, clearing his throat twice. 'We ran extensive reviews of the CCTV feeds from train stations and train footage, starting from the nearest to the prison and working our way out. The image here' – he clicked a remote towards a TV mounted at the front of the room – 'is from the CCTV of a train going between Guildford and Petersfield about two hours after Silverman escaped.' He paused and let the officers look at the image. 'This image was taken by a camera inside the prison at the time of the escape, showing what we now know to be Monica Silverman leaving the prison.' He clicked again and the screen split in half, putting the images alongside each other. The two, side by side, showed what looked like the same person, in the same clothes. He waited for a moment to let the buzz in the room subside.

'We also managed to track someone we believe to be Monica Silverman getting off the train at Petersfield and getting on a connecting train that terminated at

Portsmouth.' He played a clip of CCTV footage. It showed the person in the baseball cap stepping onto the platform, hanging around until the train to Portsmouth arrived, then getting on board. 'The cameras on this train are being analysed as we speak.' He stopped and looked at Lomas, looking pleased with himself.

Lomas stepped forward. 'Thank you, Grant, that's fantastic work. So people, we have a sighting, we have a travel route and a possible destination. Grant and the team will check to see if they can find Monica getting off between Petersfield and Portsmouth, then track her at whatever station she gets off at. We work on the assumption, for now, that she's headed to Portsmouth. Let's go through the original investigation again and see what, if anything, relates to Portsmouth. I'll contact colleagues in Pompey, we'll get word out that she may have ended up there, and get eyes on the ground looking for her. The rest of you, carry on with the lines of enquiry you're already following. Any questions?'

No one spoke.

'OK, let's get going. Thank you all – this is real progress.' Energised by this new information, Lomas went to speak to Grant Carver. 'Well done, Grant...'

'Sorry, I didn't get a chance to tell you about the additional information before we started.'

'No problem. We've got our first real lead, thanks to you and the team. Now, how quickly do you think you can pull the Portsmouth train footage apart?'

'I would guess an hour.'

'OK, fine. Let either me or Drew know the minute you find anything.'

'Will do,' Grant said, then scurried off to get to work on the footage.

'What are we going to do, boss?' Drew asked.

'We're going to speak to DCI Carlton about updating our media appeal to narrow it down to the south coast. I want Monica to feel like we're closing in on her.'

15

Monica typed 'Christina Marley' into the Facebook search bar of Lena Thompson's profile. It returned a screen full of Christina Marleys. The first one was standing in front of an altar, in a long white dress, holding the hand of who Monica assumed was her husband-to-be. The next was a close-up shot of a woman in a low-cut black top. Her face wasn't visible. Monica worked her way through the next five Christina Marleys. Two were in the USA, three this side of the pond. The seventh candidate she landed on was the right one. The profile picture was of Christina, kneeling on a beach, her arms wrapped around the neck of a Labrador. It looked like a cold day. Christina wore boots and a big grey jumper, with a blush-pink scarf wrapped around her neck. She had a glowing smile.

'Hello, Miss Marley, how nice to see you again.' Monica scrolled down, only to be frustrated by seeing that Christina had locked her personal information. She dabbed her thumb on the teacher's profile picture, and it took her to a carousel of images Christina had used before. As Monica flicked through the pictures – some of Christina solo, some with others – she came to one that looked like a favourite quote. It was on a dark background and read 'Sometimes you can't run quickly enough to escape your own darkness.'

Monica checked to see when it was posted. It was a year old. She smiled. 'You definitely can't run quickly enough to escape me, Miss Marley. Not this time.'

She moved to the next image and stopped. 'Oh, who is this, Christina?' The picture showed Christina Marley with her arm around a pretty young woman of similar age and height, with long brown hair. They were laughing, sitting at a table in a crowded bar. Monica expanded the detail at the bottom of the picture. It read: 'With Sarah Marley – I have the best little sister in the world.' Monica smiled, saved the picture to her phone and went back to the search bar at the top of the screen.

She typed in 'Sarah Marley'. An equally long list of women with the same name appeared. The first two were no good; one was a picture of a baby, the next a middle-aged woman with blue hair. The third, however, was Christina's sister. Helpfully, she used the same picture as Monica had just seen of them in the bar. She opened Sarah's profile and was pleased to see that it wasn't locked down at all. Her photos, personal information, even her friends were fully accessible to Monica, who immediately started researching.

'So, you're both teachers. Your parents must be so proud. And both so pretty too. Aw, isn't that sweet. Miss Marley loves her little school so much, she posts pictures of all their class events. I do love a nativity. Oh, and you look lovely in a bikini, Sarah.'

Within five minutes Monica had built a comprehensive picture of Sarah Marley. She saw that Sarah taught in a small primary school only about twenty minutes' drive away. She decided to go and have a look.

Monica took a direct route out of Portsmouth and joined the M27 heading west. With the radio playing quietly in the background, she swigged from a bottle of Coke as she made her way along the motorway. Taking the exit at Junction 10, she followed a tight left-hand turn that wound back on itself. She went uphill and over a roundabout, following signs to Knowle village. As Monica neared Wickham, passing a playpark at the bottom of the hill, she heard a news bulletin come on the radio. She was amused to hear that she was still the main story.

'Monica Silverman has been described by police as very dangerous. Members of the public who think they may have seen her are urged not to approach her, but to call police immediately. Silverman escaped from prison yesterday. Police have not ruled out her returning to the Portsmouth and Southampton area, and have asked the public to be vigilant. Anyone with information regarding her whereabouts should call the police immediately on 101. Alternatively, you can contact Crimestoppers on 0800 555 111. In other news...'

Monica turned the radio down and took a left turn opposite a large church. Going under a brick railway bridge she passed some picturesque cottages as she drove towards the school. She parked her Mondeo in a community centre car park, from where she could see the school through a gap in a hedgerow. Blipping the car locked, she flicked her hood over her head and walked down the path towards the school. A row of terraced houses lined the left-hand side of the path, with the school playing fields taking up the length of the path on the right, separated by a wire fence. She could hear children's voices through a door that stood open, but kept looking straight ahead. At the end of the path, to the right was a small car park. One of the cars she recognised from a picture she'd seen on Sarah's Facebook page: the white Renault Clio the young teacher had treated herself to after landing the job at the school, according to her post. Monica walked down the school driveway. It led to a quiet residential road, bungalows to her left and plenty of places to park and watch.

16

A red-faced man in a navy-blue suit, white shirt and red tie stood before the press. A tall lectern with a single microphone was between him and the mass of cameras, microphones and recording devices pointed at him. The imposing black door of 10 Downing Street was his backdrop.

'I have just finished briefing the Prime Minister on the events surrounding the escape of Monica Silverman from HMP Brookham yesterday. This is a unique situation and the police are working tirelessly to bring Miss Silverman back into custody, while keeping the public safe. There is an ongoing investigation into the circumstances of the escape, but our efforts must be focused on apprehending Miss Silverman. As you are aware, the police have issued a plea for information on the whereabouts of Monica Silverman, and have urged anyone who thinks they have seen her not to approach her but to contact the police immediately. I would echo this plea. I have every confidence in our police, and believe they will bring this regrettable situation to an end soon.'

'Minister!' came a chorus of voices, each shouting to be heard. The minister pointed at a woman from the BBC.

'Minister, could you tell us how she managed to escape from a fully manned prison in the middle of the day?'

'As I've said, there's an ongoing investigation into the circumstances surrounding the escape. That will hopefully give us the answer to your question.'

'Minister! Do you think the police can catch Monica before she kills someone else?' a scruffy-looking man in his late twenties shouted from the side of the press pack.

'I certainly hope so.'

'Minister! Is it true that the governor helped the prisoner escape?' yelled a woman in a long mac to the left of the scruffy journalist. The secretary paused briefly before answering, his already red face hiding his blushes.

'It's not appropriate for me to comment on an ongoing investigation. Thank you all for coming.' He turned from the lectern and walked back towards the door of 10 Downing Street, which was opened for him as he approached. Camera flashes went off behind him as he walked away.

* * *

'Well, that could have been a lot worse,' said Lomas to Marie Carlton as she pointed a remote control at the TV, turning it off.

'It could indeed. I thought he was going to choke when they asked him about the governor,' she said.

'I know. He held it together well though, you've got to give him credit.'

'I wouldn't want to be in Niamh Dominicali's shoes today, that's for sure.'

'I'm not loving our shoes at the moment, never mind hers,' said Lomas, standing to leave the room. 'I'm going to see what the team have found on the CCTV feeds.'

'OK, what were they looking at?' Marie asked.

'I've got them tracking Monica on and off the trains she took and looking at station and platform footage from all stations, to see if she spoke to anyone or did anything that will give us a lead.'

'Good. Let me know if you find anything. I've got to meet with the chief later and let her know what's going on. The world and their wife want briefing on this.'

'OK. If I get an update, I'll drop you a message.'

'Thanks, Lomas.'

Lomas made his way back towards his office. As he turned a corner, he nearly walked into Grant Carver. 'You in a hurry, Grant?'

'Sorry, boss. I was on my way to see you, actually.'

'Why, what have you got? Do I need to come and look?'

'You can if you like.'

They turned around and walked back to Grant's desk, collecting Drew on the way. The team that were trawling through the surveillance footage turned as Lomas and Drew walked in.

'OK, so if you have a look at this,' said Carver, turning on a large screen above the bank of PCs. An image of Monica near the exit doors of a train came up on the screen. The picture was clearer than the last one: they could see her profile clearly, her hair tucked into her baseball cap.

'That's a great image,' said Drew.

'It's really clear that it's her, isn't it?' said Grant. 'Keep watching. We've managed to stitch together the footage from the train and the footage from the platform. There was a camera virtually facing this door as the train came into the station.'

The image changed angles, and Monica could be clearly seen getting off the train.

'Great, so where's this?' asked Lomas.

'It's Portsmouth and Southsea station, boss. She got off and walked out of the main doors of the station. We lost her after that.'

'That's great work, guys.' Lomas cast a glance at the team, who had spent the last few hours trawling the feeds. They nodded and mumbled their appreciation.

Lomas took his phone and messaged Marie Carlton.

She's in Portsmouth. We've got her on CCTV getting off the train. Can we get a tactical relocation?

It didn't take long for Marie to reply.

That's great. I'll get authorisation to get the firearms moved.

He pocketed his phone. 'Thanks again. Grant, can you get a live update to the whole team that we have a confirmed surveillance sighting in Portsmouth? Drew, with me.' He didn't wait for a reply. He and Drew left the surveillance team and headed for the briefing room.

'Let's bring up the map, Drew. I want to trace the route she took from the prison to where she dumped the governor's car. From there, to Alton station and then her journey on the four trains to Portsmouth.'

'No problem.'

Lomas watched as Drew worked to plot the points that he'd had detailed on an on-screen map. He knew that Drew was really tech-savvy and it had been a close call which branch of the force she was going to specialise in. In an early chat she'd shared with Lomas that she'd joined the police after doing a computer science degree and was heading towards the cyber-crime unit when, after doing a few weeks with CID, she decided she'd rather be a detective. Her mix of determination and analytical skills had made her stand out straight away, and it hadn't taken her long to become an essential part of Lomas's team.

'Look at that – she knew we were going to track her every which way. She zigzagged all over the place,' said Lomas.

'Like you said, she's not stupid.'

'So, we have to assume she has a reason to pick Portsmouth. She's not just going there randomly. There's something in Pompey.'

'Or someone?' Said Drew.

'Yes, or someone. Even Monica Silverman must have some friends tucked away somewhere. What do we know about her past that might give us an idea as to why she's there?'

'We know that she was an only child. Her parents were married. Dad was Dr Thomas Silverman, a well-respected cosmetic surgeon. By all accounts, Monica idolised him when she was growing up, but it doesn't seem like they were that close. He seems to have spent more time on the golf course than at home. Mum, Barbara, not sure about any profession. She seems to have been a bit of a socialite and all-round lovely woman. She and Monica seem to have had a fractious relationship; Mum disapproved of her interest in weightlifting and hammer throwing, according to neighbours. Both parents are now deceased, her dad in a skiing accident six years ago and her mother from cancer two and a half years ago. As we know, Anna-May Appleby was one of her nurses. She grew up in Southampton, lived in Basset, near the top of The Avenue, went to school locally and was a star on the local athletics scene.'

'OK. What about Monica's connections to Portsmouth?' Lomas said, rubbing his chin.

'None that are obvious, with the exception of her father's sister. She was a dentist who lived in Southsea. She's also deceased – died in a coach crash in Portugal when Monica was in her early teens.'

'So no living family at all?'

'None that we could find, boss.' Drew said with a shrug as she turned away from the screen.

'Any other connections to Pompey?'

'Apart from tenuous links through athletics competitions, like I say, there's nothing obvious.'

'Well, let's keep looking. There's got to be a reason she's gone there.'

'Will do, boss.'

17

Niamh Dominicali had sat in her office for over an hour with her line manager. The crescendo of her hastily arranged meeting with the Prisons Director was him shouting at her and growing redder in the face. He'd had an earful from the Minister of Justice and was making sure that shit rolled downhill.

'You've literally backed me into a corner, Niamh. I need to commission an inquiry and I need to suspend you, pending the outcome of the investigation. The minister is furious – he's had questions from the PM and is going to have to stand in the House and answer questions on how the fuck we lost the most dangerous female prisoner the country has ever seen.'

Niamh stayed very calm. 'I completely understand. I'm sorry you've had to carry the can for this. But I was put in an impossible position, and there is no way I could sacrifice my staff. She would have killed them, Dermot.'

'I know, Niamh, I know, and if there was any other way, you know I'd take it. But I've got to think about the optics of the situation and I need to protect you from the fallout, as well as the service.' His voice dropped in volume and softened.

She knew he'd always had a soft spot for her. They'd had a drunken fumble a long time ago, but he'd been married at the time and she'd stopped things before they had gone too far. Niamh knew it popped into his head every so often when he saw her. She could tell by the way he looked at her.

'Like I said, Dermot, I understand. I know why you need to suspend me. Just promise me that you won't let them hang me out to dry over it.'

'I'll do what I can to make sure they're objective and look at it as learning, rather than scapegoating you, Niamh. You have my word.'

'That's all I can ask. Do you mind if I tell my team? I'd rather they heard it from me than an official statement.'

'Of course. I can time the paperwork an hour or so from now. That should give you time to brief your team and let them know what's happening. I'll have someone cover for the next few weeks.'

'Do you know who yet?'

'No, not yet. My first thought was Ken Bridges, but he's only six months from retirement and I doubt he'd be up for moving from the other end of the country when he's that close.'

'How about Colin?' she said.

'Jefferies?'

'Yes. He was here as deputy before he got the job in London. He's only seconded up there and he commutes. I'm sure he could be persuaded to come and cover until the investigation's finished.'

'Hmm, maybe, let me think about it,' Dermot said.

'OK, it's just a thought. It's your decision, obviously.'

'Right. I'm going to head off unless there's anything else?' He said, already putting his jacket on.

'No, I'll brief my team, put Mike Button in charge temporarily and be on my way.'

'Thanks for not making this too difficult, Niamh.'

'Not at all. It's just procedure.' She made sure he made eye contact with her as she finished her sentence. He squirmed slightly.

'Yes, like you say. Just procedure. Let's speak soon.' Dermot Jennings almost slithered out of Niamh's office. She stood behind her desk and watched him leave, deciding to let his parting olive branch hang, unanswered. As soon as her door closed, the phone on her desk flashed.

'Come on through, Claire,' said Niamh, a wry smile on her face. She knew that her PA would be itching for an update. No sooner had Niamh let go of the button than Claire was through the door.

'Are you OK?' Claire asked.

'Yes, I'm fine. He just came down to let me know how serious the situation is and to suspend me, pending investigation.'

'Suspend you? That's outrageous! You saved the lives of your team. If you hadn't acted in the way you did, who knows what Monica would have done in reception? The team won't like this – they'll think the service are hanging you out...'

Niamh let Claire vent a little then held up a hand to stop her.

'I appreciate your loyalty, Claire, but there's nothing to be done about it. The fact is I let a dangerous prisoner escape, and that has to be investigated. In the meantime, I have to be suspended. Could you arrange for as many staff as possible to come together for an emergency briefing?'

'Yes, of course, Governor. I'm so sorry.'

'No apology needed. I appreciate it, I really do. Once they've finished their investigation and realised I acted to protect life, I'll be back.'

'I'll gather the team, Governor.'

'Thank you, Claire.'

The PA left the office quietly and closed the door behind her. Niamh Dominicali dropped into her chair and let out a heavy sigh. She spun around to look out of the window, which had a view out over the prison, wondering if she'd done the right thing.

An hour later, staff were gathered in the staff dining room. There was an expectant hum to the room, with layers of conversations taking place at once. Niamh stood outside the dining room for a moment to gather herself. Behind her left shoulder stood a pensive Mike Button, who had just been told that, in the absence of a deputy governor, a position Niamh hadn't been able to recruit for due to budget cuts, he was going to act up – until the director brought in a temporary replacement for Niamh. On the opposite side was a steadfast Claire Kidson, stern-faced and clearly not amused by the actions of the Prisons Director.

Niamh took a deep breath, pushed the door open and entered the room. By the time she reached the front, there was silence.

'Thank you for coming at such short notice. I know that some colleagues are either on duty or couldn't get here. I wanted to speak to as many of you as I could personally, so that you are hearing it straight from the horse's mouth, so to speak. You'll all be aware by now that yesterday Monica Silverman killed officers Rodriguez and Bell in her isolation room. You will also know that she took me hostage and forced me to walk her through the prison. What you won't know is that before I left the isolation room with her, she had threatened to kill anyone we came across between isolation and reception – if I attempted to raise the alarm.' She made brief eye contact with Tony Davies, who'd been on reception when Monica escaped. He nodded at her reassuringly and she carried on.

'We all know how dangerous Monica Silverman is. If there had been any other way to handle this situation, that didn't put any of you at risk, believe me, I would have taken it. My assessment at the time was that the only way to keep you all safe was to cooperate with Monica and hope that she could be apprehended quickly once I had safely raised the alarm. This has proved not to be the case. She has now been out for over twenty-four hours. Although the police are working hard to find her, I fear she may have gone to ground. I deeply regret the role I played in releasing Monica back into society and I pray that no one gets hurt as a result of my actions. But, that said, they were my actions and I take full responsibility for them. With immediate effect, I will be placed on suspension pending a full investigation into the circumstances surrounding the escape. I would ask you all to cooperate fully with the investigators when they arrive. The sooner they are able to get their job done, the sooner we can return to normal. Until the director brings someone in to temporarily replace me, Mike Button will be acting up as governor. I know you will give him your full support. Thank you.' When Niamh stopped speaking a spontaneous round of applause began, first among a small number of officers, but soon the whole room was on their feet and clapping. Niamh felt herself blush, then tears began to well. She closed her eyes momentarily, took another deep breath then turned and left the room, followed by, Mike and Claire.

'Right, Mike, can you escort me to my office to collect my belongings and then off the premises, please? I don't want there to be any criticism over how we've handled this.'

'Yes, Governor, of course.' He held a door open for Niamh and Claire to walk through. Claire scurried alongside Niamh, shooting glances at her and opening her mouth to speak, but saying nothing.

Niamh tried to ignore her but eventually caved. 'What is it, Claire?'

'Sorry?' Claire spluttered.

'What is it? You clearly have something to say. We've walked the last two corridors and you still haven't said what's on your mind, so what is it?'

'Well ... It's just that I think you handled that really well. I wanted you to know that I can't imagine anyone else being as brave as you're being. And, well, I think it's spectacularly unfair. The way you're being scapegoated, I mean.' Claire's voice cracked and she dabbed her eyes with the sleeve of her cardigan.

Niamh was surprised by Claire's emotional outpouring and replied to her PA in a softer tone. 'Thank you. I really appreciate it, but don't worry about me. I'll be fine. I'm not being used as a scapegoat; I did walk Monica out of the prison. I know that if I hadn't, then lots of the people we work with would be injured or dead. And, as hard as it is at the moment, I can live with my decision to do that, as long as the police catch Monica before she hurts someone – or worse.'

'But you were acting in the best interests of your staff. That has to count for something?'

'If it does, then the investigation will bring that to the fore. Now, I need you to support Mike for me. He's going to need help to keep things running, as I don't think the director is going to find anyone to bring in quickly.' She saw Claire puff up with pride as she spoke.

'Of course. I'll help him in any way I can, Governor.'

'Thank you.' She rested a reassuring hand on Claire's shoulder.

The three of them reached Niamh's office. As requested, Mike stood at the door and watched Niamh collect a small box of her personal belongings. As they walked out of the office, Claire stepped forward and gave Niamh a hug, surprising her for the second time. She quickly passed Mike the box and returned Claire's hug, then walked with Mike to reception. When she arrived, there was a welcoming committee of her officers, fronted by Tony Davies. As she walked towards the airlock to be let out, Tony said, 'Thank you, Governor. We'll see you soon.'

She looked towards the outside then heard the door close behind her.

18

Monica waited patiently for school to end. She'd taken a slow walk into Wickham village, bought herself another bag of fish and chips and walked around the thirteenth-century square, looking through the windows of the small independent shops, particularly fascinated by a window full of tiny items of furniture for dolls' houses. She'd never had a dolls' house, and was intrigued by the idea of a small replica house, complete with little chairs and tables, perplexed about why anyone would spend their time or money on one.

She kept her baseball cap pulled down over her short, bleached blonde hair, trying to stay as inconspicuous as possible. As she made her way along a cobbled alleyway that led from the square up towards the school, an elderly woman standing at her garden gate spoke to her.

'Hello, dear. It's a bit chilly today, isn't it?'

'Yes, it is a bit,' Monica said, not looking at the woman.

'I don't suppose you would do me a favour, would you?'

Monica rolled her eyes and stopped. 'I'd be happy to help if I can,' she said as warmly as she could manage, irritated by the uninvited interaction.

'Oh, thank you. It's only a simple thing. My bin needs pulling out onto the street, or the bin men won't take it. I've overfilled it, you see, and I'm afraid I can't move it.'

Monica smiled. Without saying anything, she stepped through the gate as the old woman moved to one side for her. She popped her screwed-up chip paper into the bin, grabbed the handle and pulled the bin over the road, leaving it next to two others.

'Thank you so much. I really don't know why I filled it so much. I should have known I wouldn't be able to shift it,' the woman rattled on.

'No problem,' said Monica, waving to her and moving on towards her car.

Monica drove around from the car park and found a space opposite a row of bungalows, with a good view of the school driveway. There she sat, watching people walk by, going about their business. The road was quiet until 3 p.m. when it began to fill with cars and SUVs. Monica watched as they filled every available space, parents following each other up towards the school to collect their children. She shook her head slowly.

'There you go, marching like worker ants, happy in your entrapment,' she said.

It took less than ten minutes after the first child emerged from the school until the majority had dispersed and the residential street fell quiet once more.

Monica's patience was rewarded half an hour later when the white Renault slowly made its way to the end of the drive. She could clearly see Sarah Marley behind the wheel, and recognised her instantly from her Facebook profile pictures. Sarah turned right out of the school. Monica waited a few seconds then set off in the same direction as the young teacher, keeping the Clio in sight but not getting too close. At the end of the road Sarah took another right onto a main road that wound its way up a slight hill between dense, mature trees. Monica let two cars pass before she pulled out, the cars filling the space between them. She followed Sarah up the hill and over a crossroad, passing a garage selling camper vans and a busy greengrocer set back from the road. Metallica's 'Enter Sandman' was playing on the radio as Monica tailed Sarah off the main road, losing her buffer cars, which carried straight on. She hung back, dropping her speed a little so she didn't get too close. The tree-lined road gave way to houses on the right and a hotel on the left. Monica let a car out of a driveway to fill the gap between her and Sarah and followed her like this for another five miles until they reached the picturesque village of Corhampton. Sarah turned at a cute corner shop. Monica drove past her as she turned into a semi-circular road that faced a well-tended green. She parked between two cars in a spot where she had an unobstructed view, through her rear-view mirror, of the house Sarah had pulled up.

'So is this home, Miss Marley? If it is, it's very nice. I think maybe you live with Mummy and Daddy,' said Monica, opening a snack bar she had stashed in the door pocket of her car. 'Let's see how long you're here for, shall we? I'm in no rush. Take as long as you need.'

Dusk was starting to draw in, and there was no one around to spoil Monica's impromptu stake-out.

She sat for a couple of hours, until dusk had turned to dark and a scattering of stars peppered the cloudless sky. Just as she was starting to think of calling it a night, Sarah came out of the house. The indicators on her Clio flashed, and Monica turned in her seat for a better look. From what she could see in the glow from the house's security light, Sarah was wearing a black dress and tights, a coat over her arm. She opened the car door and threw her coat in. The fact that she'd gone in, stayed for a couple of hours then come out dressed for a night out confirmed that this was home.

Monica waited until Sarah had driven away, then casually started her car and drove slowly around the green, getting a much better look at Sarah Marley's home. There was a Land Rover Discovery and a Smart Car on the drive, a space between them where Sarah's Clio had been parked. The lawn was neatly bordered, and mature rose bushes grew up trellises on either side of the front door. Monica could see a TV flickering through the lounge window, and the shoulder of some-one sitting in a chair – she assumed it was Sarah's fa-ther.

She made a metal note of the house number and of those adjacent to it, then drove slowly out to the main road and headed away from the village.

19

Drew had spent all day chasing leads that had come in from phone calls, covering the area between Portsmouth and Southampton, to no avail. She could feel frustration building inside her as she got in her car and left the station. She drove along the dual carriageway, the huge Ikea store to her left and the docks to her right. It was unusually quiet. The tail-lights of a couple of cars glowed red in front of her.

As she made her way through the residential area of Midanbury, down a long, snaking hill and away from town, she noticed that the same car had been behind her for some time. She didn't know why it stood out, but she just had a feeling that it was following her. Drew took evasive action: she took a right then an immediate left that took her off her route. The car followed her. She slowed down, encouraging the car closer.

'OK, let's see if you go around,' she muttered.

The car slowed and stayed behind her, then its headlights flashed. Drew's heart rate quickened and she speeded up. The car following matched her acceleration and continued to flash her.

'Right, I've had enough of this shit.' Drew slammed on her brakes and readied herself to call it in. The car behind swerved around her and cut in front, blocking her way. She was about to slam into reverse when the driver's door flew open and Nick Swain got out, waving and smiling enthusiastically. Drew jumped out of her car.

'Nick, you fucking lunatic! You scared me to death!'

He laughed, 'Scared you? Why?'

'Oh, I don't know. Perhaps because we're tracking a serial killer who stalked me once and you've just followed me halfway across town?'

'Oh ... yeah, sorry. It's just ... well, I called to you as you were leaving the station and you didn't hear me and jumped in your car ... and well, I wondered if you fancied getting a drink? It's been a crappy couple of days and I thought...'

'You thought what? That I might like to be followed across town?' She smiled.

Nick looked uncomfortable.

'Nick Swain, you're never stuck for something to say.'

'Sorry, I didn't mean to scare you.'

'It's fine, really. This Monica thing has got me on edge, I guess.'

He returned her smile this time. 'So, do you fancy a drink?'

'Yeah, that'd be nice. Where?'

'There's a pub down the hill in West End. We could go there?'

'Sure. I'll follow you this time, though.' She laughed and got back in her car before he could reply.

Five minutes later they were pulling up in the pub car park. He held the door open for her as they walked into the pub. She smiled in acknowledgement. They ordered a beer each and Drew followed Nick to a table in a quiet corner.

'Tell me, Detective Swain, why the invite for a drink?' Drew asked, taking a sip of her half pint of Amstel.

'You should be able to figure that out, Detective Sergeant, or do I need to spell it out for you?'

'Maybe you do.'

'I like you. I wanted to get to know you without everyone else around. I hoped that maybe if you got to know me, you might like me too.'

'Who says I don't?'

He shuffled in his seat. 'No one, I guess. Look, Drew, about following you earlier. I'm sorry if I scared you. It was a stupid thing to do. I should have known better than to tail you through town. Especially with everything that's going on.'

'Don't worry about it. Monica really got to me last time, what with dropping parcels at my flat and writing those notes. It was pretty intense. Seeing your lights behind me, getting the feeling again that I was being followed, it made me a bit jittery. But I'm good, and I'm glad you asked me for a drink. Anyway, enough work talk. Tell me about you. How come you're single?'

'Same reason as you, I suppose...'

'What? Crap taste in men?'

They laughed.

'No, the job. It's tough to meet someone who gets it. I've been out with a few women since I've been in serious crimes, and the long hours get a bit much after a while.'

'Oh God, you're not one of those mean and moody types, are you?' she teased.

'Ha, nothing so cool. No, just a miserable workaholic, I think.'

'A quick tip – don't write that on your Tinder profile.'

'Not a winner?'

'Not the best line I've ever heard.' She waved a hand, as if displaying a banner. 'Copper, good-looking, miserable workaholic.' They laughed again.

'You did say I'm good-looking though. I'll take that.'

'Yeah, you're all right, I suppose.' She finished her beer and offered to get them another. Drew walked to the bar, resisting the temptation to look over her shoulder to see if Nick was checking her out. She stood, waiting for their beers to be poured, and thought about how she'd felt when she'd realised she was being followed. She decided to make an appointment to see her counsellor; she couldn't let what had happened when they were hunting Monica before, derail her this time. Dismissing her thoughts, she smiled at the barman, swiped her card over the reader and took their drinks back to the table.

They chatted easily for the next couple of hours, finding out that they'd grown up less than two miles apart, gone to the same school and remembered some of the same people; although Nick had been two years ahead of her.

The barman called time and they stood to leave. Nick held the door again on the way out and they walked out to their cars. As they stood by Drew's car, he stepped a little closer to her.

'I had a really good time tonight.'

'Yeah, me too. See you tomorrow.' She leaned in and gave him a quick kiss on the cheek, stroking the side of his face. He didn't try for anything more; she liked that.

Drew walked around to her driver's door. Nick was standing by his car, waiting for her to get into hers. She smiled and waved then got in her car and turned the key, feeling like a teenager with a crush. He waved at her as he reversed, then she watched him drive out of the car park.

***

Lomas was in his office, going through the call logs from the hotline team. They'd had hundreds of calls since they'd aired the initial broadcast, asking for information on Monica's whereabouts. Some were wildly implausible, like the man who'd called from Aberystwyth, on the west coast of Wales, convinced that Monica had moved in next door to him an hour after she'd escaped from prison. Others were more likely, apart from odd details that didn't add up, such as the woman who'd called saying she'd seen Monica in a corner shop in Portsmouth ... with her three small children.

Marie popped her head around his office door. 'You still here?'

'No, ma'am, I went home hours ago. This is a holographic image of me working late.'

'Very funny. Found anything?'

'Not today. We've run into more brick walls than I've had hot dinners.'

'Something will give. It always does.'

'Thanks, Marie. I hope so. The longer she's out there, the more chance there is of someone getting hurt.'

'I know, but you working yourself to death isn't going to help us catch her. You stayed here last night, didn't you?'

'Yeah. I couldn't go home. Heidi and the kids were safe, so I cracked on and had a shower and a change of clothes here this morning.'

'Well, get yourself home. Come back rested in the morning.'

'OK, will do. I just need to finish going through these call logs.'

'No, you don't, get yourself home. Go and see Heidi and the kids.'

He looked at Marie Carlton and could see it wasn't a suggestion.

'OK, OK, I'm going.' He closed his laptop and got up. He felt stiff as a board. He'd been sitting for hours and was used to being much more active. He stretched then picked up his jacket from the back of his chair. Marie was still in the doorway. 'Are you waiting to escort me out of the building, boss?'

'If I don't, you'll sit back down and carry on the minute my back's turned.'

'Fair enough.' He smiled and shrugged. They'd worked together for years; he knew she wouldn't leave without him now that she said he had to go home and get some rest. She was firm, fair and supportive and he'd ignored similar advice before when she'd headed off and he'd stayed anyway. He also knew she was right. He wanted to go home and see Heidi, and a good night's sleep would do him the world of good.

They walked out to the car park, not saying much.

'Night, Marie.'

'See you tomorrow.' She ducked into her bright red A-Class Mercedes. Lomas got into his car and headed out onto the main road. He hooked a left towards the traffic lights. He decided that, before he went home, he needed to clear his head. He pressed Play on the dashboard and the opening riff of Guns N' Roses' 'Sweet Child o' Mine' filled the VW Golf. He pointed the car in the direction of the gym and let himself become immersed in the music.

Twenty-five minutes later, he pulled up outside a familiar brick archway in the side of an old fort near Fareham. It was dark and there were no other cars around. He could see a glow around the edges of a white door with flaking paint, and knew that the owner, Mark, would still be on site. Lomas had trained at the small spit-and-sawdust gym for years. There was nothing fancy about it – and he liked that. It had been here that Lomas and his team had first arrested Monica, who'd also been a regular. Although he was already well known, Lomas had gained an almost celebrity status following the arrest. A couple of days after he and his team had taken Monica in, Lomas had gone to his favourite bench. The guys in the gym had handcuffed the bar to the bench. They all stood around, pretending not to look as he walked over to it, then the gym had erupted in laughter. Mark had given Lomas 24-hour access to the gym, leaving a key under a plant pot outside for him. Lomas had warned him against doing this but Mark hadn't listened. He'd taken advantage of the gym owner's generosity and used the gym outside hours, after a long day, on a few occasions. He was grateful for the gesture.

'Evening, Mark, didn't think you'd still be here.'

'Yes, you did,' Mark replied without turning from a mirror he was wiping down.

'Yeah, you're right. I did.'

'Besides, if I'm not, who's going to spot you when you take on something you can't lift?' He smiled and walked behind a small counter. 'I've just got a new flavour in of that protein shake you like, if you want one when you've done.'

Lomas walked through to a small changing room with his gym bag. 'Yeah, that'd be good, thanks,' he replied over his shoulder without stopping. Once he'd changed he got stuck into a back workout. He started with a few sets of deadlifts, gradually increasing the weight on the bar, set by set, until he got up to a working weight of 180 kilograms. He pulled his lifting-belt tight around his waist then eased himself into a squat in front of the bar. With his hands at opposite grips on the bar, he rolled it back until it was touching his shins. Then, with a huge effort, he heaved the bar from the floor, driving his feet down into the floor and pulling the bar up his legs until he stood, locked out at the top of the lift. He repeated this five times, each repetition felt harder than the last. Each time he fought gravity as it tried to tear the bar from his grip. After his final rep he released his grip and followed the bar down to the mat with his hands. Lomas packed another four exercises into his back workout and finished with some bicep work. During the fifty-minute session, his working day had evaporated from his mind.

'Is that you done?' asked Mark.

'Yep, all done. How about you?'

'Yeah, I'll be locking up after you. It's been a long day and I'm in early in the morning with the youngsters for some Olympic lifting.'

'How are they getting on?'

'Really well. A couple of them have real potential. You want a shake?'

'That'd be great, thanks.'

Mark made Lomas a shake in a takeaway cup and then started to flick off the lights.

'See you soon, mate,' Lomas said as he headed for the door.

'Later.' Mark waved.

Energised from his workout, Lomas drove home. He called Heidi on the way and arranged for her and the kids to meet him there. If he'd got his timing right, he should get home and be able to ensure that all was well before they arrived. Lomas knew that the longer Monica was free, the greater the potential threat to his family. He needed to speak to Heidi to see what she wanted to do; he knew it had been hard on the three of them the first time he had hunted Monica. They'd gone to stay at Heidi's parents' house. Although it was only about an hour away, it was too far for Ant and Eve to pop back and forth to see their friends – and, as much as they loved their grandparents, they had quickly run out of things to do.

As he pulled onto his driveway, he looked around. His house was in darkness. There was no sign of anyone. No unfamiliar cars on the road as he'd approached. Last time, Monica had delivered a boxed, severed body part to his house, leaving it on his driveway. That had been too close for Lomas's liking.

He skirted around the outside of his house checking that all the windows and doors were as they should be. Next he checked the lock on the back gate. It was undisturbed. Lomas headed indoors and went into every room in their house and although everything on the outside had seemed to be fine, he was still relieved to see the inside was as he'd left it.

It was getting late by the time Heidi's headlights swept across the living-room window. Lomas was watching a nature documentary: David Attenborough was describing the migration habits of blue whales. Lomas got up to greet his family as the kids piled through the door.

'Hi Dad!' they shouted, then ran up the stairs. Their bedroom doors banged shut and he heard Ant's TV go on, no doubt soon to be followed by his PlayStation. A couple of seconds later he could hear the dull thrum of

Eve's music from above. Her taste in music made him feel old. She loved Drake, Nicki Minaj and Kanye, while Lomas preferred guitar-led rock music and anything from the 1980s.

Heidi followed a minute or so later, dropping her handbag by the front door and giving Lomas a weary look.

'Rough day?' he asked.

'You could say that. Work was insane. I've been bouncing between building regs and gas safety certificates for properties that are getting too close to completion all day.'

'That doesn't sound like fun,' he said.

'Then going back to Lucy's with the kids topped it off. Ant and Tom couldn't agree what game to play, and you'd think that was the end of the world. Eve and Bee were good as gold, as usual. But it's the whole feeling – like we were intruding. Not that Lucy would ever say so.'

'I get it, hun. I know it's tough, but I don't want you and the kids to be at risk.'

'What are you saying?'

'Well, I've been thinking. I—'

'Don't say that you want us to go away again. It's not happening, Lomas.'

'I know it's not easy, but—'

'No buts. We're not doing it. I will not be driven out of my home by some psycho, just because they have an issue with you.'

'But Heidi...'

'But nothing. I'm not doing it to the kids again. Last time they were a bit younger, but they've both got exams coming up, they need to have down-time and see their friends. And, as lovely as Mum and Dad are, there's next to nothing for the kids to do there. There must be another solution.'

Lomas didn't try again. It was clear that Heidi had made up her mind. After nearly twenty years of marriage, Lomas knew when he was beaten – and, if he was honest, he understood. The upheaval last time had been massive. He knew it had impacted the kids' schooling, but Monica had been too close for comfort and he couldn't take the risk. This time though, he was being pre-emptive. He didn't know if Monica would target his family, but he did need to keep them safe.

'OK, how about I get a patrol to swing by every so often while I'm at work during the evening? But the kids are going to have to change what they do. Eve can't just be floating around in town with her mates, like they do at the weekends. If Monica did decide to target us, it's female victims she goes for, so you and Eve have to take steps to stay safe.'

Heidi's face softened. 'Of course we would. I don't want you to worry about us while you're at work. But we can't live under lockdown, Lomas.'

'No, I get that, but I have to know you're safe.'

'OK, so to be clear, you're not sending us away?'

'No, we'll work it out. But my list of fancy women won't be pleased. They were hoping I could get you out of the house.'

She threw a tea towel at him. 'Funny, Baxter! Besides, you couldn't handle a list.' She walked across the kitchen, wrapped her arms around his neck and kissed him, just as Ant walked into the room.

'Ew, get a room.'

'We will, as soon as you two are old enough to go to uni,' replied Lomas.

20

Niamh Dominicali had dragged herself through her day since leaving the prison. A girlfriend had called her after seeing her on the morning news and asked if she wanted to catch up for lunch. Niamh had regretted this about ten minutes in; all Carol wanted to do was talk about the escape and Monica. Niamh had made her excuses after the main course and headed for the safety of home.

She felt awful. The feeling that someone was going to get hurt as a result of her actions nagged at her. She'd spent hours huddled on her sofa. She pulled her knees up to her chest and dragged a blue blanket around her, tucking it under her feet. Flicking through the channels, she realised why she never watched much television. Screen upon screen of smiley extroverts, filling her TV with their faces. Temptation got the better of her on a couple of occasions and she dipped into the 24-hour news channels. Her stomach knotted when an external shot of the prison popped up, quickly replaced by her own face, then Monica's.

The newsreader was reporting on the story in suitably sombre tones. 'Monica Silverman's escape from HMP Brookham is the first by a female Category A prisoner on record. Earlier today the Minister of Justice gave a statement outside Downing Street. Miss Silverman, just months into serving multiple life sentences...'

Niamh changed the channel, unable to listen to any more.

Her phone rang and she turned it over to look at the screen. It was her mother. She rolled her eyes and answered. 'Hi Mum, you OK?'

'Never mind me. How about you?'

'I'm all right, thanks. It's been a bit of a crappy day, but I'm OK.'

'I've just been watching the news. What will happen to you next?'

'I don't know, if I'm honest. I'll be investigated and then they'll decide what they're going to do. There's not a lot I can do about it.'

'They can't criticise you for looking after your people, Niamh. It's a difficult job – don't they know the kind of pressure you're under?'

'Mum...'

'Well, I'm just saying. They can't expect you to hit all those targets and keep everything running shipshape then throw you under the bus when something goes a bit wrong.'

'This is more than something going a bit wrong, though. I helped a murderer escape. She's out there now, doing God knows what, and it's my fault...' Niamh felt tears well in her eyes, and bit her lip as it started to tremble. Then she took a breath and gritted her teeth, determined not to give in to her emotions.

'Mum, I've got to go. I'll talk you later.' She ended the call as her mum was saying her goodbyes, pulled a cushion over her face and screamed into it. Then she got up from the sofa and threw the cushion back to where she'd got it from. 'A walk – that's what I need. I've got to clear my head.'

She dressed for the elements, readying herself for a decent stomp. She left her house, jogged down the steps from her front door and walked out onto the dark street. An orangey glow from the streetlights bathed the cars that lined the street. Niamh set off towards the park at the end of the road. Halfway down the road a man got out of a car on the opposite side. He went to his boot, opened it and started fishing around, apparently looking for something. Niamh carried on towards the park. She had always walked quickly and tonight was no exception. As she passed the iron railings that marked the start of the green space, a jogger skipped around her to avoid a collision. When she jumped in surprise, her phone fell out of her coat pocket onto the ground. She bent to pick it up. As she straightened up, someone behind her shouted, 'Governor!'

She spun around to see the man who had been fishing in his boot walking towards her, carrying a camera in one hand and waving at her with the other. Alongside him were four other men, all hurrying towards her. Niamh dug her hands into her pockets and carried on walking.

'Governor!' he persisted. 'Could I have a comment on the rumour that you helped Monica Silverman escape? Governor!'

She heard the click of cameras and felt her anger building. But she was savvy enough to know that it wouldn't do her any good to show her anger. The press would just manipulate it to make her look like a loose cannon.

The journalist shouted after her for the third time. Niamh knew they weren't going to leave her alone, so she stopped and turned to face them. 'Put your cameras away. What is with the press? You can't leave someone alone for ten minutes to go for a walk?'

'This is an important story, Governor – people are interested. It's not every day a Category A prisoner escapes, especially one who's convicted of the kind of crimes Monica Silverman is.' He thrust a recording device towards her.

'The police are doing everything they can to find her, and I hope that they do so quickly.'

'Do you have anything to say about the rumour that you helped her to get out?'

'No, I have nothing to add to what I said outside the prison.'

'Is it true you've been suspended, Governor?' a fresh-faced woman shouted. She had sharp features and her hair was pulled back into a ponytail.

'Yes, it's standard procedure to suspend prison personnel pending an investigation. And, as I'm sure you can understand, the service has to thoroughly investigate the circumstances surrounding Monica Silverman's escape.'

'Are you expecting to be fired, Governor?' the woman with the ponytail pushed.

'Like you, I'll have to wait for the outcome of the investigation. Now, I really don't have anything else to say and I would like to carry on with my walk. If that's OK with you?' She cast a stern look at the journalists. None of them said anything. Niamh turned and walked on into the park, following the path.

'Fuck it, Niamh, that was a dumb thing to do. You should have kept on walking,' she muttered as she picked up her pace. She walked around the park for forty-five minutes, a hand on her personal alarm in her pocket. By the time she got back home, there were no journalists to be seen. With a hint of paranoia, she looked up and down the street, trying to spot cars that looked unfamiliar, but soon realised that she didn't pay enough attention to the cars that were normally there to know the difference. She climbed the steps to her front door and went inside, locking the door and putting the chain on behind her.

Her house was a Victorian terraced semi with a double bay window. Its original fireplaces and high ceilings had sold the house to her as soon as she'd seen it. Niamh had bought the house ten years earlier with her now ex-husband. When they divorced, she'd refused to give up the house, which had cost her thousands, but she loved it. She wandered through to her kitchen. Trailing plants hung from high white shelves, standing out against the sage-green walls. Niamh took a large wine glass down from a cupboard, pulled a rosé from her fridge and filled the glass. Without taking her hand off the bottle, she downed half the glass then topped it up.

She put the bottle back into the fridge, grabbed a bag of chocolate buttons and returned to her sofa, tucking the blanket back around her.

Niamh was surfing the movie channels when her phone rang. She picked it up and saw that it was her mother again. She let out a huge sigh, flicked the side button to silent and turned the phone upside down.

21

Monica opened the hidden side gate of the abandoned vicarage, had a quick look up and down the road, and slipped into the overgrown garden, unseen. Shadows of swaying branches were sprayed up the side of the large house from streetlights across the road. She made her way through the undergrowth, being careful not to trip. Brambles had strayed from the flower beds bordering the path to link with each other, forming a series of thorny trip-wires. When she reached the back door, Monica bent down and moved an upturned plant pot. She was pleased to see that the key she'd left was still there. She hoped that, while she'd been in prison, squatters hadn't discovered the empty house.

She unlocked the heavy door and pushed it open. Reaching round, she flicked a light switch. Nothing happened. She smiled, pleased that the power hadn't been switched on: another sign that the house had remained undisturbed.

Lighting her way using the torch from her phone, she made her way quickly through the dark house. Floorboards creaked underfoot and the smell of damp hung heavy in her nostrils. She heard a tapping sound, and stopped. Deciding it was probably an animal of some kind, she carried on. She went up a couple of flights of stairs and into the second room she reached. As she opened a faded green door, riddled with holes from mites, she flicked off the torch. Moonlight flooded into the room. A makeshift bed, made of rough cuts of wood, stood in the centre of the room. Dark patches of dried blood marked the top of the bed. The skeletonised, decapitated remains of Elinor Mary Clarke lay where Monica had left it, in the middle of the bed.

'Why hello, It's lovely to see you again, Miss Clarke. It's been a while. Hope you've not been too lonely here on your own. No? Oh good, I am glad. I'd hate to think that I left you here to fend for yourself. Well, I'm back now, so why don't I get you a room-mate? Yes? I agree – it's an excellent idea, isn't it? Who is it? Oh, you'll have to wait and see. But it will be worth the wait, I promise you. Now, as you've been in that bed for what must feel like years, you've definitely earned the right to stay there, so I'll make our new guest somewhere else to stay. Oh no, don't worry, I'll bring them in here.

Like I said, I wouldn't want you being lonely. Although it looks like the locals have kept you company.' She flicked some small bones that were lying on the floor to one side with her shoe.

'I can't believe they haven't tidied up after they've eaten, though. Rats have no manners, do they? Oh well, let's get started. Where shall we put our next guest?'

Monica tided up some blood-stained surgical tools that were lying on the floor, putting them in a corner. On one wall was a disused fireplace, either side of which were shelved alcoves. Monica turned to face Elinor's skeleton.

'I'll be back in a minute. I need to get some tools from the shed.' She left the room and headed outside. At the end of the garden she went into the shed where she'd collected her gym bag. She shone her torch on a set of drawers to the left of the door. The top was dusty and covered in cobwebs. She brushed the cobwebs away and pulled the top drawer open to reveal basic hand-tools. She took out a crowbar and a claw hammer with a wooden handle that had a crack running down it. Next to the hammer was a faded plastic bag of nails, which she also removed.

Monica made her way back into the house and upstairs to the bedroom next to the one containing Elinor Mary Clarke's remains. The floor was covered in a brown carpet that was threadbare in places. She got down on her knees in the corner of the room and tugged at the edge of the carpet. It came away easily in her strong grip and she pulled at it, walking down one side of the room, then folded the carpet back to reveal gappy floorboards. She took the crowbar, placed it under the edge of one of the boards and prised it up. It made its reluctance to being pulled up heard. Creaks from aged flooring nails filled the room. As soon as she'd created a space big enough to get her fingers under, she hooked one of her muscular hands around the end and heaved the floorboard free. She cast it to one side and repeated the action on the next five boards, freeing each one. The nails that had held them in place for years protested bitterly.

She gathered the floorboards up, carried them through to the room with the green door, then dropped them in a heap. In the opposite corner of the room was a hand saw, which Monica had used two years earlier to make the bed on which Elinor had met her fate.

She took an orange tape measure, made a couple of quick measurements, cut each floorboard to the required length then placed them in a neat pile in the corner of the room, the nails removed. She nodded approvingly at her efforts.

'Right, Miss Clarke, that's enough work for one evening. I'm off to get some food. Maybe I'll bring you a treat the next time I come over? How about a cream cake? No, I think you're more of a chocolate bar girl. Well, see you soon. Sleep tight, don't let the rodents bite.' She chuckled and closed the green door behind her.

Elinor Mary Clarke's remains had lay in the vicarage, undiscovered, since her death at the hands of Monica almost two years earlier. When Monica had been arrested by Lomas and the team at the gym, she had declined to furnish them with the information they asked for about Elinor's whereabouts. Even a heartfelt plea from Elinor's parents during the trial had failed to encourage Monica to share her gruesome secret.

Monica got to her car without anyone seeing her. Pleased with her day's work, she decided to have something healthier than fish and chips for dinner. Pointing her car towards Southsea, she headed for her hotel, via a shop.

The next morning came quickly. Monica had stayed up late, skipping between movies on Freeview TV channels, eating snacks, and enjoying not being told when to turn her light off and go to sleep.

She had a list of jobs to get through today, all of which required her to maintain her anonymity. She'd bought a hoodie that zipped up high around her face, and a new baseball cap. Her confidence was at a high. Her car afforded her the means to get around, unseen, and she'd only once had to change direction to avoid a marked police car. She showered, dressed and gave Tom on reception a cheery 'Good morning!' on her way out of the hotel. He returned it with an equally happy greeting.

The first stop of her day was a timber yard on the outskirts of Portsmouth. She drove up past the Queen Alexandra Hospital, over the brow of a hill and down through Purbrook towards Goodwillies. She drove through a set of gates painted British racing green and parked in the far corner of the car park. Monica made her way into the trade store and bought six sheets of building grade, wood board. A guy with a face set to miserable cut them to size for her, and she picked up a couple of lengths of 2×2 planed timber. She paid and thanked him, without engaging in too much conversation, loaded the car then headed back towards Portsmouth and the vicarage.

When she reached the road where her torture-den stood, she drove past the vicarage and turned into a driveway that led to a row of garages. She reversed the Mondeo estate up to the door of a grubby blue-doored garage. It was weathered with age and had moss growing around the entrance. She reached around the corner of the wall and retrieved a key from under a brick. The lock was stiff: it took a bit of persuading to get it to release its rusty grip on the garage. Eventually she pulled the door up and waved away a thick cobweb that hung down from the ceiling. Light flooded into the garage, revealing a workbench and more tools along the back wall.

Monica took a look around to make sure she wasn't being watched then unloaded the contents of the boot into the garage. She flicked on a battery powered lamp she'd bought, closed the door and set to work. She worked quickly and with skill, crafting the sheets of timber into the form she required. She measured, then measured again and cut each piece of wood to exact dimensions.

When she was done, she stood back and looked at the finished product. A five-sided box sat on the garage floor, sturdy and perfectly jointed at the corners. She nodded in satisfaction. Monica lifted the box and carried it to the car, then slid it carefully into the boot. It filled the space between the floor and roof perfectly. She closed the tailgate. It dropped into place, forming the sixth side of the box. Next she went back to the garage, opened a drawer to one side of the workbench and took out a roll of black tinting film. Back at the car, she removed the box and put it on the ground, then got into the boot. With the care and skill of a master craftsman, she applied the film to the inside of the rear windows, obscuring anyone's view into the car.

After she'd checked that it was impossible to see into the rear of the car, she opened the tailgate, slid the box back in, looped a length of thick string around the base of the wiper and sat on the edge of the boot. She shuffled backwards and reached up, pulling on the string and lowering the tailgate until it was nearly closed. If the rear of the car had been fully closed, it would have been pitch-black.

'Perfect,' she said, closing the boot once more. 'All ready for you, Miss Marley. Now to sort out your bedroom.'

Monica didn't find it difficult to transfer the hatred she felt for Christina Marley to her younger sister. In her warped mind she'd developed a plan to rid the world of the younger Marley, thus punishing Christina for escaping her clutches.

Inside the vicarage Monica worked through the afternoon, only stopping to eat a quick sandwich. By the time she'd finished, the room was as she wanted it – and ready for its next guest.

Dusk was drawing in, and the light in the bare room was starting to fade.

'Well, I think that's me done for today Elinor, what do you think?' She looked at the skeletal remains. 'I should probably find you somewhere more appropriate to rest, shouldn't I? Oh well, that's a job for another day. Righto, see you tomorrow. Sleep tight.'

22

Friday

Niamh spent most of the day at home, moving from room to room, finding things to do. She'd managed to avoid the news since mid-morning, after seeing a clip of herself in the park as she was surfing channels. She'd switched off the TV, deciding instead to put on some music and do some housework.

She'd done two loads of washing, cleaned the floors in the hall and kitchen and made an especially fragrant fish pie for dinner, all the while singing at the top of her voice to Beyoncé. She always felt better when she was busy, and regretted the wasted day on the sofa and the bottle and a half of wine she'd consumed the previous night. Niamh knew that her ability to focus on mundane tasks as a way of blocking out reality was not the healthiest way to deal with things. But it was a strategy she'd used for years until whatever was bugging her went away or, more often, she came to a solution.

Her phone rang, and she hurried to turn the music down.

'Hello?'

'Hello – is that Niamh Dominicali?'

'Yes, how can I help you?' She half expected it to be a journalist who had got hold of her number somehow.

'This is Detective Inspector Leade. I wonder if you'd be available today to come to Southampton police station and help me with some enquiries?'

'Certainly. Is it about Monica? Have you found her?'

'No, I'm not working on the Monica Silverman search. I'm carrying out an investigation into unexpected deaths in prisons, and I wondered if you wouldn't mind speaking to me about some of the recent deaths in your prison.'

Niamh felt herself go cold. 'Er, yes, of course. When did you have in mind?'

'Any time this afternoon is fine. Come to the main Southampton station and ask for me at the desk.'

'I can be there in about an hour.'

'Perfect, see you then.'

The line went dead. Niamh stood looking at the phone in her hand for a good few seconds. *What could he be looking into? He can't know about the things I asked Monica to do,* she thought. *Don't panic. The worst thing you can do is panic. It'll just be routine enquiry stuff. The system will have hit a number and it'll have triggered an investigation. Besides, the only other people who knew were Monica, Bell and Rodriguez. She's not going to call the police, and the other two are dead. Oh, they're dead – their poor families. They're dead, and it's all my fault. Why did I have to get Monica fucking Silverman to do my dirty work? Stupid bitch!*

***

Niamh had a long standing and intense emotional driver. One that saw her seek out Monica to help her right the wrongs of the justice system. When she was twelve years old she'd been out with her grandparents for the day. The three of them were walking back from spending an idyllic afternoon on the beach, when a woman had mounted the kerb in her car and mown down Niamh's grandparents, killing them instantly. She had suffered a glancing blow from the wing mirror, but had seen her grandparents bodies thrown into the air and across the pavement, like rag dolls.

When the police had arrested the driver they found that she had been over the drink-drive limit, after a lunchtime spent at the pub with friends. She also had her two children in the car with her. When the case got to court, the driver had secured the services of a smart lawyer who had done a great job of pleading the case down. He painted the picture of a dedicated mother, who after a stressful few months had made an ill judged decision to drink and drive. He'd also emphasised that she'd been temporarily distracted by her children and lost control of the vehicle. The judge had sympathised and given the woman a driving ban and a suspended sentence. The resulting impact and injustice of this decision had stayed with Niamh to this day and drove her outrage at what she viewed as weak sentencing.

***

Niamh dressed, putting on dark-blue jeans, a thin, camel-coloured jumper and knee-high tan boots. She was a fan of her autumn wardrobe and always leaned towards boots and long sleeves whenever the opportunity arose. She grabbed a knee-length brown wool coat on her way out of the door, then pulled her front door closed behind her. She stood at the top of the steps for a moment, glancing up and down the road. Satisfied that she couldn't see anything, she walked quickly to the Audi A1 her insurance company had given her – after she'd argued with the woman on the other end of the phone, who'd tried to tell Niamh that they wouldn't replace her car because she'd given her car away, rather than it being stolen. This had enraged Niamh, and she had given the woman both barrels. A very embarrassed and apologetic insurance manager had made sure that a car was delivered to Niamh's house within the hour.

An hour and five minutes after DI Leade had called Niamh, she walked into the tall, imposing police station in the centre of Southampton. At the desk, she asked for DI Leade. She was asked to take a seat. A couple of minutes later a man in his late forties, with closely cropped hair and a goatee, came and introduced himself.

'Niamh Dominicali? I'm DI Stephen Leade. Nice to meet you, come on through.' He shook her hand then turned and walked towards a glass door. He wore a pale grey suit in a way that looked as though he didn't much care for it, and had playful blue eyes. Niamh followed him into a room that had a sign saying 'Interview Room 2' on the door. He motioned to a seat on the far side of the table. A quick look around the sparse room made Niamh feel instantly nervous. She smoothed her hands down her thighs to compose herself as she sat down, smiling at Leade.

He asked her if she wanted a drink. She declined, and he sat down opposite her.

'Thank you for coming in, Niamh. Can I call you Niamh?'

'Of course.'

'Great. As I said, thanks for coming in. It's really helpful of you, given everything I'm sure you have going on at the moment.' He smiled a warm, disarming smile.

'No problem. Happy to help.'

'Excellent. I'll get straight down to it. I'm going to record our conversation, if that's OK? It makes it easier for us to talk, instead of me having to scribble notes.'

'Er, yes, fine.'

He put a handheld recorder on the table between them and turned it on. He announced their names into the recorder, together with the time and date and that Niamh was helping him, voluntarily, with his enquiries.

'Niamh, what can you tell me about Alba White?'

She caught her breath at the mention of the prisoner's name. 'Er, Alba, yes, poor girl, she hadn't been with us long. I'm sure you probably know all about her. She had an accident, we think, in the outdoor gym, although there was no one with her at the time.'

'OK, thank you. And what about Marjorie Phelps?'

Niamh paused again. DI Leade almost sounded as if he was reading a charge sheet.

'Terrible accident, that one. She fell down a flight of stairs. She broke her neck in the fall – died instantly. It was a real shame. She had two youngsters and should only have been in for eighteen months.' She regretted turning down the drink now; her mouth was dry.

Leade didn't speak much – not as much as the other police officers she'd met over the years. Normally they were a real chatty bunch. Not Leade. He just looked at her, almost as if he was waiting for her to fill the silence. She didn't.

'Yes, that's what the report said. Really unlucky – to break her neck in a fall like that, I mean. You never know, I guess.'

'No.'

'OK, and finally Rachel Sigvelt. What can you tell me about her?'

'Rachel – oh, that was another sad one. She was ever so young – barely nineteen, I think. Convicted of killing a grandmother of eight with the lead from a vacuum cleaner in a botched burglary.'

'And what happened to her? How did she die?'

'She was found in her room. Died in her sleep, by all accounts. I don't think they really know what killed her. One of those unexplained deaths.'

'Did it not raise any alarm bells with you, Governor? You know, a handful of young women dying in your prison weeks after you take in a multiple murderer?'

'Monica Silverman?'

'Why, how many more multiple murderers have you got, Governor?' Suddenly his tone had changed. Niamh felt very much under suspicion.

'None, Detective Inspector. We have no one else as dangerous as Monica Silverman, but then neither do any of the other prisons in the country. Monica is unique.'

'You almost sound as if you admire her, Governor.'

'Not at all. But in my job, you learn to have a level of cautious respect for someone as dangerous as Monica Silverman. It makes the difference between treating her like one more prisoner and staying alive.'

'Hmm. Shame that didn't work for your dead officers, don't you think?'

'I'm sorry, Detective Inspector. Is there something you're getting at?'

'It's just that you have three dead prisoners, and three dead officers, in a very short space of time. We can account for the deaths of the officers – at Monica's hands. But your inmates all apparently had unfortunate accidents or met a mysterious death. So, to answer your question, I'm not getting at anything, Governor, just stating a fact. It's a shame your respectful ethos didn't save the lives of officers Bell, Rodriguez and Anderson, isn't it?'

'I suppose it is. Is there anything else I can help you with, DI...'

'It's Leade, DI Leade. No, I think I've got everything I need from you ... for now. If I do need to speak to you again, I'll call you.'

'That's fine. Anything I can do to help.'

'Excellent. Well, I'll show you out and let you get on with your day. Again, thank you for coming in. I appreciate this is not an easy time for you.' Leade walked Niamh back through to reception.

The air was cool. She pulled her coat tightly around herself as she walked down the steps towards West Quay, where she'd parked. She'd been walking for fifteen minutes when she realised she'd passed the huge shopping centre. She saw the ferry port to the Isle of Wight was on her right and what looked like a church, which had been converted into a pub, on her left.

Her thoughts had been completely occupied by the line of questioning DI Leade had taken. She realised that her mouth was dry, and she felt as if a heavy cloud had drifted over her previously well-ordered life.

She walked into the pub and ordered a double rum and Coke with ice, found an out-of-the-way table, sank into the seat and swirled the dark-brown liquid around in the glass.

What the fuck have you done, Niamh? They're on to you, she thought as she looked into the tumbler.

The prison service investigation and the parallel police investigation felt like two high walls closing in on her, pressing her into a corner. She had to work out how to escape before she was crushed.

23

'Can I come in?'

Lomas looked up from his screen to see Stephen Leade standing in his office doorway.

'Stephen, twice in one week. Come in. What can I do for you?'

'I wanted your take on something.'

'Oh?'

'I've just spoken to Niamh Dominicali about the deaths in her prison,' said Leade.

'How did that go?'

'Well, that's just it – it went fine. I asked her about the three women who died recently, the three who were on Drew's list, and she gave me quick, almost well-rehearsed answers about all three. She knew how they'd died, which I'd expect, but her delivery was almost too smooth, if you get my drift?'

'You're saying your gut is telling you there's more to it?'

'Yeah, I guess I am. You know when you get the feeling that something doesn't quite stack up?'

'Oh yes. So how do you want to play it?' Lomas asked.

'I'm not sure yet, but I wondered if you were up for working together, if I come up with an angle that I think will fly?'

'Give me a shout when you've got something and we'll have a chat.'

'Great. How's the Silverman hunt going?'

'Too slow for my liking. We've tracked her as far as Portsmouth, but since then the trail's gone cold. I'm going to talk to Marie in a minute about doing another press statement, dropping a pin in Portsmouth.'

'Couldn't hurt. You never know – somebody might have seen her and not realised it. Do you think she's gone to ground?'

'She's smart, so my guess is she's changed her appearance, given a false name and is holed up somewhere she's familiar with or somewhere she'll blend in.'

'If there's anything I can do, give me a shout.'

'Will do.'

Stephen left, and Lomas went to get Drew. The phone lines had quietened down since the TV appeal, and Drew had been collating all the potential leads that had been followed up by uniformed colleagues to see if any of them looked promising.

'How's it going, Drew?'

'Pretty depressing, if I'm honest, boss. Loads of false sightings, and the few that match what we know, in terms of likely location or route, have all drawn blanks.'

'OK. I've been thinking. We know that she's gone to Portsmouth and we know that she's smart enough to want to stay off-grid. What's her best chance of doing that?'

'Staying solo, trusting no one, being as inconspicuous as possible.'

'How would she do that, do you think?' Lomas asked.

'I think she'll have gone to ground somewhere she knows well, and has probably changed her appearance as best she can.'

'Exactly, so why don't we have the artist draw up a couple of alternative likenesses and circulate them? They might jog someone's memory and help us narrow down the search.'

'It's worth a go. Are you concerned about letting Monica know we know she's in Portsmouth? Could it make her run?' Drew asked.

'I think she's brazen enough that she won't care how close we think we are. She believes she's smarter than us and she'll be convinced we can't find her, I'm sure of it. Come on. Let's go.'

'Go where?'

'To see Marie Carlton and ask her to hold a new press conference.'

'And I'm coming?'

'Yes. You need to get used to speaking to the brass,' said Lomas.

Drew looked a little intimidated, but grabbed a jacket from the back of her chair and followed Lomas up the stairs to DCI Carlton's office.

Lomas hung back and let Drew explain their thinking that they wanted to use some e-fit likenesses to flush Monica out in Portsmouth. At first Drew sounded nervous and she hurried the first couple of sentences. Then Lomas saw his young protégée's shoulders relax and heard her tone level out. She was clear, to the point, and gave DCI Carlton a good rationale for needing the senior officer to go back on TV.

Lomas knew that Drew had the potential to rise quickly through the ranks. She was bright, tenacious and committed. All she needed from him, as he'd told her in her review meeting, was support to build her confidence and expose her to situations outside her comfort zone. This was one such piece of exposure. Lomas knew how much Drew admired Marie Carlton, and feeling comfortable speaking to her one on one would work wonders for her personal development.

Marie agreed with the request, saying she'd arrange a press conference for later that evening.

'Oh, Drew – one more thing. You can come with me,' said Marie.

'Me, ma'am?'

'Yes, you. It will be good experience for you. Don't worry; I'll be doing the talking.' Marie nodded at Lomas. 'Is that OK with you, Lomas?'

'Fine by me. You know I don't like being up there anyway. You're both far more photogenic than me.' He laughed.

'Good, that's settled. I'll let you know what time we'll be on, Drew.'

'Thank you, ma'am.'

'Nonsense. Anyway, while I've got you here, how are you feeling about Monica being out again? I know how close this must feel for you.'

Lomas looked from one to the other.

'I'm OK, thanks ma'am. I just want to get her brought back in again.'

'And I have no doubt that you will. You're doing a great job. See you later.'

They turned and left Marie's office. As soon as they were far enough down the hall, Lomas turned to Drew. 'Well done. That was a really thorough briefing. Not too detailed, but enough to get what you needed. You carry on like this, you'll be in my seat in no time.'

'Ha ha, I don't know about that, but it did feel good.'

'So it should. Now, let's get those composites done. You need to be ready for your TV debut.'

'Yeah, I noticed you ducked out of that at the first opportunity, boss.'

'It's not my thing. Marie and Randolph, they love all that stuff. I'd much rather work this side of the TV cameras.'

They'd become closer over the last couple of years. The original hunt for Monica and the way they were both targeted, albeit in different ways, had given them a unique bond, that few could replicate. Drew was a regular visitor at the Baxter's and Lomas knew that the positive, gender role-modelling Drew provided to Eve was helping his daughter develop her own vision of the breadth of possibilities that lie ahead of her. Heidi and Drew got on so well that Lomas sometimes just left them drinking wine and chatting; sneaking off to watch a bit of sport on TV.

***

Later that evening, Drew joined DCI Carlton in front of the camera. Marie had pulled all the strings she could and had got coverage on all the local TV stations, with a guaranteed replay on BBC and ITV national news at 10 p.m.

The police artists had done a fantastic job of creating images based on the best CCTV images of Monica since her escape. The whole team had worked on them, changing Monica's hair colour to blonde and red and mocking up a couple of versions of her with shorter hair. The e-fit pictures ran along the bottom of the screen while DCI Carlton spoke.

'We have reason to believe that Monica Silverman is in the Portsmouth area. We have been able to obtain good-quality CCTV footage that shows Miss Silverman travelling into the city by train. The images you can see on your screens have been constructed by police artists and show a range of possible likenesses for Miss Silverman. I would again urge any members of the public who think they may have information relating to the whereabouts of Monica Silverman to call the police immediately on 101. Alternatively you can contact Crimestoppers on 0800 555 111. If you see, or think you have seen, Miss Silverman, please do not approach her. Call the police immediately. I'd like to thank you for your assistance. We are doing everything we can to bring Miss Silverman safely into custody.'

The images scrolled along the bottom of the screen when the studios cut back to their own newsreaders.

'Happy with that?' DCI Carlton asked Drew as soon as the cameras had stopped rolling. Drew seemed surprised that Marie had asked her, and it took her a moment to answer.

'Er, yes, that's great. Hopefully we'll get some decent information.'

'Fingers crossed. It was a good idea and it deserves to get a result.'

'Thanks, ma'am, but I can't take the credit for it. It was mainly DI Baxter.'

'Don't be so modest, Drew. You did a good job. It's not easy to pitch an idea like that and you did really well. Lomas has a lot of faith in you, and I can see why. It shows real character to be involved in something like this when it came as close to you as it did last time. You couldn't have a better mentor than Lomas. He's the best copper I know. Just don't tell him I said that – it'll go to his head.'

'No, ma'am.' They shared a smile and walked out of the TV studio to Marie's car.

24

Rain hammered on the roof of the car as Monica sat waiting for Sarah Marley to leave school. The young teacher had clearly stayed late, but Monica didn't mind. She had plenty of patience and was happy to sit in wait.

Eventually she saw an elderly chap in overalls walking down the path towards the car park beside Sarah Marley.

'Ah Miss Marley, time to go.' Monica said.

Monica moved off slowly as Sarah Marley's Clio eased down the school driveway. The road had taken on a deep sheen and the Mondeo's wipers were working hard to clear the water.

As the traffic lights at the top of the hill turned green, Monica moved away, Sarah was immediately behind her. Just beyond the junction Monica braked suddenly. Sarah Marley didn't hit her brakes quickly enough. Monica heard a crunch as the Clio hit the back of her car.

'Excellent.'

Monica drove on for another fifty metres until they were both well-clear of the crossroads, then indicated left. Sarah pulled in behind her, put on her hazard lights and got out of the car. Monica stepped out, removing the smile from her lips and met Sarah in the glow of the Clio's headlights.

'I'm so sorry – a fox ran out in front of me,' said Monica in an earnest tone.

'These things happen. I'm sorry I hit your car. Are you OK?' Sarah asked.

'Yes, I'm fine. I don't think there's much damage.'

'Let's have a quick look, and I'll give you my insurance details.' Said the young teacher.

Monica bent slightly, looking at the rear of her car, watching Sarah in her peripheral vision. As Sarah leaned down to look as well, Monica ploughed an uppercut into her face. Sarah was immediately knocked off balance and fell back against her bonnet. Monica spun towards her and hit again – once, twice, three times – in the face, with the pace and ferocity of the athlete she was. Sarah crumpled to the ground. She tried to speak, but Monica made sure the next punch hit her square in the mouth. She lifted Sarah off the ground in one swift movement and threw her into the box in the rear of the Mondeo.

Monica could see Sarah trying desperately to get her bearings, to understand what was happening. She ignored the young teacher's angst and rapidly shuffled through her pockets. She tried to protest, but Monica hit her again. She took her phone from her trouser pocket, then slammed the boot shut.

With a quick look around and a brief, but quickly dismissed thought for the Clio being found as it was, Monica got into the car and drove away. Within seconds of setting off she heard Sarah start kicking at the inside of the tailgate. The car slid to a halt and Monica yanked the tailgate open. For a moment Sarah froze, then she tried to scramble out. Monica grabbed her by the throat, ignoring the kicks that Sarah was landing on their thighs and stomach. She pulled the teacher towards her then punched her full-on in the face. She felt Sarah's body go limp in her grasp.

'Now fucking lie still, you annoying bitch,' Monica said, shoving Sarah Marley's limp body into the box. She jumped back into the driver's seat with a quick glance around to check that no one had seen her.

Satisfied that she'd managed to silence her victim, she spun the car around and pointed it in the direction of Portsmouth. Monica took the back roads through Southwick and around the back of Portsdown Hill, passing the military installations that littered the brow of the hill. As she drove past the all-night burger van that overlooked Portsea Island and the Royal Navy-dominated harbour, she contemplated stopping for a takeaway burger, then decided against it. The thought of her unconscious cargo coming to was enough to make her forgo the comfort to be gained from fast food.

Monica drove down the hill past Queen Alexandra Hospital and headed for the main road into Portsmouth. As she drove through North End, with its rows of shops, interspersed by the occasional pub, she saw three girls and two guys, all in their late teens or early twenties, staggering along the pavement. They were singing at the tops of their voices. As Monica pulled level with them, one of the girls, wearing a tiny top and spray-on skirt, staggered into the road, right in front of the Mondeo. Monica braked heavily and managed to halt, just before she hit the girl. The girl slammed her hands down on the bonnet of the car and stared at Monica. 'Oi! You should watch where you're fuckin' drivin'!' she shrieked.

Monica sat, her hands on the steering wheel, staring at the girl. One of the girl's friends, who was dressed in equally inappropriate clothing for the weather, came around to the driver's side of the car and rapped on the window.

'You nearly ran my mate over. You should watch where you're driving.'

Monica didn't look at her. Instead, she kept her eyes on the girl whose hands were on the bonnet. She eased her foot up until the clutch was at its biting point and eased the car forward a little.

'Whoa!' shrieked the drunken girl. 'She's fuckin' tryin' to run me over.'

The young woman at the window banged on the glass, and the three who had been standing on the pavement watching, walked in front of the car. One of the young men, a tall skinny guy in jeans and a short-sleeved white shirt, tattoos running the length of his arms, slammed his hands on the bonnet, next to the girl who'd started it all.

Monica looked from one to the other. The temptation to jump out and beat them all to a pulp was overwhelming. She wanted to hurt them so much that her hands were tingling. But she was very conscious that she had to avoid attracting any unwanted attention, very conscious of her hidden cargo – and becoming increasingly convinced that the gang who surrounded her car would not move without causing a scene.

She thought for a moment while they yelled abuse at her and the ones at the front of her car banged their fists against it. Slowly she moved her right hand off the steering wheel and put it on the door handle. She pushed the button on the door panel that unlocked all the doors. Then, simultaneously, she slammed her left hand hard against the horn and threw her car door open, against the girl who had been banging on the glass. The youths all jumped as the horn went off. The window girl went flying backwards into the middle of the road. Some of her friends ran to her aid. Monica hit the accelerator hard, heard Sarah Marley slide to the rear of the boot, and drove straight between the two who had been beating their fists on the bonnet, clipping the tattooed guy's arm with the wing mirror.

As she drove away she glanced in her rear-view mirror. They were making rude hand gestures and shouting at her as she disappeared into the distance.

The rest of her drive was uneventful. As she neared the vicarage, she turned off her lights and eased the car quietly into a space next to the invisible gate.

Monica sat for a minute or two, looking in both directions. There was no one around. Curtains in nearby houses were drawn and the odd bedroom was illuminated by the dim glow of lamps or the flicker of televisions. She opened the gate to the dark garden then returned to the car. She lifted the tailgate and the glow from a nearby streetlight bathed the unconscious body of Sarah Marley.

Sarah didn't make a sound as Monica hoisted her up and over her shoulder. She was a dead weight, like a sandbag at the gym. Monica controlled Sarah's body easily with one arm, closing the boot and locking the car with her spare hand.

She shut the gate behind them and carried Sarah upstairs into Elinor's bedroom, where she lay her on a rough wooden bed that she'd built next to Elinor's sparse remains. Monica secured Sarah's wrists and ankles into manacles that she had built into the bed.

'As promised, here's your new room-mate, Elinor. I'd like to introduce you to Miss Sarah Marley. She's a teacher, you know. Yes, I know – impressive, isn't it? Anyway, I'm going to leave you two to get to know each other. I'll be just downstairs. I have some letters to write.'

Monica went to the kitchen and took a small sheet of plastic from her gym bag. She laid it out carefully on the dusty kitchen table, smoothing it flat. Reaching into the bag again, she took out a pair of surgical gloves, a pen and a pad of paper.

Then in block capitals she wrote:

DI BAXTER, DS TAYLOR,

I HOPE THIS FINDS YOU WELL.
IT'S BEEN A WHILE. I'VE GONE AWAY,
BUT WHERE, I'LL NEVER TELL.
SO MUCH TO SAY, BUT WHERE TO START?
I'LL TRY TO KEEP IT BRIEF.
I REALLY HOPE THE FAMILIES
HAVE OVERCOME THEIR GRIEF.
I'M AFRAID A VISIT YOU MUST PAY
TO MARLEYS' HOUSE UPON THE GREEN,
TO LET THEM KNOW THEIR DAUGHTER
IS NO MORE TO BE SEEN.

She read the note aloud. When she was happy with how it flowed, she folded it neatly in half and slipped it into a cream envelope. She addressed it to DI Lomas Baxter and ran a gloved finger along the self-seal edge.

'Right DS Taylor, your turn. We can't have you feeling like I've forgotten you can we? Not when we got so close last time. No, that would never do, I think you deserve some special attention.' She said, carefully penning a second note in her own inimitable style.

25

Saturday

Lomas arrived at the station early, after a restless night, where sleep had come and gone in short bursts. The rest of the night, he'd lain awake, a slave to his churning thoughts, as his semi-conscious mind tried to come up with new angles they could apply to their search for Monica.

As soon as he walked through the door, his phone rang. At the same time, Nick Swain burst into the open-plan office.

'Boss, you're here! Great!'

'Slow down, Nick – why so pleased to see me?' Lomas said, ignoring the phone.

'A letter's just come for you – not delivered by the postman.'

'Slow down, take a breath. Whatever it is, I'm sure it'll make more sense if you take a breath. Now, what were you saying?'

'Sorry, boss. This...' Nick said, waving a cream envelope in the air. As he waved it, Lomas noticed that Nick had latex gloves on.

'Nick, why are you gloved up?'

'The writing – I think it's from Monica.'

Lomas took a deep breath then darted into his own office for a glove and an evidence bag. 'OK, let's put it down here, on the evidence bag.'

Nick carefully placed the envelope on the bag, then Lomas got a pair of tweezers and eased the flap of the envelope open. He pulled out the folded note and read it out loud.

'Shit! What the fuck does that mean, boss?'

Lomas heard his phone go again. He grabbed it just as it stopped ringing. He checked the display. Two missed calls from Drew. He pressed Call and waited – two, three, four rings, then Drew answered.

'Drew, it's Lomas.'

'Yes, boss, I've had a letter delivered. It's in a—'

'Cream envelope?'

'How did you know?'

'We've got one here at the station. Have you opened it yet?'

'No, I called you straight away.'

'Good. Don't open it. I'm going to get Grayson and his guys to come out to you. They can open it when they get there.' Grayson Washington, a scientific genius, headed up the forensics team in Southampton.

'OK, no problem.'

'Drew...'

'Yes, boss?'

'Are you OK?' Lomas asked.

'I'm fine. With this coming from Monica, we've got a new lead to follow?' Drew said.

'Sit tight. I'll have someone with you soon. Oh, before you go, how was it delivered?'

'It was pushed through the door. I was in the shower, so I didn't see.'

'OK, see you soon.'

Lomas contacted the forensic team and asked for someone to head to Drew's flat and another come to the office to log his note. Next, he called the officers who had been charged with looking after Christina Marley.

'She's here, DI Baxter. She's asleep at the moment – would you like me to wake her?'

'No, that's fine, thank you.' He called Marie Carlton on her mobile, knowing she would want to know about the letter.

'So who is she talking about?' Marie asked.

'I don't know. Nick is checking, but I seem to remember that Christina has a sister.'

'Keep me in the loop, Lomas. I'll let the super know.'

He hung up, then called Drew back. 'Are they there yet?'

'Yes, they've just got here. I'm just getting gloved up before we open it. I'll put you on the table for a minute.'

Lomas waited until Drew returned to the call.

'Who's there, Drew?'

'Grayson's here and one of his guys,' she answered, having clearly switched to speakerphone.

'OK, great. Grayson, I want to know what the note says as soon as you open it.'

'Hold the line, caller,' replied the familiar, deep voice of Grayson Washington.

Lomas could hear muffled conversation in the background and a crackling noise that he assumed was Drew moving the phone. Then she came back on the line.

'OK, we're opening it now,' Grayson said.

Lomas heard a gasp, then Drew's voice.

'It's definitely Monica. Do you want me to read it out?'

'Yes, please.'

'OK, it says...' She coughed, clearing her throat, then said...

'Detective Drew, long time no speak,
As I'm not counting prison.
But, like the phoenix from the flames,
I feel like I have risen.
I'm back out so no time to lose,
To pick-up where I left off.
And that means picking up with you.
I hope you've not gone soft.
No more boxed heads,
That's so last year – a relic from the past.
I'm going for a different twist,
You'd better move real fast.
Sarah's here to stay with me
Until it's time to sleep.
But unlike poor dead Elinor,
Her head ... I may just keep.'

There was silence when Drew finished reading the twisted note. For a few seconds no one spoke, then Lomas turned to Nick.

'How was this letter delivered, Nick?'

'The guys on the front desk said a taxi driver dropped it off.'

'Did they get his name?'

'Yes, and his number. Do you want me to bring him in?'

'Definitely. Drew?'

'Yeah, I'm here.'

'Did you hear that?'

'Yes. I'll be on my way in five minutes.'

'See you soon.'

They ended the call and Lomas turned to speak to Nick, but he'd already picked up the phone to call the taxi driver. Lomas called Marie again.

'Hi, Lomas. I'm in the office, why don't you come up?'

'Will do.' He took the stairs two at a time and didn't wait to knock on DCI Carlton's door.

'So, is it Monica?' she asked as soon as he walked in.

'Yes. But there's something else.'

'What?'

'She's sent one to Drew as well. It was delivered to her flat this morning, while she was in the shower. The one that came here was delivered by taxi. Nick Swain's bringing the driver in for questioning.'

'What was the content of the note she sent to Drew?'

'The same as they always are. Intimidation and threats.'

'And Drew?'

'She's OK – on her way in. Grayson's at Drew's flat, seeing if he can find any prints or trace evidence, with some more of his guys downstairs with the letter that came here.'

'Do you think she used a cab for both?'

'I would imagine so. If she's done it for one, then it make sense to do it for both. I suppose it keeps her from being picked up on camera. I hope the taxi's got an on-board camera, and it got something.'

'I'll update Randolph. Lomas, if this gets too close you'll have to take Drew off it. You know that, don't you?'

'I do.'

'Good. Let's hope it doesn't come to that.'

Lomas turned and left Marie's office as she picked up the phone to call the Superintendent.

26

A sudden noise shattered Niamh's sleep. The vibration from her phone, on the coffee table in her lounge, was intrusive and persistent. She reached out from the sofa, where she'd drifted into an uncomfortable slumber after a bottle of wine. Niamh tried to focus on the screen. When she saw that it was a withheld number, she came abruptly to her senses. She knew this wouldn't be good.

'Hello.'

'Good morning. Is this Governor Dominicali?'

'Speaking.'

'Great, glad I got hold of you. This is William Bennett.'

The name was instantly familiar to Niamh. Bill Bennett was a long-serving, well-respected prison governor who had made a name for himself over the years. He ran a tight ship, took no nonsense, and was liked by the more politically focused in the service, as he was adept at making them look good. Niamh had never met him, but she knew who he was and why he was calling.

'Good morning, William, what can I do for you?'

'Sorry to call you on a Saturday, but I've been given the task of investigating your incident. You know there are a lot of eyes on this, Niamh, and the minister is getting twitchy, to say the least.'

'I'm sure he is.' Niamh was well aware what a political nightmare Monica's escape would be. She knew her name would be mud across the service and they would be baying for her head on a stick so that they could feed her to the media.

'How would you like to do this, William?'

'Bill – please call me Bill.'

'Of course. So, Bill, what would you like me to do?'

'If you could meet me for a chat, I can get the ball rolling on the investigation. I have Maggie Sanders assisting and we're both available today, if that works for you?'

Niamh also knew of Maggie, another high-profile governor and ministerial trouble-shooter. She, like Bill, had been drafted in to turn around struggling prisons, uncovering corruption and deep-rooted poor practice on her way. This was not going to play well for Niamh, she could feel it.

'No problem, Bill. Would midday work?'

'Perfect. We've managed to get a room at Southampton Central police station. We'll see you there.'

Niamh's stomach did an involuntary flip as Bill said 'police station'. She ended the call without saying anything else. She threw her phone onto the sofa, pulled a cushion over her face and screamed.

First the police looking at deaths, now Bill bloody Bennett. I'm fucked. There's no way out of this. If the police don't dig deep enough to link the deaths, Bill is definitely going to make sure I'm fired for the escape.

27

By the time Lomas got back downstairs from briefing Marie Carlton, there was a buzz of activity in the open-plan office. Gurdeep approached him as soon as he walked in.

'What is it, G?'

'Christina Marley has a sister, boss.'

'Fuck! I thought that was the case, but I was hoping I'd got it wrong. Let's get hold of her.'

'I've already tried. She's a teacher at a primary school in Wickham. She didn't show up today.'

'Oh bollocks...'

'There's more...' said Gurdeep.

'More? Do I want to hear this?'

'Nope. Her car was found abandoned last night near some traffic lights just outside Wickham. The report said the driver's door was open and the lights were all on.'

'Where's the car now?'

'It was recovered to a compound. We're having it brought in for forensics.'

'Good work, G. OK, listen up!' he yelled, clapping his hands. Everyone in the room came to an instant stop. Over his shoulder, Lomas saw Drew walk into the room.

'We have new information that needs acting on immediately. I cannot stress how quickly we need to move, people. Two notes have been delivered to us this morning: one here by taxi, one to DS Taylor's flat, we're assuming also by taxi. Our working assumption is that they're from Monica Silverman. Both notes refer to Christina Marley's family, claiming to have their daughter, Sarah. We have confirmed that Christina has indeed got a sister. Sarah is a twenty-eight-year-old primary school teacher. She did not arrive at work this morning and last night her car was found abandoned, its lights on and door open, near some traffic lights just outside Wickham. Unfortunately, this points to validating Monica's claim to have taken Sarah Marley. I want her phone and her movements tracked. I want to know if her car had telematics and, if it has, I want the records. We need to speak to her colleagues and friends this morning. Grant, can you pull any CCTV from in and around the area where her car was found, reviewing and tracking any car that shows up in the area at the same time as Sarah. We need to move quickly, people.

We know what Monica does to young women she takes captive. We will not lose Sarah Marley. Questions?'

No one said anything. Unusually, the officers in the room did not erupt into conversation.

'Right, let's get going. Drew, you're with me.'

'Where are we going, boss?'

'To speak to Christina and Sarah Marley's parents.'

She followed him out of the room; the room erupted into a mass of conversation and activity.

'How are you doing?' Lomas asked Drew as they walked towards his car.

'I'm good. Obviously not chuffed about getting another note from my penpal, but I'm determined to bring her in. What are we going to tell Christina?'

'We need to make sure she doesn't hear any rumours about her sister before we decide what we're going tell her, as the NCA haven't picked her up to take her into witness protection yet. Can you get Nick on the phone?' he said as they got in the car.

Drew put her seatbelt on and called Nick's mobile. Her phone connected to Lomas's car, since they'd used it hands-free before.

Nick answered.

'Hey gorgeous, how you doing?'

Lomas shot Drew a sideways look and a knowing smile.

'I'm fine, Nick, but you really can't call me that in front of Drew,' said Lomas.

'Sorry, boss, I thought...' Nick stuttered.

'Never mind what you thought. Listen, we'll talk about yours and Drew's love life later. I need you to make sure that word of what may have happened to her sister doesn't reach Christina Marley. She's in the station and I don't want anyone clumsily blurting out that her sister's missing.'

'Got it, no problem. I'll go and see the team that's with her and make sure they keep her well away from everything.'

'Good man. Oh, and Nick?'

'Yes, boss?'

'Love you.' He laughed and hung up. He looked across at Drew, who was staring straight ahead.

'Anything you want to share, DS Taylor?'

'Not right now, thanks.' She smiled, refusing to make eye contact.

'Fair enough. OK, on to more important things. What are your thoughts on speaking to the Marleys?'

'That's a tough one. They're going to be devastated. I'm sure they already know she didn't come home last night, although they might not know about the car yet.

Uniform were planning to go to their address this morning about the car; they were short last night, so didn't get to them — our team stopped that when we got the notes first thing. I think we're going to have to be straight with them and let them know what we suspect to be the case,' said Drew.

'Agreed. If I remember rightly, Mrs Marley was quite fragile last time and Mr Marley is quite a matter-of-fact kind of guy, so my intention is to deliver the message gently, but directly, no beating about the bush. Then I think we sit back and give him the space to support his wife to absorb the news.'

It wasn't long before they were pulling up outside the Marleys' Corhampton home. They lived in the centre house in a semi-circular close. All the houses faced a neatly trimmed green. The grass glistened with the remnants of earlier rain. The Marleys' two cars sat on their driveway. Lomas walked between them to knock on the door. Breaking news like this was the part of the job Lomas disliked the most; there was no easy way to let unsuspecting people know that a loved one was missing, or dead.

The door was answered quickly. As soon as Beatrice Marley saw Lomas and Drew, she staggered backwards. She was a small woman, like her daughters, with soft features, blue eyes and shoulder-length blonde hair.

'Good morning, Mrs Marley. Is it OK if we come in?' Lomas said gently.

She gathered her composure, clearly dreading whatever was going to come out of Lomas's mouth.

'Yes, of course, DI Baxter, come in.' She stood back and held the door open for them, motioning for them to go through to the kitchen. 'My husband is through there. Alan, it's DI Baxter and ... sorry, dear...'

'DS Taylor,' Drew said, with the warmest smile she could manage.

Alan Marley appeared in the kitchen doorway and greeted them. He was a tall man, with broad shoulders, a military gait and close-cropped grey hair. His voice boomed when he spoke.

'Would you like some tea? The kettle's just boiled.' Alan turned towards the kettle.

'Yes, thank you. Tea would be great,' said Lomas.

Alan made the tea as Beatrice guided Lomas and Drew to seats. Beatrice then busied herself getting coasters and a packet of biscuits from a cupboard. It was clear that she didn't want to start the conversation. Lomas waited until they were seated at the table. Alan spoke first.

'We've seen the news about Monica Silverman and we're grateful to you for getting Christina somewhere safe so quickly, DI Baxter.'

'It was really important to do that as soon as we could. Christina is safe and well. I spoke to her late yesterday and she was very understanding of the situation, although understandably frustrated at Monica having an effect on her life again.'

'That's good to know. I hope she's not giving your officers too much grief.' Alan laughed.

'Oh, it won't do them any harm to be kept on their toes. Now, that isn't what we wanted to speak to you about...'

'How else can we help you?' asked Beatrice.

'We wanted to talk to you about your other daughter, Sarah.'

'What about her?' Alan took his wife's hand.

'When was the last time you saw her or heard from her?' Lomas asked, hating to have to ask, noting the panicked look that swept over Beatrice Marley's face.

'Yesterday morning, when she left for work. I think she was due to go out with one of her girlfriends last night. I assumed she'd had a couple of drinks and slept over...' said Beatrice.

'She doesn't drink and drive. Why do you ask?' interrupted Alan.

'Sarah's car was found by the side of the road just outside Wickham last night. The lights were on and the driver's door was open.'

Alan and Beatrice exchanged worried glances.

'Then, first thing this morning we received two letters, which we have good reason to believe are from Monica Silverman, stating that she has taken Sarah.' Lomas paused, allowing the enormity of what he'd told the couple to sink in. 'We've checked with her school, and she hasn't arrived at work this morning. We're working on the basis that the letters are genuine, I'm afraid. We've mobilised all our resources to establish Sarah's whereabouts.' He stopped again, taking a sip from his mug of tea.

The Marleys had gone from sitting, holding hands, to hugging each other. Silent tears ran down Beatrice Marley's face.

Drew looked at Lomas. They both knew there were no words that would alleviate the Marleys' suffering or lift the dark cloud that had just descended over their lives. They sat silently for a little while, Alan kissing the top of his wife's head as he stroked her hair. Then in hushed tones he spoke. 'Does Christina know?'

'No. We've made sure that word doesn't get to her. I wanted to come and speak to you first. Would you like me to arrange for you to speak to her? Or would you prefer me to tell her then arrange a call with you?'

'I think it may be better if it comes from you, DI Baxter. Please don't take that the wrong way, but I wouldn't know where to start,' Alan said.

'Are you sure it's her? Monica, I mean?' Beatrice's voice wavered.

'We're as sure as we can be at the moment. Unfortunately, our experience of dealing with Miss Silverman gives us a reasonable amount of confidence that the letters and the claims in them are genuine.'

'You will find her, won't you?' she continued through her tears. 'She's such a happy girl, and Christina was so damaged by what happened to her.'

'We'll do everything we possibly can to bring her home, Mrs Marley,' Lomas said. 'Do you have a recent photo of Sarah that we could have, please?'

Alan fished his phone out of his pocket, dabbed at the screen and turned it towards Lomas and Drew. 'This was taken last weekend at the Fisher's Pond pub. It's the most recent one I have.'

'Perfect. Could you send that to my phone, please? We'll use it for public appeals for information – just so you're not surprised when you see it on TV,' said Drew.

Alan fumbled with his phone for a moment before admitting that he didn't know how to send the photo. Drew took his phone and airdropped the photo to hers.

'Will you need us to do another TV appeal, like we did for Christina?' asked Beatrice, wiping her tears with the sleeve of her cardigan.

'I think that may be something we'd like to do reasonably quickly, if you're OK with it.'

'Whatever we have to do to get our daughter back safe and well, DI Baxter, we'll do,' said Alan.

'Thank you. I'd also like to move you both to a place of safety. Monica is very dangerous and clearly has some kind of vendetta against your family, for whatever reason. I don't want to risk anything happening to either of you. DS Taylor will arrange to have a car come and collect you. In the short term, we'll take you to the station.'

'DI Baxter...' Beatrice began.

'Yes?'

'Please break this to Christina gently. She's been through enough. This will be really hard for her to hear.'

'I will. Once I've spoken to her, you'll be able to spend some time together without being surrounded by police officers. I'm so sorry this is happening to your family,' said Lomas.

Alan Marley coughed and cleared his throat. 'Thank you, DI Baxter. I can't imagine how difficult it must have been, coming all the way out here to tell us this.'

'I just wish it hadn't been necessary, Mr Marley.'

They made awkward small talk until the unmarked car arrived, with an officer to take the Marleys to be with Christina. When they got into their car, Lomas let out a sigh and let his head drop back against the head-rest.

'Poor, poor people. I can't imagine what they're going through right now.'

'I know – the look in their eyes as you were telling them was heart-breaking. How unlucky can one family be?' Drew replied.

'We'd better get back and tell Christina before the news leaks.'

As they made their way back, Lomas called Gurdeep to see what progress they'd made on tracking Sarah.

'We've had a result on her phone, boss. We pinged it off a tower and got a location, close to where her car was found.'

'We're not far away. Have you got anyone heading out there?' Lomas said.

'Yes, Grayson and his team are already en route. Shall I let him know you'll be joining him?'

'Yes please. We'll head straight there. Good work, G. Can you put me through to Nick now?'

'Will do.'

Drew turned her head and looked at Lomas while they were waiting for the call to be transferred.

'Don't worry, I'm not going to give him any more grief. I just want to know if he's spoken to the taxi driver yet.'

'Sorry, boss. About me and Nick – it's all quite new, in fact, very new, like this week. I'd have mentioned it...'

'I know. Don't worry, it's all good. Nick's a good guy...'

They were cut off by Nick answering the phone, rather sheepishly. 'Hello?'

'Nick, hi, have you managed to speak to the taxi driver yet?'

'He just left the station. I took a statement, for what it's worth.'

'What do you mean?' Lomas asked.

'He has no CCTV in his car and can't describe the person who gave him the envelope. Said she wore a hoodie, zipped quite high up to her face. She paid in cash and gave him a note with the address on – which he binned because he knows where the station is.'

'And the other letter? The one that went to Drew's?'

'He said there was another cab behind him. He guessed she gave the other letter to that cab. He didn't deliver it.'

'OK. Where was he when he picked up the letter?'

'At the front of a taxi rank, near the guildhall in the middle of Pompey.'

'Good. Let's pull all the CCTV from the surrounding area. Could you tell us anything that might confirm it was Monica who gave him the letters?'

'Will do, boss. As far as ID, only rough height and build and the fact that she was hiding under a zipped hoodie.'

'OK. Thanks, Nick, well done.' He ended the call and saw a police van parked alongside some trees on the strip of road in front of them. Lomas parked behind the van and saw Grayson Washington get out of one side, and one of his forensic team get out of the other. Washington was a good-looking, athletically built black guy in his mid-thirties. He had a shaved head and designer stubble that was always perfectly trimmed. Lomas had a huge amount of respect for the forensic scientist, who was meticulous in his pursuit of evidence and insisted on the same discipline from his team.

The area to either side of the road was covered in dense woodland. Lomas could see the traffic lights and crossroads at the top of the incline. About a hundred metres behind them was a garage selling motorhomes. He made mental note to get Drew to ask for their CCTV footage or security cameras. As they got out of the car, a fine rain started to fall. Lomas grabbed a grey coat from the boot of his car, pulling it on over his suit jacket. There was no pavement along the edge of the road. Lomas and Grayson met in the space between their vehicles, closely followed by their partners.

'What have we got, Grayson?'

'A rough location ID for Sarah Marley's phone, in this area to the right.' Grayson motioned towards the woods.

'That's a lot of woodland. Just as well we get decent data these days. I remember when you'd have been searching a couple of miles either side. Lead on, sir,' Lomas said, waving an arm towards the woods.

The four of them made their way in through a clearing in the trees. Raindrops clung to the branches as if not wanting to fall to the ground, for fear of being lost. The ground was covered in bracken and golden leaves. They didn't have to go far before Drew stopped and pointed into the woods. 'Look – what's that?'

Light was reflecting off the screen of a phone in the undergrowth. Grayson asked his partner, a man in his mid-twenties, with blond surfer curls, to tape off the area and start marking and photographing around the phone.

'We're going to head back to the station and leave you to do your thing,' Lomas said to Grayson.

'No worries. I'll let you know what we find later.'

28

Sarah Marley struggled to open her eyes. Slowly they let the light in but it hurt – it hurt so much. A searing pain started in her eyes and made its way around her head, forcing her to close her eyes again. Her body ached after the beating she had been given, and being thrown around, unconscious in the box. She tried to move her hand to her face, but couldn't. It stopped dead. The metal restraints that held her in place registered in her consciousness. Sarah tried in vain to fight against their grip, thrashing her arms around, but each time they were snatched back into place by the manacles. She felt a searing pain in her head and a cold sweat start to envelope her body. Her heart raced in her chest, feeling like it was thumping against her ribs.

Her eyes were open now. She turned her head. She was lying on a wooden bed. The heavily grained wood near her face looked gappy and old. It smelled like musty carpets. She raised one hand slowly and saw the metal shackle that held it in place. She worked her fingers around the metal chains that held her wrists in place.

Sarah turned her head in the opposite direction and gasped. She was too terrified to scream at what she saw. Lying on a makeshift bed like the one she was on was the skeletal remains of a person. She closed her eyes and turned her head away. Her chin creased and her bottom lip began to tremble uncontrollably. Hot tears began to stream down her face.

Her attention was ripped away from the remains as she heard footsteps on what sounded like a wooden floor. They were getting closer, louder. Heavy, purposeful steps, striding in her direction. They stopped, quite close by. Silence. Sarah strained to pick out other sounds, but there was nothing. Then, a key in a lock. She looked to her left, towards an old green door. It opened quickly and in walked a big woman. She was thick-set, wearing a black Adidas hoodie that hugged broad shoulders and jeans that clung to muscular thighs. She had short-cropped, bleached blonde hair, a square jaw and blue eyes. The woman made eye contact with Sarah as soon as she walked in.

'Ah, Miss Marley, you're awake. Excellent.'

Sarah didn't reply.

'What's wrong? Cat got your tongue? Oh well, suit yourself. Allow me to introduce you to your room-mate. Miss Sarah Marley, meet Miss Elinor Mary Clarke. Elinor's been here for a couple of years now and she was just dying to meet someone new. Weren't you, Elinor? Nothing from you, either? You'll both get to know each other, I'm sure, probably when I'm not around.'

Sarah considered whether to speak or not. *Could it do any harm? I'm already chained up. It might help to humanise me – I've read that helps people who have been abducted. Build a rapport with her.* She took another look around. *Fuck it. Why not?*

'You didn't say who you are,' she said, trying to sound friendly.

'Oh, my apologies. I thought you'd know – what with your family history and all.'

This confirmed what Sarah had already suspected.

'You're Monica Silverman.'

'Got it in one. Gold star for Miss Marley. Do you still give out gold stars in school? No matter. It's a pleasure to make your acquaintance. I've read so much about you.'

'It was you at the traffic lights, wasn't it?' Sarah asked, feeling pain wash over her body again.

'Yeah. Sorry about the damage to your car. I had to think of a way to get *your* attention without attracting attention, if you know what I mean.'

'But why?'

'Why what?'

'Why did you need to get my attention? What do you want with me?'

'Well, it's like this. Your beloved sister was never meant to get away the way she did. And I'm pretty sure that as soon as I managed to free myself from that wretched prison, DI Baxter will have moved dear Christina somewhere safe. So, since I can't get to her physically—'

'You'll get to her mentally, by taking me.'

'Gold star number two. You really are very bright. I dare say, even brighter than your sister.'

Sarah ignored the fake flattery – or dig at her sister – by Silverman and thought quickly. How far should she push the conversation? Given what she knew about Monica, she decided that she probably planned to kill her. She should stick with her original plan: fuck it and carry on.

'So what are you going to do with me? Chop me up and deliver me to my family?'

'No, no, I think I can be much more creative with you. I have lots to do and you're not going anywhere, so why rush to repeat the things I've already done?'

'So where *am* I?' Sarah turned her head, casting a glance around the room.

'Somewhere out of the way, where no one will find you.'

'That's vague.' Sarah tried to bait Monica.

'It's the best you're getting for now – and if you carry on like that, I'll put you to sleep again.'

'So, are you saying that if I scream, nobody will hear me?' Sarah asked.

Monica strode over to Sarah. 'If you scream, Miss Marley, no one will ever hear from you again. Are we clear?' Her tone had changed from conversational to menacing.

'Clear.' Sarah turned her head away from Monica, disengaging from the dialogue. She felt Monica standing next to her for another few seconds in silence, then she turned and walked back to the door.

'I'll leave you two to get to know each other.' Monica slammed the door and left Sarah alone with Elinor's remains and only her thoughts for company.

Sarah slammed her fists down in frustration, then instantly regretted it, as a splinter dug into the fleshy part of her fist. Images of Christina popped into her head. Was this how her sister had felt when she was held captive? Had Monica used the same menacing tone and playfully intimidating dialogue with her? She knew that Christina had shared a room with another of Monica's victims. Anna-May Appleby had been alive when Christina had been abducted. Christina had told Sarah about the conversation they'd had the night before Anna-May was killed. But Sarah remembered something else: Christina had told her that Monica had blindfolded her and tortured her.

But Sarah had no blindfold, or gag.

Why was that?

29

Monica closed the green door behind her and left Sarah Marley for a while. She was starting to get agitated with Sarah's questions and needed some space to think about what to do with the teacher next. Should she leave her without a gag? She decided that she'd either knock Sarah out or gag her before she went out.

She had things to do.

She knew that Lomas and Drew would have received their letters by now, and they would have started a desperate hunt for Sarah. This would take up a big chunk of their time – time that would have otherwise been spent looking for her.

Monica had been particularly pleased with the idea of using taxi drivers to deliver the notes. Although both cabbies had looked at her like she was mad, she knew it was sensible to remain a safe distance from DI Baxter.

Monica opened a bottle of water and took a swig, sitting on a wooden stool in the kitchen. The room had none of the normal kitchen features: no utensils or pans, no plates draining next to the sink, no fruit bowl.

Instead it had dust, cobwebs and burgundy cupboard doors, some ajar, some hanging off. Knowing that the kitchen couldn't be seen from the road, since it was at the back of the house, behind the high fence, she'd set up a camping stove and a battery-powered light at one end of the worktop. In a shopping bag next to the stove were some basic provisions, some of which she'd bought with Sarah in mind. Others were for her.

Monica heated a tin of baked beans on the stove and pondered her next move. She needed to derail the investigation into her escape, she'd thought of a couple of ways to do that. She plotted as she ate the beans, thinking that they weren't even as good as prison food.

She got out the mobile phone she'd taken from Paul Daniels – his awkwardness when explaining that it really was his name made her smile, like it did every time she thought about the interaction.

She opened a gym timer app she'd downloaded and set it to time five sets of exercises, with one-minute intervals and thirty-second rest periods. Then she put the phone on the end of the kitchen worktop, facing her. Monica took off her hoodie and draped it over the stool. She pressed Start on the screen, and a seven-second countdown began. At the beep, she sprang into action. minute of burpees, followed by a minute of push-ups. Sixty seconds of tuck jumps came next, then a minute of shadow-boxing. She was breathing heavily by the end of the first round, and her jeans made it difficult to move as quickly as she'd like. She made a mental note to get a pair of joggers the next time she passed a charity shop.

Monica repeated the circuit five times. By the end she was sweating and out of breath, but she felt good. Exercise had always been a great way for her to centre herself. The act of pushing her body, finding its limits with heavy weights or intense bursts of cardio, gave her a familiar sense of achievement. She had excelled physically her whole life: always faster, stronger and with better endurance than her peers.

Her mother had hated it. She'd never been proud of her, had always been scathing about how 'lifting weights and all that sweating isn't ladylike'. When she'd been brave enough, Monica had mocked her mother, telling her that she only hated exercise because she was too weak and feeble to enjoy it. But inside, her mother's disapproval ate at her. She knew her mother would have preferred her daughter to be a prissy, petite, well-manicured, polite girl. Instead of the hulk she'd turned into. She'd heard her mother talking to friends on the phone on various occasions as she'd been growing up.

The night Monica found out that she'd been selected to represent England in the hammer-throw, she'd heard her mother tell a friend that 'Monica isn't doing a proper sport; she's just going to throw things'. This scathing remark, coupled with her mother's scornful laugh, had been one of many similar occurrences that had cemented Monica's hatred for her maternal parent. That and all she seemed to stand for, or value. Her love of preening, of perfect hair and make-up. In Monica's view, she had wasted countless hours socialising, floating around like a social butterfly, obsessed with clothes and jewellery. All of these things Monica had grown to despise.

The ultimate evolution of her hatred was the list she drew up of those who had developed friendships with her mother. Friendships deepened by their shared love of the finer things in life, of pointless socialising and preening and vanity. Some of these women — who unbeknown to them were noted in Monica's mental list — were regular guests at the Silverman home and had been all too keen to join in with her mother's humiliating mockery of Monica's athletic pursuits.

It was time to start working on the list.

Monica swilled the pan she'd eaten her beans from with some water from a bottle, and put it on top of the bag of groceries to dry. She grabbed a fresh T-shirt from her gym bag and pulled her hoodie over her head. She bounded up the stairs two at a time and made her way to the green door. As she opened it she saw Sarah Marley jump, woken from what must have been an uncomfortable nap, chained to the makeshift wooden bed.

'Right, Miss Marley, I'm off out. Since it looks like you're nice and comfy, you can stay here and keep Miss Clarke company.'

Sarah didn't reply. Monica shrugged and strode over to the bed. She held the T-shirt she'd been wearing for her workout. She saw Sarah look from her to the shirt and back again.

'You're wondering what I'm doing with this? Let me show you.'

She took the shirt in both hands and ripped it along the side seam. It tore easily in her strong grip. She then ripped a strip off the bottom edge of the T-shirt, using about ten centimetres of the material. Monica held the strip of cloth out for Sarah to see, like a magician showing a prop, mid-trick. Still, Sarah didn't speak. Her eyes were wide, and Monica could see the fear in them. Monica tied one knot, then another, in the centre of the cloth. Then in a swift movement she flicked it over Sarah's head, pulled the big knot around to the front and stuffed it into her prisoner's mouth. Sarah gave a muffled scream as Monica tied the gag tightly around her head.

'Oh, shush now. I need to go out and I can't have you upsetting the neighbours by making a racket, can I?'

This was met with an attempt at muffled speech which, if Monica had tried, she'd have been able to work out. But she didn't.

'Now lie still, be quiet, and don't make me have to do anything else to keep you quiet.'

Sarah's eyes were wide and fearful. She was clearly thinking through the other ways she could be silenced, and obviously decided not to push her luck. She remained still and quiet.

'Good, that's better. I'll be back later. Don't run away.' She laughed and left Sarah Marley on her own.

30

The traffic was steady as Lomas and Drew drove along the dual carriageway that ran parallel to the docks. An opulent-looking cruise ship was visible above the shipping containers as they headed towards Southampton police station. It was a little after 11 a.m. when he and Drew went inside, to meet Christina Marley.

She was sitting on a functional-looking black sofa, chatting to a uniformed officer as they approached. She looked up and made eye contact with Lomas. He knew from the way she returned his look that she sensed something was wrong. Their conversation stopped and the uniformed officer stood to greet Lomas and Drew.

'Morning, sir.'

'Morning. Could I have a word with Miss Marley, please?'

'Of course. I'll be in the kitchen around the corner. Would you like a cuppa?' He looked at Drew then Lomas.

'That would be great, thanks. It's been a long day already,' said Drew. The officer nodded and left them.

'Christina, how are you doing?' Lomas asked. She looked different to the last time he'd seen her. Her hair was much darker and a thick fringe hid the scars that Lomas knew ran across her forehead: a permanent souvenir of her encounter with Monica Silverman.

'I'm OK. Do you know how long I'm going to be here for?'

'It shouldn't be too much longer. We have a division that deals with witness protection and they should be here later today, I hope. They'll take you somewhere safe – that isn't a pull-out bed in a police station.'

'So I can't go home yet then?'

'No, I'm afraid not. Monica hasn't been found yet and it wouldn't be safe for you to be at home while she's still at large.' He paused. Christina let out a long sigh and the uniformed officer brought over three mugs of tea.

Christina hugged her mug and looked from Lomas to Drew and back again. 'There's something else, isn't there? You didn't just come to tell me that I couldn't go home yet.'

'No, we didn't, you're right. There is something else I want to talk to you about.' He paused again, searching for the right words, but knowing they didn't exist.

'There's no easy way to tell you this, Christina, but your sister, Sarah is missing.'

'Missing? What do you mean, missing?'

'Her car was found abandoned on a road near the school she teaches at last night. It was clear from the way it was left that it hadn't been parked there.' He sipped his tea. 'Christina, we have reason to believe that Monica Silverman has abducted your sister. We're doing everything we can to find her.' He stopped again.

Christina didn't react at first. It was like she couldn't find the right words either. 'But why? Why do you think it's her?' she asked finally, tears welling in her eyes.

'Do you remember the note you received when you were in hospital?'

'Yes, the one in the flowers.'

'Well, we received something very similar this morning. It was written in the same style as the letter you got, and whoever wrote it claimed to have Sarah.'

Lomas watched as Christina's gaze darted from side to side. Her hands were shaking. Drew reached forward and gently took the mug from her, placing it on the table in front of them.

'Why would she take Sarah? It doesn't make sense, unless ... oh my God! She's taken her because she couldn't get to me, hasn't she?'

'We don't know why Monica has targeted Sarah. There's no way to know for sure,' said Drew, placing a hand on top of Christina's. 'None of this is your fault, Christina. Not what happened to you before – and not what's happening now.'

'But there can't be any other reason for her to take Sarah. It's because I got away. She got out of prison to finish me off. She's not going to stop until I'm dead, is she?' Her eyes were fixed on Lomas, wide and unblinking.

'You're safe here. We won't let anything happen to you,' he reassured her.

'But, Sarah isn't. She's got her, and she does terrible things to people. I know – I spoke to Anna-May. I heard what she did to her. I heard her get...' Her voice trailed off before she could verbalise the acts of torture Monica had inflicted on Anna-May Appleby as Christina lay chained to a bed not two meters away. Her face was awash with tears, her eyes red, and the only noise coming from her was a soft sob.

'You will find her, won't you, Detective Baxter?'

'We're doing everything we can, Christina.'

'What about Mum and Dad? Do they know?'

'DS Taylor and I told your parents earlier this morning. Would you like me to arrange a call for you?'

Lomas and Drew sat, helpless, as Christina sobbed. Her whole body shook. She'd given up trying to wipe the tears from her face and just let them flow. She pulled her hand out from under Drew's and put both over her face, her sobs becoming louder.

Gurdeep came rushing into the room. Lomas looked round.

'Sorry, boss, could I speak to you for a moment?'

Lomas glanced at Drew, but didn't need to say anything.

'It's fine, I'll stay with her,' said Drew. Lomas stood and walked out of the room with Gurdeep.

'What is it, G?'

'We've had a call from a couple of kids in Portsmouth. They say they've seen Monica. Apparently she took their phones.'

'How genuine do they sound?'

'They gave a pretty good description and seem sure it was her. The timings match with how long it would have taken her to walk from Portsmouth station after getting off the train, and the time we saw her on CCTV.'

'Great, let's get them in.'

'Already on it, boss. I've sent a car to pick them up and bring them in. They should be here in about an hour.'

'Good work, G. Give me a shout when they get here, would you?'

'Will do.'

Just over an hour later, Lomas and Drew were in an interview room, sitting across the table from a scrawny-looking Paul Daniels and Damian Mansell, with Damian's mum. Karen Mansell was a thick-set woman with heavily bleached blonde hair scraped up into a messy bun. She wore black leggings and a bright red Helly Hansen puffer jacket that made her look disproportionately top-heavy.

'Is this gonna take long?' Damian asked around a mouthful of gum.

His mum slapped him around the back of the head and smiled at Lomas. 'Don't be so cheeky, Damian.'

Damian rubbed his head but didn't reply. Clearly, he knew better.

Lomas waited for the exchange between mother and son to play out, then made sure that all three of them understood why they were there. He told Paul that, because he was eighteen, he could be interviewed without an adult present, but as Damian was sixteen his mum had to be there. They all nodded, then Lomas started the interview.

'Paul, let's start with you. Could you tell me when you saw the person you believe to be Monica Silverman?'

'It was 'er!' interjected an enthusiastic Damian. Another clip round the ear followed.

'It's OK, Mrs Mansell, I've got a son the same age. I'm used to their outbursts,' said Lomas, hoping to save Damian from a headache. 'Now, Paul, tell me what you can remember.'

'Well, we was on our way into town, weren't we, Damo?'

Damian nodded.

'We were walking down this alley, minding our own business, when she came round the corner and robbed us.' Daniels had a shifty look about him as he spoke, his eyes focused everywhere but on Lomas, and he twisted the middle finger of his left hand back and forth as he recounted his version of events.

'Is that how you remember it, Damian?' asked Drew.

'Yeah. Like he said, she came out of nowhere and robbed us, innit.'

'OK, well, you two are very lucky. I'm sure you've seen the news and have heard why Monica was in prison. So tell me, Paul how did she rob you?' Lomas spun his pen around the back of his thumb.

'What d'you mean?'

'Well, how did it play out? Did she speak to you? I'm sure you didn't just hand over your stuff, did you?'

'Nah, course not. She told us she wanted our phones an' cash – an' if we didn't give 'em to 'er, she'd kill us.'

'She threatened to kill you? That's a bit more serious than it appeared when you called our officers. You said she'd robbed you, but you didn't mention that she'd threatened to kill you. That throws a very different light on things,' said Lomas.

'How d'you mean?' Karen Mansell asked.

'If Monica threatened to kill the boys and beat them up, which is what they told our call handler, that could be attempted murder, Mrs Mansell. In which case, this becomes a very different kind of interview, because the implications are very different. For example, when we find Monica and bring her in – and we will find her…' He looked sternly at the two boys. 'We'll ask her to give us her side of the story. It could be that we end up charging her with attempted murder and taking her back to court. This means you'll both be asked to give evidence, in court, regarding her threats to kill and subsequent assault on you.'

Damian and Paul exchanged a worried glance. This wasn't lost on Karen Mansell. She turned so that she was facing both of the young men. 'You better tell them the truth. Don't go makin' any shit up to make you sound better. If that's not what 'appened, you'd better say so now. If I have to call your mum and get 'er down here, Paul, I will. Don't think I won't. Now, tell the fuckin' truth.'

Paul and Damian both looked embarrassed as Karen Mansell tore a strip off them. Paul squirmed uncomfortably in his chair. Damian, who was obviously being led by his mate, just looked at Daniels, waiting for him to speak.

Lomas waited and let Karen do his job for him. He knew a more realistic version of events wasn't far away.

'OK, well … it weren't quite like that,' Daniels started.

'Go on. Why don't we start with where exactly you were? And which way were you heading? Where did you meet Monica?' Lomas prompted before Karen could say anything. She fixed Daniels with a glare, then shifted it to her own son.

'Yeah, well, me and Damo were on our way into town to get some stuff—'

'Stuff? What stuff?' interrupted Karen.

'Please carry on,' countered Lomas.

'Yeah, like I said, we were on our way into town.' Damian glanced up at Lomas. 'We were headin' through

Landport on our way towards town. We were takin' a shortcut through the alley, when she came in the opposite direction.'

'Coming from Portsmouth?'

'Yeah, that's right. She was definitely comin' from town. Anyway, we – well, I – decided she looked like an easy target, so we got in her way...'

'When you say "easy target", could you elaborate for us?' Drew asked.

'Eh, you know, to get some cash, or a phone, or somethin'.'

'Ah, so you mean you intended to mug her?' Drew clarified.

'Yeah, s'pose.'

'OK. Carry on, Paul,' Lomas said.

'We told her to give us her phone and her cash.'

'And what did she do?'

'She laughed at us and gave us some verbal. Then she punched me in the throat, put a choker on Damo and threw him on the floor. She was so strong and fast, it was fuckin' scary.'

Lomas could see from Paul's face that this was more like the truth. He stayed quiet and let him continue.

'So, when she'd given us a kickin', she told me she wanted both *our* phones and wallets. Damo was out cold, so I got his out of his pocket and I gave her my phone. But I don't carry a wallet, so I gave her my foldin'.'

'You gave her phones and cash?'

'Yeah.'

'How much, roughly?'

'It was about three hundred quid.'

'Where the fuck did you get three hundred quid?' shrieked Karen Mansell.

Paul and Damian looked at each other, but didn't answer her.

Lomas gathered that the cash wasn't from a legitimate source, but his priority was Monica's movements.

'What happened then, Paul?' Lomas asked.

'She asked for my phone PIN and our addresses. She said if we told anybody, she'd come and get us. Then she chucked me twenty quid and told me to get Damo some painkillers. Then she walked off.'

'She threw you twenty pounds for painkillers?' Lomas asked, baffled.

'Yeah, she looked at Damo and me on the floor, and said to get some painkillers.'

'Right, thank you, Paul. Damian, do you have anything to add to what Paul just said?'

Karen fixed Damion with another stare, but this time didn't say anything.

'Nah, it's like he said, innit?' Damion said.

'It sounds like you boys had a lucky escape,' said Drew.

'Lucky? How'd you figure that?' Paul asked.

'Because Monica Silverman is a killer, and I don't think she'd have taken very kindly to you two trying to mug her. So the fact that you're still breathing? I'd take as a bonus if I were you.'

Lomas looked from Damian to Paul. Both boys looked suitably flustered, and Lomas was convinced he'd got as true an account of their brush with Monica as he was going to get.

'Do you have anything you'd like to ask these gentlemen before we let them go?' Lomas asked Drew.

'What direction did Monica go when she left you?' she asked.

'Er, she carried on through the alley towards Fratton.'

'And have you got the boxes from either of your mobile phones at home?'

'Ha, yeah, I'm bound to have mine at home. Mum never throws anything out. She always keeps boxes for stuff,' said Daniels.

'Perfect. When our officers drop you home, could you go in and find the box and give it to them, please? It might help us locate your phone.'

'Shit, are you gonna do a trace thing?' asked Damian, suddenly coming to life.

'Yes, we should be able to track the phone using the information from the box,' Drew said with a smile.

'That's sick!' said the scrawny youth.

Lomas wrapped up the interview and thanked them for taking the time to come to the station – especially Mrs Mansell. Then Drew got one of the uniformed officers who had collected the three to take them home, giving them strict instructions to collect the phone box from Daniels before returning.

31

Bill Bennett greeted Niamh warmly in the reception area of Southampton police station. He wasn't what she'd been expecting. Bill was shorter than she'd imagined him to be, with a friendly face, balding head and metal-framed glasses, which gave him more of a favourite school-teacher look. He wore a burgundy V-neck jumper under a grey tweed jacket, a checked shirt collar peeking out of the top, and navy chinos.

'Niamh, lovely to finally meet you. I just wish it was under different circumstances. I've heard lots about you, all very good. I'm sure we can get through this quite quickly.'

'Thanks, Bill. It's nice to meet you too.'

'Do come through. They've been kind enough to give us an interview room, just through here.' He motioned towards a door that led further into the station. A stern-looking police officer behind the reception desk nodded at Bill as he buzzed the door to let them through. Bill held the door open for Niamh. She smiled at him as she walked through.

'Maggie is waiting for us in the room. Have you met Maggie before?'

'Yes, we met a couple of years ago at a conference.'

'Excellent, that should make introductions quicker.'

Niamh got the impression that Bill's emphasis on moving things along was going to spill over into the interview. Again, he held the door to the interview room for her.

Maggie Sanders stood to shake Niamh's hand as soon as she walked in. She was in her early fifties, with great skin and perfectly straight, white teeth. Her dark inverted bob had a healthy sheen, and her fitted white shirt and navy pencil skirt showcased a figure that she clearly worked hard to maintain. 'Niamh, lovely to see you again. It's been ... two years?'

'Hi, Maggie. Yes, it was the women in leadership conference in Birmingham, pretty much two years ago this month, I think.'

'How are you? This must be quite an ordeal,' Maggie continued, with a tilt of her head.

'I've had better weeks, I've got to be honest.'

'I can imagine. Luckily I've never been through anything quite like this.'

Niamh shot Maggie a knowing look. Maggie smiled and took a seat.

'Please take a seat, Niamh,' said Bill, taking charge of the meeting. He poured them a glass of water each and opened a soft-bound notebook in front of him. Niamh hung her jacket on the back of a chair, opposite Maggie and Bill, and sat.

'So, Niamh, I think the first thing to acknowledge, as Maggie has just said, is that we recognise how difficult this situation must be for you. If you need a break at any time, please just say.'

'OK.'

'I'm going to record the interview. It will be transcribed and you'll get a copy to review for accuracy.'

Niamh nodded, aware of the process.

'OK, let's dive straight in.' Bill introduced himself, then asked Maggie and Niamh to do the same, making it clear that he was the lead investigator.

'Niamh, could you tell us what happened on the day of the escape? Please, take your time,' Bill began.

'Well, it had been quite an intense day or so leading up to it. Two of my officers had been hospitalised and one had died as a result of an attack by Miss Silverman—'

'In her cell?' Maggie clarified.

'Yes. She attacked three of my officers in her room, with devastating results. I wasn't in on the day of the attack, so the next day I wanted to go and see her and find out whether this was a pattern of behaviour that was likely to repeat itself, or a one-off. Officers Bell and Rodriguez accompanied me to Miss Silverman's isolation cell.'

'To speak to her.' Maggie interjected again.

'Yes.'

'Sorry to interrupt,' began Maggie.

Bill gave her a sideways glance, which Niamh read as frustration at Maggie's style of questioning.

'But, at this point, had you commissioned an investigation into the attacks and the death of your officer?'

'No. I'd spoken to members of my team who had been on site, and I'd read the incident reports.'

'And then you decided you wanted to go and speak to Miss Silverman yourself? Directly?' Maggie pushed.

'Yes. As I said, I wanted to understand the potential risk to the other prisoners and my officers. That seemed to me to be the best way to achieve this...'

'OK, sorry. Please carry on.'

Niamh watched as Maggie made notes in a small notebook. She took a sip of water. Bill sat with his fingers steepled in front of his face.

Niamh continued. 'Bell, Rodriguez and I went to the isolation cell and, following protocol, entered the room. Miss Silverman seemed genuinely surprised when I told her that Officer Anderson had died. She expressed regret at the outcome. In her words, she was "having some fun with them and didn't mean for anyone to die".'

'Did that surprise you?' Bill asked, before Maggie had the chance to ask anything.

'That she saw it as having fun with them?'

'No. That she was surprised to learn that Officer Anderson had died and appeared to regret the outcome?'

'Not really. I knew that she liked Bob, and from early reports it seems that Bob died of a heart attack brought on by the stress of the situation, rather than Monica beating him to death.'

'Thank you. Please continue,' said Bill.

Niamh decided against telling the pair that she'd told Bell and Rodriguez to stand outside the room while she spoke to Monica, as it was against protocol and would set hares running with the pair. Instead she started with Monica grabbing her around the neck. 'So, after speaking to Miss Silverman for a couple of minutes I turned to leave, and it was then that she grabbed me from behind, around the neck. Bell and Rodriguez moved to restrain her, but she tightened her grip and told them not to come any closer or she'd kill me.'

'That must have been very scary,' said Bill, with what sounded like genuine concern.

'It was. Miss Silverman is the strongest person I've ever been that close to, and her grip around my neck was restricting my breathing. I know it's not in any training, but I instinctively tried to defend myself by stamping on her foot and driving my elbow back into her ribs. Neither had any effect. She spun me around and punched me in the face. I was knocked unconscious and I'm not aware of anything else that happened in the room until I came to.'

'By which time, Bell and Rodriguez were both dead?' Maggie asked.

'Yes. When I came round, Bell was in Monica's bed and Rodriguez was in the corner of the room. Both were dead.'

'They suffered significant injuries,' Bill said. 'Bell sustained a broken nose, jaw and four ribs. He also had a broken wrist and elbow. According to the coroner's report, his cause of death was a broken neck. Rodriguez suffered a broken nose, his jaw was broken on both sides, and he had a fractured skull. The coroner said in his report that the blows Rodriguez sustained were similar to blunt-force trauma with a large hammer, such was the force inflicted by Miss Silverman. The report says he died of suffocation: it would appear that Miss Silverman murdered him in cold blood.'

'Looks like you were lucky to get out alive,' Maggie said without looking up from her notebook.

'I believe the only reason I'm not dead is because Monica needed me to escape.'

'Well, we're all grateful that you're not,' said Bill as Maggie and Niamh glared at each other. 'Would you like a break, Niamh?'

'No, thanks, I'd rather get this done.'

'Very well. Please tell us what happened when you came round and found your officers dead?'

'When I came round, I was handcuffed and Miss Silverman was wearing Bell's uniform. She was crouched down in front of me when I opened my eyes. She kept me cuffed until she'd told me what she wanted me to do. She told me that if I didn't do as instructed, she'd kill me. She said that if I tried to raise the alarm once we were out of the room, she would kill me and any of my staff that were in the immediate vicinity.'

'And what did you think at this point, Niamh?' asked Maggie. Niamh downed her water and refilled her glass before answering Maggie, using the time to try and hold her temper in check.

'What did I think? Let me see, Maggie. I thought I was going to die. I thought that any number of my officers were going to die. And I thought about what I could do to minimise the impact of this incident on my team.'

'And from that thought process, you decided to go along with her plan and help Monica Silverman, one of the most prolific serial killers in our country's history, to escape?'

Niamh snapped. 'Yes, Maggie, that's *exactly* how I thought about it at the time, with two of my officers lying dead in front of me and my hands cuffed behind my back. I thought, how *can* I help get a killer back on the streets? Jesus, Bill, what is this? Have you two decided to play good cop, bad cop, and Maggie drew the short straw?'

Maggie just looked at her. Bill lowered his hands to the table. 'Now, Niamh, we know this is stressful for you, but we must ask you these questions to fully understand what happened, what you went through, and how we came to be in this position.'

'But *we're* not in this position, Bill, are we? I am.'

'Why don't we take five minutes then reconvene?' said Bill, remaining calm and looking at Niamh over his glasses. She took a deep breath and agreed.

Niamh walked around outside the station, filling her lungs with the cool air. She knew that Maggie was trying to get under her skin on purpose. She also knew that she needed to keep her emotions in check, or it would work against her when it came to them writing up their report.

Bill popped his head out of the station door and asked if she was ready to come back in. She paused for a second before answering, conscious that she was biting her bottom lip, something she never did.

The rest of the interview played out in the same way, with Maggie interrupting either Niamh or Bill, scoring cheap points off both.

As Niamh got to the part where Monica had taken her car and driven away from the prison, she felt sweat trickling down her back, which was pressed against the back of the chair. She was biting her lip again, and Maggie was giving her an almost-sympathetic smile.

It took another half an hour for her to talk through reporting the escape and how she felt about it. All the time, she could feel her body temperature creeping up. Niamh had pretty much finished the jug of water on her own. She felt a bead of sweat break on her forehead and, without warning, run down the side of her face. Simultaneously, her mouth began to water in the way that only meant one thing. All of a sudden, Niamh was fighting to stop herself throwing up. The room began to spin and her forehead was covered in sweat.

'Niamh, are you all right?' she heard Maggie ask. But she sounded as though she was speaking from fifty metres away.

'Niamh?'

Her head was swimming. She didn't know if she could hold it back any more. She staggered to her feet, pushing her chair out behind her with the back of her knees, and ran for the door.

'There's a bathroom straight across the corridor,' she heard Maggie say.

Niamh burst through the door into the ladies' toilet and made it into the cubicle just in time. She crumpled to her knees in front of the toilet bowl, heaving up what remained inside her. The sweat that covered her whole body grew chilled in the breeze from the open bathroom window. She shivered and raised her head from the toilet seat.

Get a grip, for fuck's sake, her internal dialogue chastised her.

Half an hour later, feeling like absolute crap, Niamh sat in her car, her hands on the steering wheel and her head resting on her hands. Bill had wrapped up the interview very quickly once Niamh had returned from the toilet. Judging by Maggie and Bill's reaction to her as she'd walked back in the room, she had clearly looked as bad as she felt.

She was about to start her car when her phone rang. 'What the fuck is it now?' she muttered, fishing in her bag for her phone. 'Hello?' She didn't bother looking at the screen to see who it was.

'Governor, it's Mike. How are you?'

'Mike. Ha, funny you should ask, actually – I feel like crap. What can I do for you? You know you shouldn't be calling me?'

'Yes, I know, but ... well, I thought you'd want to know, and I figured you wouldn't tell anyone I'd called.'

Niamh's nausea suddenly abated. 'OK, what is it?'

'We've just had a DI Leade here at the prison. He's investigating—'

'The unexpected deaths of prisoners.'

'You know?'

'Yes, I've already had the pleasure of meeting him. What did he want?' she said.

'We had a long chat. He's given me what he described as a "starter list" of people he wants to interview.'

'And?'

'Well, I wondered what you wanted me to do.'

Niamh wasn't surprised by the question. 'Do as he asks. There's no point being obstructive. It will just put you in his sights and I would imagine you've got enough heat coming from up top without the police adding to your problems.'

'It has been pretty intense. I'm not kidding, I don't know how you manage it. The director has been on the phone what feels like every half hour. Then there's the press outside the gates – and the rumours flying around among the team are rife,' said Mike.

'What's the rumour mill saying?'

'That you're not coming back. That you're going to get scapegoated to save the minister's and the director's arse.'

'Sounds about right to me.'

'But that's out of order. You saved the lives of God knows how many of our staff. Don't they see that?'

'It doesn't matter whether they see it or not. It's how it looks. Look, thanks for letting me know, but just do everything by the book and you'll be fine.'

'Will do.'

'Oh, and Mike? You probably shouldn't call me again. We log all outgoing calls, remember?'

Mike Button sounded sheepish as he ended the call, and Niamh thanked him again for letting her know about DI Leade.

32

Drew was making a coffee when Nick Swain came into the kitchen, checking over his shoulder as he closed the door.

‘Detective Constable Swain, can I help you?’ she asked with a smile.

‘I can’t believe the boss answered the phone earlier when I called you.’

‘I know, you did sound a bit shocked.’ Her smile broadened as she stirred her coffee.

‘Did he say anything?’

‘He asked if there was anything he should know…’ said Drew.

‘And what did you tell him?’

‘I told him I didn’t want to talk about it.’

‘What? And he left it at that?’

‘Yes, apart from telling you he loved you before he hung up, he’s not mentioned it again. Don’t worry about it. It’ll be fine. I’ll talk to him when I’m ready – if there’s anything to tell.’ She turned to face him.

'Well, since you mentioned it. Do you fancy grabbing a bite to eat when we're done tonight?' Nick asked.

'Maybe I do.' She flicked his tie, picked up two coffees and walked off. Drew took the second mug through to Lomas, who was going over what Mansell and Daniels had told them.

He took the cup from her, blew it and took a sip. 'Oh, that's a good coffee, thanks. I was just going back over what our Pompey lads said.'

'Do you believe them?' she asked.

'Once they stopped trying to be Billy Big Balls and told us what actually happened, yeah, I think I do. How about you?'

'Same. I wouldn't want to be Damian Mansell when his mum gets him home.'

'Ha ha, no, me neither. She wasn't impressed, was she? I've asked the team to track the phone as soon as we have the box. We should be able to use the IMEI number to track where Monica has been – maybe even where she is. I would imagine she's ditched their SIM cards.'

'On a separate note, I saw DI Leade floating around again earlier. What's he up to? Is it related to our investigation? I sent him the info you asked me to send.' Drew asked.

'He's looking into suspicious deaths in prisons and he's interviewed Niamh Dominicali, so yes, it might have a link back to Monica being inside. Who knows? We've got enough to be concentrating on.'

***

Stephen Leade sat at one of the station's hot-desks, looking through his notes. The interview with Niamh Dominicali was still bugging him, but he couldn't put his finger on why. The more he thought about it, the more he came back to the conclusion he'd shared with Lomas: her answers were just too well rehearsed. He didn't like it, not one bit.

He was in a long open-plan office. To his left were two uniformed officers, talking about some visitors they'd let in earlier during a shift on reception. He hadn't meant to eavesdrop, but when he heard Niamh Dominicali's name mentioned, he leaned back in his chair. It creaked in protest. He cradled a mug of tea and listened. The younger of the two was saying that he'd signed Niamh in and that she looked fitter in person than she did on TV. Leade tried not to shake his head too obviously. The officer then said that she'd been shown through to an interview room they'd been asked to book for a prison service interview. He carried on to tell his colleague that halfway through the interview he'd been in the corridor when Niamh had come running out, white as a sheet, straight into the women's toilet – he guessed to throw up. He laughed and his colleague shook his head. 'Must have been some interview to make her throw up.'

'Excuse me, gents,' said Leade. 'I couldn't help overhearing your chat. Did you say you'd let Niamh Dominicali into the interview room? Sorry, I'm DI Leade.'

The one who had been speaking looked a little uncomfortable, but confirmed what he'd said.

'I don't suppose you know who she met from the prison service, do you?'

'Er, yes, there were two of them. One male, one female: a Mr Bennett and I think Mrs Sanders.'

'That's great, thanks. Oh, and do you really think she's fitter in person than on TV?'

The younger man looked really embarrassed. His older colleague laughed and playfully clipped him around the ear. 'Come on, idiot. That'll teach you for gobbing off.'

Leade smiled as they walked away. His chair groaned again as he straightened himself up. He called down to the front desk and asked them to confirm that Bennett and Sanders had visited the station, then asked for their contact details. It turned out that Bill Bennett had left his full name and contact number. Leade scribbled down the number and thanked the officer on the desk.

Turning his focus to his laptop, he typed in 'Bill Bennett, prison service'. It gave him a couple of hits, but not what he'd expected. He amended his search to 'William Bennett' and by the miracle of Google, he was presented with a LinkedIn profile and links to articles Bennett had published on prison life, the effectiveness of long prison sentences, and governor fatigue, among others.

'Excellent,' Leade muttered. 'Now, let's give you a call, Mr Bennett, and see what you can tell me.'

Bill Bennett answered his phone within a couple of rings. He was only too happy to speak to DI Leade, once he'd emailed Bennett confirmation of his ID. They talked for over half an hour. As an experienced governor, Bill was keen to hear about the investigation Leade was conducting into prison deaths, and by the end of the conversation they'd agreed a joint working approach. This would see Leade get far closer to the investigation into Niamh Dominicali's conduct regarding Monica's escape. He figured it might give him some insights that would help with his own investigation. Bill was also keen to work closely with Leade to take action against Dominicali.

Leade thanked Bill for his time then did some research on Maggie Sanders, who seemed equally impressive.

The smell of warm pizza drifted under his nose as two officers walked by with a Domino's box. This made him realised it was hours since he'd eaten. Leade grabbed his jacket from the back of the chair and headed out to get something to eat and figure out his next move.

He remembered there was a Subway on the other side of the train station, so he walked over to the crossroads that dominated the landscape outside the police station then across a bridge towards the takeaway. He loved the smell when you walked in the door of a Subway: the mix of melted cheese, toasted sandwiches, freshly cooked bread and all the fillings. Definitely one of his favourite smells, although he knew that bread was no good for his waistline.

Once he'd got his foot-long tuna melt, he walked up to see what was on at the nearby Mayflower Theatre. A bit of mayo squeezed out of his sub onto his navy suit jacket. He cursed and rubbed at it with a napkin until it had all but disappeared.

His lunch finished, he made his way back towards the station, working out the best way to move his investigation forward. His gut was telling him that Lomas's hunt for Monica Silverman and his own investigation into the deaths inside prisons, were going to cross over. He knew Lomas would be up for collaborating, but he needed to clear it with DCI Marie Carlton. Leade and Carlton had endured a rocky relationship in the early part of their career, which neither of them had ever seemed to move beyond.

As up-and-coming young detectives, they'd jockeyed for position on more than one occasion. Both were stand-out talents and both wanted to get to the top. It was only when Leade realised the level of politics involved in the top jobs that he'd eased off and decided he didn't want to go beyond DI. He hadn't spoken to Marie for five years. The last time they'd spoken, things had got heated: he'd told her she was wrong about the direction she was taking on an investigation she was heading up. That in itself wouldn't be a problem for someone like Marie, but Leade had done it in front of the whole briefing room. That *had* been a problem. She'd taken him to another room and ripped into him. He knew she was within her rights to do it, but it hadn't sat well.

He needed to figure out the best way to approach her – and he knew who to speak to for advice.

33

Sarah Marley had been unable to sleep since Monica had left her gagged and chained to her makeshift bed. But she *had* managed to work the three screws loose on the restraint that held her right hand in place. She'd gently moved the base from side to side until, if she'd wanted to, she could have lifted the restraint clear of the bed.

Then she heard an unfamiliar noise. She held her breath. Then, with her thumb, she made sure that the screws were still in place, just in case the noise had been Monica returning.

During the time she had been lying there working the screws loose, she'd also figured out that the room she was in did not face a road. She'd heard vehicles passing intermittently, at a distance, and in the silence of the room Sarah had identified the direction of the sound.

She'd also paid attention the last time Monica had left, and was pretty sure that she was two floors up. Sarah turned to her left and looked towards the door. As she did, she saw again the remains of Elinor Mary Clarke. For a moment she lost control of her imagination. *How on earth had the ribcage come to be left behind on the bed?* she wondered wildly. Beyond the bed, a collection of tools was piled up on the floor. Some were stained with what looked like old blood. Sarah forced herself to look at them for long enough to work out exactly what was there.

Her dad had included her and Christina in various DIY projects as they were growing up. Out of the pair, Sarah had always enjoyed DIY the most. As she'd got more experienced with various tools, she'd become confident enough to take on her own projects.

When she was thirteen she'd designed and built a pine trunk, complete with dovetail joints and hinges that held the chest open. She'd stained it by hand, applying multiple coats of wood stain, until it was the exact shade she intended. She'd taken the trunk when she went to university and it came home with her when her relationship with her uni boyfriend, Kyle, had fallen apart.

She'd had a good look around the rest of the room. Judging by the windows' state of disrepair, the dirt in the room, and the old, peeling wallpaper, Sarah figured she was in a derelict house. It smelled of old wood and she could taste damp in the air. There was a chill in the room; it was clear that it was only the sunlight coming in through the window that warmed the space she was in.

When she was satisfied that the noise she'd heard wasn't Monica returning, she lifted her right hand, wriggling the restraint clear of the bed. She took the three screws out and placed them carefully, where she could get to them quickly.

Reaching over to the manacle holding her left arm in place, she worked fast and freed the screws attaching it to the old wood. They came away after about ten minutes of working the base back and forth, the way she'd done with her right. With both hands free she sat up, feeling the rickety bed move beneath her. Sarah sat still for a moment, listening. Silence. When she looked down at the chain holding her left leg, she saw that her earlier thrashing about had already loosened the fixings, so she could turn them with her fingers. She speedily undid them and laid them next to her foot. She could feel her heart beating harder in her chest as she worked her way towards freedom. Within a couple of minutes all the chains were lying on the bed and Sarah was standing in the middle of the room. She felt a bit dizzy at first, but that wore off quickly. She picked up one of the small bones from the bed next to hers and put it in her pocket.

'I'll make sure they come for you, Elinor,' she whispered.

Sarah darted to the corner of the room and grabbed a blood-stained crowbar she'd eyed up earlier. She made her way over to one of the dirty sash windows and jammed the tip of the crowbar between the bottom of the window and the frame. From her bed, she'd seen that the old frames were nailed shut along the bottom and had looked for a tool capable of helping her. The wood splintered and broke around the crowbar, crumbling away to the floor.

'Shit!'

She tried again, this time nearer the corner, where the frame looked a bit less rotten. The hard steel bit into the wood and Sarah levered the bar downwards, forcing a crack of light to appear between sash and frame. She moved the crowbar along a few centimetres and repeated the effort. Again she was rewarded with movement from the window. It broke free of the nails; old, dark wood splintered to the floor. She put the crowbar down. Feeding her fingers into the gap she'd created, she heaved the window up. It moved steadily, the swollen wood of the window gripping the timber frame. Slowly but surely the window opened further and further, until Sarah was sure the gap was wide enough for her to fit through. She poked her head out. There was a deep sill, with flaking green paint that more or less matched the paint on the bedroom door. As she looked down she saw that below her windowsill was brickwork and a drop that went all the way to the ground floor. The garden was overgrown and looked to Sarah as if it had been untended for a long time. A high fence surrounded the garden. From her vantage point, she couldn't see an exit. Beyond the fence was some scrubland, trees and what looked like a railway embankment.

The window was too high to jump from. She looked to her right. Along the wall was an old cast-iron drainpipe. She didn't know whether she could reach it, but decided she had to try. Sarah glanced back into the room and saw some old rope: it was frayed and tatty but it was all she had. She tied one end around the radiator on the wall just under the window, and tied the other end around her waist. There wasn't enough rope to lower herself all the way to the ground, but there was enough to stop her falling too far.

Sarah edged out onto the window ledge, her hand hooked inside the open window for balance. She inched her way to the end of the sill and reached out, still gripping the corner of the open window, afraid to let go. She looked down. It was a long drop. The drainpipe was just beyond her reach. She checked the rope to see how much slack she had; she figured she had about a metre, or so. Even though it was cold, she could feel sweat starting to bead down her spine. The pipe had a bracket holding it to the wall about half a metre down from where she stood. She figured if she could jump to the pipe and grab it, she might be able to slide her feet down and onto the bracket.

Sarah pressed herself against the wall and let go of the window, immediately feeling vulnerable. She thought about the alternative for a few seconds. Monica returning and torturing her until she was dead. She was not going to die here, in this disgusting room with the bones of another young woman beside her. Without any more thought, she leapt for the drainpipe. Her face slammed against the cold metal and she grabbed it, desperately trying to wrap her hands around the pipe. She missed, her left hand grabbing at fresh air. Her foot landed on the bracket then slipped off it, the cast-iron attachment scraping her calf and hitting her knee as she slid down the drainpipe. The rope stopped her falling too far, and dug into her waist when it reached its full extension. This was enough for her to wrap her hands around the pipe and press her knees tight against it. With her left hand, she pulled at the knot she'd tied in the rope. It came undone and she let go. As she did, she began to slide towards the ground, half holding on to the drainpipe, half falling.

Sarah hit the ground – hard. The impact knocked the wind out of her, but she was alive. She lay on the ground for a moment, looking up at the window she'd crawled out of and at the wall of the house. Hot tears began to stream uncontrollably down her face.

Come on, Sarah. Move.

She scrambled to her feet, trying to ignore the pain that shot from the injuries she'd sustained both from Monica and the fall. Sarah looked along the fence, first left, then right. It curved around the huge, overgrown garden, looking like it went on forever. She stood with her back to the wall and tried to get her bearings. She knew there was scrubland beyond the fence in front of her. That meant that the road she'd heard was around the other side of the house. Quickly she made her way along the fence, staying away from the house in case Monica came back. She thought the grass might be long enough to hide in if her captor returned. Her heart was racing and her breath was fast and shallow.

Sure enough, when Sarah reached the other side of the house, she could see rooftops above the fence.

There are houses! I'm nearly there.

She heard a car, then another. She flattened herself against the fence, then crouched low. She could imagine Monica walking through a gate Sarah was yet to find, catching her trying to escape and killing her there and then.

She was moving quickly now, running her hands along the fence panels. Before long she was going back around the house, the road behind her. There was no gate. No exit. No way out.

Sarah had been getting progressively faster until she'd almost broken into a run. Sweat was running down her face. Where was it? There had to be a gap. How did Monica get in and out?

Then she felt it.

There was something different about one of the panels. She'd run past it twice. She'd run past the whole fence twice. But this panel wasn't flat like the others. Then she saw it. There was a bolt two-thirds of the way up. She studied the panel. At the very top, she saw a hinge. She followed the line of the fence down. Half hidden in the grass was a hinge. It was a gate! She pulled back the bolt and it opened just a crack. Sarah grabbed it and swung it open. She ran out towards the houses, checking the street as she went. She couldn't see any-one. More importantly, she couldn't see Monica.

Her tears of pain were being replaced by tears of relief and desperation. She had to get away. To be anywhere but there. She had to get to the police.

Sarah ran across the road and banged on the first door she saw. No answer.

'Someone, please help me!' she shouted as she ran to the next house, her bare feet slapping against the cold pavement. The second house – again, no reply. At the third house, someone answered. An elderly man who sounded as though Sarah had just woken him from an afternoon nap.

'Can I help you?' he said as he opened the door. When he saw her, he stopped dead and looked Sarah up and down, his eyes wide. 'My dear, what on earth has happened?'

'Please help me,' she said through sobs of desperation.

'Come in, come in.' He showed her through to a small living room, cluttered with ornaments and pictures. Sarah looked around her, her heart was pounding in her chest, her tears were flowing freely. The image of what she'd escaped horrifyingly clear in her mind's eye. She couldn't take in enough breath to speak clearly and she knew that she had never been so grateful to see another living soul in her life as she had the old man.

She was safe.

34

Two and a half hours later, Sarah Marley was in Southampton. The old man had driven her there from Portsmouth. She'd had a medical examination and been given painkillers. The police medic had spoken to her at length before agreeing that she was fit to speak to Lomas. A red-headed detective who introduced herself as DS Drew Taylor had come to meet Sarah. She was patient and calm and made Sarah feel safe. Drew explained that her sister, Christina, was at the police station and that they'd take her to see her as soon as they'd spoken.

They walked through to an interview room, but it didn't look how Sarah had expected it to. It had soft furnishings and was carpeted, with pictures on the walls – not at all like the bare rooms she'd seen on TV. When they walked in, DS Taylor introduced someone that Sarah felt she already knew, from all the conversations she'd had with her sister after her abduction. Detective Inspector Lomas Baxter.

***

Lomas composed himself before walking into the interview room to speak to Sarah Marley. He knew that it was wrong to walk into the room with a beaming smile, an outward sign of the elation he felt at Sarah having managed to escape the clutches of Monica. But he was so pleased that the call he had just made to the Marley's was one confirming that their daughter was safe and in the police station. Nick had been dispatched to let Christina know, while Drew had gone to collect Sarah for interview. He could feel the tide turning on Monica.

Lomas took a minute to allow Sarah to get comfortable on the sofa before he began. She had visible welts around her wrists, and bruising to her face. Lomas thought how much she looked like her sister, and remembered the state Christina had been in when they'd found her in the cottage, chained to a makeshift bed. Even before he'd asked his first question, he knew that Sarah had suffered similar treatment.

'Sarah, are you sure you're OK to talk us through what happened to you?'

'Yes. I want to tell you everything while it's fresh in my mind,' she said, taking a sip from the mug of tea that Drew had given her.

'All right. If at any time you need to stop or take a break, please let us know.'

She nodded. Lomas got the formal parts of the interview out of the way and began.

'In your own time, could you tell us what happened to you, starting from you leaving your car near the crossroads just outside Wickham?'

Sarah looked surprised. She took a deep breath and began to explain that she had run into the back of Monica's car.

'I bent to look at the back of her car and she punched me really hard. I couldn't get away, she was so strong. She hit me over and over again and I fell to the ground. I felt so helpless.' She paused and took another deep breath.

'It's OK, take your time,' Drew said.

Sarah nodded and gave a half-smile. 'I was on the ground between the two cars, then she just picked me up and threw me into the back of her car. I tried to fight her off, but it was like fighting a brick wall. She went through my pockets and took my phone, then she hit me again and shut the boot. I knew I was in the boot of the car, but it was different...'

'Different how?'

'It was like I was in a wooden box. I could feel the rough wood against my hands. I started kicking at the back of the box. We couldn't have gone more than a few hundred metres before she stopped the car, opened the boot and punched me again. It was even harder than before. She must have knocked me out, because I don't remember anything else until I woke up, chained to the bed in Portsmouth.'

'That's great. You're doing really well,' said Lomas.

He watched as Sarah ran her hand over the marks on her wrists, wincing. Her gaze darted around, struggling to stay focused on one thing for too long, as she relived the traumatic memories.

'I hadn't been awake long when Monica came into the room.'

'Monica?'

'Yes, Monica Silverman. She introduced herself to me – well, sort of. She mentioned Chrissie.'

'Could you describe her?'

'Yes. She has a muscular build, above average height, short bleach-blonde hair.'

Lomas and Drew looked at each other.

'Do you think you'd be able to describe her in more detail if one of our police artists helped you?'

'Yes. I can see her in my head, as plain as day.'

'That's great. Carry on,' said Lomas.

'Once she'd introduced herself, she introduced me – if that's the right way to describe it – to some ... human remains that were lying on a handmade wooden bed. It looked similar to the one I was chained to. She said it was someone called Elinor Mary Clarke.'

Lomas and Drew exchanged another glance.

'But from what I could see, there was only a ribcage and ... and a few smaller bones.' She sniffed and welled up.

'Shall we take a couple of minutes and refill that tea for you?' asked Drew.

'Yes, please, if that's OK.'

'It's absolutely fine, we're in no rush. We understand that this is difficult to talk about. But whatever you can tell us will help us track Monica down and stop her hurting anyone else.'

They resumed ten minutes later. Lomas gave Sarah the time and space to recount everything that had happened: Monica's threats to kill her. The conversation they'd had about Monica taking Sarah because she thought Lomas would have moved Christina somewhere safe. Sarah Marley was mentally, one of the strongest witnesses Lomas had ever interviewed. Even though she was clearly traumatised by her experience, she described everything in as much detail as she could remember, including how she escaped. Lomas and Drew listened intently. Sarah perched on the edge of the sofa, fidgeting and repeatedly checking her wrists as she spoke. But she spoke with purpose, and the detail she shared with them blew Lomas away. After nearly two hours, Lomas wound up the interview.

'Sarah, that's been really helpful. Thank you for taking the time to go through what happened to you. I know it can't have been easy, but you've done really well and it's given us lots to go on. Just one more thing — the gentleman who brought you into the station gave us his address, could you confirm exactly where in relation to his house you escaped from on this map?' Lomas asked laying a zoomed street map on the table, with the old man's house marked up. Sarah pointed without hesitation to a building across the road from the old man's house, Lomas nodded.

'Thank you. Why don't we take you through to see your sister?'

'That would be good.' Her bottom lip began to tremble at the mention of Christina.

'Drew will take you through to Christina, then we're going to arrange for you both to be taken somewhere safe.'

'What about our parents? When Monica finds out I've got away, she might go after our parents.'

'Don't worry – we'll make sure your parents are safe. I'll have an officer go and collect them this afternoon and bring them to see you both.'

Sarah nodded her thanks and stood to leave the room with Drew.

'Drew, could you join me in the briefing room once you've taken Sarah to her sister?'

'Will do, boss.'

Lomas stood and took Sarah's hand in both of his. 'Don't worry, Sarah, you're safe now.'

'Thank you, DI Baxter.'

As Lomas got back to his office a very excited DC Grant Carver came bounding around the corner. 'Ah, boss, good, I caught you.'

'You did. What is it, Grant?'

'We've managed to get a hit on the IMEI number from the box of Paul Daniels' iPhone.' Grant paused.

'And? Don't keep me waiting; it's not a game show.'

'Sorry, boss. We got a hit off a couple of towers around Portsmouth and narrowed it down. We've tracked its movements and can give you a couple of locations where the phone was on for a period of time. We're confident, having looked at the area, that we know where the locations are. The most promising one is a hit that has come up at night only, but for significant amounts of time. It's in the area near the seafront and Florence Road. Now, we've checked the surrounding area and there's a hotel or B&B on the end of Florence Road called Southsea Rocks. We think that's where whoever has the phone might be staying.'

'That's great. Let's have the details.'

'That's not all, boss. We also tracked the phone to the area near Sarah Marley's parents' house in Corhampton.'

'That's awesome, Grant – well done. Right, we've got work to do, and quick. Can you pull all that information together in an easy-to-share format? We need to tell the troops. Can you also speak to your team, who did such a great job of tracking Monica on the train CCTV, and get them to pull all the CCTV camera feeds in the area surrounding this hotel in Southsea?'

'Will do.'

Drew joined them and Lomas updated her on the developments.

'Drew, could you get Grant the address that Sarah Marley just pointed out please? Grant, when you've got that, could you check it against the tracking you've done with the phone and let me know if you get a hit?'

They nodded. Grant Carver scurried off.

'Once I've got Grant that address, what do you want me to do next?' asked Drew.

'We'll get everyone together and update them on what we've learned from Sarah and Grant. Then we'll coordinate two teams – one to go to the house where Sarah was held, one to go to the hotel. Hopefully, Grant's team can get a CCTV image we can match with Sarah's description, then we can get that out on our media channels,' Lomas said.

'I'll bring everybody in.'

'Great. I'm going to see Marie, to get search warrants for both places. We need to make sure the teams are prepared to bring Monica in, if they come across her. I'm going to ask Marie to get firearms authorised. I don't think Monica will come in without a fight. We also need to hit both addresses at the same time. I'll get in touch with Portsmouth and coordinate using their video surveillance gear.'

'On it.' Drew left and Lomas walked towards DCI Carlton's office.

35

Monica spent the afternoon tracking Lydia Bartholomew. Monica despised her. She had been good friends with Monica's mother, and Monica had spent years listening to them cackling at each other on the phone. She'd been on Monica's 'list' for years now. Monica was convinced that her mother had been more toxic and nastier to her after she'd been around Lydia. It seemed to her that Lydia fuelled Beatrice's disappointment in her daughter. Lydia had been childless despite trying, from what Monica had gathered from her mother's conversations with Lydia and Monica was convinced this had made her bitter and was the reason she'd been such a cow to her when she was growing up.

As she watched the older woman go about her business on the edge of Chichester, Monica was taken back to times in her childhood when her mother had been particularly horrible to her. They had often involved Lydia. One time, when she was eight, Monica had been playing in the garden. She never had many friends, so often played on her own. The day in question was a bright, sunny summer's day. Monica had got a small axe from her father's shed and some offcuts of wood – tree stumps and the like. She'd amused herself by pretending to be a circus act, throwing the axe into lumps of wood, bowing to rapturous applause from the crowd, and creating a world where she was the greatest axe thrower ever.

Her concentration had been rudely interrupted by Lydia Bartholomew's grating cackle. When Monica looked around, she saw her mother and Lydia sitting at a garden table, under a parasol, drinking wine. Lydia was pointing at Monica and laughing so hard that she snorted. Monica turned around and carried on throwing the axe – although, in her mind's eye, the lump of wood had now become Lydia's head. Their chatter and laughter got louder until Monica turned around and shouted at them to leave her alone. Beatrice got up from her patio chair, put her wine glass down and stomped down the garden towards Monica. Over her mother's shoulder, Monica could see Lydia craning her neck to get a better look at what Beatrice was going to do.

'What are you doing, you idiotic child?' her mother shrieked.

'I'm axe throwing, in the circus.'

'That would be about right – you belong in a circus, you little freak. Now give that axe to me before you hurt someone.'

'I'm not going to hurt anyone! Leave me alone!' Monica shouted in reply.

Beatrice glanced back over her shoulder at Lydia. 'How dare you raise your voice to me? Give me that axe!' Snatching the axe from Monica's hand, she turned it around quickly and hit Monica around the back of the head with the axe handle. Monica's head rattled and she felt herself wobble. But even at eight, she was determined not to fall and give her mother the upper hand. She steadied herself against the side of the shed.

'Get to your room and don't come out until I tell you, you insolent little bitch.'

Monica had done as instructed. She walked past Lydia, who had grinned at her with her crooked teeth. Oh, how she'd wanted to hit her. She didn't, though; she did as instructed and went to her room. Her room was her sanctuary. It was full of her books. She'd worked out that if she slid the chest of drawers in front of the door, no one could get in and disturb her. Her mother didn't let her out of her room for two days after that incident.

Monica returned to watching Lydia. She'd aged and put on weight.

'Oh, how Mother would disapprove of your unsightly weight gain, Lydia. You were always so Jane Fonda-fit. You and your fucking awful leggings and gaudy make-up. It's definitely your time.'

She watched Lydia walk over to a silver Range Rover. She had a small dog sticking out of the top of her trolley, which she pulled along behind her. Hanging off the side of the trolley were Waitrose shopping bags.

'What the fuck is that rat sticking out of your bag, Lydia? Surely you've not gone all soft in your old age? Do you need the company of an ickle pet?' Monica sneered. She was boiling with resentment at the sight of Lydia. Her heart beat a little faster and her palms grew sweaty.

Monica waited until the Range Rover drove past her, then tucked in behind it. She followed Lydia north, out of Chichester, passing some sports fields and a private hospital where she remembered her father working once. Houses gave way to open fields. Monica kept about a hundred metres behind Lydia. Lydia hung a right past a quaint-looking B&B with rambling roses growing in its well-kept garden. The road was lined with trees and Monica could smell the cow manure in the fields that sat behind them.

She checked in her mirror. There hadn't been anyone behind them since they'd left Chichester. Monica picked up speed and moved closer to the Range Rover. She pulled out fast, overtook Lydia's 4×4, then cut back in and slammed on her brakes. She saw the Range Rover nosedive as Lydia braked; Monica braced for the impact. It didn't come. The big 4×4 stopped faster than Monica expected. It didn't change her plan. She jumped out of her car, pulling on gloves as she did so. As she walked towards Lydia, she could see the rage on the older woman's face. It was the same indignant face Monica had despised throughout her childhood. As she got closer, she saw a flicker of recognition on Lydia's face. She paled visibly and her eyes widened. As Monica reached the driver's window, Lydia was scrabbling in her bag; Monica guessed she was searching for her phone. Monica wagged her finger at Lydia, who looked terrified. She stared directly at Lydia, holding her gaze. Then Monica took a centre-punch out of her pocket, placed it against the bottom corner of the driver's window, and pressed. It took a minimal amount of strength to pop the window. Lydia shrieked. The dog yapped.

'Hello, Lydia, how lovely to see you. My, haven't you aged?'

'Wh-what do you want?' Lydia whispered.

The dog yapped some more.

'Isn't it obvious? I've come to visit with my mother's dear friend, Lydia.'

'I saw you on TV. I know you've broken out of prison. They'll catch you – you know that, don't you?'

'Oh shut up, you supercilious bitch. Now, open the fucking door, or I'll drag you out through the window. And make that scrawny little rat shut up.'

'You won't get away with this. They'll get you. Whatever you do to me, it will come back on you. Karma has a habit of catching up with people.'

'I couldn't have said it better myself. You can call me Karma, if you like. Now, this is the last time I'm going to ask. Open. The. Door.'

Lydia did as requested and gingerly pushed the door outwards. Monica pulled it fully open. The dog was getting more and more stressed, yapping faster and louder as Monica pulled Lydia from the Range Rover. Monica glared at the dog and slammed the door shut. She walked Lydia to the back of her car and waved a foot under the bumper. The tailgate lifted silently.

Lydia looked confused. 'What the hell are you doing? You strange girl.'

'Now, now, Lydia, there's no need to be hostile – and not so much of the girl, please. I stopped being a little girl that you and my mother could bully a long time ago.'

'You're pathetic. Oversized, masculine and pathetic.'

Monica slapped Lydia with the back of her hand. The old woman fell to the ground. Monica stood on her ankle, pinning her in place.

'Right, let's see what you have in your boot.' She moved the Waitrose bags to one side and lifted the floor panel of the boot. 'A tow rope – very handy. Roger does make sure you're well looked after, doesn't he?'

'Roger's been dead for years.'

'Oh, I am sorry. Really, I am. He was the nicer one of the two of you. How he put up with you, I'll never know. Lucky escape for him, I guess.'

'It doesn't matter what you say or do. You'll always be the pathetic, friendless child who broke your poor mother's heart with your weight lifting and all those poor dead animals she always knew were your doing. She deserved better than you.'

Monica slapped Lydia again, then hoisted her to her feet. She felt an involuntary twitch in the corner of her right eye and an overwhelming urge to punch the old woman. Instead, she perched her on the edge of the boot. Squeezing her face between her thumb and forefinger, she said, 'Go on, keep talking. Get it all out of your system, you vile old witch. Now, sit there and stay still.'

Monica took her bowie knife out of her pocket and unsheathed it. Then she cut the tow rope in half. The large tailgate of the Range Rover canopied over them, held in place by two thick hydraulic struts.

Monica tied the ends of the rope in strong knots around Lydia's wrists. Then she looped the other end around where the struts met the 4X4's bodywork and pulled on the them. Hoisting the old woman up off her feet, with her arms being pulled out in a crucifix position. She stretched Lydia's arms as far as they would go. As Monica pulled the second rope tight, Lydia's feet lifted off the ground. The backs of her calves rested on the rear bumper and she let out the quietest of cries.

'No smart or abusive comments, Lydia? I am disappointed. I heard your critical voice and your fucking cackle for the whole of my childhood – and now that it's just the two of us, nothing? I expected better from you.'

She took the knife and cut each of the buttons off Lydia's royal-blue blouse, exposing a white bra and a slightly rounded stomach which, due to the angle she was hoisted at, hung over the top of her trousers. Monica slid the blade of the knife under Lydia's chin and lifted her head so the old woman was looking at her.

'Any final words?'

'I hope you burn in hell, you pathetic excuse for a human being. Your mother should have given you away – she'd have been better off. You're a disgrace to your family.'

'That's more like it. I'm so glad you didn't let me down.' Monica grabbed a fistful of Lydia's hair, forcing her head back. Then, with the very tip of the knife, she began to slowly cut Lydia Bartholomew's forehead. Lydia let out a high-pitched squeak every time the knife tore into her skin. When Monica had finished, she dragged the knife down the centre of Lydia's face, then her neck, and stopped at the centre of her sternum. Lydia's eyes grew wider and she was beginning to hyperventilate. Fresh blood ran from the cuts on her forehead.

Monica tipped her head to one side as she stared at the old woman's blood stained face. Then she moved the blade down and in one swift movement, plunged it between Lydia's ribs, into her heart. The older woman jerked back, as if trying to get away from the knife. Monica grabbed Lydia's hair and wrenched her head back, holding the knife in place with her other hand.

'Your years of ridicule, of torment and of you turning my mother against me have finally caught up with you, Mrs Bartholomew. When I remove this knife, your chest cavity will be pumped full of blood and you'll go into cardiac arrest. I'll stay with you while you go – more to make sure you're dead than to keep you company.' She pulled the blade from Lydia's heart and stood watching her body convulse.

When she was sure that she was dead, Monica wiped the knife clean on Lydia's blouse and walked casually back to her car, leaving her mother's friend hanging by her wrists.

36

Mike Button sat in the dining room of his small, two-bedroom house. The furniture was tired and shabby, and the decor could have easily been from the 1970s. He sank his third neat whisky in a row and was holding the bottle over his glass to refill it when his phone rang. He rolled his eyes as he answered it.

'Mike, it's Tony.'

'What can I do for you, Tony?' Button filled his glass.

'You sound cheerful.'

'Like I said, what can I do for you?'

'I've just got into work and got your note saying the plod want to interview me. I've asked around and there's a few of us—'

'So you're phoning me to find out why?' Button interrupted.

'Well, yeah. What do the plod want *us* for?'

He took a sip of whiskey. 'They're investigating unexpected deaths in prisons. After they'd looked through the rota information I sent them, they gave me a list of people they want to talk to. You and the others were on that list.'

'Oh, is that it? I thought it might have been—'

'Well, you were wrong.' He cut Tony off again.

'Well, that's good then. Shall I let the others know?'

'Yes, Tony, fill your boots. I'm sure you would anyway, even if I said no.'

'What the fuck's eating you?'

'Nothing. It's Saturday night and I've got better things to be doing.'

He heard Tony snort on the other end of the phone. 'See you next week, Tony.' He ended the call before Tony could say any more.

On the table in front of Mike was the list of officers that DI Leade wanted to interview. The person he was most concerned about was the top one: Mike Button.

For the last couple of years, Mike had been running a highly lucrative drug and extortion racket in the prison. He'd known officers like Tony O'Bryan for years – a long time before Niamh had arrived. He knew their personal circumstances and how to get them to do what he wanted, when he wanted something done. He also had a significant amount of influence on the overtime rota, which meant that those closest to him were the ones who regularly picked up the extra shifts – and pay.

He'd been approached in his local. A guy had sidled up to him and begun chatting. He worked for a Southampton drug dealer and knew intimate details of Button's life. The guy knew about his divorce, his debt, the payments he made every month for his ex's house and car. More importantly, he knew that Mike had been gambling money he didn't have on back-street poker games, and was in debt up to his eyeballs to a Chinese gambling syndicate.

The man, Larry, had calmly told Mike that he could make it all go away – or he could make it all come crashing down around Mike's ears. It was up to Mike to choose which way it went.

Button had agreed. Within two months the drug gang had woken the sleepers among the prisoner and prison officer population.

The drug train had started, with a semi-regular supply coming in via the officers who were now part of Mike Button's in-house gang. They would bring drugs in to pass on to prisoners, who were scattered across the wings. The prisoners had all been planted in the prison by the drug dealer. They were a mix of frequent offenders and ex-homeless people who found life inside easier than out. The money would be passed back to the officers and finally to Mike, who would hand it to a contact of the dealer, or sometimes to Larry himself.

It hadn't taken long before Mike was spending as much time coordinating the drug business as doing his actual job. When the director brought in a new governor, he'd figured the best way to keep up his side-line was to be as helpful as he could to Niamh Dominicali.

To date, this strategy had worked.

But now, faced with the police investigation into the prison and the prison service investigation focusing on Niamh, Mike didn't know how to keep things going – and secret. He tried to tell his employers that they needed to back off for a while. They'd refused. They were having their best year to date and they intended for it to continue. If Mike didn't want to be thrown to the Chinese syndicate, he'd keep his head and make it work.

The thing that had really driven Mike to drink was that, after years of running the drug train and making a decent cut, he had nothing to show for it. Instead of using the money to build a nest egg or pay off his debt, he'd taken it up to the casinos in London and gambled it all away, hoping to double his money and clear all his debts in one go. He didn't even have enough money to walk away from his day job.

As this thought went through his head for about the fiftieth time that evening, he tapped the bottle on the edge of the glass and watched the golden liquid pour into the tumbler once more.

He looked around the room. He hated this house. It held so many memories – none of them good. The whisky was starting to hit him; a familiar warm flush moved over his body. His head was starting to get fuzzy. It was always the same. He looked at the glass, pushed it away, then pulled it back towards him and carried on until he fell asleep, his head on the table. Tonight was no different to all the other nights.

37

It was starting to get dark when Lomas and Drew joined officers from the Portsmouth Police Investigation Centre in their video surveillance suite. They'd been quick to agree to Lomas's request to help with accessing the vicarage where Monica had held Sarah.

Uniformed officers from Portsmouth had been deployed to watch the building from a safe distance in an unmarked car. They were under instruction to stay out of sight and immediately raise the alarm if they spotted Monica. They had reported back that all was quiet.

Paul Daniels' phone was constantly monitored, but there was no more activity. It was assumed that Monica switched it off when she left the property.

Armed police with body cameras had been authorised to lead the team going into the vicarage, based on the level of threat Monica presented. Lomas and Drew would watch the images live from the Portsmouth police base.

The police had also contacted the navy, who agreed to help. As the officers on the ground checked their cameras and comms gear, Lomas could hear the occasional clack of the Royal Naval air-support helicopter circling over the area.

Lomas felt an excited – or nervous – flutter in his stomach when the team on the ground confirmed they were ready.

Across in Southsea, Nick Swain and Gurdeep, with a uniformed officer from Portsmouth, armed with a Taser, were waiting to be given the go-ahead to go into the Southsea Rocks Hotel on Florence Road. A tactical firearms team was close by, sent over in case Nick and Gurdeep made contact with Monica. The intelligence that Grant and his team had managed to gather suggested that Monica was only in the area late at night. So they decided it was less likely she would be there now. Grant also managed to provide them with a near-perfect CCTV image that they would use to find out whether Monica had been staying there.

Drew gave them the all-clear to go into the hotel.

Simultaneously, the firearms lead checked with Lomas that they were good to go into the vicarage.

Both teams moved in. From the vicarage, live images were transmitted to the video suite. Using the hidden gate that Sarah had told them about, they moved into the overgrown garden. The team of nine fanned out as they entered. They moved cautiously around the large house, splitting into two teams to cover both doors into the property. Lomas and the team watching the video feed could see everything clearly.

'Armed police, come out!' shouted one of the officers, then waited. 'We have no answer from inside the property,' he said, for Lomas's benefit.

'Armed police, come out!' he repeated.

When he got no reply, he changed his command. 'Stand back from the door – armed police. I repeat, stand back from the door – armed police.'

There was an almighty crash. Lomas saw both doors into the vicarage burst open. No one moved, then a dog appeared on camera.

'We are sending a police support dog into the building. Come out!'

Again there was no reply from inside the house. The officer repeated the instruction, then the handler released the dog. It raced into the house. Lomas felt himself holding his breath. The dog's body camera showed rapidly changing images as it ran from room to room, scanning the environment with a speed that Lomas found mesmerising.

Drew tapped his arm. 'Boss, they've got a positive ID from the hotel. The guy behind reception says he's positive it's Monica, but she's booked in as Lena Thompson.'

'That's great. Ask them to contact Grayson and get her room sealed off until his team get there.'

'Will do.'

He heard Drew relaying his instructions and turned his attention back to the video. The police dog was running around upstairs now, pushing its way into all the rooms with open doors, checking the rooms in the same way it had on the ground floor. It sniffed outside any doors that were closed. It wasn't long before it hurtled back down the stairs to its handler, to be greeted with lots of fuss.

'The dog hasn't found anyone. We'll go in and clear the building,' said the officer leading the team. They made their way in, carefully sweeping each room as they moved through, calling, 'Clear!' every time they were satisfied there was no one in a room.

On camera four, Lomas saw the team open a green door on the second floor. He saw two wooden beds. On one of them were some bones – if Sarah's account was right, the remains of Elinor Mary Clarke. He glanced at Drew, who looked sad. She glanced at Lomas, and they shared the unspoken sorrow of not being able to save Elinor.

At the far end of the room, Lomas saw the partially opened sash window that Sarah Marley had escaped from. The officer's body cam panned around. Lomas asked him to stop. 'Could you go closer to that corner, please?'

The officer did as requested, and the video frame was filled with an image of the tools and implements that were piled in the corner of the room.

'OK, thank you, I've seen enough. Once your team have cleared every room, let's get everyone out and get it sealed off, ready for the scenes of crime team. Thank you.' He carried on watching the video feed until the team had exited the house. It was dark by the time they got outside, and they immediately started to tape off the house and its grounds.

'One step closer, Monica,' said Lomas.

38

The air felt different as Monica stepped out of her car, around the corner from the Southsea Rocks Hotel. There was a chill in the air, and she felt a sense of disquiet. As she rounded the corner, two unfamiliar men got out of a grey BMW and headed into the hotel, not locking their car behind them. The hairs went up on the back of Monica's neck – and not because of the chill breeze. She stopped dead and eased back into the shadow of a house front, the darkness swallowing her. Pulling her hood over her head, she stayed motionless.

After ten minutes, one of the men came out, took something from the boot of the car then headed back into the hotel – again without locking the car.

Monica had seen enough. Convinced they were police, she turned and headed back to the Mondeo, pointed it in the opposite direction to the hotel and drove slowly away.

'Fuck it! How did they find the hotel?' she fumed. 'Right, let's pop in and see that Miss Marley is OK.'

She drove out of Southsea towards Fratton, slamming her hand on the steering wheel as she drove. As she made her way along the road to the vicarage, she noticed that there was an unusual amount of activity on the road. There were people out in the street, talking over garden walls; teenagers were out in big groups, their faces illuminated by the glow of their phones.

The uneasy feeling returned. Monica decided to park the car down a side road and walk the rest of the way. She pulled her hood low over her head and dug her hands into the pocket of her hoodie. Despite her build, she blended in well with the groups of hoodie-wearing teens milling around. She slowed to eavesdrop on a conversation between two neighbours, pretending to be looking at her phone.

'There's police everywhere,' said one woman, with a distinctive Pompey accent.

'I know, they've bin there ages. It's that spooky old vicarage, innit?' replied her neighbour.

'Sheila up the road, she said some young woman was bein' tortured in there. She banged on old Bernard's door, woke him up, screamin' that she needed help.'

'There's some weirdos out there. Imagine kidnappin' somebody and then torturin' them. It's bloody sick, if you ask me. They need lockin' up.'

'Yeah, throw away the key too, innit babe.' They took a drag on their cigarettes.

Monica had heard as much as she needed to. Staying out of the way, she walked until the vicarage came into sight. Her fists were clenched in her pockets, her brow furrowed and her face set in a scowl.

The secluded house where she'd left Sarah Marley was alive with police. Crime scene tape surrounded the property and officers in white overalls were flitting in and out of the garden – a fence panel had been removed, granting them easy access. Across the road, Monica could see TV cameras and journalists setting up and taking pictures. She turned on her heel and hot-footed it back to the safety of her car, her heart pounding.

She got to the car and slammed her fist down on the roof. The metal dented under the force of the blow and didn't pop back out. Monica got in the car and punched the steering wheel repeatedly. She could feel the blood coursing through her veins and sweat popping from her pores.

'Fuck!' she yelled. 'Lomas fucking Baxter, I know you're behind this. You and your fucking sidekick. How the fuck did she manage to get out? What the fuck happened? You'll pay for this Baxter, you and Drew-fucking-Taylor!'

She dug her phone out of her pocket, making sure it was switched off. Her paranoia had spun into overdrive. 'Right, DI Baxter, you've found my hiding places. Now it's time for me to disappear.' She checked up and down the road and carefully eased out. Her car didn't have Sat-Nav and she was smart enough to know that her phone was a useless piece of metal and plastic – so long as it stayed switched off. She also knew that Portsmouth was crawling with CCTV – and now there were police everywhere, and they were looking for her. She needed to get away without being spotted, and quick.

She made her way along a series of residential streets that eventually brought her out at a roundabout that went under the motorway. She'd made a subtle change to the number plate on the Mondeo, copying another grey one that she'd seen on her travels, and hoped this would be enough to keep her under the police radar. Assuming that even if someone thought they'd seen her in the car, a plate check would lead elsewhere. She headed over the back of Portsdown Hill, passing the military bases which overlooked Portsmouth. Down she went, sticking to quiet country lanes, confident there would be no CCTV out there.

Her thoughts went to what she'd left in her hotel room. Her cash, clothes and DNA – but she figured that, if Lomas knew she'd been there, he wouldn't find anything that would tell him any more than he already knew.

A police car shot past her, going in the opposite direction. Monica held her breath, her eyes fixed on the rear-view mirror, until the car disappeared. She needed to find a place where she could think about what to do next. There was nowhere else she could use as a bolt-hole. She needed to find somewhere new, but out of the way. Monica headed into the countryside and found a lay-by tucked out of sight, behind a thick tree-lined verge. She parked close behind an articulated lorry, whose driver was clearly sleeping. The back doors were pinned open to make it clear to would-be robbers that there was no cargo on board. She climbed into the back seat of the car and pulled her hood over her head and covered her face as far as it would go. She bunched up a hoodie that had been on the back seat into a makeshift pillow and tucked her head into the corner of the seat.

39

Sunday morning

Niamh was lying in bed, watching the light start to bleed around the edges of the blinds that cloaked her bedroom window. Sleep had not come to her; the night had dragged laboriously into dawn. She threw herself onto her side, like a five-year old having a tantrum, to face away from the window. She grabbed her phone and blinked as the screen popped into life. It was just coming up to 6 a.m. She was not amused.

Her head ached from another night of red wine, downed in front of the TV. After Mike Button had called her to let her know about DI Leade taking a heightened interest in the prison, she'd felt claustrophobic, trapped: the dual investigations were closing in around her.

Her mother had called her just after 10.30 the previous evening, innocently asking how she was feeling. Niamh had bitten her head off.

Sighing, she threw the duvet off and swung her legs over the side of the bed. Her head pounded as she pushed herself upright and she brought her hands up to her temples, cradling her skull.

'Come on, Niamh, get a grip, for fuck's sake,' she muttered. 'Get your arse up and get a shower.' Her head throbbed, and she decided to shower after a coffee. She took her dressing-gown from the back of the bedroom door and padded downstairs to the kitchen. The daylight hurt her eyes as she filled the kettle. The wine glass from the previous night was by the sink, and she caught a whiff of what had been a functional Merlot. She closed her eyes, took a deep breath, and poured the leftover wine down the sink.

Just as the kettle was coming to the boil, her phone rang. She retrieved it from her pocket and saw her mum's number on the screen. She stabbed the Decline button. She slid the phone onto the counter and took a cup from a cupboard. Her phone rang again. 'Mum' flashed on the screen again.

'Can't I even get a coffee in peace, woman?' She snatched the phone from the counter. 'Hi Mum, it's six in the morning! What the hell's so important at this time in the morning?'

'Niamh, it's Aunty Joy,' came the unexpected reply.

'Aunty Joy? But why are you calling me this early, from Mum's?' She felt her throat go dry.

'Niamh, it's your mum – she's gone, love. She passed away in the night. I got a call from a neighbour who saw her TV and lights on really early this morning...'

Niamh didn't hear the rest of what her aunty was saying. The world spun away from her and she sank to the kitchen floor, clutching the phone to her chest. Niamh wanted to disappear into a dark hole and never come out. Her mum had got on her nerves over the past few days, fussing about her, but Niamh spoke to her mum every day – even on days she didn't have anything to say. Her thoughts went to the last conversation they'd had, and a wave of guilt washed over her. Her bottom lip wobbled, and tears pricked her eyes. In her mind's eye she could see her mum's face, hear her voice comforting her.

'Mum ... no, not now, not like this. Why now? I need you, Mum,' she wailed. Niamh stayed on the kitchen floor, unable to get up, for what felt like an eternity. She cried until she had no more tears left and her face was sore.

She had never felt as alone as she did now. Suspended from work. Being investigated by the police and the prison service – and now her mum, taken from her without warning. Without a chance to say goodbye. To tell her how much she loved her. She felt truly broken.

She dragged herself to her feet and redialled her mum's home number. Her aunty picked up after a couple of rings.

'Sorry, Aunty Joy, I don't know why I...' The tears came again.

Her auntie's voice was soft and soothing. 'Shh, it's OK. I didn't see it coming either. We only spoke yesterday evening. She was worried about what was happening to you – your escaped prisoner and the stress you were under.'

Niamh gathered herself as Joy spoke. She sounded a lot like Niamh's mum. The sisters were close, and they lived not far from each other. Niamh suddenly felt like she needed to be there for Joy, rather than the other way around.

'Are you OK, Aunty Joy?' Niamh asked.

'I'm a bit shocked...' Joy's voice trembled, but it didn't break. 'But I'll be all right. They said they think it was a stroke. They don't think she suffered.'

'I'll get dressed and come over. Will you still be at Mum's?'

'Yes, I think I'll be here for a while yet. Drive carefully, love. I'll see you soon.' Joy's voice wobbled again then the line went dead.

Niamh splashed cold water on her face and caught her reflection in the kitchen window. She needed to get cleaned up before she went anywhere. She headed upstairs and turned on the shower.

Forty minutes later, she was on her way out of the door. She got to the end of her path and saw a car door open across the road. One of the journalists from the park scurried across the road towards her, holding a recorder out in front of him as he approached.

'Governor Dominicali, Monica Silverman is still on the loose. She is thought to be in Portsmouth. Do you have anything to say to the people of Portsmouth who may be at risk because you let a Category A prisoner escape from your prison? How much of a threat do think Monica Silverman is? Do you think she'll kill again?'

Niamh ignored him and walked towards her hire car.

'Governor, do you feel embarrassed that she escaped on your watch? How will you feel if innocent people are murdered as a result of your prison's incompetence?'

She couldn't help herself. Her fist clenched almost without her knowing. She spun around and the pursuing journalist nearly ran into her. She punched him square in the nose. He dropped his recording device and let out a cry, his hands going to his face.

'What's wrong with you fucking people? Have you got no thought for anyone? Maybe, just maybe, there's more going on in people's lives than your sordid, headline-grabbing stories.'

'You assaulted me,' he said through his hands. Blood was trickling between his fingers.

'Put that in your story and fuck off!' she yelled, getting in the car and slamming her door. She left him by the side of the road, clutching his bloody face.

'That was stupid, Niamh. That's not going to help, you know that,' she said as she drove down her road.

40

The sun was barely peeping above the horizon when Lomas decided he'd had enough of trying to get some sleep. He rarely slept well when the stress of an investigation started to build, and the second hunt for Monica Silverman was no exception. He'd got home at 2.30 a.m. The adrenaline from the successful raid on Monica's lair, and the slightly lower-key discovery of the hotel that she was staying in, had kept him awake when he first got home. But when he finally got into bed and Heidi rolled towards him, laying an arm across his chest, he was still unable to settle. His head was buzzing with theories and scenarios playing out, over and over, as he tried to figure out where Monica had gone and what she would do when she realised that Sarah Marley had escaped.

Lomas rubbed his hands through his hair and sighed quietly. He got out of bed slowly, so as not to wake Heidi, pulled on a pair of pyjama bottoms and headed downstairs to boil the kettle. He made a cup of tea, got a bowl of cereal sat at his kitchen table, then heard a stair creak. He looked round to see Heidi walking down the stairs, her dressing-gown pulled around her and a sleepy smile on her face. He loved how she looked first thing in the morning – always had. Even though she insisted she looked like crap.

'Want a cuppa?' he asked, getting up, anticipating her answer.

'Mmm, please,' she said, her voice croaky. She pulled out a chair next to his and leaned her head on her hand. 'Couldn't sleep?'

'No, not really. Sorry – did I wake you?'

'I turned over and you weren't there. I figured you'd come down. Rough night?'

'No, it was a good night. We found out where Monica's been staying and the woman she kidnapped, Sarah – she managed to escape. It was incredible. She told us where she'd been held.'

'Wow, that's amazing. So why the lack of sleep?'

'We raided both places, but there was no sign of Monica. I've been trying to figure out where she might have gone.'

'So, you got no sleep then?'

'Not really.'

She wrapped her arms around him and laid her head against his. 'You have to get some rest, or you'll be no good to your team.'

'I know. I'll try to get home at a reasonable time tonight. Maybe we can get a takeaway and a bottle of wine.'

'Mmm, Mr Baxter, that sounds like a plan,' she said, kissing him. He lingered for a while, enjoying the moment. When he was with Heidi, she made all the worries in the world disappear, regardless of how bad things were.

He was at the station by 7 a.m. The night team were working flat out, trawling any CCTV they could get their hands on around the vicarage and the hotel. The image Grant had got to Lomas the day before was a good clear facial shot, but they knew Monica had a vehicle. Sarah Marley had told them about it, and they were trying to link the addresses to a car. If only they could get some footage of her going to a car, they could put a flag on the ANPR system and track the number plate through the network of cameras.

Lomas wasn't surprised to see Drew also in early, working with Tina Ashford, the Investigation Manager. Tina was a short blonde-haired woman with a kind face. An experienced copper in her late forties, she was in charge of pulling together all the evidence gathered from the various lines of enquiry, keeping everyone informed on all the strands of the case, and making sure briefing room materials were up to date. She was solid, reliable, mega-organised and Lomas's go-to for managing the flow of information on all his big investigations.

They looked up as Lomas walked into the room. Drew scraped her long red hair up into a ponytail and Tina leaned back in her chair. She had a casual, relaxed air about her which Lomas had always thought was a perfect contrast for how seriously she took her job.

'Morning, boss,' said Drew.

'Morning ladies, what have we got?'

Drew looked at Tina, who began. 'Initial findings in the Southsea Rocks Hotel are promising. One of Grayson's team, supported by a couple of officers from Portsmouth, is working the room that Monica has been staying in. They've found cash, SIM card carriers and clothes, some worn, some clean – along with some half-empty bottles.'

'Sounds like they're doing a good job. What are SIM card carriers?' asked Lomas.

'They're the plastic cards that hold SIM cards and micro-SIMs that you see in the shops.'

'Ah I see, so do they have detail on the carriers that means we can track the numbers and pull any call data?'

'I would think so, but I'll check.' Tina made a note.

'OK, thanks. And what about the vicarage?'

'Grayson is there with a team of three. He says it's going to take him about four days to go over the place fully. They've also got a garden shed to search, and a neighbour has told one of our officers that there's a garage that belongs to the address,' said Drew.

'Great. Any news on the remains?'

'Sherlock has confirmed they're human, but he'll have to run tests to confirm that they belong to Elinor Mary Clarke.'

'So far, so good. Now all we have to do is find Monica,' he said with a shrug and a smile.

'Yeah, not much of a task there then, boss,' said Tina.

'We'll find her – we just have to look in the right places. Or get the public looking in the right places. I don't think she'll go far,' he replied. 'I'd like to have a briefing first thing, bring everybody up to speed with what happened yesterday and share the new CCTV image of Monica. Then I want to talk them through what we need to do next. Can you be ready for nine?' He looked at Tina, then at Drew.

They looked at each other. 'Yes,' they said in unison.

'Right people, listen up,' began Lomas. 'It's safe to say that we had a good day yesterday, but let's not get complacent. I want to bring everyone up to date. Yesterday, Sarah Marley escaped from captivity and managed to get herself to us. She'd been chained to a wooden bed and would have undoubtedly been tortured and killed by Monica, had she not escaped. While she was in captivity, Monica told her she'd taken Sarah because she knew we'd have made Christina Marley safe. As a result, we've got uniform cover for all immediate family members of Monica's previous targets, or victims. The Marley family are now in our protection, and colleagues from the NCA are going to move them somewhere safe this morning. Grant's team have managed to find a new CCTV image of Monica, and this has been positively identified by Sarah.' He pointed at an image on the large TV screen behind him: Monica, with short bleached blonde hair.

'As you can see, Miss Silverman has been savvy enough to change her appearance, which we suspected she would. This image will be sent to your phones. It will also be shared in a TV broadcast later today. We can now narrow Monica's recent movements down to an area around Southsea and Portsea Island. Sarah Marley gave us the location of the house where she was held.' He pointed to another image that Tina had popped onto the screen. 'It's an old vicarage. According to neighbours, it has been derelict for a number of years. We're doing background checks to find out how and why Monica was able to use it. Grayson and the scenes of crime team are going over it with a fine-tooth comb and we'll update details as we get them, but it's not going to be quick. With support from the tactical armed unit and the Royal Navy, we raided the property late yesterday. Needless to say, there was no sign of Monica.' He paused for a drink of water. A rumble of conversation started in the briefing room. Lomas stood silently for a couple of seconds, and the chatter died away.

'In addition, two young men from Portsmouth came forward after the most recent TV appeal. On the day of her escape, Monica assaulted them, stole their mobile phones and money. We managed to get the IMEI number for one of the phones and, after triangulation of the handset, we located an area around the Southsea Rocks Hotel, on Florence Road, where the phone had been used. Last night, Nick and Gurdeep visited the hotel and the manager confirmed that Monica has been renting a room there for the past few days. We have another forensics team in her room. So far, they've found a range of items proving that Monica was there. Any questions so far?'

He scanned the room. All the officers were either focused on him and the TV behind him, or were making notes.

Before he had a chance to start to dish out tasks and assignments for the next phase of the hunt, a uniformed officer rapped on the door and came in. 'DI Baxter?'

'Yes.'

'I've been sent up by the desk sergeant. There's an urgent call for you – he told me you'd want to be disturbed.'

'OK, Drew, can you take over?' Lomas ushered the officer out of the door and followed him to the nearest phone. He snatched the handset and jabbed the button for reception. 'It's Baxter.'

'Lomas, it's Jim. I've got a DI Richards from West Sussex on the line. Says it's urgent.'

'You'd better put him through.' He paused for a beat. 'DI Baxter, how can I help?'

'DI Baxter, this DI Ben Richards from West Sussex. We've had an incident over here that I think you'll want to come and have a look at.'

'What makes you think that?'

'Well, I remember your initial investigation into Monica Silverman and some of the injuries she inflicted on her victims. Am I right in thinking that she left a calling card – an etching on their forehead?'

'You've got my attention. Yes, that's right – they all had etched foreheads, with a range of symbols. Why?'

'A member of the public called in. They said they'd found a woman hanging, dead, from the tailgate of her Range Rover. When officers arrived, they found exactly that. A woman in her sixties, hanging by the wrists from the hydraulic struts of her tailgate. She'd suffered a fatal stab wound to her chest and had symbols engraved on her forehead.'

Lomas was silent for a second or two.

'DI Baxter?'

'Yeah, I'm here. Have you got photos you can send me?'

'Of course.'

'And have you identified the victim?' Lomas pressed.

'Yes, her name is Mrs Lydia Bartholomew. I thought she might be—'

'Connected to Monica? We're on the same page, Detective. If you get a couple of pictures of the injuries sent over, I'll get my team who processed the original crime scenes to compare them with the engravings on the foreheads of the previous victims. One more question, DI Richards.'

'Yes?'

'Where was the killing and what time, roughly?'

'Just outside Chichester. Our pathologist estimates that Lydia was killed late yesterday afternoon or early evening. She wasn't found for a while, as the car was on a quiet country road. Does that help?'

'Yes, it helps a lot, and unfortunately it points towards your theory being plausible. Thanks for letting me know. Let me have your number and I'll give you a call as soon as we've checked the photos out.'

They exchanged mobile numbers and Lomas hung up. 'Shit!' He headed for the briefing room. Drew was just wrapping up as he walked in.

'OK, live update, people, we may have a new victim. Gurdeep, can you find out everything you can about a Mrs Lydia Bartholomew? She's in her sixties, resides near Chichester. DI Richards from West Sussex can give you more detail if you need them. Drew, DI Richards is going to email us some photos. As soon as they land, can you get them to Sherlock and ask him to compare them with the injuries sustained by Monica's initial victims? If the information I've just been given leads us where I suspect it will, Monica Silverman has killed her first victim since escaping from prison. Lydia Bartholomew was found late yesterday, hanging by her wrists from the hydraulic struts on the back of her Range

Rover. She'd sustained a fatal stab wound to her chest and has symbols engraved on her forehead. The time she died fits roughly with the time between Sarah Marley escaping from captivity and us raiding the vicarage and identifying the hotel in Southsea where Monica has been staying. We cannot let up for one second. Monica Silverman is the most dangerous person I have ever come across – and it's up to us to bring her in before anyone else gets hurt. Now, Drew has let you know what needs doing next, so let's get to it.' He clapped his hands.

41

The artic rumbled into life. As it moved away, the early morning sun poured in through the windscreen of Monica's Mondeo. She shielded her eyes with her fore-arm from the shafts of light, that pierced the gap between the driver's seat and the headrest. Her night had been made up of a series of broken naps; she had been disturbed by every vehicle that passed the lay-by. Her hypervigilance and paranoia made it impossible to rest. She grunted and turned over to face the back of the seat, but quickly gave up the idea of getting back to sleep. A couple of minutes later she was standing next to the car stretching in the cool, morning air. She took a couple of deep breaths, closed her eyes and felt the sun's rays on her face. Her surroundings had that fresh, early morning smell and it occurred to her that, regardless of how lovely it was, she couldn't hang around here for long. Without the blanket of darkness, she was far too exposed. And now that Lomas Baxter had found her refuge, she had to keep moving.

In between trying to sleep, her anger at losing her vicarage and hotel bubbling, she'd worked up an outline of what she needed to do next.

She jumped into the driver's seat and headed off to execute her plan.

'Good morning, how can I help you today?' said a cheery woman from behind the counter of a village corner shop.

'Do you sell hair dye?' asked Monica. Her hood was pulled down to the bridge of her nose.

'Yes, we have a small stock. If we haven't got the shade you're looking for, I could order it in for you,' the woman replied helpfully, pointing to a shelf in the far corner of the shop. Monica stared at the boxes of hair colour, sneering at the pictures of beautiful women with radiant smiles and full, lush locks. She picked up a box of L'Oréal Colorista bright red permanent hair gel. Monica read the back of the box and dropped it into her basket.

'Those ones go on really well. All the girls round here like them,' said the woman, who'd appeared by Monica. Monica looked over her shoulder at the woman, who wore a soft-looking pale blue jumper and knee-length skirt, but didn't reply.

'Is there anything else I can help you with?'

'I'd like to write my grandmother a letter. Do you sell paper and envelopes?' she asked.

'We do, just around this side. It's such a lovely thing to do. Letter writing, I mean. It seems like a bit of a forgotten way of communicating, but I remember the excitement of getting handwritten letters in the post as a girl. Emails aren't the same.'

Monica followed her, grabbing a sandwich and a big bottle of water as she passed them.

'Here you are.' She passed Monica a blue lined writing pad and a pack of small envelopes. She paid and thanked the woman, watching as she fussed over packing a carrier bag, as if the contents were the Crown Jewels. Monica wondered how many customers came through here in a day. It was quiet and out of the way, but probably essential to the village, she mused. She thought briefly about breaking the woman's neck, so that she would be unable to identify her, but the thought passed and she took the bag with a thank you.

For the next forty minutes Monica drove around, looking for an open community centre or public toilets. She ended up in a village called Bishop's Waltham, where she found a toilet block in a car park tucked behind the high street. She felt unusually nervous as she parked her car in a corner, under a tree. She walked with her head down to the disabled toilet and locked herself in. She wasn't disturbed as she once again changed the colour of her hair. Using a T-shirt from her gym bag to roughly dry her hair, she looked in the mirror. It hadn't come out like the box – in fact, it was more of a muted orange – but she didn't care. She wiped down all the surfaces she'd touched with paper towels and headed back to her car. Monica drove out of the village, avoiding main roads and major buildings, trying to avoid as many CCTV cameras as she could.

***

In the nearby village of Fair Oak, about a hundred metres down the road from where she'd followed Drew Taylor nearly two years earlier, Monica sat watching. There was a marked police car between her and the block of flats. Occasionally a uniformed officer would get out and walk along the road. Monica was convinced that this was for her benefit: they were clearly making their physical presence felt.

'Well, that won't work, will it, DI Baxter? It didn't stop me before. All you've done is put another one of your officers at risk,' she mumbled.

While she sat, watching, she wrote a couple of notes on the blue lined pad. She folded each neatly and placed them in envelopes. As she finished addressing them the involuntary eye twitch she'd felt earlier in the week returned. She rubbed her eye with the back of her hand, trying to ignore it, but it wouldn't stop. She knew from a well meaning counsellor she'd seen in her early twenties that the twitch was a stress reaction. The counsellor had tried to help Monica use meditation to reduce her stress levels, and take away the twitching, but she could never get the hang of it and had eventually accepted her frustrating tick.

'Right, things to do, Monica,' she said, starting the engine.

42

DI Leade showed his ID to the reception staff at the prison and took a seat, waiting for Mike Button to come and meet him. The acting governor looked a lot less cheerful than he had the previous day, as he greeted Leade with a forced smile and a handshake.

'DI Leade, good morning. You're bright and early.'

'Morning, Governor. Yes, I like to get an early start on a day as busy as this one is going to be. This is my colleague, DC Tomlinson.' He motioned to his partner.

Janette Tomlinson shook Button's hand. She was roughly the same height as Leade, which made her a tall woman, with Scandinavian features, blue eyes and white-blonde hair. She had a keen ear for a lie and a dark sense of humour, that Leade had needed to rein in a couple of times.

'Morning, Governor. Nice place you have here.' She smiled. Mike Button looked at her quizzically but didn't reply.

DI Leade coughed and brought Button's attention back to him. 'So, where shall we set up for the day?'

'Er, this way,' Mike said, opening the door for them to pass into a long corridor.

'Is this the corridor Monica Silverman walked down on her way out of the prison?' Janette asked. Button looked uncomfortable with the question, which Leade was sure had been Janette's intention.

'Er … yes, it would have been. Just for my own clarity, you're here investigating the deaths that have occurred here at the prison, not the escape of Miss Silverman?'

'Yes, that's right. I'm sure DC Tomlinson was just curious, Governor. You know, getting her bearings, first visit and all that,' said Leade.

'Hmm,' said Button.

Leade shot Janette a look that said 'Don't wind him up', but he doubted she'd take any notice. He'd worked with Janette for two years and she had a natural talent for rattling people, especially those with something to hide.

Button led them into a vacant room that was used for interviews or confidential visits, with lawyers and the like. Tomlinson set up the recording equipment they'd brought with them, and Leade turned to Mike Button.

'So, Governor, how did you get on with our list? I hope it wasn't too much trouble bringing the officers in?'

'No trouble at all. We're always happy to help the police wherever we can. We're all on the same side, after all,' Mike replied.

'Absolutely, thank you.' Leade pulled a folded sheet of paper from his inside pocket and opened it out on the table, far more slowly than was necessary. 'Can we just compare notes and check we've got the same names?'

'Yes, of course,' said Mike, taking a scruffier-looking sheet out of his trouser pocket. He smoothed his hand over it as he put it down next to Leade's. They took a moment to silently cast their eyes over both, then Leade nodded his approval.

'Excellent. Let's make a start then, shall we?' He looked at Janette.

'Yes boss, let's crack on.'

They looked at Button, who still looked uncomfortable and slightly sweaty.

'I'll get some coffees brought in for you. The first person on the list will be about ten minutes.'

'Perfect. Thanks for your help, Governor. I'm sure you have plenty on your plate at the moment, what with the national press crawling all over the story about Monica and the suspension of Governor Dominicali. It can't be easy,' said Janette, with a smile.

Button didn't give her an answer; he just nodded and left the room, closing the door behind him.

'Did you see the look on his face?' Janette asked as soon as the door had closed.

'Yep. He was visibly uncomfortable when you mentioned Niamh Dominicali and the press.'

'I thought he was going to lay an egg when I said he had a nice place.'

'Are you going to wind everyone up today? Just so I'm prepared.'

'Would you have me any other way?'

'No, I suppose not. Although I'm sure Governor Button might not agree.'

'Well, if he'd had less corpses in his prison, he wouldn't have to meet me, boss.'

The door opened. A prison officer – who looked as though he was a few years past retirement and unimpressed at playing waiter – bought in their coffees on a tray, with a handful of milk and sugar sachets. He put the tray down on the table without a word, turned and left.

'Get the feeling we're not popular visitors?' said Janette.

'It's starting to feel that way, isn't it?'

Fifteen minutes after they'd finished their coffee, the first prison officer knocked on the door and came in. Roger Coleman was the one who'd brought their drinks. Leade and Tomlinson exchanged glances.

This is gonna be interesting, thought Leade.

'Good morning. Officer Coleman?' he said.

'That's right.'

'Take a seat. Thank you for taking the time to speak to us,' DI Leade began.

'Ain't really got a choice, have we? Is this going to take long? I've got loads to do.'

Leade's tone hardened. 'It will take as long as it takes, Officer Coleman. We're here to speak to you about the deaths of people who were detained in this prison. People who were in the care of you and your colleagues. If you think that warrants me being concerned about how long we keep you here for, then you're sadly mistaken.'

Coleman didn't reply.

The interview was fruitless. Coleman gave a series of grunts or single-word answers. He didn't have, or didn't want to share, any information about any of the women who'd died, except to confirm that he'd been on shift at the times they'd all died and that the prison staff always followed procedure. After half an hour, Leade terminated the interview, which was about five minutes after Tomlinson had put her pen down, as Coleman was giving no information for her to make notes of.

'Thank you, Officer Coleman, that will be all. If we think of anything else we want to ask you, we'll let you know,' said DI Leade.

'You won't get anything else out of any of the others. We have each other's backs round here,' said Coleman as he stood up and turned to leave.

'Why would you need to have each other's backs, Roger?' asked Janette.

He turned back to look at her. 'I know what you're up to. You're looking to pin those deaths on one of us, an' it ain't gonna happen. We did nothing wrong. You have no idea what it's like bein' in here all day, every day. Some of these women are fuckin' mental – and the ones that aren't are scared to death. So you do your investigation and ask your questions. But you're not gonna find anythin' to pin on us.' He glared from Tomlinson to Leade.

'So let me get this straight. You didn't answer my questions because you think we want to pin the deaths of these women on you and your mates?' Janette said.

'Why else would you be here? It's obvious that you're tryin' to fit somebody up so the governor doesn't take the fall. You're gonna hang it on one of us.' His hands gripped the back of the chair, his knuckles turning white.

'Wow, talk about paranoid. So tell me, Rog. What have you got to hide that you don't want us to find out? Why do you need to cover your mates' backs? What have they been up to?' Janette leaned forward in her chair, keeping eye contact with the older man.

'You fuckin' jumped-up—'

'Let's take it down a notch, shall we, Roger?' Leade interrupted, his tone soft and conciliatory, his palms open and facing the angry officer. 'Why don't you sit back down? You clearly have things you want to say, and we've got all the time it takes to listen. And to be clear, I am not looking to hang the blame one of the officers to get the governor off the hook. It's clear to me that there have been some unusual deaths here. Now, you've been around the block a few times, Roger. How long have you worked here?'

'Twenty-eight years this December,' said Roger, still holding the back of the chair, but gripping it less tightly.

'Wow, so you've seen some changes.'

'Yeah, just a few. I've seen governors come and go too.'

'I can imagine. So, how do you rate Governor Dominicali, among the ones you've worked for?'

'Pfft, she's all mouth, that one. Talks a good game – about how we're a unit an' we need to work as one, an' all that old crap. But she's in it for herself – an' only her favourites are part of her team.'

Leade motioned for Coleman to sit back down, which he did. Coleman looked over at Janette. He still looked pissed off, so Leade continued. 'Look, DC Tomlinson didn't intend to wind you up. But I can see that someone who's been around as long as you have, and committed so much of your working life to the prison, might be offended at the suggestion that you've done something wrong.'

'Well. Yeah,' said Coleman.

'We can see that you're a straight-shooter, Roger, and that's what we need to help us get to the bottom of these deaths. If it turns out these women just died, and they were accidents, just coincidence, then so be it. But if they weren't accidental, then the person or people responsible need to be held to account, don't you think?' Leade said.

'Yeah, I suppose.'

'Good, so how about we start over and see if you know anything that might help us reach a conclusion one way or the other?'

Coleman let out a sigh. 'OK, what do you wanna know?' His voice had a low, forty-a-day rasp to it.

The following half an hour was much more useful. Roger Coleman's frustration at the Dominicali regime was clear. He neither rated, liked or trusted the governor – or her immediate team.

'OK, so tell me, Roger, where were you on the day that Alba White died?' DI Leade asked. Roger Colman looked pensive when Leade said Alba's name.

'She was a good kid. I know she did some horrible stuff, but still...' Coleman began. 'She was one of the ones I was talkin' about: she was scared to death. Everybody she tried to get to know took the piss out of her. By the time she'd been here a couple of weeks, everything she'd been allowed to bring in with her had disappeared from her room. She'd given stuff away to try an' make friends, but the other women didn't care. They're all just out for what they can get.' He paused and took a sip of water. Leade looked at DC Tomlinson, who gently prompted Roger to carry on.

'She'd been quite excited that day. Her little sister had been added to her approved visitor list an' she was really lookin' forward to seeing her. Anyway, I'd been on the landin' with Bell and Rodriguez. We'd been sortin' out who was goin' for visits and who was goin' for exercise. I was with Maria Gomez. She's – she *was* – two rooms down from Alba. Then Bell and Rodriguez went past me, with Alba. I thought that it was a bit weird; it's not like she needed a double escort or anythin'. Anyway, not long after that, the alarms went off, an' one of the others told me Alba had had an accident in the yard. I guess she was trying to work out – you know, get stronger so she could stick up for herself.' His eyes glazed as he recounted his last memory of Alba White.

Stephen Leade nodded to Tomlinson to continue.

'Roger, I understand this must be difficult to go over, but can you tell me where you were when Marjorie Phelps died? You were on shift that day too, is that right?' Tomlinson asked.

Coleman sighed and shook his head. 'Yeah, I was on that day too. She was a different kettle of fish, though. Tough as old boots. She was in for settin' fire to a house with her ex inside. Torched him an' his kid – really sad, but she didn't give a fuck. Crowed about how he deserved it for cheatin' on her. She had a smart-arse lawyer though. He got her a reduced sentence, so I'm guessing she helped you lot somehow.' He shrugged and carried on, clearly not looking for a response. 'She used to rule her floor. I mean, literally, she scared the shit out of the girls either side of her. 'Course, she was smart enough not to get caught doin' anythin', but she was up to no good from the minute she got here.'

'That's really helpful, Roger. What can you remember about the day she died?'

'It was busy – I mean, really busy. We'd had about six newbies turn up and they all needed settlin' into the wing. I was on with Gill O'Leary, Bell and Rodriguez. We were flat out, then Rodriguez said they needed to take Marj over to the library.'

'They?'

'Yeah, him and Charlie Bell. Said they needed to take her over there to move some stuff. She worked over there. I think they were goin' to help her with some books, or shelves, whatever. Anyway, she'd have talked them into helpin' her – she had a way of doing that with some of the younger ones. She was a bit of a charmer.'

'What happened next?'

'They were escortin' her to the library. Next thing I know, there's alarms goin' off and Beth Jeffries came runnin' onto the floor sayin' that Marj had fell down the stairs and wasn't movin'. Turns out she broke her neck when she fell. What a way to go.' He shuddered.

Leade glanced across at Tomlinson. She was still making notes.

Coleman was more vague about the third death they asked him about. Rachel Sigvelt had been in another part of the prison. All he'd heard were the alarms again and talk of her being found dead in her room.

'That's been really helpful, Roger. Is there anything else you'd like to tell us, or you think might be helpful, that we haven't covered?' Leade asked.

'Only what I said before – you won't get much out of some of the others. Maybe you should start by explainin' that you're not out to get any of us. Or to get the governor off the hook. They might open up a bit more then.'

'Thanks again, you've been a great help,' said Janette. They stood and shook his hand. As the door closed behind Coleman, Janette let out a long breath. 'Well, that turned around a bit, boss.'

'Yeah, I thought we were in for a day of getting blanked until you wound him up,' said Leade.

'It wasn't difficult – he's a big teddy-bear, really,' she said with a smile.

'I thought he was going to lump you. So, what do you think?'

'I think we should play the others like Coleman suggested. Take five minutes explaining why we're here and that we're not here to fit any of them up. He really doesn't like Niamh Dominicali, does he?'

'No, I can't imagine him stumping up for a leaving collection for her, that's for sure. I agree about the approach. You can lead on that. Then I want to dig a bit on this "getting the governor off the hook" stuff. There's something else going on here. It might not be linked to the deaths, but my gut tells me there's something. Coleman went back to it too many times. And I want to find out who her "team" are. Do you reckon Button's one of them?'

'Could be. Although, with the way he looked this morning, I think he's more "team JD and Coke",' Janette said, raising her eyebrows.

Next through the door was Gill O'Leary. Her thick glasses made her eyes look bigger than they were. She sat down opposite Leade and Tomlinson, looking nervous and alert. She rested her left arm, which was encased in a cast, on the table.

Janette started by outlining why they were there and, more importantly, what they were *not* there to do. Gill nodded silently.

DI Leade paused while Gill filled her paper cup. 'Gill, can I start by asking how long you've worked at the prison?'

'I've been here for eight years. It's the best job I've ever had. I mean, it's hard work, but it's so rewarding, especially when you see the girls going back home to their families. Some of them have their kids come in and visit, and they're so upset when they leave.'

'Do you have children, Gill?'

'Yes, I've got four – two boys, two girls.' She beamed as she answered.

'Aw, lovely, how old are they?' asked Janette.

'They're between seven and fifteen.'

'Wow, I bet that's a handful on top of working here. Do you have a partner?'

'Yes, my husband, Joe. He works for the council, he's a plumber.'

'And how are things at home?' asked Leade.

Gill looked a little confused, but she answered anyway. 'We have the same problems as everyone else with four kids and a mortgage.'

Janette stepped in, picking up on Gill's answer, her tone sympathetic. 'I can imagine that's really tough. It's not cheap these days bringing up kids. And as for keeping a roof over their head.' She paused briefly. 'I guess having enough money to go round is a big problem.'

Stephen Leade watched as Gill O'Leary's eyes suddenly teared up. She was looking at Janette, not Leade.

'Isn't it for everybody? We work hard to make ends meet, but there's always something the kids need. New shoes, a laptop, money for a trip, a day out with friends. We both do extra, but sometimes it's just not enough.'

Janette passed her a tissue from a packet she had in her pocket.

'Thank you.' Gill sniffed.

'It's OK, Gill, take your time. I'm sorry, we didn't mean to upset you.'

'It's fine. It's just that things around here have been really tense these last few days. You know, since Bob died and Monica escaped. It's like the whole place is under a massive microscope.'

Leade let Gill take a moment, then he said, 'You were in the room with Bob when he was attacked, weren't you? Didn't Monica attack you too?'

She sniffed and wiped her nose with the tissue. 'Yes. It was really scary. She's so fast and strong. We made the mistake of putting her between us and the door, and when she realised that, she just lost it. She threw herself back at us and knocked us over, like she was ten-pin bowling. Then she went mad. She kicked poor Beth in the face, stamped on my arm.' She lifted her cast off the table as she spoke. 'Then she gave Bob a real beating...' Her voice cracked again. 'He never stood a chance.'

'There was nothing you could have done, Gill. Monica Silverman is a very dangerous woman,' Janette said.

'Did you feel like you had the right amount of support to be dealing with someone like Monica Silverman, Gill? From the prison, I mean.'

Gill shook her head. 'We told the governor she was too much. She didn't listen. She never listened.'

'How do you mean?' Leade asked.

'We'd told her before that we needed to have Monica locked down, in isolation, but she wouldn't hear of it. She told us that just because we were scared of a prisoner, it didn't make them more of a threat. Bob tried to tell her more than once. Her – and Button.' Her tears had gone now. She had venom in her voice and a steely look in her eyes.

'Mike Button?'

'Yeah.' She sneered. 'He's just her puppet. There's no point talking to him. He just does what she says. He'll be struggling now without her around, that's for sure. Especially with two of her team gone.'

Leade looked at Tomlinson.

'Her team?'

'Yeah, she's got her favourites. Bell and Rodriguez were part of her team. They did most of her dirty work for her—' She stopped abruptly.

Leade didn't allow her to change subject. 'You were saying?'

'Er, well, she just had favourites, that's all.' Gill took a swig of her water.

'And, Bell and Rodriguez were two of them?' Leade pushed.

Gill didn't answer for a minute or so. Leade and Janette looked at her without breaking eye contact. Then Janette spoke. 'Gill, you remember what I said when we started talking?'

Gill nodded.

'We're here to find out what happened to the women who died. Some of them had families – children who are never going to see them come home. Never going to spend another birthday or Christmas with them. That can't be right, can it, Gill? They didn't come to prison to die. They came here to pay their debt to society and then go back to their kids.'

Gill's eyes darted from one to the other. She was twisting the tissue in her hands and the nervous look she'd come in with had returned. But she didn't say anything else.

'You were on shift the day Alba White died, is that right?' Leade said.

'Yes, but I didn't see what happened to her.'

'So what *do* you remember from that day?' Leade followed up.

'I was on the lower floor, with Bob. We were getting prisoners ready for work placements and learning. Bell and Rodriguez came past me with Monica Silverman.'

'Where were they going?' Janette asked.

'I don't know. She had to exercise on her own, under supervision, so they could have been taking her to the yard, or the gym. Or maybe they were taking her somewhere else. I honestly don't know.'

'Then what happened?' said Leade.

'About twenty minutes later, the alarms went off and the response team ran through the wing. I know now that they were on the way to the exercise yard, where Alba was found.' Her gaze dropped to the table, and she fiddled with the paper cup.

'What is it, Gill?' Janette asked.

'Alba was a sweet girl. She had a youngster – a two-year old, I think. Seems such a waste.'

'Can you tell me what people might mean by saying that we're here to get the governor off the hook?' Leade asked, motioning to himself and Tomlinson.

'I don't know.' Gill shrugged. 'Maybe they thought that the governor had pulled some strings with her high-up friends and got you to come in and find someone to pin it on.'

'Hmm, and who would we pin it on? If we were here to do that?' Leade said.

'I don't know. Someone who was on shift every time someone died. Anyone who moved attention away from the governor, I guess.'

'What about Bell and Rodriguez?' Janette said. 'You said they did the governor's dirty work. What did you mean by that? What's going on here that we don't know about?'

Gill shifted in her chair, then grabbed the water jug and refilled her cup again. Her hand shook ever so slightly as she poured.

'It's obvious you know something we don't, Gill. It could be something important. I know you don't want the deaths of these women on your conscience,' Janette continued.

Gill shook her head. She was chewing her bottom lip and turning the cup around in her hand. 'I'm not going to get in any trouble, am I?'

'I don't know. Have you done anything wrong?' said Leade.

'Not really – not as much as some of the others.'

Leade nodded at Janette.

'Why don't you tell us what you know and we'll see what we can do to help you?' said Janette in a soft, reassuring tone. They waited for a minute or so then Gill spoke, quietly at first. 'It was just a bit of gear. Bell would bring it to the staff room and dish it out to a couple of us who helped him, and he would pay us in cash – once we'd delivered it to the right rooms.'

'By gear, you mean...' Leade started.

'Drugs. Cannabis and cocaine, mainly. It was in small bags – small enough to fit in your pocket without being spotted. I never collected any money for it, though. I just delivered it, I swear. Am I gonna get fired?' Gill's eyes welled up.

'How long has this been going on?' Leade asked.

Gill's voice shook as she replied. 'Er, I've been involved for about four years. I don't know how long before that.'

Leade and Tomlinson looked at each other. 'OK ... how was it coordinated? There must have been someone higher up, pulling Bell's strings,' said DI Leade.

'I don't know. I figured it must come from the top, but if I'm honest, I think it was going on before the governor got here.'

43

Lomas stood at the end of Sherlock's work bench. The forensic pathologist's real name was Dr Alan Paisley. He was a font of knowledge; Lomas had worked with him on various cases over the years, including the original Monica Silverman investigation.

Sherlock held a printed version of one of the pictures that DI Richards had sent over from West Sussex next to his laptop screen, which displayed an image of Christina Marley's forehead.

'What do you think?' Lomas asked.

'They look very similar, that's for sure.' Sherlock zoomed in on the image. 'Look here,' he said, pointing to the top of a star-like shape etched into Christina's skin.

'You see the way this shape is formed in the skin? It's almost identical to the one in the centre, here.' He waved the picture of the marks in Lydia Bartholomew's head.

Lomas leaned in and took a closer look at the screen. He could clearly see, in 150% zoom, the torn skin of

Christina's forehead. A memory suddenly surfaced. Finding Christina Marley chained to a wooden bed, her head bound in disinfectant-soaked bandages, jerking in terror at the sound of them crashing into the room she'd been held in.

Sherlock's voice tore Lomas away from the memory.

'And take a look at this.'

Lomas looked at the screen. Sherlock had zoomed back out.

'What am I looking at?'

'This.' Sherlock ran his finger across the screen from right to left, then held the printed picture underneath the screen.

'Although the engravings weren't identical, as there are differences in the sizes and angles, the basic pattern looks the same – same shapes, in the same order. Look.'

'Sherlock, you're a genius.'

'Yeah, I know,' Sherlock said with a smile.

'She's spiralling. That's not good.'

'How so?'

'She left this woman, Lydia Bartholomew, hanging from the tailgate of her Range Rover. Didn't attempt to abduct her or torture her over time, like the others. It's like she was angry with Lydia. I don't know. This one feels more rushed, more personal.'

'Anything else I can do?' asked Sherlock.

'Do you think West Sussex would be happy for you to take a look at the body?'

'I don't see why not. I'm sure Marie could get it cleared. What am I looking for?'

'I don't know. Anything that someone else might have missed, or not thought was significant enough to let us know about. We've got to find Monica before too many more people get hurt. I'll talk to Marie and get her to square it with West Sussex.'

'OK. I'll finish up here and get over there.'

***

Lomas joined Drew in DCI Carlton's office. He ran through what Sherlock had told him, for both their benefit, and Marie agreed to call a colleague to arrange for Sherlock to examine the body. Drew updated the DCI on their searches of the hotel and the vicarage, then asked if Marie could go on TV again, using the CCTV image of Monica.

'Are you putting me to work, DS Taylor? Lomas, you're clearly training her well,' Marie said with a smile.

'Can't have you getting bored and feeling left out, can we, boss? Managing up, I think they call it. And don't worry – she does it to me as well,' replied Lomas.

Drew smiled. They left DCI Carlton and headed back to see Tina Ashford, the Investigation Manager.

'I hope you haven't come in here with any curve balls to throw at me?' Tina said when Lomas and Drew walked into the briefing room. It looked a lot bigger without the whole team assembled in it.

'Not exactly,' said Lomas, with mock hesitation.

'What is it?'

'Can you pull all the interviews from the first investigation? Monica's and Christina Marley's? Then Sarah Marley's.'

'Of course. What are you looking for?'

'Any reference to Lydia Bartholomew.'

'And the Marleys?'

'I want to see how they described their interactions with Monica. I know they both spoke to her during captivity, but they had different experiences. I think she's starting to spiral, and I'm looking for something that might give us an indication of how she might act when she does.'

'On it. I'll call you when I've got them. Who do you want to go through them?'

'Do you want me to do it?' asked Drew.

'No, you can come with me, Drew. Tina, can you ask Gurdeep to go through them, please?'

'Will do.'

Lomas and Drew left Tina to start digging out the interview records.

'Where are we off to, boss?' asked Drew as they headed outside, dashing to get to the car and out of the pouring rain.

'We're going to see Elinor Mary Clarke's parents and let them know we've found their daughter's remains. Sherlock has gone through the bones that were found in the vicarage and matched them to Elinor.'

'That's good news, I guess.'

'Hopefully it will give them some closure and they can finally put her to rest.'

They weren't at the Clarkes' house for long. When they broke the news, Mrs Clarke had stared blankly out of the window and Mr Clarke had sobbed silently. Neither of them tried to console the other. They didn't have many questions. Just, where was she found? When they could they collect the remains?

'Thank you, Detective Baxter. Ray and I are so glad you have found our little girl,' Winnifred Clarke said to them at the door when she saw them both out. She turned to Drew before Lomas had time to answer and took her hand, holding it tightly.

'Elinor would have been about the same age as you, DS Taylor. Such a waste. Make the most of every day, my dear. Life is the most fragile and priceless gift.' She released Drew's hand, gave a smile and closed the door. Lomas and Drew exchanged a glance but didn't say anything until they got back to the car.

Drew spoke first. 'That was a bit weird.'

'Yeah, I thought that. They're very different as a couple to how they were the last time we saw them. I guess losing Elinor has put quite a strain on them.'

'They were definitely closer the last time we saw them. It must be really hard, not being able to move on.'

'Near impossible, I would think. It seems you struck a chord with Mrs Clarke too. So, DS Taylor, how *are* you going to make the most of today?' he said as he started the car.

'Oh, I don't know. I might take the rest of the day off and go to a spa,' she said, smiling and clicking her seatbelt into place.

'If you figure out how to do that, let me know. Anyway, changing the subject, I'd like you to do the press conference again later with Marie. Are you up for that?'

'Yes, of course, but why me?'

'A couple of reasons. One, it's good for your development. You will have to get used to being in front of a camera if you stay in serious crimes, and the more you do it, the more comfortable you're going to be. Second,

I want Monica to see you front and centre, showing her that you're not fazed by her threats. It might wind her up and make her do something careless. At this point, with her hotel room and hiding place not available to her, she'll be starting to feel under pressure. I would imagine that paranoia is setting in too. We could do with her being more reactive and spontaneous, less planned. Seeing you and Marie sharing a CCTV image of her and giving details of where she's been and what we know might spook her. But you need to be comfortable with that.'

'I'm in,' she said without hesitation.

'Good. I'll talk to Marie when we get back.'

'You mean you haven't spoken to her about it yet?'

'No, but it'll be fine, I'm sure.' His phone rang. Heidi's name popped up on the car's media screen.

'Hey, you, how's your day?' Lomas said.

'Lomas, where are you?' The tension in her voice was clear.

'I'm just outside Winchester with Drew, on our way back to town. Why? What's wrong?'

'Can you come home? Now?'

'Yes – what is it?'

'I've just had some flowers delivered, and you need to see them. Lomas, I'm scared.' Her voice wavered.

'Heidi, it's fine. I'm on my way, and I'll send a uniform there now. Where are the kids?' he said, putting his foot down.

'They're in their rooms. Ant was going to go out, but the rain put him off.'

'OK, good. Stay in, lock the doors and don't answer to anyone. Heidi?'

'Yes.'

'Who delivered the flowers?'

'It was a florist delivery. There's a card, but I haven't opened it.'

'All right. I'm going to make a couple of calls. We'll be there in about fifteen minutes. It'll be fine. I promise I'll be there soon.'

'OK.' She hung up. both Lomas and Drew were silent for a moment.

'Call the station, ask them to get the nearest car to my house, tell them to wait outside,' Lomas said. Drew nodded and plugged her headphones in, knowing that Lomas would be using the car phone.

Lomas commanded the car phone to call Grayson Washington. He answered after three rings. 'Hi Lomas, how are you?'

'Grayson, I'm not sure. Are any of your team free at the moment?'

'Er, most of the team are working on the vicarage. What do you need?'

'Heidi's just called me. She'd had a flower delivery that's freaked her out. I don't know any details yet, but I expect it's Monica-related.'

'Say no more. I'll leave the team here and meet you at yours.'

'Thanks mate, see you soon.'

Lomas broke every speed limit on the way home. Drew sat next to him, after calling for a uniformed officer to go to Lomas's house. A marked car could be there within five minutes. Next she called Grant Carver to see if Monica had been using the mobile phone. He said she hadn't used the phone since the previous day, and they were trawling the local CCTV feeds. She relayed both conversations to Lomas as he sped towards his house.

He swung into his driveway. The marked car was parked on the opposite side of the road. A uniformed officer raised his hand as they pulled in. Lomas didn't respond.

He was out of the car and at the house before Drew had closed her car door. Lomas unlocked the door and burst through it, leaving it open for Drew.

'Heidi!'

'In here,' she replied, her voice shaky. He went through to the kitchen and stopped dead in his tracks. On their dining table was an arrangement of pure white chrysanthemums spelling out the words RIP HEIDI.

Lomas dashed over to Heidi and threw his arms around her, pulling her to him as she burst into tears. Her body jerked with the force of her sobs. Lomas ran a hand over her hair, her head pressed against him. He looked round to see Drew standing in the doorway, staring at the flowers.

'Drew, can you check on the kids, please? They're up in their rooms. I'm guessing they've got headphones in. Thanks.'

Drew nodded and headed for the stairs.

Lomas guided Heidi to a chair and crouched beside her, gently wiping the tears from her cheeks with his thumbs.

'Heidi, I need to know what the florist said.'

In between sobs, she said, 'Th-they said that they had a delivery for Mrs Baxter. I s-said that was me and he nodded, went to the back of his van and came back with – *that*.' She pointed at the floral arrangement and turned her tear-stained face away from it. 'I asked him who it was from and he said he didn't know, he was just the driver, but there was a card. Then he said he was sorry for my loss and left.'

'And what did you do? Did you open the card?'

'No, I put them there and called you. Then I sat here, just staring at them. It's her, isn't it? It's Monica.'

He didn't answer her. He pulled a chair up next to her and held her close. The flower arrangement dominated the room. Lomas couldn't drag his eyes away from it. He felt his stomach start to tighten and resisted clenching his fists. Feeling her sobs beginning to die away, he kissed the top of Heidi's head. There was a knock at the door. Heidi jumped. As Lomas stood to answer it, he heard Eve and Ant speaking to Drew upstairs. Through the glass panel in the door, he could see the athletic frame of Grayson Washington.

'Hi Lomas, everything OK?' Grayson asked. His deep voice sounded more suited to voice-overs than being a top-notch forensic scientist.

'Heidi's freaked out, understandably.'

'And your kids?'

'They're upstairs. Drew's chatting to them.'

Grayson nodded and smiled as he stepped inside and slipped his shoes off. Lomas realised that he still had his on. He followed suit, then walked through to the kitchen with Grayson. The forensic scientist stopped when he saw the flowers, the same way Lomas and

Drew had done. They stood out against the wooden dining table, looking every bit as sinister and out of place as they were intended to look.

'Hello, Heidi,' Grayson said as he approached the table.

'Hi Grayson.' She wiped her face with a tissue.

'Has anyone touched the flowers?'

'Only Heidi, to carry them through, and the florist delivery guy. Heidi says there's a card in there but we haven't touched it.'

'Good. If they're from who we think, I doubt she'll have touched them either, but you never know.' He snapped on a pair of gloves and laid a plastic sheet around the floral arrangement. Then he took some photos and picked the small card from the centre of the flowers, using a pair of tweezers. He laid it on the plastic, took another photo and then lifted the flap of the envelope. Grayson eased out a small card, with a picture of a purple flower on the front and 'With sympathy' printed across the front in gold. Opening the card, he looked across at Lomas.

'You'll want to see this, Lomas.' He nodded towards the card. Lomas lifted his hands from Heidi's shoulders; she stood to follow him.

'I'm coming to look. I want to know,' she said.

'OK.' He moved to one side for her to stand beside him and put an arm around her shoulders. Written across the card in capital letters were the words 'SLEEP WELL. SEE YOU SOON – MS'. Heidi took in a sharp breath and covered her face with the tissue. Instinctively, Lomas's arm tightened around her. He nodded at Grayson, who closed the card.

'If we can find out from the florist who wrote the card, that may rule out the need to do any work to check the handwriting.' Grayson said, slipping the card into its envelope.

'OK. Can you bag the flowers and take them away, please?'

'Of course. I'll have them out of here in five minutes.'

Grayson was in the process of wrapping the floral arrangement when Lomas heard footsteps on the stairs. Seconds later, Eve, Ant and Drew appeared at the kitchen door. She gave Lomas a look that said 'Sorry – I tried'. He smiled, grateful that she'd kept the kids occupied for as long as she had. The smell of the flowers was filling the room.

'What's this, Dad?' Ant asked, stepping forward to see what Grayson was doing.

'Don't get too close, please. It's evidence, and Grayson is just about to take it away,' Lomas replied.

'No worries. Hi, Grayson,' said Ant as he moved a bit closer.

'Hello, Ant, how you doing?' replied Grayson with a casual air that Lomas was a bit surprised by, but pleased with, given what he was in the middle of doing.

'What's in the bag? Smells like flowers,' Ant persisted.

'Like I said, it's evidence. Now let Grayson finish what he's doing and I'll tell you all about it.'

'OK, cool.' Ant shrugged, seeming satisfied.

'Mum, are you OK?' asked Eve.

'Yes, I'll be fine, sweetie,' Heidi said.

Eve didn't look at Heidi as she replied; her eyes were on Grayson. Lomas knew that Eve had a crush on Grayson. She had since she was about fifteen and Grayson had been over for a barbecue in a tight white T-shirt and shorts that showed off his athletic legs. Since then, every time Lomas had mentioned Grayson around Eve she'd either blushed or asked a never-ending list of questions about him.

Lomas smiled and turned to Heidi. 'Why don't you and the kids go through to the lounge for a couple of minutes? Drew and I will help Grayson finish up in here.'

Lomas saw Heidi's gaze follow his eyes and pick up on Eve's fixed stare.

'Yeah, sure. Come on, kids, let your dad get sorted out in here.' She ushered them out of the kitchen.

'Thanks for getting here so quickly, mate,' said Lomas as he held the door open for the forensic scientist to leave.

'No problem. I'll get them back and logged and catch up with you later about the vicarage.'

'That'd be great. Thanks again.' He closed the door and asked Drew to find out what she could about the florist the flowers had come from. Had they seen Monica? Who'd written the card. Then she was to call Marie Carlton and let her know. She was also to ask for the marked car to stay outside for a while. Drew nodded, logging the list of instructions, letting Lomas know about a couple of additional calls she was going to make, then went through to the kitchen, closing the door behind her.

Lomas joined his family in their lounge. Heidi sat in the centre of the sofa, with Eve beside her and Ant in a chair opposite.

'What happened, Dad?' Ant asked straight away. 'Drew said we had to wait to speak to you, then she changed the subject to school and stuff.' He was clearly unimpressed at the lack of information.

Lomas explained what had happened, leaving nothing out. Eve hugged her mum as Lomas spoke and Ant took on a serious expression, reminding Lomas of himself. He noticed Ant gripping the arm of the chair as Lomas explained the events of the previous hour or so. Once he'd answered their questions about the delivery, Eve asked if they were in danger.

'I don't know, love. You know how dangerous Monica is. The fact that she's targeting us again puts you all at risk—'

'I'm not being driven out of my home again, Lomas. These flowers being delivered don't change that. Didn't you say that she's unlikely to do something like this herself for fear of being spotted?' said Heidi.

'I did, but who knows what she'll do if she starts to get careless? I can't risk you all being put in danger.'

'Can't we get someone to watch the house?' asked Ant, pointing out of the window at the marked car.

'Possibly. Look, I'm doing my best to keep you all safe and to catch Monica before someone else gets hurt.' He crouched in front of Heidi. 'I'll talk to Marie, see what she can do. But if Marie decides you all have to go somewhere else to be sure of being safe, she won't ask my permission; she'll have you picked up.' He didn't move his gaze from Heidi as he spoke. She nodded, and he hoped she trusted him enough to know that he'd do everything he could to protect them.

44

Niamh had sat in her car, fifty metres down the road from her mum's house, for nearly half an hour, unable to move or open the door, paralysed by fear of going into her mum's home, knowing she wouldn't be there to greet her with a hug and a smile. She knew that Aunty Joy needed her. Joy had never married, instead devoting her younger years to doing foreign aid work in far-flung parts of the world. When she was a child, Niamh had loved hearing her stories and seeing photos of where Joy had been. She would sit on her lap for hours, listening to her tales about families in the developing world and their struggles. For a while she'd wanted to follow in Joy's footsteps, but then her prison career had taken off.

Niamh's mum had been married, briefly. Niamh's father had been in the army. Her mum always said he had swept her off her feet – until she landed with a bump and realised he wasn't there to catch her. The marriage had lasted less than a year. Niamh had seen a few photos of her father when she was younger, but he'd never been in touch with her. She'd asked her mum about him from time to time as she was growing up. He sounded like a nice guy, but the truth was that Niamh didn't even know if he knew she existed.

She'd always had her mum and Joy, and she'd always made friends easily. Some of her close friends' dads had become father figures and male role models for the young Niamh. When she'd heard her friends moaning about their dads being too strict, or not interested enough, she felt lucky not to have those issues to contend with. As she was growing up, her mum had dated occasionally, but there had never been anyone serious.

Niamh looked at her phone, which was on the seat beside her. For a second she thought about calling her aunty and saying she couldn't face it, then she thought better of it. She closed her eyes, took a few deep breaths and got out of her car.

Opening the gate to the red-brick terraced house that she'd grown up in, she reminded herself that her mum wasn't there. The house looked different somehow.

'Hi, Aunty Joy,' she shouted as she let herself in.

'Hi, love. I'm through here.' The reply came from the dining room.

Niamh glanced through the lounge door as she walked past. That looked different too. The furniture – always so neat and tidy – was out of place; the coffee table had been pushed to one side. The work of the paramedics, she guessed.

Her auntie sat at the round dining table, paperwork strewn in front of her. She looked up at Niamh, fresh tears in her eyes. 'I know she had a funeral plan all paid for, but I'm damned if I can find it.' Her face crumpled, and Niamh rushed to her side to comfort her.

'It's OK, we'll find it, there's no rush,' she said, sitting beside her aunty. She looked at the mass of paper on the table and the open filing box on the floor, and knew she would be the one to sort the formalities of her mother's passing. 'How about I make us a tea and we leave all the paperwork for now?'

'That sounds good,' Joy said with a sniff.

They walked through to the kitchen together. Niamh hadn't been prepared for what she saw when she got there. Her mum was normally so tidy, but all along the worktop newspapers had been laid out. Each one was open at a story to do with Niamh or Monica's escape from prison. There must have been at least ten newspapers.

Niamh raised a hand to her mouth to stifle any sound that might leak out, and felt Joy's hand on her shoulder.

'She was really worried about all the coverage you were getting and how the press were hounding you, especially after the scene in the park.'

'I knew she was worried, but I had no idea...'

'It's not your fault, love, it's how she dealt with things. She's always been the same. If something got stuck in her head, she'd go out of her way to find out as much as she could about it, reading everything. Even as a girl, she was the same. That's why she was top in every class that interested her when we were at school.'

'But what if the stroke was brought on by all this? By stress, by me? What if I killed her, Aunty Joy?' She broke down in tears, burying her head in her aunty's shoulder, just as she had as a girl when she fell, or needed comforting.

'Shh ... you can't think like that, love. These things happen. There's no rhyme or reason to it. When your time is up, it's up. Today was your mum's day, but I know she wouldn't have done a thing differently and she was so proud of you. So very proud.'

45

The next five interviews DI Leade and DC Tomlinson carried out all helped to add to the picture they were starting to build. A couple of the officers had started off prickly, like Coleman, but once they understood that Leade and Tomlinson weren't looking for a fall guy, they seemed only too keen to unburden themselves.

Leade had asked officers who made sure the right people were on shift to ensure the drugs coming into the prisons were distributed by the right people. The officers had looked confused when Leade had hinted about the governor being the one in control.

'What do you think?' asked Janette Tomlinson as the last officer left the room.

'I think we've ended up with two investigations in one. There's clearly a well-organised drug distribution network, being led from the top, but no one is willing, or able, to point the finger specifically at Niamh Dominicali. We'll need to flag what we've found out and see if the boss wants us to follow that line of enquiry to see where it leads. With regard to the deaths, it seems that everyone has seen Bell and Rodriguez every time someone died. And it looks like they were the closest to Niamh Dominicali. I think her team was a small group of officers she trusted. It wouldn't surprise me if she had something on each of them. Let's look into the finances and family lives of Bell, Rodriguez and Button – see if anything stands out.'

'OK, will do. What about Button? He's our last interviewee, due in about ten minutes. How do you want to play it?'

'I think we'll miss out the "we're not looking for a scapegoat" bit and see how he responds to our initial questions. If he doesn't open up, then let's see if we can rattle him a bit. Maybe drip in the odd line about drugs, or rota tampering,' said Leade.

'When I reviewed the rotas and overtime logs, it was Button who signed most of them off. That could give us a route into those, as he clearly authorises who's in and when. Makes sense to me that he'd be the one coordinating the drugs being pushed around the prison. When Gill was talking about it, she said it had been going since pre-Niamh Dominicali.'

'OK, sounds like a plan. Why don't you start and we'll see where it goes?' said Leade.

Mike Button was five minutes later than his allotted time. He came into the interview room sounding overly cheerful and engaging. 'Hello again. How's your day gone? Hopefully my officers have been open and helpful?'

Tomlinson began, as planned. 'Yes, thank you, Governor Button, they've been very helpful. Now, we know you're a busy man, so we're not going to take up too much of your time.' Tomlinson waded straight in. 'Tell me, Governor, what can you remember about the day that Alba White died?'

'No preamble there, DC Tomlinson,' he said with a wide grin. Neither Leade nor Tomlinson answered him. He coughed and dropped the smile. 'Erm, yes, Alba, very sad. Let me see. I was on shift, but you know that already.' Another smile, more nervous this time. 'I was checking through some rotas, making sure we had cover for the upcoming weekend, I think. We'd struggled for staffing that week and I wanted to make sure we had safe numbers on shift.'

'Do you do that often, Mike?' DI Leade asked.

'Do what, sorry?'

'Check the rotas and shift cover?'

'Er, yes, I did at that time, when Governor Dominicali was here. It's an important part of the job – making sure that shifts are covered, that you've got the right people in the right places. Some officers work better in different areas of the prison, depending on their skills.'

'And you've been here a while, so you're well placed to know who has what skills and who to place where?' Leade followed up.

'Yes, yes, I suppose so. You get to know your team well when you've worked with them as long as I have. You know what makes them tick and, importantly, what pushes their buttons, pardon the pun.' He gave a nervous laugh.

'Let's stay with that for a minute. We've heard a lot today about the different "teams" in the prison,' said Tomlinson.

'Oh? In what way?' Button frowned.

'Well, it would appear that people have differing views of what *team* they're in. Some seem to think that Governor Dominicali had her own team. Is that something you were aware of?'

He shifted in his chair, unable – or unwilling – to make eye contact with Janette or Leade. 'I'm not sure she had a team, as such, but there were some officers that worked more closely with the governor, I suppose.'

'And you, Mike? Would you say you were part of Niamh Dominicali's team?' asked Leade.

His gaze darted between the detectives. 'Er, yes, I suppose I was. I was one of the management team – we all report to the governor, so yes, I'd be one of her team.'

'What about Bell and Rodriguez?' Leade continued.

'What about them?' Button's tone had hardened.

'Well, they weren't part of the management team, but we have evidence to suggest they were involved in all three of the unexpected deaths we're investigating. Would you say they were in her team? You know, as an insider who'd know these things?' asked Leade.

Button rolled his head around as if to loosen his neck muscles, and ran a finger round inside his shirt collar. 'I-I don't really know.'

'Oh, come on, Mike. You just said you knew your officers well, what made them tick, who should work where. So what about Bell and Rodriguez? What were their special skills? Where did they work best, Mike?'

'I, I...' He wiped a chubby paw across his forehead.

'Or were they part of your team? Were you the one making sure they were free to escort guilty women to their deaths? Is that what they were good at, Mike? Did something go wrong the day Monica escaped? The day Bell and Rodriguez escorted the governor down to Monica's isolation room?'

Button drained his paper cup then immediately refilled it, emptying it again in one go. His gaze darted from Leade to Tomlinson.

Janette jumped in, her tone softer than the one DI Leade had used. 'We can see how much this is weighing on you, Governor Button. The pressure of running this place, under the scrutiny of the prison service, the press and now us. It must be really tough. Let us help you. Tell us what's been going on.'

Still, Mike Button said nothing. Janette carried on softly. 'Do you know what the next steps in our investigation are, Mike?'

He looked at her, the colour rising in his cheeks.

'We're going to pull everyone's bank records and family details. Then we're going to look to see which of your staff might be vulnerable to blackmail, or coercion. How many of them have debt they can't afford, houses, cars, credit cards? Kids at private schools that they couldn't pay for on their prison salaries? Or expensive divorces ... or gambling debt?'

Leade saw Button's eyes flicker at the last part – an involuntary look down and away from Janette when she mentioned divorce and gambling.

'What are we going to find when we look at your finances, Mike?' Leade asked in a flat, neutral tone.

Button undid his tie and collar and put his head in his hands. Leade silently raised a hand to Janette. They sat, looking at Button, waiting.

'Look, I don't know anything about the deaths, but if you say Bell and Rodriguez were involved – well, that's nothing to do with me. The governor used to send for them directly through Claire, her PA.'

'OK, we'll speak to Claire. What else did you want to tell us, Mike?' Janette asked.

'The background checks. What happens to what you find? I mean, what do you do?' Button asked.

'That depends what it is. Why? What are we going to find?' she asked.

'Gambling, the house, car, a divorce, credit I can't afford. Most of the things on your list,' he blurted out.

'Mike, we need to know what kind of trouble you're in, if we're going to be able to help you,' said Leade.

'I've got some pretty big gambling debts. I owe a lot of money to a Chinese gambling syndicate. My ex-wife cleared me out, and I pay for her car and a mortgage on her place. She left me when the gambling got out of control. Then a guy approached me in the pub. He knew everything about me. He said he could make it go away. I should never have got involved, but I needed a way out. I didn't mean for it to carry on so long – just long enough to get a big win and pay all my debts off for good.'

Leade wanted Button to keep talking, and for that they needed silence. He looked at Janette Tomlinson and saw her acknowledge his unspoken instruction. For once she didn't jump in with a question. It took nearly two minutes of silence before Mike Button was uncomfortable enough that he felt the need to fill it. 'He told me all I had to do...' He took a deep breath. 'All I had to do was arrange to have certain officers on shift at specific times. They would bring in some gear and pass it to some of the prisoners. He told me they already had sleepers – staff and prisoners. It was insane. He said that if I didn't go along with it, he'd throw me to the Triads.'

'So, what did you do?' Leade prompted.

'I did as he asked. I took the list of names, I reworked the rotas so that the right staff were on shift at the right times, and it worked like clockwork. The gear came in, it got passed to the prisoners, they sold it on, I got paid.'

'When you say "gear", what do you mean?'

'Er, cocaine, weed, sometimes heroin.'

'Mike, we're going to need that list of names,' said Leade.

Button swallowed hard. His eyes were as red as his cheeks and he looked as if he might be sick. Then he reeled off the names of twelve prison officers, as if he was reading a shopping list. Of the twelve, Leade and Tomlinson had interviewed four that day, including Gill O'Leary. Bell and Rodriguez were also on the list.

When he'd finished, Leade thanked Button for his cooperation, then cleared his throat. 'Mike Button, I'm arresting you on suspicion of supplying Class A drugs. You do not have to say anything, but it may harm your defence if you do not mention when questioned something which you later rely on in court. Anything you do say may be given in evidence. Do you understand?'

There was a pause.

'For the benefit of the recording, Mr Button has nodded,' said Leade. 'Now, Mike, we're going to take you to the car and drive to the station so you can be interviewed. Because I don't want to spook anyone whose name you've just given us, or place you in any unnecessary danger, I will not be handcuffing you, so walk with us to the car without any fuss. Is that clear? Any nonsense and we will handcuff you.'

Button nodded again.

'Mike, is that clear?'

'Yes, yes, it's clear.'

46

From a dense wooded area, a playing field between her and Lomas Baxter's house, Monica watched the commotion she'd caused starting to take hold. First there was the florist's van, adorned with the name of the shop and floral vinyl pictures. Monica had a clear line of sight, but was satisfied that she couldn't be seen. She had tucked herself in behind the trunk of a tall oak tree, about three rows back into the woods. She saw a woman who she assumed was Heidi Baxter come to the door, but couldn't see her reaction. Then she saw the florist pass Heidi the floral arrangement.

'I bet that's a bit confusing, Mrs Baxter,' she muttered. Then Monica waited patiently for the cavalry to arrive. She wasn't disappointed. First came a marked police car, closely followed by Lomas swinging his car fast onto his driveway. She was silently smug at the sight of Lomas and Drew arriving. Then, when she saw another police vehicle arrive and the man who got out getting some kit out of the back, she knew that her flowers had had the desired effect. She stayed behind the tree until she saw the guy leave, carrying what looked like the flowers. The marked car was still there, and the officer inside it hadn't moved. She figured they'd been posted there to keep an eye on Lomas's family. Very wise, she thought.

Lomas clearly wasn't leaving in a hurry, and Monica decided she had better things to be doing with her day. She drove back towards Drew's flat, which was in Fair Oak, near Eastleigh. Monica stuck to the back roads through Durley, and Horton Heath. When she saw a large pub facing the road, with neat gardens and a fenced-off seating area, called the Brigadier Gerard, she knew that she was heading in the right direction. She also knew she was taking a risk, as she came into the village of Fair Oak. There could be CCTV cameras. She turned left at a pub called the Old George then found a spot where she could see the flats where Drew lived without looking conspicuous.

Monica noted the presence of a marked police car on the road outside Drew's flats. She was convinced it was there because of her. She moved, and parked behind a convenience store next to Drew's block of flats, separated by an access road. There was no one around as Monica parked in the furthest corner of the car park, her car facing a thick hedge, a fence to her left.

Checking that nobody was around, Monica pulled herself up and over the fence in one smooth, athletic movement. She stayed close to the hedge that surrounded the large garden belonging to the flats, and made her way to the rear of the block. A neat panel of buzzers, each labelled with the resident's name, was screwed to the wall by the door. Monica ran her finger down the labels until she found one that said 'Taylor – 12'.

'Flat twelve it is, DS Taylor,' said Monica, pressing the buzzer, knowing full well that Drew was with Lomas at his house. She stood back and looked up at the windows that overlooked the garden. There was movement in a window on the middle floor. Since there were eighteen buzzers and three floors, she worked out that there were six flats in each floor, and pressed the buzzers of eight, nine and ten before she got an answer.

'Hello?' came a bright, cheerful voice through the metal speaker.

'Hi, could you buzz me in please? I've got a delivery for flat fourteen.'

'Sure.'

'Thank you.' The door buzzed and Monica yanked it open. She made her way quickly along the corridors and up the first two flights of stairs. The landing was clean and bright, with white walls and a light grey corded carpet. The apple scent of a plug-in air freshener filled the air. A silver plaque on the wall indicated that flat twelve was through the door in front of her. Monica opened the landing door and checked the corridor for cameras. Seeing nothing obvious, she made her way in. Sensor-operated lights lit up as she passed.

Outside flat twelve was a brown mat with the word 'Welcome' written across it in black lettering. There was no one around and no noise coming from adjoining flats. Monica stood for a moment, looking at the front door of Drew's flat. She traced a finger around the chrome-coloured numbers in the centre of the door. She tried the handle; it didn't move.

'Oh well, worth a try.' She gave a shrug and an amused smile.

Monica took one of the small envelopes from her pocket and tried to slide it under the door. It wouldn't go. She checked the seal that ran between the door and the frame and slid the envelope lengthways into the thin gap, resting the bottom edge of the envelope on the door handle. Just as she was checking it was in place and not about to slip out, a voice came from behind her.

'Tom's away for a couple of weeks, I think.'

Monica turned slowly to see a woman, probably in her late fifties, with curly shoulder-length hair, glowing white teeth and great dress sense, smiling at her.

'Tom? I was meant to deliver this to a Miss Drew Taylor. The button downstairs said Taylor was number twelve.'

'Oh, it is, but Tom Taylor lives in number twelve. Drew lives upstairs next to me at number eighteen. I can pop it outside her door if you like?'

'Number eighteen, you say?' said Monica, ignoring the offer of help.

'Yes, up to the top floor and left. Drew's is the end flat,' said the smiley woman, helpfully opening the door to the stairwell for Monica.

'Thanks. That could have been embarrassing,' said Monica, trying to sound relaxed.

'She won't be in either, she'll be at work,' said her impromptu guide as they walked up the stairs. Monica walked a step behind the woman as they ascended to the top floor. The landing was identical to the one below, and even smelled the same. Monica held the door open, allowing Smiley to walk through first. They turned left and walked past flat sixteen on the left. A thumping bass line emanated from inside. Monica could hear Eminem spitting the lyrics to 'Sing for the Moment'.

'His music's always that loud. It doesn't bother me, though, I quite like a bit of Eminem. Anyway, this is me,' said Smiley, putting her key in her door.

'Thanks for your help. I appreciate it,' Monica said, coming alongside the woman.

'No problem.'

Just as Smiley pushed her door open, Monica's hand shot out and grabbed a fistful of the woman's hair. Monica smashed her head against her door. She briefly saw the shocked look on the woman's face. It was instantly replaced by fear as Monica slammed the side of her face against the door for a second time. The music coming out of flat sixteen made it impossible for anyone to hear the attack. Monica threw her victim through the doorway. The woman collapsed in a heap on the floor and tried to scramble to her feet. Monica punched her, hard and fast, in the temple and the woman crumpled back to the floor, unconscious.

Monica turned, removed the keys and closed the door behind her.

'Right, Smiley, you looked at my face for far too long – *and* you live next door to the lovely DS Taylor. Double whammy for you, I'm afraid.' She picked up an envelope that lay on a white console table near the door.
'Michelle Batchelor, nice to meet you, I guess.' She took

hold of the back of Michelle's fitted leather jacket and lifted her upper body up off the floor. She dragged her along the floor into an impeccably tidy lounge-diner, noticing how light she was. Monica pulled a pale grey chair out from a glass dining table that had a vase of white lilies in the centre. She still held Michelle in her other hand. Without any real effort, she sat her on the chair. The woman slumped forward as Monica released her grip, forcing her to stop Michelle falling off the chair. She leaned her back. Her head lolled to one side. She was still out cold.

Monica looked around the flat, keeping half an eye on her unconscious captive. It was beautifully decorated in greens and greys, with carefully selected pictures and ornaments. 'It's a lovely place you have here, Michelle,' she said, wandering through an archway into an equally well appointed kitchen. She opened a couple of drawers and quickly found a new-looking role of packing tape and a bright green microfibre cloth. She took them back to the unmoving Michelle. Pulling her arms behind the chair, Monica wrapped the tape around the woman's wrists several times, binding them together. Then she opened Michelle's mouth, pushed the cloth in and secured it with a piece of tape. Monica looked at the silent, gagged and bound woman, then she ran her thumb gently along Michelle's face.

Satisfied that she wasn't at risk of raising the alarm if she came to, Monica left Michelle for a minute. She popped out of the flat to Drew's door and repeated the delivery method she'd attempted at flat twelve. This time she wasn't disturbed; music still boomed from flat sixteen. The envelope wouldn't wedge in between the frame and door, so she set it on the door mat, leaned it against the door and returned to flat seventeen. Monica had only just got through the door of Michelle's flat when she changed her mind.

'I think I'll hold on to this, DS Taylor. I might just keep an eye on you first.' She retrieved the note. Monica looked in the fridge and took out four eggs, some milk and butter, then proceeded to make scrambled eggs. Michelle's kitchen was intuitively laid out, and Monica found her way around easily. The pans, plates and even the pepper were all where she would have expected to find them. She worked quickly and was just plating up her eggs onto a couple of slices of toasted granary bread, when Michelle started to stir.

'Oh fuck, really, Michelle? Now you're going to wake up?' she said.

Monica took a seat opposite Michelle at the dining table and tucked into her eggs. She looked up from her food to see Michele blinking her eyes into focus, looking groggy. She saw the familiar panic set in when Michelle realised she was gagged and bound. She started making the muffled screams and shouts that, again, Monica had heard many times before.

'Hush, Michelle, I'm trying to have some lunch. Just sit there and be quiet. I'll answer all your questions in the fullness of time.'

Michelle tried to stand up, but her arms were bound too tightly to the chair and she couldn't swing herself forward far enough. Monica rolled her eyes and put her fork down. When she stood up, Michelle kicked out at her.

'Fine, have it your own way,' said Monica, grabbing the roll of tape with one hand and one of Michelle's ankles with the other. She taped the woman's ankles to the chair legs. Despite her attempts to kick and struggle, it didn't take long.

'Now I'm going to finish my eggs. Then we'll talk.' Monica did exactly that. When she'd finished she took her plate through to the kitchen and washed it, putting on the draining board and drying her hands with a tea towel that matched the lemon kitchen accessories.

'I'm going to take your gag off, but if you scream or shout, I'll hit you so hard you'll wish you'd stayed quiet. Do we understand each other?'

Michelle nodded vigorously.

'Good. OK then.' Monica removed the tape and slowly pulled the cloth out of Michelle's mouth. The woman did as instructed and didn't scream.

'Who are you, and what do you want?' she asked, gasping for air.

'Oh good, two easy ones to start with.' Monica's tone was chatty. 'My name is Monica Silverman.' She saw the reaction on Michelle's face that she'd hoped for, and smiled. 'And what I want is for your neighbour, Detective Sergeant Taylor, to be dead. Which she will be, as soon as I get her on her own for long enough. Next question.'

'What do you want with me?'

'Well, nothing, really. You're just in the wrong place at the wrong time, as they say. It was very helpful of you to let me know that DS Taylor doesn't live downstairs. It would have been embarrassing if her neighbour had got the note I've written for her. Death threats don't have the same ring when they're third-hand.' She smiled at Michelle, who was clearly struggling to comprehend what she was being told. Her teary gaze darted around the room and she pushed against her bindings, trying to move, but to no avail.

'Are you going to kill me?'

'I had thought about leaving you alone when you spoke to me at first. But then, when you told me you were DS Taylor's next-door neighbour – well, you made it impossible for me to walk away and leave you. I'm sure you understand. You've not only seen me, but you've spoken to me – and now look.' She waved an open hand up and down in front of Michelle. 'It's just all gone a bit far, hasn't it?'

'No! I don't have to tell anyone you've been here. I don't talk to Drew much – she's hardly ever in. I can just avoid her. No one has to know you were here.'

'Oh, but they will. The minute I turned my back and the immediate threat to your life you're feeling now, had subsided, you'd be straight on the phone to the police, doing your civic duty. Then the police would come knocking and would want to know what you'd seen, and you'd just blurt it out. I know you would.'

'I wouldn't, I really wouldn't. I'll never tell another living soul.'

'Oh, Michelle, I wish I could believe you. But I don't. Tell me, do you have a shower, or a bath?'

'A bath, with a shower over it. Why?'

Monica didn't answer. She stuffed the cloth back into Michelle's mouth and reapplied the tape, despite the woman shaking her head in protest. Michelle was taking deep panicky breaths in through her nose, which

Monica knew would subside after a few seconds. She waved a calming hand. 'Shh, control your breathing or you'll hyperventilate, and that would be really difficult to manage with a gag in your mouth.'

Michelle did as she was advised. Monica turned and went to check the bathroom. A mustard and grey hand-towel was draped neatly over a chrome towel rail and a spotless glass shower screen ran halfway along a pristine white bath.

A minute or two later, Monica returned to her terrified captive. 'You really do have a lovely, lovely home,' she said to Michelle as she lifted her, chair and all, and carried her through to the bathroom. She lifted her over the side of the bath and set the chair down in the middle of it.

'Oh, you look confused. Bless you. I guess I've had more practice than you. So, you're sat here so that you don't make a mess – and if you do, it's easy to clean up. I wouldn't want to spoil your lovely flat.'

Monica reached down to the bathroom floor and picked up a large knife she'd taken from the kitchen. Michelle saw the knife and her eyes widened. She began to shake her head frantically.

'Now, now, try to calm yourself. It will make things much easier and it won't even hurt that much. Anyway, before you go, I want to thank you for being so helpful and for letting me use your flat. It will make my getting to your gorgeous neighbour so much easier.'

Monica placed a hand on the top of Michelle's head, holding it still. Then she raised the knife, placing the tip to the right of Michelle's windpipe. Michelle tried in vain to move her head, desperate pleas coming from her gagged mouth and tears streaming down her face.

In one swift movement Monica drove the knife into Michelle's neck. The blade severed her terrified captive's carotid artery and blood pumped from the hole in her neck as soon as she withdrew the knife.

She stood and watched as blood soaked Michelle's body, the bath and the tiled wall. Michelle's eyes swam as the blood drained from her body. As any remaining muscle tension ebbed away and Michelle's head fell forward, Monica wiped the blade of the knife with a handful of toilet roll. She flushed the blood-stained tissue and left Michelle's body in the bath, returning to the kitchen, where she filled the kettle and flicked the TV on.

47

Lomas had a knot in his stomach as he drove back to the station, leaving Carl, the uniformed officer, in his house with Heidi and the kids. He was under strict instructions to let no one in, and Heidi had reluctantly agreed to the three of them staying in, and away from the door, for the rest of the day.

On their return, Drew had gone to join Marie Carlton and prepare for the TV appearance. He'd told her to break a leg and smirked as she flicked her hair theatrically and stalked off as if she was on a catwalk.

Lomas had heard back from Grayson relatively quickly. He could find no evidence to suggest that Monica had touched the flowers, or card, as they'd suspected. She was brazen, but not stupid.

While they'd been at the house, Drew had tracked down the mobile number of the owner of the florist. Calling them was Lomas's first job.

The phone was answered quickly by a woman called Sue, who sounded surprised when he introduced himself. 'You made a funeral arrangement earlier today, saying “RIP Heidi”. Can you tell me about the person who ordered it, please?’

‘Yeah, sure. It was a woman in a big hoodie and jeans. It was a little bit weird, if I’m honest.’

‘Weird how?’

‘Well, she had her hood pulled down low over her face and didn’t really make eye contact. But I guess we all deal with grief differently, I suppose, poor thing.’

‘Would you recognise the person you met if you saw a picture of them, Sue?’

‘I would imagine so. She was quite a big-built woman – you know, stocky.’

‘Great. Do you have time to pop into Southampton police station today? It would be really helpful.’

‘Er, yes, of course. I need to sort dinner out for my kids, but I could come in this evening.’

‘Perfect. Ask for me when you get here. I’m DI Lomas Baxter. I’ll come and meet you in reception. Thank you.’ He ended the call.

Next stop was Grant Carver, to see how the CCTV trawl was going. Grant was zooming in on an image when Lomas reached his desk. He spun around in his chair. ‘Hello, boss. We’ve had a bit of a result with the local cameras around Florence Road.’

‘Really? What have you found?’ Lomas asked.

'To start with, nothing. The local shops and street cameras didn't catch Monica after the camera on the door of Southsea Rocks Hotel lost her. But a couple of the guys went door-knocking around the immediate vicinity and we've got some coverage from a couple of households and a pub – the Florence Arms. It's on the corner of Florence Road and St Catherine's Street. We've managed to piece together some footage that shows her leaving the hotel, on the hotel camera, then walking around onto St Catherine's, on the pub camera. Then she crosses the road and two cameras on the back of houses, on the end of Onslow Road, pick her up getting into a car that's parked in an off-road space. I sent the footage over to Lisa, our gait-analysis specialist, and asked her to compare it to the video of Monica leaving the prison. Lisa confirmed that, based on the way she walks, there's a high likelihood that this is Monica. I was just zooming in on this when you walked in.' He pointed to the screen.

'Sounds impressive. Don't let me slow you down, Grant. Let's see you in action.'

'Er, yeah.' Grant zoomed in on the image of the car. Lomas leaned in to get a better view. 'Can you clean that up?'

'Yes, I'm pretty sure I can. The new cameras are quite good quality. I should be able to make it clearer.' He worked as he spoke, and the car became clearer in the centre of the screen.

'That looks like a Mondeo estate, which would match the style of car Sarah Marley described. Can you zoom in on the registration?'

Grant played around with the image some more , focusing on the number plate.

'EH10 VDU,' Grant read aloud. 'Do you want me to run that through PNC, boss?'

'You read my mind.'

It didn't take long for the car to be confirmed as a grey Mondeo estate, registered to a Mr Brian Evans of North End, Portsmouth. It was taxed, MOTd and insured.

'Great work, Grant. Let's get someone round to pay Mr Evans a visit. Look's like Monica's cloned his plates. Can you set up an ANPR alert on that reg and see where it pings?'

'I'll do it now.'

Lomas patted Grant on the shoulder then left to speak to Gurdeep, to see what he'd found in the historic interview records.

'Both sisters gave similar accounts of Monica flying into a rage quickly when challenged, or when they answered back,' said Gurdeep. 'They both talked to Monica during their captivity and both gave really clear accounts of her reaction to any kind of back-chat or non-compliance.'

'That's what I thought. Thanks, G.'

Lomas hotfooted it up to Marie Carlton's office to update her on what the team had found so far and to fill her in on his current direction of thought. 'I'm hoping that us taking the hotel and the vicarage, and plastering her face all over the TV – with you and Drew later today – will push her into making mistakes. She doesn't have the greatest control over her anger and her paranoia must be off the scale. The Lydia Bartholomew murder was out of character. It was rushed and risky – not Monica's usual style at all.'

'How's Heidi doing?' Marie asked.

'She's OK, thanks. Not happy about having to stay indoors and having one of our uniforms on duty. But she'd rather that than her and the kids having to clear out again, like they did last time.'

'How about you? How are you managing all this? It can't be easy Monica getting so close to home again. I'm pretty sure I know where your head's at with this, but you know that if you want off the case, you've only got to say the word.'

'I appreciate that, Marie, I really do. But all it does is make me more determined to catch her.'

'I know, but make sure you keep talking.'

'I will, thanks. Anyway, what time are you and Drew on TV tonight?'

Marie smiled. 'Subtle change of topic there. We're on local BBC and ITV news straight after the six o'clock news, with a national pick-up likely on the ten o'clock. They've managed to put together a simultaneous broadcast on *South Today* and *Meridian*, so we cover as much ground as possible. They've also teed up a couple of minutes with the Minister of Justice straight afterwards. They're keen to keep the ball rolling on the Cat. A escapee angle, and were more than happy to have something fresh to put out there. I was going to get Drew to do the localised information part of the press conference, focusing on Portsmouth and linking in the CCTV footage – she did that well the last time – and I'll top and tail it with the formalities. What do you think?'

'I think she'll be fine. You might just need to run it through with her before you go live, but I'm sure she'll come across well again. I also think that if Monica sees it, it'll push her buttons, seeing Drew up there with you again.' Lomas said.

'OK, let's run with that then. She's gone off to get something to eat. I'll talk her through it when she gets back.'

'I'm going to give Sherlock a call and see how he got on in West Sussex, examining Lydia Bartholomew. And I'm hopeful that we'll get an ANPR hit on the car.'

***

The TV slots went smoothly and the Minister of Justice, live from Downing Street, immediately after Marie and Drew's segment, spoke in sombre tones about how Monica's escape was a matter of the utmost concern to the prison service. He also made a point of emphasising that the prison were supporting the police's efforts to bring Monica back into custody. He dodged a couple of questions by the assembled press about how the investigation was going and how he would feel if people died as a result of prison service incompetence. He disappeared behind the door of Number Ten after concluding his speech.

The TV news cut back to the newsreader, who began her recap. 'Monica Silverman has been at large for five days. Hampshire police believe they have narrowed the search for Silverman to the Portsmouth area...'

Lomas flicked off the TV in the briefing room and turned to his team. 'Right, people, we've taken some huge steps over the last couple of days. Obtaining the clear CCTV image you just saw Drew put out for the public, the hotel in Southsea and the vicarage in Portsmouth. But we have another dead body added to Monica's tally and a whole host of people under our protection. We must capitalise on our momentum. Grayson's team have finished with the hotel room. They found plenty of evidence of Monica being there, including a spare phone, which is not the one we've been tracking, and over £8,000 in cash, stuffed in a bag. In the last couple of hours we've also had a result from CCTV analysis that Grant and his team have been doing. We now believe that Monica is driving this grey Ford Mondeo.'

Tina flashed two images on the screen as Lomas spoke: one of the car and a close-up of the registration number.

'We know she's cloned the plates of another Mondeo, which belongs to a Mr Brian Evans of North End, Portsmouth. We've been in touch with Mr Evans and his car is legal and in his possession. However, we've set up an ANPR alert on the plate and we'll check in with him and check his whereabouts if we get a hit. The net is closing on Monica Silverman, ladies and gents, and she must be starting to feel it. We know that her normal methods of operation are both well planned and carefully executed. With her options starting to become more limited and her face all over national TV, she may start to act out of character. She may become spontaneous, reckless and desperate. This could lead her to make mistakes.'

A hand went up at the back of the room.

'Yes, Pete?'

'Is it true that Monica has targeted your family again, boss?'

Lomas exhaled and he felt the knot return to his stomach. He nodded to Tina. 'The image you can see on the screen is a floral arrangement that was delivered to my wife earlier today by a local florist. The owner of the florist is on her way in for an interview, but it looks like Monica ordered these flowers in person.

Tina changed the image to a close-up of the card.

'Grayson has examined both and has found nothing that indicates that Monica touched, or handled, the floral arrangement or the card. This has been confirmed by the owner of the florist. Any questions?'

Lomas cast a slow glance around the room. Satisfied that there were no questions, he ended the briefing.

48

Evening was drawing in by the time DI Leade and DC Tomlinson got back to the station from the prison. Mike Button sat quietly in the back of the car. He hadn't said a word since he'd been arrested. He remained quiet as they led him, by the arm, through to the custody sergeant's desk, who took him through the formalities of his detention after DI Leade had explained the grounds for his arrest.

'Yes, I think I should probably have a solicitor,' said Button when the desk sergeant explained his rights to him.

Tomlinson carried out a brief search of Button, taking his wallet, keys and prison ID, passing them over the desk to be bagged. Leade watched Mike's face the whole time. His expression didn't change; he had the demoralised look of someone who was broken. He barely lifted his head when he spoke, and his gaze was fixed on the floor in front of him.

As the cell door banged shut, Leade looked in through the observation panel. Button had gone straight to the bench-like bed that ran along the back wall and flopped down on it, burying his face in the thin mattress.

Stephen Leade went to grab a coffee from a pot that one of the CID team had just brewed. When he walked into the kitchen, the rich, nutty smell pulled him in. He stood for a moment, cup in hand, contemplating the twist their investigation had taken.

With three prisoner deaths so close together, Niamh Dominicali's prison had the highest percentage of unexpected deaths per head of prison population in the UK. Red flags were flying for Leade. But now, he had the added complexity of the drug network in the same prison. He chugged the coffee, refilled his mug and primed the percolator ready for the next person, then made his way over to the hot-desks he and Tomlinson had been given while they were in Southampton.

He'd given Janette the green light to go and get some food while they waited for the solicitor who would be appointed to represent Mike Button. He sat at his desk and removed his notebook from his bag.

Scribbles and lines linking people's names ran across his notebook like a partly formed spider's web. But the picture he was building had gaps in it. He could see how Button could have been running the drug ring – that much was clear. He was a down-on-his-luck gambler, in debt up to his eyeballs. It wasn't a stretch to imagine him being tapped up to orchestrate the supply of drugs into the prison. Leade had seen similar stories before, and Button fitted the brief. Drug gangs were adept at picking off the weak and easily manipulated, then exploiting them until they'd served their purpose. Leade was also pretty sure that once they'd pulled the background information on the twelve officers Button had given them, they'd find similar reasons for their involvement in the corruption. The lines on his pad ran from the starting point – Button's name – to the others, with notes by each name.

But the dead prisoners? No, he didn't see Button being involved with them. He was positive that the deaths were suspicious, but not linked to the drug dealing. The more he thought about it, the more he came back to the other starting point on his web of lines – Niamh.

As he was swirling the last of his coffee in the bottom of his mug, he saw Lomas walk past. He stood and half walked, half jogged, to catch up with him.

'Lomas?' he said as he got closer.

'Hello, Stephen. How's it going?' Lomas stopped and turned towards him.

'Have you got five?'

'Sure. Come on through. I was just going to get a cuppa – want one?'

Leade thought briefly about the two mugs of coffee he'd just had, but said yes anyway, figuring the extra caffeine wouldn't do him any harm. They got their drinks, making small talk about family and the weather, then walked through to Lomas's office. Leade closed the door and took a seat opposite Lomas.

'I wanted to pick your brains about something,' Leade said.

'Oh?'

'Janette and I were at the prison today, interviewing the officers that were on duty on the days the three women died. The last one we interviewed was the acting governor—'

'Mike Button.'

'That's him. Anyway, a few of the officers referred to there being more going on at the prison than met the eye. To start with, they all thought that we were there to find a scapegoat, to clear Niamh Dominicali. But, once we got past that, they started to talk and to open up to us about a drug network in the prison.'

'That took a bit of a turn, then?' said Lomas.

'Just a bit. They don't trust each other, and I think a couple of them figured that if they spoke up first, it would look better for them. When we got to Mike Button, we were pretty sure that he'd played a role in something – either the deaths or the drugs. When we pushed him, using the threat of financial records as leverage, he caved and basically confessed to being the person behind it. He's got massive gambling debts to a Chinese syndicate and an ex-wife who sounds like she's bleeding him dry.'

'Wow, so what have you done?'

'We've arrested him. He's downstairs in a cell. We're going to do a more in-depth interview with him once his lawyer gets here. The thing is, I don't think he's behind the deaths.'

'Do you think the deaths are suspicious?'

'I do, but I can't see Button being involved. He's already far enough out of his depth with the drugs, never mind dead prisoners. But the officers made quite a big thing out of there being cliques and special teams within the prison, and on more than one occasion they hinted at Dominicali having her own team of her favourites.'

'So where's your gut taking you?' Lomas asked.

'Well, you know the two officers that Monica killed when she escaped?'

'Bell and Rodriguez?'

'Yeah. Now, it appears, from what I've heard today, that they used to be summoned by the governor via her PA. But no one knew what for. *And* they were the last ones to be seen with all three dead women. More than one of our interviewees can place Bell and Rodriguez with the dead prisoners in the minutes before they died, but none of them could give us a definitive answer as to why they were with them, or where they might have been going.'

'So, you have a link between the governor and Bell and Rodriguez. And you have positive links between those two and the dead women?'

'Yep.'

'So, again, what's your gut telling you?' Lomas asked.

'That Niamh Dominicali was pulling the strings of Bell and Rodriguez and they're directly linked to the suspicious deaths of all three women. The only thing I can't figure out is why. What possible motive could there be for killing three prisoners? And how did they actually die?'

'I don't know about motive, but if you want another opinion on how they died maybe Sherlock could have a look at the reports?'

'I'd need to get them from the original coroner.'

'It sounds like you've got a strong enough reason to me. I'm sure you could get sign-off on it,' said Lomas.

'So, what do you think?'

'About which bit?'

'About the motive. If they were killed and those three were in on it, why?' Leade asked, rubbing a hand over his head.

'I don't know, mate. Have you done background on the three dead women to see if they're connected in any way? And similarly with Dominicali, Bell and Rodriguez? There might be a link there we don't know about yet.'

'We haven't done that yet. Sounds like we've got more work to do.'

'Is it worth pulling Dominicali in under caution and seeing if she cracks?' Lomas suggested.

'Maybe. I might give Bill Bennett a call too.'

'Who's Bill Bennett?' Lomas asked.

'He's the lead investigator for the prison service investigation into Niamh's actions around the escape. They interviewed her about it yesterday.'

'Got to be worth a shot. See how it went, what he thinks of her.'

'Cheers, mate. That was really helpful,' Leade said.

'I'm not sure I did anything, but no worries.'

Leade left Lomas's office and headed back to his desk. He flicked through his notebook and found Bill Bennett's phone number, at the same time taking a bite out of a digestive biscuit from a packet in his drawer. He brushed crumbs onto the floor and dialled Bill's number.

'Mr Bennett, DI Leade here. We spoke recently about the investigation you're doing into Governor Dominicali.'

'Ah yes, hello, Detective Inspector Leade. How can I help you?'

'Sorry to call you on a Sunday evening, but I wondered if you could let me know how your interview with Niamh went. What was your impression of her?'

'No problem, you're not disturbing me – there's nothing much on TV these days. Is there anything you'd like to know specifically?'

'How did she present to you? What was her demeanour during the interview?'

'To start with, it was fine. She was very professional and clear in her answers, then she and my co-investigating officer, Maggie Sanders, began to rub each other up the wrong way. Things became a bit tetchy and I took a break for a few minutes.'

'What did Niamh do during your break?'

'She went outside to get some air, which was understandable, given the circumstances and the questions she was facing.'

'Of course. And after the break?'

'More of the same, I'm afraid. There were quite a few heated exchanges. Then it ended quite abruptly...'

'How so?'

'Well, we were close to wrapping up anyway, but after answering one of Maggie's more pointed questions, Niamh began to sweat and became very pale. Then she ran out of the room across the corridor to the ladies' toilet, and I believe she was sick.'

'Physically sick?'

'Yes. She looked awful. I put it down to a stress reaction, brought on by reliving the events surrounding the escape.'

'What happened then?'

'As I say, we'd pretty much covered all the ground we needed to cover and I ended the interview.'

'Can I ask what conclusion you and Maggie drew from your interview?'

'Well, on the face of it, Niamh made a decision to help a convicted killer and Category A prisoner to escape. She presented some mitigation in terms of her fears for the safety of her team, but there are protocols in place for such an event, which she didn't follow. Now, I don't know whether that was due to the stress of the situation or, as she said, the belief that by cooperating she would save the lives of her staff. The fact remains, she is responsible for her actions. I will be recommending that there's a disciplinary hearing to determine her future.'

'Thank you, that's really helpful. Mr Bennett, could I ask your opinion on something else?'

'Certainly.'

'As you know, I'm investigating a number of unexpected deaths in the wider prison service and how they were dealt with. As part of my investigation, it's become clear that HMP Brookham had the highest number of unexpected deaths in the shortest period of time.'

'Right...' Bill said, his tone enquiring.

'After further investigation, it would appear that the same officers were on shift – and indeed, with each of the dead prisoners – in the minutes before they died.'

'Really?'

'Yes. It appears that the two officers in question seem to have been part of a small team of trusted staff who – how can I put it? – worked more closely with the governor than others. And on every occasion, other officers we questioned placed these two with each of the dead women, as I said earlier, just before their deaths. What they haven't been able to clarify is why the officers were with them, or where they were going.'

'Oh dear. That really doesn't sound great, does it? So what would you like to ask me?'

'I wondered if you'd be happy to join me in a further interview with Niamh Dominicali, to try to establish if there's a link between her and the two officers. Or between her and the dead prisoners?'

There was a pause which was longer than Leade expected, then Bill Bennett answered. 'Yes, I'd be happy to. To be clear, this is part of your investigation and I'd be assisting you? You would be leading the interview. In what capacity would I be there?'

'As a technical expert in prison procedure and protocol. How does that sound?'

'That works. When were you thinking?'

'If we can arrange it, I'd like to bring Niamh back in tomorrow. Does that work for you?'

'Yes, I can be available tomorrow. Just let me know what time.'

They rounded off the call and Leade took another biscuit from the packet just as Janette appeared, holding aloft a bag of KFC.

49

Monica lay on Michelle Batchelor's sofa, her foot on the corner of a knotted grey footstool. She emptied the remains of a large pack of cheesy Doritos into her mouth and flicked through the TV channels, looking for something to watch that wasn't a true crime programme or a cooking competition. She sighed and started her trawl again from BBC 1.

'Monica Silverman has now been on the run from police for five days. Police are confident that they are closing in on the multiple murderer. They have narrowed her whereabouts down to the Portsmouth area following successful night-time raids on two properties in the city yesterday. We're now going to a live press conference being held by Detective Chief Inspector Marie Carlton and Detective Sergeant Drew Taylor,' said a newsreader.

'Huh – closing in, really? Let's see what you have to say, neighbour,' she said, unscrewing the lid from a bottle of Coke Zero.

The press conference started with DCI Carlton giving a confident appraisal of the police's activity to date, including the successful identification and securing of two properties. 'We would urge members of the public to come forward with any information they may have as to the whereabouts of Miss Silverman. However, and I cannot stress this enough, if you do see, or think you've seen, Miss Silverman, do not approach her. She is very dangerous. Call police immediately. I'll now hand over to Detective Sergeant Taylor, who will give more information.'

The camera panned to show both detectives, then zoomed in tighter on Drew. 'Yesterday afternoon a woman escaped from an address in Portsmouth where she was being held captive. Forensic officers are now searching the property. Through her tenacity and courage, she was able to escape and raise the alarm. She is safe and well and is now under police protection.'

Monica could feel her eye twitch returning as Drew spoke. 'Fucking bitch!' she yelled at the TV, throwing the bottle of Coke across the room. 'Tenacity and courage? More like blind luck.'

'We are exploring other promising lines of enquiry at the moment. As DCI Carlton has said, we ask any members of the public who believe they may be able to help us locate Miss Silverman to contact us immediately.

Crimestoppers has offered a reward of £50,000 for information leading to her arrest and conviction.'

The picture cut to a full-screen, zoomed-in image of Monica taken by what looked like a CCTV camera.

Monica screamed, leapt off the sofa, picked up the footstool and hurled it across the room. It smashed into a shelving unit, sending ornaments and framed pictures crashing to the floor. Every muscle in her body tensed. She took two giant strides across to the shelves, grabbing them with both hands and hurling the unit across the room. She spun around, snatched up a glass vase from beside the TV and smashed it against the wall. The destruction only fuelled Monica's anger further. Sweat popped from her forehead as she drove her elbow, then her fist, through the lounge door. Lumps of wood splintered and fell to the floor on the other side.

'Who the fuck do they think they are? Fucking closing in on me? I don't think so, DS Taylor. You wait until you come home – you'll be more than closing in then,' she spat.

She stalked through to the kitchen and threw open a cupboard door, banging it against the one adjacent to it. She recalled seeing some bottles of alcohol in the cupboard when she'd been looking for food earlier. She took out a bottle of vodka and a glass, half-filled it and topped it up with Coke. Monica downed half the glass in one go, shuddering at the strength of the drink, then raised it again and drained it. She refilled it straight away and sat at the dining table, bottle in one hand, glass in the other.

'Think, Monica, think. What could they mean by "lines of enquiry"? What could they have found at the hotel or vicarage? Maybe they've spotted the car somewhere? Fuck!' She took another drink, again reacting to the strength of the vodka with a shake of her head.

Someone began speaking on the TV. 'Monica Silverman escaped from this prison on Wednesday.'

She looked up to see a man in a suit and tie standing outside the prison gates. 'We understand that the governor, Niamh Dominicali, is suspended, pending an investigation. Earlier this week, Ms Dominicali responded aggressively to reporters who tried to speak to her outside her home about her involvement in the escape. The Minister of Justice, who spoke outside Downing Street, is said to be receiving constant updates on the progress of the police investigation into Miss Silverman's escape.'

Monica laughed and took another swig. 'Sounds like you're having a pretty shitty week too, Governor.' She raised her glass to the TV. 'Good. Fucking corrupt bitch.'

Her senses were prickling as the newsreader moved on, speaking to his colleague. 'As you've heard, Kate, the police are now confident that they are narrowing down their search for Monica Silverman. We'll keep you up to date on this tense and fast-moving hunt as it develops. Roger Shepperton, *BBC South Today*.'

Monica launched the near-empty vodka bottle at the TV. It bounced off the wall just to the right of the screen. She tried to blink away the fuzzy feeling that was developing. Monica had never been much of a drinker; she'd never seen the point in it, and it hadn't done anything to help her athletic endeavours. Grabbing the TV remote, she changed the channel. A woman with a mouthful of very white teeth and a game-show smile popped up on the screen.

Monica groaned, curling her lip in disgust. Just then, she heard a door closing out in the hallway. She dashed through and pressed her face against Michelle's front door, looking through the peephole. The Eminem fan at sixteen, who had been conveniently playing his music so loudly when Monica had attacked Michelle, was locking the door to his flat. He was tall and skinny and wore a smart blue suit. Monica was surprised by his appearance; she'd expected him to look different. As he turned to walk away she could see discreet EarPods hanging from his ears. He began to whistle as he disappeared from view.

Monica returned to the kitchen. Opening the drinks cupboard again, she scanned the eclectic mix of alcohol, looking for something else to drink. She picked an almost full bottle of Kraken spiced rum and took it over to the sofa, where she'd left the half-empty bottle of Coke. She poured an unhealthy amount of rum into her glass and topped it up with the mixer, taking a slug as soon as she'd poured it.

She settled on a movie channel showing *Terminator 2. This should kill a couple of hours,* she thought, resting the glass of rum against her stomach. She glanced up at a metal-framed clock on the living-room wall, closing one eye to help her focus. 9.30 p.m. She started to plan her next moves, letting the movie play in the background like a soundtrack to her evolving thoughts.

50

Leade and Tomlinson went to collect Mike Button from the custody sergeant and take him for interview.

'How's he been, Frank?' Leade asked the sergeant.

'Fine. He hasn't really moved, except for when his brief came and he had his phone call.'

'How long did he spend with his solicitor?'

'Not long. He was in and out pretty quickly. She's waiting upstairs.' Frank rolled his eyes at the mention of the solicitor. 'You should probably know about his call, though.'

'Oh? How come?'

'He called Niamh Dominicali. Got quite agitated too.'

Leade saw anger flash across Janette's face.

'Why the hell was he allowed to call her?' she asked.

'He said he was giving me his ex-wife's number. But then he started shouting at her. Telling her that he knew what she'd done with Bell and ... and...'

'Rodriguez?' Janette offered.

'Yeah, that's it. I think he'd have gone further if he hadn't realised I was listening to him. Anyway, when I clocked it wasn't the ex, I ended the call,' said Frank.

'Hmm, OK. Thanks, Frank. Can we have him, then?' said Leade, wanting to move things on.

'I'll go and get him.'

They walked a very sombre-looking Mike Button to an interview room, where they were met by his solicitor, a woman in her late forties, with heavy make-up and frizzy brown hair. Leade had met with her briefly to outline why Button was being detained, and he'd noted that she wore the familiar stressed look of a court-appointed solicitor, who had too many people on their caseload and not enough hours in the day.

They dispensed with the formalities of the interview. Before Leade had a chance to say much, the frizzy-haired woman chipped in. 'I've advised my client to be more considered with his answers than he was earlier on, Detective. I think you may have caught him at a particularly difficult time, given the stress he's under at the moment.'

'I would echo your sentiments, Mrs Levison. I think your advice to be considered in his answers is definitely in his best interest.' Leade gave the lawyer a smile, which she didn't return.

'So, Mike, let's talk about your finances. We've done some checking and you're in quite a predicament. You're up to your neck in gambling debt to the Chinese. Your ex-wife. And, from what we can tell, quite a wide selection of credit cards. Tell me, how do you make ends meet?' Leade sat back in his chair and folded his arms.

Button looked at his solicitor, who gave a subtle shake of her head. Then he looked back across the table at DI Leade and DC Tomlinson, who were silently waiting for his response. A full minute passed. Then, without looking back at his brief, Mike Button unburdened himself of every detail of his role in the drug ring he'd been running on behalf of what he assumed was a south coast drug dealer. It all went straight on record, including the names of the officers involved.

Despite Leade pushing more than once for the identity of the person pulling the strings, Button maintained that he didn't know and had never met anyone who he would class as being in charge. Leade sat listening intently, watching Mike Button's body language as he spoke. He could see the pressure the acting governor had been under for so long, trying to keep his head above water, not knowing how to get out of the mess he found himself in. Out of the corner of his eye, Leade also saw Button's solicitor look exasperated at her client's apparent need to tell all. He felt a little smug that there was clearly nothing she could do to stop Button once he was in full flow — he'd had his fair share of no comment interviews.

Mike stopped and took a drink of water, and DI Leade took the opportunity to bring up the call. 'Mike, tell me why the one person you chose to call, to tell them you'd been arrested, was Governor Dominicali.'

He saw shock wash over Button's chubby face, but he didn't offer a reply.

'It just seems a bit strange that when you have one call, you don't call a family member, or a lawyer. You called your suspended boss. A bit odd, don't you think?'

Button glanced nervously at his solicitor.

'You don't have to answer,' she said.

'No comment,' Mike said for the first time.

'It's just that the custody sergeant overheard you saying ... what was it again?' He looked at Tomlinson.

'Er, I think it was "I know what you did with Bell and Rodriguez". I think that was it, boss,' said Janette.

'That's it, thank you, DC Tomlinson. So, what are we to make of that, Mike? There are clearly things you know that we don't. So why don't you enlighten us? What *has* the governor been up to?'

'No comment,' he repeated.

'Oh, come on, Mike. We know that "no comment" isn't your style. You've been open with us about the drug dealing, the mess you're in with the syndicate *and* your ex, and that's to your credit.' Leade raised a finger for each of the points of honesty he was crediting Mike with. 'So what else has been going on?'

'No comment.' Mike folded his arms.

'OK, have it your way. We'll just pull Niamh Dominicali and the officers you've named in your statement in and ask them. Someone will tell us.' He let the sentence hang in the air, waiting for a reaction.

'No comment.'

Acknowledging that they weren't going to get anything else out of Button, Leade shrugged and wrapped up the interview. Mike Button looked like a broken man. His round face was flushed as his gaze returned to the table in front of him.

Leade and Tomlinson walked him back to the holding cells. As the custody sergeant opened the cell door, Button paused and cast a look along the row of closed cell doors, then into the one he was about to enter. Leade registered this and held up a hand to Frank.

'Have a good look around, Mike. These are going to be the kind of views you're going to have for a long time. Why don't you do yourself a favour and talk to me about whatever the governor, Bell and Rodriguez were up to? We know that you know. It might even help you when it comes to sentencing. The fact that you cooperated with us and helped us with our enquires might make a judge take a more lenient view.'

Button turned to face him, then backed slowly into his cell. 'No comment, DI Leade.'

Leade nodded at Frank to close the door. It clanged shut with a heavy, permanent sound.

***

Leade and Tomlinson picked up a coffee each. Janette offered the bucket of leftover KFC to Leade. He declined. She shrugged and tucked into a piece of chicken.

'So, what do you think?' she said between bites.

'About which bit?'

'The ranting down the phone at Niamh Dominicali.'

'Well, according to the work you did on the rotas, Bell and Rodriguez were on shift every time there was an unexpected death. That's supported by the statements we got from the officers at the prison. Also, some said that the pair were with seen with each woman just before they died. So, my money is on the two of them either being the actual henchmen or being directly involved with Dominicali and the deaths...'

'And they're dead, so we can't pull 'em in,' Janette interrupted.

'Yeah, that's mildly inconvenient. But we also know that there were cliques and teams within teams – and everything points to Bell and Rodriguez being part of Niamh's team. Put that together with Button choosing to call Niamh when he's in here, and either they were in on it together and he's pissed that he's in here. Or she was behind it somehow and he found out. But the bit I can't get my head around is why? Are there any other links between Dominicali and the dead women?'

'None that I've managed to find so far.'

'Any connection with each other?' Leade asked.

'Nope. Their only connection is being in prison at the same time and all being dead.'

'How about with Bell or Rodriguez?'

'Same again. The only thing they had in common was that they all did some pretty horrendous things.'

'Let's go over their crimes, see if there are any links there then,' said Leade.

'Erm, hang on a minute.' She shuffled through her notes. 'Here it is. Alba White – she found her boyfriend and best friend in bed together. Stabbed them to death with a kitchen knife. She claimed it was a crime of passion and diminished responsibility. Prosecution stated that she knew they were there, had got the knife in advance, and it was premeditated. The judge went with diminished responsibility and gave Alba a lower sentence than expected,' said Janette.

'OK. Who's next?'

'Marjorie Phelps – she set fire to her house with her ex inside. He burned to death, but his nine-year-old daughter was with him, and she also died in the fire. Marjorie, in her own words, had a smart-arse lawyer who helped her to get off lightly. Apparently, according to the people I've managed to speak to about it, she was proud of the fact she'd killed her ex, and wasn't bothered about the girl.'

'She sounds like a piece of work.'

'Yeah, doesn't she? Then there's Rachel Sigvelt – she killed a grandmother of eight with a vacuum cleaner cable in what her defence claimed was a burglary gone wrong. They also played on the fact that, at the time of committing the offence, she was only eighteen and had her whole life ahead of her to become a useful, contributing member of society. There was a bit of an uproar about the judge giving her the very minimum allowed in the sentencing guidelines.'

‘I remember that one. The tabloids came out in support of the family of the deceased, but it didn’t get them anywhere,’ said Leade.

‘That’s the one.’

‘So, we’ve got three women, all dead. Their only connection is that they were in Niamh Dominicali’s prison, had all killed people, and all had sentences on the light side.’

‘That, and they were in at the same time as Monica Silverman,’ said Janette.

‘Interesting – maybe coincidental, but let’s play that out a bit further. Why would Dominicali want these women dead? And what’s the connection with Monica?’ Leade posed the question.

‘What if Dominicali had an issue with the judiciary handing out sentences that were too light, relative to their crimes? She then has people in her prison who aren’t being punished as much as she thinks they deserve to be…’ said Janette.

‘So she decides to dish it out herself…’ Leade continued her thought.

‘And who better to save you getting your hands dirty than an in-house serial killer?’

‘Wow, that’s quite a theory.’

'It is, but it hangs together. Why don't I look into how many times the governor met with Monica?'

'OK, but tread carefully. It won't do us any good if people start clamming up. I'll go and let Lomas know we have a theoretical link between Dominicali and Silverman. Then I'll give Niamh Dominicali a call and ask her to come in tomorrow.'

51

When Drew returned from the TV press conference to the open-plan office, the whole team stood and began a slow, deliberate clap. She waved graciously, acknowledging the sarcasm in the applause but unable to stop a grin cracking across her face. This widened as she reached her desk. Her colleagues had clearly been busy. In the centre was a mocked-up Oscar, with an envelope leaning against it. In capital letters across the front were the words 'And the winner of the Oscar for most convincing police officer goes to DS Drew Taylor'. Next to the Oscar was a bottle of prosecco, a ribbon tied around the neck. To finish the ensemble, taped to her PC monitor was a screenshot taken of Drew from the TV broadcast earlier that evening.

'Thank you – you're all very kind,' she said with a mock-royal wave.

'OK, back to work, you lot,' said Lomas as he approached Drew. 'You did a really good job. Well done.'

'Thanks, boss. The DCI briefed me to within an inch of my life before we went live, and I'm glad she did. It helped take the edge off the nerves.'

'Well, it clearly worked. In fact, you did such a good job, she might even stop asking me to do them.' He smiled.

Drew started to dismantle the display on her desk. She liked it to be clear.

'Stephen Leade arrested Mike Button for supplying drugs into the prison while you've been out. He just called to say that he and Janette are exploring a theory linking Niamh Dominicali, and possibly Monica, with the three dead prisoners.' Lomas spoke while she tidied up.

She stopped what she was doing. 'Really? That would be a hell of a thing to pull together. How have they arrived at that?'

Lomas explained Leade and Tomlinson's theory. Drew nodded along as he spoke. 'It sounds plausible. What about the vicarage? How are Grayson's team getting on?'

'He called me about half an hour ago. They've identified plenty of evidence, they believe, that will link Monica and the previous victims to the address.'

'Wow, that would be good – when we catch her, that is.'

'We'll catch her, don't you worry.' He seemed very positive. The progress they'd made in recent hours and days had really put a spring back in his step. 'Oh, and the florist came in and positively identified Monica. It was definitely her that ordered the flowers for Heidi but, as we thought, she didn't touch anything. Even asked the florist to write the card the way she wanted it done, said she'd hurt her hand.'

Drew caught sight of Nick over Lomas's shoulder. He made eye contact with her and gave her a smile. Lomas must have noticed her return the smile, as he glanced over his shoulder.

'Why I don't let you finish up tidying your desk and catch up with your colleagues?' he said with a smile. 'Great job this evening. Why don't you get off home?'

She felt like a naughty schoolgirl; being caught smiling at someone across a classroom, but it passed quickly. She knew Lomas was realistic enough to accept that coppers often began relationships with other officers, and she was pretty sure he trusted her to keep it out of the office, which she would, whatever *it* was.

Lomas walked off towards Tina Ashford who, Drew figured, must be working flat out to pull the evidence strands together.

Nick came over with a tentative smile on his face. 'You good?'

'Yeah, I am. Were you behind this?' she asked, waving a hand over her desk.

'Maybe some of it.' His smile broadened. 'You did really well on TV tonight. The boss was well impressed.'

'Aw, thanks, that's sweet. I'm getting out of here in a minute – it's been a long day.'

'I'll be done soon. Don't suppose you fancy getting a drink?'

She glanced at her watch. 'It's half ten. We're not going to get a drink anywhere tonight.'

'Oh yeah, suppose not.' He looked crestfallen.

'Do you fancy coming over to mine? For a drink, I mean.' Drew felt the need to be clear.

'Er, yeah, sure, that would be great. I've got a few things to finish off, but I'll only be about another quarter of an hour...'

'Well, I'll get off. You come over when you're done.' She grabbed a yellow sticky note and a pen from her desk. 'Here's my address and here's the door code. It'll save me buzzing you in.' *It'll also give me a chance to make sure the flat's tidy*, she thought as she jotted down her home address.

'OK, great, see you soon.' Nick said, his smile still firmly set. She watched him walk away, noting the muscles of his back and shoulders pushing against his blue shirt.

Drew cleared the rest of her desk, picked up the prosecco and headed for the door. 'Night, boss,' she said cheerfully as she passed Lomas.

'See you tomorrow, Drew, bright and early. I'd like us to get over to the vicarage in the morning.'

She got into her pale grey Audi A1 for the twenty-minute drive home, which took her over Cobden Bridge and through Midanbury, where Nick had followed her the last time they'd gone for a drink. She used a cut-through down Allington Lane past the nurseries, singing along to Uprising by Muse.

It wasn't long before she was pulling into her parking space behind the flats. Drew felt a sense of excitement at the thought of Nick coming over. She'd enjoyed the evening they'd spent together, chatting easily about everything and anything. He seemed like a genuinely nice guy. Which, based on her recent love life, was novel.

She jogged up the stairs to the top floor. As Drew reached her door and slid the key into the lock, she heard a door open behind her. She turned, expecting to see Michelle, or Ethan from number sixteen, and did a double take.

Monica Silverman was emerging from Michelle's flat. Drew scrabbled with her key in the lock, fumbling, clumsy, trying to focus on the fast-approaching Monica. Her door didn't open quickly enough. Before she knew it, Monica's fist was flying towards Drew's head, and she was screaming like an animal.

Monica's eyes were wide with rage as she threw the punch at Drew. Drew was quick enough on her feet and, thanks to years of kickboxing, was good at ducking. She dodged the punch. But, standing at the end of the corridor, with a wall behind her and nowhere to go, she couldn't stop Monica from barrelling into her. They slammed against the wall. The smell of alcohol was heavy on Monica's breath.

Drew tried to throw Silverman backwards, but she was solid. Instead Drew ducked under the bigger woman's next wild swing, putting Monica into the corner. Drew fired off a double jab, as hard and fast as she could, to Monica's head, and followed up with a kick to her stomach. The kick rocked Monica backwards, but didn't have anywhere near the impact it usually had on other people.

Shit! she thought, as Monica gave her a maniacal grin and hunkered down into a charging position. The powerful woman launched herself towards Drew, arms outstretched as if in a rugby tackle. Another loud scream tore from her wide open mouth.

Drew knew that if Monica overpowered her, she'd struggle to recover. She skipped back far enough to be out of range. Then she turned and ran for the stairs. She was out of the door and into the stairway much quicker than Monica. Drew took the stairs two at a time. Behind her, she heard the door slam against the wall and could hear Silverman hurtling down. As she was halfway down the last flight, the door from the car park opened and in walked Nick. He looked up and saw Drew hurling towards him.

'It's Monica! She's here!' yelled Drew.

Nick held out his arms. Drew used him to stop her as she leapt the last few steps. There was no time for any more words as, piling down the stairs, hot on Drew's heels, came Monica. Drew and Nick exchanged a look, nodded, and launched themselves towards Silverman. Instinctively, they went for opposite sides of the muscular woman, stopping her dead and pushing her backwards. She crashed back onto the stairs.

Drew and Nick piled on top of Monica. She screamed like a wild animal, thrashing and fighting to throw them off. Monica pulled an arm clear and punched Nick in the side of the head sending him crashing against the stair wall. She then rounded on Drew, who was temporarily distracted by seeing Nick get hit. Monica grabbed a fist-ful of Drew's top and lifted off her feet. Drew instinc-tively kicked the bigger woman, planting a solid foot in the side of Monica's ribs. She felt Monica buckle from the blow, but she still had a firm grip of Drew's clothing. Suddenly, Drew saw Nick get to his feet again. He didn't pause, he catapulted himself at Monica forcing her to release Drew as they all crashed onto the stairs.

Drew used every ounce of strength she had as they both wrestled to pin Monica to the stairs, knees and forearms pushing her down as hard as they could.

Monica's face was pressed against the edge of a step. She screamed and struggled some more, but her fight was subsiding. Drew could feel it ebbing away.

She and Nick were winning.

They carried on holding her down. All the time, nei-ther of them had spoken. All three were breathing hard. Then Monica had a sudden burst of energy and tried to push herself up with her hands. Drew yanked the killer's arm out from under her and her face slammed back down onto the step.

'You fucking bitch! I'll fucking kill you!' Monica screamed, thrashing about in her prone position, pinned by the two detectives.

Nick wrestled Monica's other arm out from under her, they both pulled them hard behind her back, then Nick put his knee on top of Monica's wrists, grabbing a fistful of her hair and forcing her head against the stairs.

'I'm arresting you for escaping from prison...' Drew couldn't quite believe they'd got her.

'You OK? I've got her. Call for back-up,' Nick said, panting.

'Yeah, I'm good.' Drew laid across the backs of Monica's legs and called 999.

'This is DS Drew Taylor. Officers need urgent assistance at Linford Court, Fair Oak Road. We have arrested Monica Silverman and need urgent assistance and transport. Please inform DI Baxter, and please hurry.' She looked at Nick and silently mouthed 'thank you'. He nodded and smiled. Underneath them, Monica lay completely still.

A few seconds after Drew had made the call, she was amazed to see the outer door open and Lomas, Gurdeep and Pete all walk in. They stopped dead when they saw Drew and Nick on the floor with Monica.

'G, Pete, get some cuffs on Monica, would you?' Lomas said. 'Grant got a hit on ANPR earlier on today. Monica's car – just around the corner from here. When he tracked it, it didn't show up on any other cameras either up or down the road, so we figured that she must have stopped really close by,' he explained before Drew had the chance to ask how they'd got there so quickly.

Drew stayed across Monica's legs until Gurdeep had put handcuffs on her, then Nick hauled her to her feet.

Drew looked at Lomas.

'Go on, this one's yours,' he said to her.

'Monica Silverman, I'm arresting you for the abduction and false imprisonment of Sarah Marley. You do not have to say anything. But, it may harm your defence if you do not mention when questioned, something which you later rely on in court. Anything you say may be given in evidence. Do you understand?'

Monica stared blankly at Drew, then turned her attention to Lomas and grinned. 'Did Heidi like her flowers, Detective Inspector Baxter? I do hope so. Quite a lot of effort went into choosing the right mix of blooms.'

Drew watched Lomas, but he didn't answer Monica. 'Keep her there until the van gets here, gents. Drew, can I have a word?' He walked towards the door to the car park.

Drew followed him outside.

'You OK?' he asked as the door closed behind her.

'Yes, boss, I'll be fine. If Nick hadn't had turned up when he did, I'm not sure what would have happened, though.'

'How did she get in?' As soon as the words left Lomas's mouth, a wave of realisation crashed over Drew.

'Shit. She was in Michelle's flat.' Drew spun back towards the flats. She yanked the door open and ran at full pelt past Pete, Nick, Gurdeep and Monica. Taking the stairs two at a time, she hurtled upwards. She tore along the top-floor corridor to her neighbour's flat and crashed through the front door, Lomas hot on her heels.

'Michelle! Michelle!' she yelled. She ran through to the lounge, checking the kitchen and doubling back towards the bedroom. When she came out of the empty bedroom, she saw Lomas coming out of the bathroom. She didn't need to ask. The look on his face told her everything she needed to know.

'Oh no. Not Michelle.'

Lomas held out an arm, blocking her access to the bathroom. She pushed it down and walked past him, stopping and clapping her hands to her mouth when she saw Michelle Batchelor.

She felt a strong arm across her shoulders. 'Come on, Drew. We need to keep it clear for forensics,' Lomas said in a soft, sympathetic tone.

'But she didn't do anything to anyone. All she did was live next door to me,' Drew said. They walked out into the hallway. Drew felt numb. Lomas was saying something to her, but she couldn't make out the words. His voice was like a distant echo. Her head began to swim and she slid down the wall, ending up on the floor with her head in her hands. The smell from the bathroom was hanging in her nostrils and the image of Michelle, bound and bloody, was imprinted on her mind's eye.

When Drew and Lomas made their way downstairs Nick and the rest of the team had moved the handcuffed Monica to the inside wall to the right of the doorway. Drew guessed it was in case she tried to make a run for it. She glared at Monica as they reached the foot of the stairs.

'Ah, DS Taylor, you must have found the lovely Michelle. She's been quite the hostess today. So accommodating – pretty much let me have the run of her flat.' Monica grinned.

Drew lunged towards her, but Lomas darted in front of her and turned her away. 'She's not worth it, Drew.

There'll be plenty of opportunity to make sure she gets what's coming to her.'

'Oh, you're such a spoilsport, DI Baxter. I quite enjoyed fighting her earlier. If lover boy here hadn't turned up, who knows what might have happened?' Monica tipped her head towards Nick, who grimaced. Drew saw Gurdeep and Pete look at Nick, but both looked away quickly.

'Oh, sorry, did they not know?' Monica continued. She had clearly seen the look too. 'Oops. Well, he did show up before you'd called for help, so I guessed you'd invited him. Not sure he's your type, though.' She shrugged. 'What do you think, DI Baxter? Is he DS Taylor's type?'

'Shut it, Monica,' said Lomas.

A police van and two marked cars screeched to a halt in the car park and a team of officers swarmed towards the door.

'Oh look, the cavalry's arrived,' Monica cracked her neck from one side to the other.

Three uniformed officers came into the foyer to take Monica from Nick and Gurdeep. As soon as they were close enough, she kicked one of them in the balls. Drew saw Nick and Gurdeep tighten their grip on Monica's arms and then march her past the fallen officer and out through the door. One of the officers opened the back of the van and they bundled her into the cage. Nick slammed the door shut.

52

Monica was checked in by Drew and the custody sergeant, Frank, with four police officers flanking her. Two of the biggest officers Lomas had ever seen were holding on to her arms and a stocky pair, each armed with a Taser, stood beside them.

After going through the familiar drill of grounds for arrest and legal representation, the team walked Monica into the first cell. They made her kneel on the floor before they backed out quickly. Two female officers came into the cell and got Monica to remove her clothes, which they bagged, leaving her with a pair of grey joggers and sweatshirt. As the cell door finally closed, Lomas felt a pent-up sigh escape from his lungs.

'I know how you feel, boss,' said Drew.

'Are you OK? You should get checked out,' he said.

'I'll go and get checked out once we've questioned her.'

He recognised her stubborn streak as being similar to his own and decided not to push the matter. 'I'm pretty sure I know what the answers is, but, given how close your relationship is to Michelle, are you—'

'I'm fine, boss. And there's no way I'm letting anyone else interview her.'

He smiled. 'Right, come on then. Let's go up and speak to the others.'

When Lomas, Drew and Nick walked into the briefing room, it erupted in a buzz of positivity and congratulations from everyone in the team. At first they started to praise Lomas, but he stood to one side, leaving Drew and Nick front and centre to take the plaudits. The pair stood side by side, looking slightly embarrassed but with broad smiles. As the acclaim subsided, Lomas stepped forward.

'OK, thank you, guys. I think we can all agree, Drew and Nick did an amazing job tonight. For those who aren't aware, earlier today Monica gained access to the flat next door to Drew's, owned by Michelle Batchelor. Unfortunately Michelle was killed in her flat by Monica. The forensic team are on their way over there now to start processing the scene. This was clearly a ploy to enable Monica to lie in wait for Drew to return home. What she didn't bargain on was Drew being so capable when it comes to self-defence – or that Nick would be there too. However, the upshot is that Monica Silverman is now in a cell where she belongs, and no longer on the streets. You have all done a fantastic job. I want to thank you for the countless hours you've all put into this investigation. It has been a superb team effort.' He paused to allow the team to congratulate each other. 'Now, Drew and I will question Monica in the morning, so there's loads to do in terms of pulling the various strands together. Those of you who are working with Tina, let's get cracking. The rest of you, get yourselves off home. You can pick up in the morning.' He turned to Gurdeep. 'G, could you find out who Michelle Batch-elor's next of kin are, please? We need to contact them.'

'Will do, boss.'

'Thanks. Nick, get yourself checked out. I saw you wince as you pulled Monica up onto her feet,' Lomas said.

Nick nodded. 'Yeah, I'll go now.'

'You both did a great job tonight. It took guts to take on Monica Silverman. Well done.' He patted Nick on the arm, then left him and Drew alone.

As those who were going home dispersed, Lomas closed his office door and gave Heidi a quick call. Even though it was well after midnight, he knew she'd want to know.

'Hey.' She sounded sleepy.

'Hey. Did I wake you?'

'Not really; I was dozing on the sofa. You going to have a late one?'

'Yeah, it's going to be a long one for sure. I just wanted to let you know – we've got her.'

'Who? Monica?' She suddenly sounded awake.

'Yeah, we brought her in a couple of hours ago. We've just taken a break from prepping for interview, so I wanted to give you a quick call.'

She sighed with relief. 'That's great. You must be really pleased. Is everyone OK?'

'Yeah, the team are all fine. It got a bit hairy, but they're all good. I don't want to keep you up – why don't you get some sleep? I'll see you in the morning. Love you.'

'Love you too.' She ended the call. Lomas sat with his phone balanced in the palm of his hand. The reality of the situation was starting to kick in.

He sank back into his chair, resting his head against the seat back and closing his eyes. He took a couple of long, slow breaths and allowed himself a moment of silence.

Drew popped her head around the door to see if he wanted a cuppa.

'I was going to do that, but I got side-tracked calling Heidi.'

‘How is she?’

‘Relieved. I’m trying to park the fact that Monica threatened you and Heidi until we get what we want from her. I don’t want her to get a rise out of us when we go down that path.’

‘Understood.’ She turned to get their drinks.

53

Monday morning

It was just after dawn when Lomas and Drew sat in the interview room across from Monica and her appointed lawyer, who looked nervous.

'Here we are again, Monica.' Lomas began. 'More people dead. You're looking at another trial and then the rest of your life in prison. Tell me, was it worth it?'

Monica, who'd been looking up at the camera with a blank expression on her face, turned towards Lomas. She gave him a broad, toothy grin. 'Absolutely, Detective Inspector Baxter. You have no idea how monotonous the days in prison can be. Conversation isn't exactly intellectually challenging – not that I got let out much. And the women in there are either pining for their families or they think they're all that. Neither of which is particularly entertaining.' She looked sideways at her solicitor, a wiry, bespectacled man in his late forties, with a brown suit and uninspiring face.

'I can't believe you're the best they could come up with,' she said to him. He didn't answer, but bristled at the insult.

'OK, Monica, let's talk about your escape from prison. We saw you briefly before you got out, following Officer Anderson's death. What happened between us speaking and you deciding you were going to get out?' Lomas asked.

'I'm not sure where you want me to start. I guess you want to work your way around to asking how I killed the two officers in my cell, so let's start there. Bell and Rodriguez were, to say the least, irritating.'

'Is that why you killed them? Because they irritated you?' Drew asked.

'DS Taylor, the lenses that you and I view the world through are very different. You see everything in black and white, right and wrong. To me, the world is much more complex. Yes, they were irritating. But, on the day they died, they could have been anyone. They were standing between me and the door. That's all.' She shrugged.

'So what makes you say they were irritating?' asked Lomas.

'Because every time I saw them, they came with a task or message for me – and every time they delivered the message, they were irritating. Bell's displays of machismo. Rodriguez's nasal, whiney voice. Like I say, irritating.'

'What kind of messages did they bring you?'

She let out a heavy sigh. 'Not so fast, DI Baxter. I want to know what's in it for me before I go blurting out useful information.'

'Like you started to when we visited you about Bob Anderson?' asked Drew.

'You see, that's what I like about you, DS Taylor. You're sharp, and clearly you listen. *And* you have a good memory. I can see why you've kept her around, Lomas,' said Monica, nodding in Drew's direction.

'You're not in the strongest bargaining position here,' said Lomas.

'That's merely a matter of perspective, Detective. Ha – I'm a poet and don't know it. Or do I?'

'That's enough amusing yourself at our expense, Monica. What do you think the information you have is worth?' Lomas asked.

'I think, given the coverage our lovely Governor Dominicali is getting on the news, and the red-faced statement from the Minister of Justice I saw on TV ... I'd say it's got to be worth consideration being given to my living arrangements once I go back inside. I'm not going to be getting out, I know that. So, while I'm inside, I want to be comfy. You know – creature comforts. TV in my room, decent bed, decent food, that kind of thing.' She leaned her forearms on the table and fixed Lomas with a glare.

'OK, let's say, for argument's sake, I can influence that. It's all being recorded so your request will stand. What have you got to tell me?'

'As I reckon you're a man of your word, I'll trust you to try and make something happen for me.' She rolled her head from side to side, and it cracked. 'So, once I'd settled into prison life, the governor had me brought to her office...' Monica went on to explain her arrangement with Niamh Dominicali. She told them about the handwritten instructions delivered by Bell and Rodriguez. She also explained that she'd kept a copy of one of the notes – and that it was in her hotel room in Southsea.

Monica admitted to the murders of the three prisoners. She sounded matter of fact. 'I'm in prison for the rest of my natural life. How else can you punish me?' Throughout, Lomas noted how – just like the first time they'd caught her – she was completely devoid of emotion when she explained how she'd taken the lives of the three inmates. She narrated the killings as if she were telling him what she'd bought from the supermarket.

'Thank you for being so open, Monica. Now, let's talk about your escape. As I keep reminding you, you are still under caution,' said Lomas.

'Of course. What would you like to know?' She shrugged and fired a disdainful look at her silent lawyer.

'Well, you've told us that you killed Bell and Rodriguez because they were in the way and, according to Niamh Dominicali, you forced her to help you get out.'

'That's correct.'

'So you admit threatening to kill Governor Dominicali and any staff that tried to stop you getting out?'

'I do.' Monica nodded slowly.

'So, what happened once you got beyond the wall, in the governor's car, heading away from the prison?'

'Oh, let's not go over that. It's far too dull and tedious. There are much more entertaining things to talk about.'

Lomas caught her solicitor rolling his eyes, and chose to ignore him.

'OK, so what would you like to talk about?'

'How about ... er ... my lovely vicarage, or my nice, quiet hotel room? Both of which you now know about,' she said in an almost playful tone.

'OK, Monica, I'll indulge you. Tell me about getting to Portsmouth and how you came to use the vicarage.'

'It took quite some working out – jumping on and off trains trying to give you lot the slip. But of course I managed it, and disappeared into the backstreets of Portsmouth. Oh, I nearly forgot, how are Paul and Debbie?'

'Debbie?' asked Lomas, not recognising the name from their investigation. Had they missed another victim.

'Paul Daniels and Debbie McGee. The two who tried to rob me after I'd got off the train. Now, that was magic.' She waved her hands over the table.

Lomas resisted cracking a smile and assured her that both were fine. 'The vicarage?' he prompted.

'Oh, yes. That's been owned by my family for generations. Dad always hated it and never went near the place. It was left to him by an uncle, who used to be in the clergy, but was disgraced, I think. Anyway, when I graduated from uni I asked Dad if I could renovate it. He handed me the keys. We never did any formal paperwork and you would have never found it, I think it's still in my uncle's name, or maybe my Dad's. Anyway, it's just mine. And very handy it is too.' She gave a smug grin. 'Or was...'

'Our forensic team have been working their way through the vicarage over the last couple of days. What can you tell us about the human remains we found in the front bedroom on the second floor?'

'That would be Elinor. You remember her from our last little outing, don't you?'

Lomas ignored the quip. 'You're saying that the remains in the vicarage are those of Elinor Mary Clarke?'

'Yes, and she would have had company too, if bloody Sarah Marley hadn't managed to get away. Note to self: check the manacles next time. Schoolgirl error.' Monica mused, swaying from side to side, her eyes closed, as if listening to music.

'Monica, are you OK? Would you like to take a break?' Lomas asked.

'Er ... yes, I think we should. Could I get something to eat, please?' She looked at her solicitor. 'Well? Can I?'

'Yes, yes of course,' he said, his voice rusty. 'Could my client get something to eat, Detective Inspector?'

Monica rolled her eyes. 'There you go – now you're earning your money.'

Lomas paused the interview and Monica was escorted back to her cell.

***

Lomas and Drew regrouped in the office, where they were joined by Marie Carlton. 'How's it going?' asked Marie.

'Well, so far. She's admitted to killing Bell and Rodriguez, and the three women prisoners that Stephen Leade is investigating. So we're going to have to take those on as well, now that she's admitted to them. She's also put Niamh Dominicali in the frame for instructing her to kill them – says she's got proof at the hotel. We'll have to talk to Stephen and tie in his investigation. She's also confirmed that the vicarage is hers, the remains are Elinor Mary Clarke's, and she abducted Sarah Marley.'

'Wow. That's quite a list,' said Marie.

'Yeah, and we're not done yet. I need to let Stephen know about the deaths and Niamh's involvement. He had his suspicions.'

''Course he did,' said Marie, her tone giving away her dislike of Leade.

'He's a good copper, Marie,' said Lomas.

'I know, I know. He's not going to be chuffed at handing over the prison murders and Niamh Dominicali, though. Anyway, what's happening now?' she asked.

'A quick break for something to eat, then we're going back in.'

'Keep me in the loop. I'll let the super know. Good job tonight, Drew.'

'Thanks, ma'am,' said Drew.

'And Nick too, I hear.' She smiled. Lomas looked at her and she shook her head slowly, turning to leave before Drew could reply. 'Keep up the good work, guys,' she said over her shoulder.

Drew turned to Lomas as soon as Marie had gone. 'Boss, you know that Nick and I – well, it's not…'

'Not anyone else's business. Don't take any notice; she's only winding you up. Go and grab something to eat while I give Stephen Leade a call.' He pulled up Leade's number on his mobile. 'Stephen, hi, it's Lomas. We've had a bit of a breakthrough this morning. I thought you should know about it.' He told DI Leade all that Monica had admitted to, and about the alleged evidence that supported Niamh Dominicali being the one who was pulling the strings.

'I've got Niamh coming in later for interview. Shall I go ahead with it?' Leade asked.

'Yeah, I don't see why not. We need to pull the investigations together into one, but you're already involved and have been chasing this one down, so it makes sense for you to interview her.'

'OK, will do. We'll catch up when I've spoken to her.'

Drew came back in with a couple of sandwiches and a fresh tea.

'OK, that's him up to speed. I'll have this and then we'll get cracking.' Lomas opened his sandwiches.

***

Half an hour later, they were once again sitting in the interview room with Monica and her solicitor.

'Monica, can you tell us about the abduction of Sarah Marley?' asked Drew.

'Oh, you're getting to take the lead for a bit, are you? Very developmental of you, DI Baxter.' Monica smirked.

Lomas didn't answer, so Monica turned her attention back to Drew. 'Why of course, DS Taylor, what would you like to know?'

'Why don't we start with why?'

'I thought that would have been obvious to a bright young detective like you. But if I must explain it to you...' She held up her hands in mock exasperation. 'It was quite straightforward. I never managed to finish the job with her sister, did I? Thanks to you two rescuing her when I was mid-flow. By the way, that was most infuriating at the time. But it's water under the bridge now. Anyway, I knew that once I was no longer a guest at the pleasure of her majesty, you would move Christina somewhere safe, which I assume you did.' She looked from one to the other. They didn't reply. 'Spoilsports. So the only way I could get to Christina was to get to someone close to her. Who better than her sister? It was simple enough. I tracked her down on Facebook without too much trouble. For teachers, they're both a bit dim. When she ran into my car at the traffic lights, she was so apologetic, I almost felt bad for punching her.'

'Almost?' asked Drew.

'You should know by now, DS Taylor, that displays of emotion aren't my strong suit.'

'Carry on.'

'There's not much more to tell. I put her in the back of my car, took her to the vicarage, made her very welcome – I even introduced her to Elinor. She clearly didn't like her surroundings, because while I was out the next day, I assume she worked the fixings loose on her bed and then ran away. I'm guessing she's also safe now.' Again she paused, looking for a reaction. None came. 'Huh, you two are no fun, are you? Come on, play the game. I tell you something, you tell me something. That's how this works.'

'We're not here to play games, Monica. We want to know what you've done and to whom. Besides, it seems that you know all the answers,' said Lomas.

She gave him a smug smile and sat back in her chair. 'You sound almost surprised that I know what you've been doing. It's not difficult to figure out. You see, you have rules, guidelines to follow. You need to keep people safe. Me? I was just trying to have a bit of fun while I could.'

'Is what you did to Lydia Bartholomew your idea of fun?' Drew asked, putting a picture of Lydia on the table. 'Torturing and murdering a defenceless old woman?'

Monica's face contorted. Her eyes darkened and she fixed Drew with a glare. 'You know fuck all about that bitch!' she spat. 'That fucking manipulative whore made my childhood a nightmare. Looking down her nose at me because I didn't want to play with dolls, or go dress shopping with her and my mother. She deserved everything she got. If I could have made her death last longer and be significantly more painful, I would have done.'

'So why didn't you? Her death wasn't your usual style.'

Monica's teeth were gritted. 'Because just seeing her made my skin crawl. And when I confronted her with what she'd done, she turned it all back on me, just like she always did when she was with my mother. That fucking bitch should have died years ago. I had plenty of chances.'

By the time she'd finished talking, she was breathing heavily. Her fists were clenched and she was staring down at the table.

Drew looked at Lomas, who nodded for her to continue.

'Monica, what can you tell us about what happened yesterday, in Michelle Batchelor's flat?'

Monica glared at Drew, but didn't speak.

'Come on, you've been doing so well. Why were you in Michelle's flat?'

Still she stayed silent.

'Did you kill Michelle Batchelor?'

Monica moved her stare from Drew, to Lomas, then back again. 'Yes.'

'OK, why?'

'Because I couldn't find anything to watch on TV.' She folded her arms and slumped back into her chair.

'But everything else you do is so well planned. Wasn't that a bit random? Killing Michelle, I mean.' Drew maintained her composure as she said her neighbour's name.

'She wouldn't have got hurt if she hadn't been so bloody helpful.'

'What do you mean?'

'She stopped me putting a note through the door of number twelve. Apparently another Taylor lives down there....'

'Tom.'

'Yes, that's what she said. Tom. Anyway, she was only too happy to show me where you lived when I said I had to hand-deliver a letter for you. Clever you, not having your name outside on the buzzers.' Monica gave her a small, patronising clap.

'So what happened then?' asked Drew.

'Well, it occurred to me that if I waited in Michelle's flat, I could surprise you when you got home, and finally repay you for getting me locked up. But my mistake was in helping myself to Michelle's drinks cupboard. If I hadn't had anything to drink, you and lover boy wouldn't have been able to overpower me, just to be clear.'

54

'Jesus, really? She said all that?' said Janette when Stephen Leade brought her up to speed on what Lomas had shared with him earlier that morning.

'Yep, and she says she's got proof. Apparently, she kept one of the handwritten notes that Dominicali sent her via Bell and Rodriguez. The forensic team are at the hotel room, looking for it.'

'That's amazing. So we've got her then.'

'We're getting pretty damn close, that's for sure. Bill Bennett is in later. Once he gets here I'll fill him in, join the dots between his investigation and ours, then we're ready to arrest and interview Niamh. Hopefully forensics will have found the note by then. This is all going to have to be wrapped up into Lomas's case now, since it all links back to his case against Monica Silverman.'

'No way of avoiding that, I suppose,' she said with a shrug. 'I can't wait to see her face when we put that note on the table.'

'I know. It sounds like our theory was right. Monica told Lomas that Dominicali was pissed off about the sentences that some of the women got, and decided that death sentences were more appropriate.'

'That's some God complex.'

'Isn't it just? Right, let's get ourselves sorted. Can you go over the notes from her last interview? It might also be worth having a look at Mike Button's notes as well. There's some stuff in there I want to talk to her about. I'm still not convinced she wasn't involved in the drugs,' said Leade.

***

Niamh picked out her favourite Boux Avenue underwear – a black set that always made her feel better about herself. She figured she'd need all the help she could get today. She took out a suit, as if she was going to work, then decided against it and grabbed a pair of fitted jeans and a lilac jumper. Her hair and make-up were perfect by the time she headed downstairs and out of the door to go to the police station.

Thoughts of her mum had been hitting her in waves for the last twenty-four hours. There was a darkness that she couldn't shake: a muted numbness that, ever since she got the call from Aunty Joy, had enveloped her.

She hoped she could hold it together while she spoke to DI Leade.

She steeled herself as she stepped out of her front door. There were still a couple of press photographers lingering on her street. She'd noticed them waiting in parked cars, unashamedly raising their long-lens cameras every time she ventured out. She decided to ignore them, in the hope they'd get bored and go away.

As she started her hire car, the radio sprang into life. George Michael and Elton John belting out 'Don't Let the Sun Go Down on Me' didn't do anything to lift her mood.

The echo of her mum asking how she was the last time they spoke rang around inside her head, overpowering the music. She teared up but managed to stop herself from weeping as she drove, dabbing her eyes with a tissue.

Niamh was abruptly dragged back to reality by a newsreader. 'Hampshire police are believed to have captured Monica Silverman. More on this story as it unfolds.' She stopped the car dead.

Niamh sat with her hands on the wheel, staring blankly ahead. Her mind began racing, considering the implications for her. *Did they really have Monica? What had she told them?* Her mouth was dry and a nervous flutter that hadn't been there before took over her stomach. Her head was swimming. She began to scratch at her forehead, trying to put her jumbled thoughts in order.

A beep from behind her caught her attention. She instinctively held up a hand and moved the car to the side of the road. She was vaguely aware of a man in a red van, revving his engine as he overtook her, ranting silently from inside his vehicle and shaking his fist.

Niamh checked her watch. It was 1.20 p.m. She needed to be at the police station to meet DI Leade in twenty-five minutes. She took a deep breath as she felt the weight of her situation pushing down on her shoulders. Niamh sank back against the driver's seat and unclipped her seatbelt. Tears welled in her eyes once more, this time not initiated by thoughts of her mum. She couldn't hold them back. They flowed freely down her face, and her body shook.

'What have I done? What am I going to do?' she sobbed. Niamh could feel her well-ordered world collapsing around her. She could hear her mum's voice in her head, telling her to 'do the right thing'. It didn't help. She dragged the back of her hand across her eyes, smearing tears and make-up over her face. She started the car and began to drive.

Fifteen minutes later she found herself pulling up outside her own house, with no recollection of the journey. In a daze, she got out of the car, closing the door behind her but not locking it.

To her right a camera clicked. She turned towards it, startled, raising a hand to cover her tear-soaked face.

'Governor, what do you make of the reports that the police have captured Monica Silverman? Is it a relief, Governor?'

Niamh didn't acknowledge the questions. She opened her gate and staggered to her front door. Her keys felt heavy in her hands as she struggled to locate the lock. Eventually she stepped into her home and closed out the world. She leaned against the door and slid down to the floor. A mixture of grief for her mother and the stress of her situation created an overwhelming maelstrom of emotion inside her.

After a little while, she pushed herself up to her feet and wandered through to her lounge. Picking up a photo of her mum and clutching it to her chest, she sank into her sofa.

Mike Button's words were rattling around in her head. He had screamed at her that he knew what she'd done. The knowledge that he too was in police custody made the weight even heavier.

He couldn't really know, could he? She thought she'd been so careful: only using Bell and Rodriguez, making sure no one else had been around whenever she spoke to Monica. She'd even waited until Claire had been out of the office, to avoid her eavesdropping.

Her phone rang and wrenched her out of her waking nightmare. DI Leade's name flashed up on the screen. She'd saved it after the last time he'd called her. Her thumb hovered over the phone as she considered answering. She decided to let it ring out – she knew it would go to voicemail. The time on her phone screen told her she was an hour late for the interview. She had no idea where the time had gone.

There was no voicemail notification. Instead Leade rang again, straight away. She let it ring again. This time there was a familiar ping, telling her she had a message.

'Niamh, this is Detective Inspector Leade. We were supposed to meet at one forty-five. The time is now two fifty. Please give me a call when you get this message. It's important that I speak with you today.'

The message ended and gave her the usual option to save or delete. She chose neither. Once again emotion overcame her. She pulled the photo in tight against her, rocking back and forth, staring into space. Then she held the photo of her mother in front of her and traced a finger around her face.

'What am I going to do, Mum? They know everything. They know about the dead women, the deal with Monica, Bell and Rodriguez – all of it. How could I have been so stupid? Oh Mum, I miss you. Why did you have to go? Why now? I can't go to prison. I'm sorry, Mum, I know it's the right thing to do, but I just can't.'

A sense of hopelessness swept over her, like a dark, inescapable wave.

Niamh picked up the photo of her mum and kissed her face. She carried it upstairs. Her phone rang on the sofa as she walked away.

In her bedroom, she placed the picture on the dresser, facing out. She pulled the cord from her dressing gown and took the stool from under her dresser. Niamh placed the stool behind the bedroom door and looped the dressing-gown cord over the top, tying one end to the outer handle. She closed the door from the inside and stepped onto the stool, wrapping the noose around her neck.

Tears filled her eyes as she felt the cord tighten, digging into her skin. Niamh blew her mum a kiss. 'I'm so sorry, Mum.'

Then she kicked the stool away.

No Remorse

Thank you !

Thank you for taking the time to read No Remorse, I hope you enjoyed reading it as much as I enjoyed writing it.

If you could take 5 minutes to leave a brief review I'd really appreciate it.

Quick link to amazon shorturl.at/qBDFR

Thanks Again.

Heath

Follow me on socials using the links below

Instagram – instagram.com/heathgunn1

Facebook - Heath Gunn Author page

Twitter - Heathgunn

Or join my mailing list - The Gunn Club, at

www.heathgunn.com

And I'll keep you up to date with what I'm up to next.

Other Books By Heath –

Prisoner

DI Lomas Baxter is used to dealing with the criminal underbelly of the south coast and has built his career from hunting down and catch- ing murderers. He is also a dedicated father and husband who strives to keep his family and "the job" separate.

As the arm of victim three is fished from a stream, Baxter knows he has to hunt down and stop a sadistic serial killer. One who is relentless- ly abducting, torturing and murdering young women. With the death- toll mounting, DI Baxter and his team race to save the lives of inno- cent victims, while being taunted by a seemingly untouchable foe.

Can Baxter capture the killer before the threat moves closer to home and his two worlds collide?

If you like gripping, fast paced crime thrillers, and you're a fan of greats like Rankin, McDermid and Patterson, you will love Prisoner, a debut novel by Heath Gunn.

Khan

When the body of Inzamam Khan is dumped onto a busy Southampton street, it marks the fall of a dark empire.

Khan is a successful restaurateur, married to an equally successful and beautiful wife, with two loving teenage daughters.

He is also one of the country's biggest drug dealers who rules by fear and has a habit of making enemies on all sides.
As the last week of his life and the events leading up to his death are replayed - there's only one question to answer...

WHO KILLED KHAN ?

Khan is the second crime novel from **FIVE STAR author,** Heath Gunn.

If you like fast paced crime fiction, with dark forces at play, you'll love *Khan!*

Buy Khan today and immerse yourself in a world of intrigue.

Coming in 2022 is the eagerly-awaited sequel to Khan!

Read the first chapter now...

Working title - Khan II

1

She could feel his presence, even without looking she knew he was getting closer. Her eyes darted around the area that they were able to pick out, in the subdued lighting. Her pulse began to quicken and she felt the familiar tensing of her muscles, the visceral preparation for fight or flight.

Then, as if from nowhere a forearm was thrust around her throat, pulling her in. She could smell the musky scent of her attacker. Feel his body-heat against her back. There was no flight response. She took hold of the clenched-fist around her neck, and with both hands twisted it, rapidly, jarring the wrist-bone of her assailant. Next, she stamped her heel down onto his toes, twisting as it made contact. Then with a lightning spin, she ducked and flicked her body under the arm, simultaneously pulling it with her and forcing it up behind her attacker's back. With well-practised precision, she drove her foot into the side of his knee. As she sent him crashing to the floor, she dropped a knee onto his throat.

Suddenly, bright lights flooded the room and a slow, but firm clapping filled the air.

'Well done, Kamila, as ever, our best are no match for your speed and agility. Now, please let poor, Assan go, he is beginning to go a bit pink.'

Kamila Khan looked down at the man she had pinned to the ground and sprang to her feet. 'Thank you Dadda.' She took a step towards her grandfather and put her arms around the old man's neck.

'Now-now child, these men will think you have a soft side.' Malik Khan said with a smile. She heard a grunt from the man who was still struggling to get up, but didn't give him the satisfaction of a reply — instead looping her arm through her grandfather's and walking with him out of the training room.

It had been four years since her father, Inzamam Khan, had been brutally murdered and dumped on a busy Southampton street, only a day after the death of her mother, Husna. She had died after her car had been run off the road, in the New Forest, orphaning Kamila and her sister, Muna within 24-hours.

Kamila had known that her father, as well as being the front-man for the family's successful restaurant business, had also had his fingers in some less-than legal pies. But he was still her father, and on the day Malik had told her and Muna of Inzamam's murder, she had vowed to find the people responsible and make them pay.

During her teenage years, Kamila had found out about her grandfather's involvement in the Taliban training regime, in camps outside Pakistan. She had been carrying out a research project, for school and had come across details which coincided with places and times she knew her father's family had been living in Pakistan, in the years before they came to England. On a day-out shopping, when it had just been the two of them, she had asked Malik a direct question about it. At first he tried to fob her off, but she had always been good at reading people, even as a child. She had pushed him to tell her the truth and after swearing her to secrecy, Malik had told his granddaughter the basic details of his involvement in the Holy-War. He did so with a sense of pride in his voice, that stuck with her as something that jarred against her previous image of her grandfather.

It had taken six-months after the death of Inzamam, for Kamila to convince Malik to train her. He had started by telling her the training he used to oversee was not for women. This had only outraged her and made her more determined to prove to him that she was every-bit as tough and capable as any man. Eventually, when he realised she was not going to relent, and, knowing that she had kept the original secret he had trusted her with, he had agreed to secretly train her. He only put one condition in place — that it did not effect her schooling, and if it did, he would stop immediately. She had agreed and since then, she had spent every day, for three and a half years, training in martial arts, unarmed combat and becoming familiar with a wide range of weapons.

At twenty-years old, Kamila, tall, slim and with her mother's looks, had three kills to her name and a level of calculated intelligence that gave her a distinct advantage over many of her older, more experienced, male counterparts.

She had also aced her A-levels and accepted a place on a medical, surgery and primary care degree-course at Southampton University, which allowed her to carry on with her training, alongside her studies. Her grandparents had been glowing with pride, when the offer from the university had come through.

Kamila and Malik walked arm-in-arm out into the sunshine of a warm August afternoon. The training took place in an industrial unit, on a small estate under the Itchen Bridge, in Southampton. They reached the back of

Malik's shiny, black, S-class Mercedes and he passed his granddaughter the keys. She smiled and spun the keyring around her finger.

'Thank you Dadda, where to?'

'Home. I think your grandmother is expecting us and the restaurant is fully booked tonight.'

'Well, that's no fun.' She said with a playful smile, firing the big car into life.

'You worked well today. I think we may have to change-up your training. You are getting too advanced for the training-partners we have available to you.'

'Oh? What did you have in mind?'

'I have a friend who is ex-special forces. He would be able to enhance your unarmed combat and your weapons knowledge, and he owes me a favour.' He winked at Kamila.

'Doesn't everybody?'

'Not quite everybody, but enough people.'

As she pulled away from the unit, Kamila put Circles, by Post Malone on the stereo - Malik shook his head and smiled.

Khan II coming 2022

Printed in Great Britain
by Amazon

71538012R00285